Whitney,
Have a fantastic
read. Enjoy the story
when you get a spare
moment in your schedule.
Bonne aventure & good
luck. Kat Jaske

FOR HONOR

An Adventure of What Might Have Been

Book One of <u>BY HONOR BOUND</u>

Kat Jaske

Coming new books by Kat Jaske

Gambit for Love of a Queen

Righting Time

Out of Phase

FOR HONOR

ISBN 0-7414-2057-0

Library of Congress Catalog Card Number: 2004110000

Published by:

INFI∞ITY
PUBLISHING.COM

1094 New Dehaven Street, Suite 100
West Conshohocken, PA 19428-2713
Info@buybooksontheweb.com
www.buybooksontheweb.com
Toll-free (877) BUY BOOK
Local Phone (610) 941-9999
Fax (610) 941-9959

Printed in the United States of America

Printed on Recycled Paper

Published June 2004

Prologue
1636 A.D.

Chilling cold settled itself more fully upon the barren landscape. A bone-chilling type of cold that seemed to fuse itself into the marrow of one's being with an almost human bitterness. Not even the solace of falling snow pierced the stillness of the frigid panorama. No, it was quite simply too cold to snow, if such a thing were possible.

Rather than descending as fluffy white flakes, snow lay packed and trampled so heavily on the ground that it had been polished to a thick, rough slab of ice. And all this in early November. 1636 was turning truly vicious.

Through this bleak and barren terrain, two figures trudged as fast as their legs could carry them—fast enough so that the exertion might bring some needed warmth to their numbed bodies. Perhaps it would bring enough heat to withstand the biting cold— to ward against the icy fingers of air seeping through their breeches and leggings and multiple layers of clothes and deep into every muscle fiber and into their very bones.

The smaller of the two figures reached up to steady the taller man—actually the very tall man—as he stumbled over a stone frozen in the icy snow.

"Papa." The boy's eyes searched his father's face as if seeking signs to assure himself that his father was all right, considering their most recent travails in the duplicitous world of espionage. That they had managed to escape the insidious designs of the powers that be—with their lives and the documents—was nothing short of a marvel.

Especially after such stratagems as they'd been obliged to adopt in their flight, he had no intention of letting his father freeze to death, even if he had to rely on sheer stubborn willpower to ward off the chilling hand of death. Christophe's mouth drew into an even tighter line as he addressed his father. Splotches of healthy tinted skin stood out on the older man's face—a hollow consolation that attested to the life that still animated him.

The older man, with grey-streaked brown hair, stopped short every so often and leaned with his hands on his knees as his son's steadying hands left him. "Christophe, you must go on without me. I slow us down too much, and I will not be the cause of both our deaths." He paused as the frigid air stung his throat, and then his eyes shifted back to the tall, proud boy with shoulder-length blond hair. "I thought I told you to get going."

Christophe d'Anlass rolled his blue eyes and opted to ignore his father's last few words. Instead, he urged his father to stand straight. Reluctantly, through an immense effort of will that had often served him in good stead, Thomas d'Anlass stood taller.

"*Bon*," Christophe concluded with an expression of determined satisfaction. "I don't wish to and won't abandon what's left of my family. Now come, we must hurry. There's no telling how close to us those Prussians have gotten, and I refuse to be captured."

Christophe crossed his thin arms across his chest and tapped a foot on the ice. That he had a cousin by his father's deceased sister, he conveniently decided to forget since the young man was well on his way to squandering everything he had ever had and becoming a drunken, gambling wastrel—and that perhaps was an overly positive evaluation of his cousin's flawed character.

Of course his intense dislike of the useless specimen of humanity could have something to do with the fact that Thomas was doing and had done all within his not inconsiderable power to cut Christophe's cousin out of his will and completely out of the line of inheritance. *No wastrel bastard is going to stand a chance to inherit my lands and my title, even if I must cash in all my favors with the king*—as Christophe's father had once stated. Christophe uncrossed his arms and gestured impatiently. "Well, come on already. We've got to get out of the Germanic territories, into Belgium, and meet with this Mazin you mentioned."

Thomas endeavored to conceal his abrupt start and shivered, trying futilely to ward off the intense cold. He should have known that after these years of dragging his child around with him on his various spy missions for the king of France the boy would latch onto any names very quickly and remember them, even if they had only been mentioned once in passing.

Thomas was on the verge of arguing again when he caught that defiant look in the eyes of his only living child—the one that bespoke of imminent and stubborn rebellion. *So much of his mother in him*, Thomas thought, as he often did. Then he quickly dismissed the thought. Thérèse may have been years dead, but the pain was still too fresh. "I know you won't let me freeze. Well, give me your hand. Let's move quickly. *Vite*." Thomas repeated the injunction to be quick in his native French rather than the German they had been speaking on this latest mission for king and country. He didn't need to mention that those Prussian agents were still tracking them and that very soon those same agents would likely be upon them; nor was he in any shape to deal with them. And then . . . well, freezing might easily be a more merciful end.

Without further conversation, the pair proceeded on their course towards Belgium, the smaller figure helping to pull the larger on with the gentle, persistent pressure of his hand. The blond-haired boy, who appeared to be anywhere between eleven and three and ten, ducked his head as the wind suddenly kicked up and flung random loose particles of snow and ice into his partially covered his face. Just as quickly, his free gloved left hand went up to shield his face from the missiles.

Thomas made no sound. It was challenge enough for him to continue to put one foot in front of the other—forward little by little. *Nom de nom*! It felt good to allow himself to think in French again. He was old of a sudden. Or at least he felt abominably old. Too old to have buried four children and three wives and to have gotten himself into scrapes many a younger man would have fled from. At any rate, he felt far too old to perform covert services for his *majesté*, the king and Compton; maybe he should have retired from the spy service years ago.

Stubbornly the aging spy forced any emotion or thought from his mind. His eyes rested ever so briefly on the hand that grasped his and through persistent tugs encouraged him to continue. A sigh escaped his chapped, weather-cracked lips. Hard to believe there had been a time when he had once been as determined as his son, a time when he had thought he could conquer the world and set all injustices right, not to mention live through it all. Life was even more fickle than society if one could believe that fine irony.

How long the odd pair trudged along in that wasteland neither had a clue. They simply walked in a rough quick shamble, though there was probably nothing simple about it.

After the interminably long period of wind gusts the boy looked up and squinted his eyes. "*Mon Dieu,*" he whispered, not bothering this time to try to hold back the statement the Church might call using God's name in vain.

Could it be? Could it possibly be what he thought it was? His labored steps took him closer, and the snowcovered wooden structure persisted to register to his senses. At that instant Christophe tugged his father's hand and yelled at him to hurry, for there was shelter close ahead.

Thomas, Marquis de Langeac's head snapped up as his child's words finally registered.

A surge of adrenaline rushed through his limbs, limbs suddenly awash with sensation after being deadened for so long. He dropped his son's hand, and both advanced more quickly than they had thought possible towards the only dwelling in the ice-covered expanse. A mere few steps ahead of his son, Thomas made it to the solid wooden door, and scarcely a second later he was knocking upon the portal.

Time ticked by, and no one arrived. Christophe's father turned from the door, and his shoulders sagged; that door was too strong for him to break down in his present pitiful condition. Nor could his clumsy hands pick any lock until the warmth had been restored to them.

However, Christophe was not so complacent. Muscles worked at his jaw. One way or another he would find a way in. Christophe was not his father's child for nothing. And with his temper simmering to the surface, that way in could well be anything. The boy slammed his fists against the door, yelling in German as he did so, spewing a long stream of virulent language that sounded out of place coming from such a young citizen of France. Nor was it marred by any trace of a French accent.

So absorbed in his tirade was the boy that he did not hear the bolt slipping from its place, and he was therefore caught off guard when the door creaked open. He tumbled forward a step before catching his balance and then found himself looking up into a pair of piercing eyes set in the face of a dark-haired man who was somewhere in his early thirties.

Had he been in a more temperate or less desperate state of mind, the boy would have cowered upon facing the imposing, evidently bad-tempered man. Instead Christophe plowed on in flawless German, apologizing briefly and then pleading for his father and explaining how sick Thomas was.

The dark-haired man glanced at the man the boy was speaking of, coldly assessing him. The older man did appear to be quite unwell and could die without immediate help. In all likelihood he would pass on anyhow. But Peter trusted no one during this turbulent time of war. Christophe saw the hardening in the Germanic man's face and knew that he was going to be condemned to be shut out in the cold unless he did something.

That was all it took. What was left of the boy's frazzled control on his temper snapped, and he threw several choice insults at the large man, insults that made even Peter cringe. Boys did not speak that way. Nor did many men. If this were his boy he'd—

Peter's hands snaked out to grab the wiry boy. Just before he could get a good grasp on the insolent upstart, strong hands stayed him. "Peter, *nein*," an attractive blond-haired man of some twenty years commanded. "I will handle this," the second Germanic man informed Peter with an authority that was unquestionable. The blond-haired young man surveyed Christophe and shook his head. "Qiara," he concluded so softly that only the boy heard.

Christophe froze as his eyes took in the young man's friendly face. "Péale," he mouthed without sound. It was Mickael. But the Prussian had left for England. Christophe had seen his ship leave. Yet here he was standing in front of the boy and obviously nowhere near England.

"Help the boy's father," Mickael, better known to most of his countrymen as Erik, told Peter. "I'll take care of the boy. I know them," he added by way of assurance to the dark-haired man.

Upon these words the marquis and his son were ushered into the warmth of the building and were attended by the two Prussians.

As soon as he could manage it, the man known as Mickael or Péale snatched away Christophe from his father. Wry amusement sparkled in Mickael's eyes. "You have always had quite a way with words. But you had best watch that colorful vocabulary of yours or you'll never survive to see the coming of the next decade. Not to mention that politeness is next to godliness as well."

"Where are we?" A single stern look of warning Thomas shot from across the room prevented his son from saying anything more than those three stilted words.

Mickael propped his elbow against the wall, still looking every inch a gentleman. "Technically you're in Belgium, but in the area of land which many Germanic princes have laid claim to."

"In short . . ."

"Disputed territory," the handsome young Prussian concluded for Christophe.

"Figures," the boy grumbled and then dropped to a mulish silence. "*Danka.*" Christophe belatedly remembered his manners, this time in German, and a moment later asked to be excused so that he could rest as the weight of exhaustion suddenly crushed down on him. The young man nodded and watched as the youth curled up and quickly dropped into a deep sleep. Whatever had possessed Thomas to continually take his only child around with him on such dangerous missions? Of course they were Mickael's friends, and he owed them his life, but . . .

* * * * * * * * * * *

Thomas raised his hand and gestured for his son to approach. Their pursuers had to be dangerously close was the thought he left unvoiced. This time Thomas was well prepared for a battle. No child of his was going to delay any longer than the day he'd already spent here.

Christophe came to stand by the bed where his father was propped up. Already the marquis looked greatly improved, but it would still be a few days before he was back up to adequate strength. Thomas gestured again for his son and heir to come closer still so as to provide a measure of privacy. Reluctantly the boy complied.

"You will go with Peter," said Thomas firmly. Christophe looked nothing short of mutinous. Thomas snapped, *"Non, mon petit,* you will go with Peter, immediately, to the heart of Belgium and then you will make your way back to France. Enough. You will listen! I will not be responsible for your death, and I will not have your uncle or cousin ruling over my lands as your guardian or in any other capacity. Do not bring that fate upon our family, especially not after all my efforts to avoid that outcome."

Another protest was clipped short by Thomas' resolute look. "I repeat, if nothing else youngster, do not stoop to dishonoring your family name and heritage. Now you were saying?"

"Papa," Christophe insisted in a hushed tone. "I intend no dishonor, and I have grown up on this lifestyle. I will not die if I stay to help you. And I can help you get out of here. I beg of you."

"A lifestyle I should never have brought you into," barked Thomas. "Silence! I've done you no favor in raising you this way. You'll always be too wild and too headstrong for proper society. I should have had you trained properly, but since I can't change that, at least I will ensure that you survive this mission and that my holdings have a proper heir. Plus, they search for a man of my description fleeing with a boy. If we split up, we can better disguise ourselves and will increase the odds that we both escape. You *will* go or I will see to it that the marriage that was arranged for you years ago will go through."

Christophe fell abruptly silent again. How could he, after he had promised that his son could choose his own spouse! But he had no doubt as to the earnestness of the marquis' words. Check and mate. He would go, and heaven forbid anything happen to his father. Mechanically Christophe rose to his feet and was on the verge of going to Peter when his father touched the boy's hand.

In Thomas' hands was a collection of papers. "Take them," Thomas told his son. "Anything at all that is found on me will condemn me, and I have every intention of coming back to you alive and well. Watch my estate until I return." Langeac, Christophe knew his father meant, as it always had been the most precious of his father's holdings, at least to Thomas, regardless of its humble size compared to his other numerous holdings.

Without a word the boy snagged the papers so deftly that neither the man better known as Erik nor Peter saw the exchange. Rapidly, his anger at having his hand forced still simmering, Christophe gathered his belongings and bundled himself tightly against the cold before joining Peter. The pair was on the verge of departing when Christophe rushed to his father and hugged him fiercely before returning just as quickly to the door.

In dry-eyed silence Christophe followed Peter out the door, and as he passed, Erik said, "Do not fear, Qiara, I will do what I must, and your father will be safe. I give you my word."

The young Prussian watched as Peter and his charge made their way towards the safety of Belgium. At least the boy would be out of harm's way he concluded and turned back to Thomas.

Blasted intrigue! He wasn't very good at it, but he had given his word that he would see to it that Christophe's father would safely escape. Of course if Christophe knew the half of it. . . . Best to deal with that hurdle when he or Thomas ran into it. No doubt they'd never hear the end of it—if they managed to get out of this quagmire alive.

SECTION ONE
1638 A.D.

He was an uncommonly attractive, intriguing man. And, yes, even beautiful, though the first person to tell him so would probably find a sword thrust through his or her gut. Well maybe not her gut. He was a gentleman. Perhaps one could best describe him as a stranger of unknown origin, virtually impossible to keep in one place.

Some claimed he was a first-class rake, completely lacking moral scruples, a consummate lady's man devoted to charming each pretty woman he met. Others swore he was a saint—God's gift—an ideal protector who was loyal, honorable, and virtuous to a fault. Regardless of his perceived character, the man was not lazy and indolent, although his current posture—his body propped against the wall—almost supported that erroneous conclusion.

Then again, the man was considered an enigma by even those who knew him well. Did anyone truly know the man who was a complex mishmash of the flirtatious seducer, an all-around lady's man and a compelling, sensitive, honorable and loyal soul devoted, above all, to God and country? Often enough even he doubted that he really knew himself. Could explain why he always seemed to be searching for something that defied definition and could never seem to tolerate staying in one place for long. In that way he supposed he was just like his best friends: duty and honor bound and always ready for the next adventure.

But duty was so often a poor—no, a paltry comfort. And wine, women, and good food were only invigorating for so long before they lost their novelty and appeal. He sighed and shifted upon the balls of his feet. His recently polished and sharpened sword tapped rhythmically against his right leg.

Bored, that's what he was, completely bored. No mission to occupy his time, no scandal, no plots to foil. Made one almost wish for a great deal of excitement or another plot to kill the king or queen, or simply to get out of Paris. At least then he could have something useful to do instead of whiling away his days feeling utterly lazy and useless. Maybe he was just getting old, finally. It could have waited longer to catch him, he groused internally as he absently kicked a pebble.

"Aramis," someone called, and the man turned to face the direction of the hail, temporarily setting his brooding aside. If he weren't careful, he was bound to start following in Athos' tracks, and the musketeers hardly needed another brooding and lonely and guilt-ridden man. Come to think of it, Aramis couldn't remember the last time he'd seen Athos truly happy since—must have been around the time he'd first become a musketeer. No, he had no desire to fall into that type of melancholy.

"What can I do for you?"

"Aramis." The big man descended upon his fellow musketeer with a mock scowl of disapproval. "What would the lovely Queen of America say? You know, you're going to ruin that handsome face of yours if you continue this brooding. Then what would I do with all the ladies who would have to turn to me? I couldn't let them down, but to be in such demand . . ."

"I think you can handle it, *mon ami*," Aramis informed Porthos, grasping the large man's shoulder for a brief moment. "That is hardly a problem you would have to deal with, *mon cher* Porthos, even if I did lose my looks or decide to enter the priesthood. Now young D'Artagnan, well, that is another matter."

Porthos took a step back and placed his hand on the hilt of his cutlass. "That cocky young pup," he replied. "Do I sense an insult to my powers of attraction? I just may have to call you out."

"Very well," Aramis agreed. "Just please be so kind as to leave my face unblemished. I would like the ladies to remember me as I am now."

The large man nodded his head ever so slightly, and the two opponents drew their swords, saluted, then engaged.

"*Sacrebleu*," D'Artagnan cursed under his breath; that had to be broken up immediately before it became bloody. Quickly, he endeavored to sheathe his longsword, so quickly he nearly missed the scabbard in the process.

No sooner had the young man finally succeeded in sheathing his sword than a hand on his shoulder stayed his effort to interfere in the battle between his two companions. "Athos," the young man protested. "We can't just stand by and let those two try to kill one another. They're fellow musketeers and our friends."

Athos, however, obviously felt no compulsion to try to peaceably end that fight. He didn't even display the slightest unease. "They won't kill each other," the blond-haired man said with an eerie lack of emotion. "D'Artagnan, you're an excellent swordsman and as honorable as your father, but you have much to learn about the musketeers. About our friends in particular."

"What's to learn?" The youth insisted and tried ineffectually to pull away from his fellow musketeer. "They're going to kill each other unless we do something."

The young man finally shook off Athos' restraining hand and moved to head towards his dueling companions. "D'Artagnan," Athos' voice halted him for a moment. "Just remember that Porthos and Aramis take their bouts very seriously. Almost as seriously as Aramis takes death. Wait and see."

Right as the youth came upon the fighters, they bowed and re-sheathed their swords and then turned their attention to young D'Artagnan. "And what can we do for you, *mon beau jeune ami*?" Still slightly out of breath, Aramis inquired of his handsome young friend

At D'Artagnan's look of baffled confusion, Porthos nudged Aramis with his elbow. "I believe the young pup is quite confused. We just may have to set him straight."

Aramis nodded and straightened the crucifix that hung from the chain around his neck. "Shall I do the honors, or shall you?"

"Look." D'Artagnan interrupted their exchange, not in the mood to listen to Porthos and Aramis banter back and forth indefinitely, as they were obviously capable of. "I don't care who tells me what's going on, but someone better tell me and *soon*."

"Impatient and cocky," Porthos commented to no one in particular and then decided to take his version of pity on the young lad. He slung a brotherly arm around the youth and began a long narrative about when he had joined the musketeers and first met up with Athos and Aramis.

Aramis watched his companions silently, simply listening to the tale that the large man was weaving. The intense look he fixed on his companions might have led one to conclude he was at least somewhat amused by the way his older companion was embellishing the original tale.

Porthos hadn't even gotten to where Aramis had joined the musketeers when D'Artagnan held up his hand for a moment, and

Porthos' hand dropped from his shoulder. "Wait," he began. "Just what does this have to do with anything?"

"Very little. Porthos has always been long-winded, as you have probably observed already by now," another voice intruded, and D'Artagnan glanced aside and caught sight of Athos.

"And he has a habit of taking liberties with the original tale, shall we say?" Aramis interjected smoothly in his oddly expressive deadpan voice.

Porthos was on the verge of protesting when the blond-haired Athos absently ran fingers through his beard very quickly in what could be construed as a gesture of annoyance. Three pairs of eyes focused on the man who carried himself with almost unconscious regal bearing. Athos fixed his steady blue-eyed gaze, which unnerved many or made them squirm, on the large man, ignoring Porthos' tortured expression. "May I do the honors of completing the tale?" he asked, knowing he'd be allowed to do so before even Porthos signaled him to complete the story.

"About a year after Porthos and I met one another," Athos began, "a young man who had been training under the cardinal as his student and a member of his guard appeared at *Monsieur de* Treville's door." The older man halted and looked over at Aramis for a long moment before the would-be-priest shrugged his shoulders ever so slightly.

"*Monsieur de* Treville was informed that this young man was being sent to him temporarily because in a duel he'd inadvertently killed a man whose brother had a great deal of influence and who had demanded that Aramis be expelled from the order," Athos explained. "So young Aramis was sent to train with the musketeers until the scandal blew over and he could return to his studies under the cardinal and eventually become a priest. However, Porthos and I became attached to the young man and had no desire to see him return to the cardinal and take the orders.

"One day Aramis announced his withdrawal from the musketeers and his intention to return to the Church in the cardinal's service. Porthos took it badly, and he and Aramis had a horrific argument that ended in a duel. I stopped the duel in time to inform them about a plot by the cardinal to discredit the queen. Ever since foiling his eminence's plot, Aramis has hated the cardinal. Still, as Porthos would say, 'Aramis has an unnatural desire to join the priesthood.' Thus, anytime Aramis gets to brooding and contemplating taking the orders, he and Porthos engage in a mock duel. Now I can't say that it actually prevents Aramis from leaving us, but it does break up his boredom a bit."

Aramis, who'd been silent the entire time, chose that moment to speak. "I will become a priest someday—probably within the next year or two, before I reach thirty," which was still a good ways off, but this particular time his friends refrained from telling him that he had more than six years before he reached that age. "I never did intend to become a fighter for the better part of my life."

"Pay him no mind," Porthos whispered loudly to D'Artagnan. "He's always saying he'll become a priest soon, but he'd never leave me and Athos until Athos retires from the service or I quit or some combination like that."

"Gentlemen." A fifth man interrupted, and they all turned to see the commander of the musketeers, *Monsieur de* Treville. "I hate to break up your little party, but I need all of you to join me in my office. I've got a task for the four of you."

"He can't be serious," D'Artagnan griped as he checked the supplies he had in his saddle pack to be sure he had everything including lots of ink and paper so that he could write Constance; dear sweet Constance, whom he had to leave for weeks to do some stupid mission anyone could do.

The giant, brawny, older man glanced at the youngest of the four men as he cinched his saddle and prepared to mount. "Ah, but you must remember, *mon jeune ami*," Porthos began, emphasizing 'young,' "that *Monsieur de* Treville gets his orders from the King of France, and if *Cher* Louis wants the best musketeers to guard a shipment of precious spices, he gets the best. Of course that only changes if a more pressing duty comes up. . ."

"Such as protecting the queen from being disgraced or framed," Aramis added.

"Or," Athos added, "protecting the king from a plot to overthrow him."

"Or some such combination as that which puts our beloved sovereigns in mortal danger," Porthos concluded, flourishing his hat with gusto.

"So basically what you're saying is that we are stuck escorting this caravan to Marseille, and there is no way out?" D'Artagnan was sorely tempted to sulk. For this duty he'd be away from Constance for at least a fortnight! Most likely longer.

"Didn't I tell you he was a bright lad?" Porthos commented cheerfully in his usually loud and forceful manner, and Athos and Aramis smiled into their carefully clipped beards as they made their final preparations for the journey.

"*Mince*, thanks," D'Artagnan thanked him sarcastically as he tugged briefly at the buff jerkin before slipping on his gauntlet gloves. His clothes adjusted, he mounted his horse and guided the animal towards the waiting caravan. He paused to glance back and say, "Well, come on you three. Let's get this over with as quickly as we can."

"*Oui, monseigneur*," Aramis replied courteously to the young *comte*, unable to keep the smile from playing about his lips, and the four men made their way through the streets and towards the merchants they were responsible for escorting safely to the coast.

* * * * * * * * * * *

The blond-haired woman struggled to push herself to her feet. *Parbleu*, she was weaker than a newborn babe even after all these months. Of course she supposed that she was incredibly lucky, to say the least, to have survived her plunge from the cliffs into frigid, rock peppered waters.

Soon, though, very soon she would be well enough again to resume activities. Only how she was going to pay for her lifestyle was something she cared not to contemplate—could be tricky. Well, maybe not. She sighed and immediately winced at the darts of pain shooting from her bruised but mending ribs. Apparently she would be going back into the service of the cardinal or whoever else would be requiring her unique and deadly skills of subterfuge.

Except, Athos could prove a very prickly problem. He and his three friends had foiled her mission and nearly ended her life. Athos. Definitely a problem. On so many levels. He was supposed to have died, but obviously those reports had been premature. Turns out he'd only turned his lands over to the king and lost himself in near anonymity. Now he had to be dealt with. Yet how? The woman chose not to examine that thought too closely.

She scowled, wrinkling her lovely brow. Blast his overdeveloped sense of honor and duty. They had brought her to this end and nearly killed her several times over. Nor was it at all unlikely that that same sense would get him killed before he reached his fortieth year. Actually, she amended her conclusion: it could well get him killed by his thirtieth year, and he wasn't far off that mark.

A door opened and a kindly faced woman in her early thirties, by all appearances a peasant, hesitantly entered the bedchamber carrying a basin of water. While humming, the lower-class woman set the cracked basin on the nightstand and dropped a cloth beside. A moment later she said, "Milady, you shouldn't be outta bed. You look as if you're 'bout to fall over if you try to move a step."

With a posture that would have done a queen proud, the injured woman leveled a supercilious gaze on the commoner but said nothing. A slight waver caught the peasant's eye. Her patient looked none too steady on her feet. A moment she paused, frozen by uncertainty. The patient wavered again, and that stumble made the peasant's decision for her. The kindly faced woman reached towards the injured woman and looped her strong arms underneath the other woman's shoulders in order to support her weight.

Slowly she led the patient back to the bed and asked, "Can I be getting you a glass of water?"

"*Oui, s'il te plaît*," the aristocratic woman replied condescendingly, not bothering to formally use *vous* to address the woman who was so obviously not of her exalted rank. For several seconds she labored to catch the breath her modest exertions had sapped from her.

The peasant carefully filled a glass with fresh water from the basin and handed it to the blond-haired woman, who gulped it down and set the empty glass on the nightstand before dropping back against the pillows. Sleep quickly claimed her, and the older woman whispered, "Sleep well, milady," as she quietly crept from the room. Some things about the aristocracy never changed no matter how bad off they were.

* * * * * * * * * * * *

The rhythm of horse hooves plitting on the road and wagon wheels rattling against the rugged ground grated steadily on D'Artagnan's nerves. Someone should have warned him that caravans moved with excruciating slowness and were trying on what little patience to which one could lay claim. Of course, it was his duty, and he really shouldn't complain. But what a lousy duty, especially since it was his first real duty since becoming a musketeer and a very tame task at that. Still, he refused to disgrace his uniform and his new friends by complaining.

If they could endure, so could he. Was definitely going to be a very long trip. Nothing but delays and petty quarrels. Already five days had passed, and they were scarcely more than halfway to Marseille. And that estimate could well be no more than wishful thinking on his part.

The young man glanced up as grey and black clouds rolled across the sky obscuring, the sun. Just what he needed, what they all needed, a nasty storm to make their travels even slower, more uncomfortable, and more dangerous. As if responding to his negative thoughts, the wind kicked up, and rain burst from the clouds, tumbling down in sheets and transforming the roads into mud-churned slop.

Each step became progressively harder than the last, and D'Artagnan's horse labored to lift its hooves and continue forward. A vicious gust of wind swept stinging rain into his eyes and face, and he struggled to see through the downpour, but could discern the path no more than a few arm lengths in front of him.

If he and his horse were having such difficulty, the wagons must be having even more; they had to find a place to shelter until the storm passed over and before late afternoon soon became night. The brim of his hat drooped under the weight of the cascading water, and the youth bowed his head in an effort to shield his face from the biting pellets of rain.

D'Artagnan glanced up as a rider pulled up alongside him. Both riders slowed their horses further, and Athos leaned closer to the younger man. "To the southeast," the older musketeer said loudly and pointed, "there is a road that leads to a country estate. We should be able to appeal to the local lord for shelter and stay there for the night." The younger man nodded in acknowledgment as Athos pulled away and took the lead. Taking a deep breath, he began urging his charges to follow his fellow musketeer.

The tall, lanky lad looked up from the horse he had secured just before the full fury of the storm had let loose and saw a small procession approaching the estate. "*Ce n'est pas* possible," he muttered softly in tamer language than was his wont. "Not possible." he repeated again to himself. Time and circumstance always did seem to conspire against him.

"This storm would have to bring travelers needing shelter." Apparently even backwater country estates couldn't avoid all visitors, particularly during a nasty storm. He rushed from the stable and ducked in through the servants' entrance. His wet body very nearly collided with the butler, who fixed the youth with a frown of disapproval. The lad hushed the servant before he could say a word. "No time now to lecture me on appropriate deportment. We've got guests, or will have guests, seeking shelter from the storm. They'll be here very shortly, and I can't receive them in this state."

The butler asked stiffly, "What exactly would you have me do, ma—"

"Gerard," the young master interrupted, "you must pretend to be my father and extend them assistance and hospitality."

"I will not masquerade as your father," the servant protested. Well he knew the penalties for one who tried to usurp a higher station than he had a right to claim, even if this headstrong child had forgotten.

"But I can't just turn them away. They have nowhere else to go, and you know what would happen if I were the only one on hand as the proprietor of this estate." The young aristocrat turned pleading blue eyes on the butler, all the while trying to ignore the feel of the wet tunic and doublet squeezing tighter to his frame. "Even I don't want to dare flout conventions to that extent, and it could be dangerous for them to know I am the only one here. . . . I beg of you."

The butler sighed in reluctant agreement. "I'll pretend to be your father for the duration of their stay, but in return you must endeavor to take up your proper role when this is over. You will do that. It is what your father would want." The youth regarded him silently and then nodded even as he hurried the butler to get prepared for the charade before rushing off to change into dry clothes. Perhaps that loose-fitting leather jerkin he used to wear when he had hunted with his father.

A temporary butler answered the rap at the door and ushered the musketeer into the hall. "What can I do for you?" he inquired in a tone that implied the man had best have a good reason for being here or he'd regret his stopping here for days to come.

In an automatic gesture, the musketeer removed his formerly high crowned hat and asked pardon for his disgraceful appearance.

"My party and myself have been caught in the storm and are desperately in need of any shelter you might be able to offer us," the blond-haired man said. "Is your master at home that I could appeal to him?"

The butler eyed him suspiciously and was about to speak when a young, aristocratic lad appeared, a lad that apparently did not care overly much for convention. He sported a cavalier hat indoors, a hat that looked as if it would be more at home on an older man. "Claude," he said, "I'll handle this. Have Stephanie prepare for guests."

The lad turned his attention to the wet and disheveled musketeer. Thank God for small favors, and God's small unexpected favors were welcome, this time. The man's waterladened mantle proclaimed him a musketeer, and he possessed the demeanor of a true gentleman. Moreover, there was something about him that inspired more trust and more confidence than Christophe usually accorded anyone. "You need shelter for the night?" the lad inquired and Athos nodded. "And you are?"

"Athos," the musketeer replied and sketched a bow. "In the service of his *majesté, les mousquetaires de* Louis XIII."

The boy's intelligent eyes surveyed the bedraggled man. If what little he had heard of this man's reputation was true, he was indeed a man who was unfalteringly loyal to the king and country to which he had pledged his service and honor. Very rare. "*S'il vous plaît*, please, *monsieur*, follow me. I can't have you standing there and catching a chill," the boy said as he guided Athos to a fire. The musketeer took his first opportunity to survey the lad as they stood by the fire. Tall and thin and unmistakably genteel. Though, with that hat and the lad's stance, Athos couldn't really get a good look at him.

"I cannot presume to stay here without your father's permission."

"My father should not begrudge that to you. He should be along shortly. I'm sure Claude went to fetch him. I do not honestly think he would turn travelers out in a storm; nor would he turn musketeers away without very good reason."

At that moment Gerard entered the room, decked in finery he was scarcely accustomed to: a fine waistcoat set off by lace, long-legged breeches tied off with ribbon, and soft leather boots. The lad turned his attention to his would-be father. "Papa."

"Christophe," the older man acknowledged brusquely, turning his attention to the musketeer.

"Papa, may I present to you *Monsieur* Athos of the king's Musketeers. He and his party are seeking shelter from the storm."

Gerard extended his hand "Thomas, Marquis de Langeac." Athos shook the marquis' hand firmly and introduced himself again. "You may consider my home at your disposal for the next day or so. Christophe will assist you while my servants help your men get settled." Athos murmured his profound thanks, and with Christophe's assistance went to get himself settled for what could prove to be a long, cold summer night.

"I must protest," said Gerard to his noble master. "It is one thing for me to masquerade as your father, but for you to continue this masquerade is unpermissable, *Maîtresse* Laurel!"

"Gerard, I've been over this before. It's not a wise idea for these gentlemen to be aware that I'm the mistress of this house. The fewer people who know Lady Laurel Christophe d'Anlass is here and that her father is not, the better. I don't wish to attract attention to the fact that I've returned. It could well bring the men who have been searching for my father here, and I'd rather not bring that danger to my doorstep any sooner than necessary." Not to mention, if the wrong people knew her father had been gone so long, the estate could wind up in her unsavory cousin's hands all too quickly.

"But to pretend to be a young boy, Laurel. That's not wise." And wouldn't be possible for much longer. Already her body was becoming too feminine for the masquerade. If only she hadn't been such a late developer. If only her father had raised her in a more mundane manner.

"What other choice do I have?" asked the young woman who was still dressed as a lad. Similar conversations had transpired numerous times over the last fourteen months, but this time she had more ammunition. "*Monsieur* Athos and his companions already believe that the only child of Thomas is a lad by the name of Christophe. I cannot suddenly reveal that there is no Christophe, but rather a lady of some nine and ten years. It quite simply cannot be done, Gerard," Laurel concluded, and the butler departed with a scowl of disapproval etched upon the planes of his face.

Laurel pulled off the large-brimed hat and set it on the dressing table. Unwound her hair from the tight bun, and the long blond braid fell just short of her mid-back. Her scalp ached. At least no one questioned why she, as a lad, had such short tightly pulled back hair. Rather they assumed she had her hair tied in a tight queue at the base of her neck. Plus, with the hat, her hair didn't look too unusual to pass for a boy's. The young woman pulled off the jerkin, so that she was wearing only her linen tunic.

She frowned as the mirror showed her that the linen shirt was definitely not enough protection to cover the fact that she had bound her small breasts tightly. No, the bindings could be seen through it. But at least her hips and waist were still narrow, boyishly so, although she wondered how much longer such luck as she'd had would hold out. Seeing as her breasts were becoming more full, she knew it was only a matter of time before the rest of her body became more feminine. Apparently even she couldn't elude fate indefinitely, no matter how she might try.

She sighed and rubbed her eyes with the palms of her hands as she recalled her rather unwise promise to Gerard. She was used to playing a lad; she'd been playing at being a lad for the greater part of her life since her father could not really carry out his duties with a daughter tagging along, and he had refused to leave his child at home since he felt he was the only one who could really protect her from the enemies he had gained in his line of work.

Papa. If only she knew where he was now. She hadn't seen him in more than a year, closer to two, and she herself had barely escaped her pursuers with her life intact. She shivered at the thought. He couldn't be dead; she simply refused to believe that she would never see him alive again. The marquis was inordinently good at his chosen profession and always had been. Besides, Erik had promised that her father would be safe, and she refused to contemplate any other alternative.

Swiftly she got up from her seated position on the bed and accidently knocked a basin to the floor. It fell with a loud clatter, and Laurel unsuccessfully stifled an exclamation of pain as she jammed her stocking-clad foot against the bedpost. The young woman bounced back on the bed grabbing her tender foot and praying to God she had not foolishly broken anything.

"Are you all right?" D'Artagnan rushed into the room and stopped short at seeing the blond-haired woman dressed, or rather half undressed, in male attire.

"*Mince* and blast! Don't just stand there. Close the door, quick. Before anyone else comes to see what happened." The young musketeer complied and then promptly froze facing Laurel, a look of bafflement in his light blue eyes.

"I, I, I . . ." he stuttered.

Laurel completed the examination of her foot and concluded nothing was broken despite the soreness. "It's not broken." At the young man's continued look of confusion she explained. "My foot, I didn't break it. I was afraid I might have, but it's only bruised." Laurel put her clenched hand to her pursed lips. What was she going to do? "I see you've discovered my little secret."

"Why?" D'Artagnan finally managed to get out, struggling to come to terms with the unorthodox situation. It was definitely improper for a musketeer to remain alone in the chamber of a young, single woman. He shouldn't even be here in the first place.

"My father's out of the country," she began in a measured tone, "and a lone woman could hardly welcome a group of strange men to her home. Nor could I allow you to remain out in this weather. So I did the only thing I could think of: had a servant play my father and became a lad for my own protection." Her deep blue eyes met his, and she carefully looked him over. No more than one and twenty and probably not even that old, but strong, beardless, boyishly handsome with a bearing that indicated breeding. "Your word, *monsieur*."

"What?"

"*Votre parole monsieur.*" She searched for the name that would fit his description and stumbled upon it. "D'Artagnan, please, promise by your sacred word as a gentleman that you will not betray my secret. I'm putting my reputation completely in your hands." And my life, she added silently. No telling what fiasco she might have accidentally embroiled this young man in.

A musketeer and a gentleman didn't destroy a lady's reputation, but to allow his friends to remain in the dark about who was really their host, and unaware of the truth of the situation . . . She waited silently, and finally he responded. "You have my word as a gentleman that your secret is safe with me."

True to his word the young musketeer revealed nothing, and the following afternoon he and his party left while Laurel and Gerard looked on. As she watched the procession depart she wrapped her arms around her body. She had a very bad feeling not unlike the one she'd had when she and Peter abandoned Thomas to his fate some year and a half earlier.

Exhausted, Laurel wearily crawled under the sheets and pulled the blanket to her shoulders. Swiftly she blew out the candle by her bedside and settled back to her pillows in preparation for much-needed sleep when she felt an ominous presence in the room.

Her still open eyes registered shock as they perceived a shadow looming over her bed. Her first coherant thought was that she should have listened to that bad feeling she'd had days earlier.

The young woman attempted to reach for her dagger. Not soon enough. A strong hand clamped over her mouth, "*Non, ma petite.* Don't scream."

"Papa," she whispered, limp with relief, when the hand had been removed. "What are you doing here?" She shot up and heard her father's grunt of pain. "You're hurt."

He waived her hands away. "No time for that, *chérie.* I'll be all right. Of that you can be sure," Thomas reassured. "But you're not safe here. The Prussian agents aren't just looking for me anymore. They are also looking for you."

"It's those papers you gave me before I fled Belgium, isn't it?" Sudden enlightenment struck her. How could she have been oblivious for so long? Didn't say much for the intelligence she was so proud she had cultivated.

Her father didn't respond, but she knew it was the truth. "Then we both must flee as quickly as we can to the Netherlands." The Netherlands had frequently taken in political refugees, and they'd be unlikely to turn two wealthy French aristocrats away.

"*Non.* You must give me the papers, and I can get the rest from the agents in Brussels, Marseille, and Luz. Then I can take them to the king and warn him. Quick, Laurel, get the papers, and you must prepare to leave for Uncle Joseph's estate immediately." There was still his old nemesis to capture, and that was not a depraved character he wanted his daugther to have to tangle with.

"*Non.*" She would not go to the estate of her father's deceased sister. Joseph, her uncle by marriage, and his wastrel, profligate son were not to her liking. Nor did she have a desire to be pressured into marriage with her cousin. Disgusting, filthy man.

"Look, you must—"

"*Non,* papa. You're in no condition to be relaying secret papers back and forth, and I won't permit it. Don't you argue with me," she said, shooting to her feet. "I may only be your daughter, but you raised me on campaigns such as this. You taught me the tricks of your trade, how to take care of myself. I'm taking those papers to Compton in Marseille." Also, she quickly reminded him that her fluency in several other languages was quite beneficial and would aid her in completing the task.

"Laurel, you mustn't get involved. They'll kill you too, even though you're a woman. They may even do worse than kill you."

"I am aware of the dangers," she countered solemnly. Her temper fled quickly, though her stubbornness remained implacable. "Besides, that is immaterial. I'm already involved. You said so yourself. And . . . they won't be able to recognize me if I go as Christophe." Seeing by his expression that Thomas was not going to allow her to have her way, she defiantly leveled her best argument. "Need I remind you that only I know where the papers are now? If you don't give me your permission, I'll go anyway, and you won't have those documents, so I implore you to tell me everything I need to know."

Thomas shook his head gravely. "Laurel, you have no idea what you are asking of me. *Oui,* I know you'll do as you say. Very well, *ma fille,* contact Compton in Marseille and tell him '*les trois coronets.*' He'll give you further instructions. In the meantime, I still will head for Luz and Brussels. I expect you to post me a letter addressed to the estate of the merchant Jacques Devré in Brussels. Also, I will try to meet you somewhere near Boussac, if possible. Understood?"

Laurel nodded and pressed her father no further. They both knew better than to belabor the issue; there was no time, and it would serve no purpose.

Two stubborn souls were not likely to change their ways anytime soon; had there ever been such a case of like father like daughter previously? And they had more urgent matters, like figuring out exactly how they could orchestrate the passing of messages between the two of them so that Thomas could relay his daughter important information not yet in his possession and she him. Pray God his old nemesis would not catch on to their game or give Thomas the slip this time.

* * * * * * * * * * *

23

The pungent smell of well-roasted food mingled with alcohol and tobacco swirled in the air. Lights flickered and serving wenches wandered from table to table, delivering ale and meals. Sometimes more than that.

As he was known to do, Porthos was giving D'Artagnan another lesson on how to woo women while Aramis looked on in what some might construe to be mild amusement. Still, one could hardly ever be sure what the man who wanted to be a priest was truly thinking. Not that the youngster needed much instruction as far as Aramis was concerned. With that pretty face and body of his and those eyes, not to mention the alluring recklessness, he already had captured much female attention. It seemed to matter little that he was more brash than charming, more bold than subtle. Ah, well, not to worry; D'Artagnan could take care of himself more often than not. Plus, the boy was already basically bested with Constance Bonacieux, so the lad was in no danger of becoming enamored of an unsuitable woman.

No, D'Artagnan could handle himself well enough. It was Athos Aramis was worried about. Man had been drinking hard. True, he took his drinking very seriously, but he was drinking more than usual, and the man was like the devil under the influence. In that condition he could well strangle or shoot or break the neck of anyone who wasn't a good friend and might accidently set off his ire. Not to mention, he ended up saying things he would later regret.

Still, Aramis couldn't much blame Athos. Highly unlikely, Aramis admitted to himself, that he would be in any better shape had he run into a wife he thought was long dead and then discovered she was an agent of one's own worst enemy. Nor could it be easy to watch her jump to her death. Very hard. And very hard was assuredly an understatement.

Of course Aramis was not married—never had been—so he couldn't quite understand the depth of grief Athos must be feeling. Aramis gently shook off a serving wench's arm and excused himself from the table. Wenching could wait for another night. There were plenty of beautiful and willing women he could choose from. More often than not they threw themselves at him. Methodically, he made his way to the far corner of the darkened room and halted the server.

The would-be-priest shook his head firmly. "No more drinks for him. I'll take care of him. You just see to it that everyone else stays clear of him." The girl backed away, and Aramis sat himself across from his old friend.

"Ah, Aramis, come to drink a toast with me," Athos said, filling a glass with a shaking hand. Already starting to show signs of intoxication—in short not holding his liquor very well. Not a good indication for it took a lot of drinking before Athos usually revealed his intoxication. After a brief pause the inebriated musketeer pushed the filled glass towards the man with raven-black hair and then took another healthy swig from his tankard. He wiped a dribble of ale from his lip with his sleeve and then took yet another drink.

Aramis' deep brown eyes flecked with gold regarded the older man. He hated to see the usually fastidious Athos reduced to this state. It was like watching his older brother drink himself to death all over again. "*Non. Merci*, thanks, Athos. I have had enough to drink."

"Ah, *oui*, I forgot," Athos said in a condescending tone, "no more than one cup of ale a day for the would-be-priest. Wouldn't want to offend God by drinking more than in moderation. Could be damned for it."

"That's enough, Athos," Aramis said in a soft but firm voice while grabbing the other man's hand and preventing him from lifting the tankard to his lips again. The younger man's eyes were cold and unreadable. "We should be turning in for the night."

"Listen, Aramis, you may not want a drink for some damned, blasted and mistakenly noble or moralistic reasons, but that's no reason to stop others from taking their pleasures as they please. I'll drink when I choose. Now let go of my hand, and go get yourself stinking drunk for once or better yet go screw some new bitch like you're always doing."

Aramis slammed Athos' hand onto the table, shattering the tankard and cracking the table. Athos moved to throw a punch at the other man. However, his reactions were slowed by drink, and Aramis easily blocked the punch. "*Ca suffit*, that *is* enough, Athos," he said struggling to control his temper with moderate success. "You have had too much to drink, and I am not *saying* that just because I choose not to drink much. Do you not see what it does to you, man?" He leaned closer to Athos. "I do not like seeing you this way, and I do not want to watch you drink yourself to death. I have already watched my brother do that, and I have no desire to lose one of my best friends the same way."

By this time all eyes were focused on the two men. Tension gathered more tautly in the air, waiting and shivering to see blood spilled. Or spoiling for a fight. D'Artagnan followed Porthos' lead and bought drinks for the rest of the guests and focused his efforts on distracting everyone's attention from Athos and Aramis.

The blond-haired man swallowed tightly, almost as if it were hard for him to do so, as if something were lodged in his throat. "I'm sorry, Aramis," he finally said very quietly. "I didn't know." Athos pushed away from the table and rose to his unsteady feet. "If you'd be so kind as to help me to my room, I think I should sleep this off." Aramis nodded and went to assist his friend. As the pair passed the proprietor, Athos and Aramis both flipped him several pistoles and said, "Sorry about the mess."

Porthos halted Aramis. "Is he going to be all right?" Porthos asked, his tone uncharacteristically sober.

"He is still asleep," Aramis informed both his fellow musketeers. "I told the caravan leader that since our duty was discharged, he was welcome to leave us, and we'd find our way around Marseille and back to Paris. My guess is Athos will not be getting up until at least midday at any rate. Even then he is probably going to be suffering from a nasty headache. I daresay we will not be leaving any sooner than tomorrow." Aramis glossed over the hangover with his customary aplomb.

The other musketeers nodded. D'Artagnan addressed the would-be-priest. "What'd you say to him?" Concern was evident in every inflection of his voice.

"That is a private matter between Athos and myself. I cannot tell you that sort of thing. I am sorry." His tongue traced his even white teeth. "I know you are worried about him, D'Artagnan. We all are. Just be careful what you ask Athos. The man does not like dwelling on any part of his past, and I especially doubt he will want to talk about milady."

"Well, if it isn't the pot calling the kettle black," Porthos commented. For, if anything, Aramis was just as reserved as Athos about revealing his past. In fact, they knew less about Aramis than about Athos. Seemed even the best of friends kept secrets from one another. Maybe even the apparently completely open D'Artagnan was more secretive than he appeared to be.

* * * * * * * * * * *

"Where's the Marquis de Langeac?" the man with a hawklike nose asked the two men standing before him. "You were charged with finding the marquis and those papers that he gave to his daughter. Well?"

"We done our best, *monsieur*," one man said. "It was hard enough to find out his identity, and then discover that he'd given the documents to his daughter." For a prominent, old, and established family, remarkably little was known about the marquis or his family.

"I don't pay you to devise excuses, Joseph. You would do well to remember that fact. Now what about the good marquis and his daughter?"

"As far as we can tell," the other man, Guillaume, said, "Thomas d'Anlass contacted his daughter and warned her to flee. So when we arrived at the estate, only the servants remained."

"Really," his superior observed. "I see I have a great deal of incompetence to deal with. A situation which must be rectified."

"*Monsieur*," Guillaume said. "It was not a total loss. Thomas was injured, and we know he and his daughter did not leave together. In fact, we have reason to believe he enlisted her help and that she is seeking to complete his contacts and deliver the documents in his stead. Nor does Thomas even have all the papers. We know that. So we have an idea where he might be going so he can get the complete information."

All of which did very little good unless they knew where the woman might be heading. The hawk-nosed man turned his back on Joseph and Guillaume and stared out the window into the peaceful, moonlit night.

Thomas d'Anlass. He pondered the name and what he knew of the man several moments and then turned his thoughts to the marquis' daughter. If he was recalling correctly, she must be between eight and ten and twenty years, and single. Laurel—that was her name. A blond-haired blue-eyed girl who was raised more as a son than a daughter, he suspected. "I'll take care of finding Laurel d'Anlass. I have enough contacts in the places she might go for aid. You two will see to it that no messages find their way to Paris or the king, and alert my agents in Belgium and Austria. I want the marquis found."

27

"*Oui monsieur.*" They replied in French rather than their native German and scurried from his presence to carry out his bidding. The marquis would be found. Now they knew how to track him.

* * * * * * * * * * *

"Milord." The servant entered the well-appointed study.

"Valent." His lordship acknowledged the servant and then looked up from his morning paper. He took a brief pinch of snuff and set his morning papers aside. "What can I do for you?"

"Milord, there is someone here insisting to see you."

"And this person is?"

"That's just it. The lad won't give his name. He says he won't talk with anyone except for you, and he refuses to go until you've seen him. He's gone so far as to threaten to create a nasty scene."

"I assume he won't say what he wants to see me about either." Valent nodded in confirmation. "What *did* he tell you?"

"Well, *monseigneur*, I don't know if it's important." When the servant paused, his lordship gestured for him to continue, and that he'd be the judge of how important the information might or might not be. "He kept mumbling something about *les trois coronets.*"

"Did you say '*les trois coronets*'?" his lordship repeated and Valent nodded. "Send the boy in here immediately, and see to it that no one disturbs us. Absolutely no one."

Valent bowed and exited. Moments later he entered the room with a lad who was sporting a full cape and hat pulled low, hiding his face. "Please be seated and make yourself comfortable. We should not be disturbed. What news is it that you bring?"

"You are Milord Compton," the contralto voice inquired and he confirmed he was the half English, half French lord. The lad still hadn't taken off his hat and cape. Did he have no manners, or was he something he wasn't supposed to be? He reached under his desk for the flintlock pistol he had recently procured and loaded it as he surveyed the visitor. Better to be prepared in his line of work. He'd learned that much over his decades in control of France's spy network. One reason for his longevity.

The lad set his cape aside and removed his hat to reveal he wasn't a he at all, but rather a she. The poorly fixed blond hair tumbled down her back, and she fixed a steady gaze on Compton.

Compton put the gun back into the compartment without making a sound. "Please excuse my appearance and the deception, Milord Compton, but there was no other way I could reach you without the charade. My father, Thomas d'Anlass, sent me to you. He told me that you would give me further instructions."

"*Mademoiselle* Laurel," his lordship half asked. Clearly the woman was Thomas' daughter, and equally as obvious was her expectation that she would be able to simply step into a role very similar to the marquis'. Never had his long-time friend done or permitted anything so asinine before. "*Parbleu*, why did your father get you involved in this international tangle? He should not have subjected you to such danger."

"Milord, with all due respect, I have always been in danger, whether I stayed at home or accompanied my father on his missions as a spy for King Louis XIII. I do not think that the danger to me now is significantly greater than it has been in the past." From inside her doublet she withdrew a portfolio of papers and presented them to the man. "These are the documents my father and I obtained upon our last visit to Brussels more than a year ago. I put them in your safekeeping until such time that they can be safely delivered to his *majesté*."

"So now you'll have me turning a marriageable, single lady into a spy. You are what . . . scarcely nine and ten?" He didn't wait for an answer. He knew Laurel had just reached that age a fortnight earlier, though she'd obviously played at being a young lad on the verge of manhood for years. "I'm sorry, *mademoiselle*. I cannot permit it. I'll have to send someone else." It'd be hard to find someone else, particularly someone who worked well with Thomas, but it had to be done. How dare his old friend and the best spy in his network put him in this untenable position!

"I'm not so young, milord. I am already nearly an old maid, or have you forgotten that I am no longer a girl and no longer a very desirable catch on the marriage market?" Save for the impressive dowry that came with her, but she chose to overlook that fact. "I may only be a woman, but especially in this I am more capable than most any man you will find. No, you'll send no one else, Compton," she stated and stood, leaning her hands against his desk. "No one else knows where my father is or how to reach him. I do. Unless you send me, you'll never get in touch with Thomas d'Anlass again. Nor will you ever get your hands on the last of the information he has gone to acquire."

A vein throbbed in Compton's temple as he stared at the defiant woman before him. He didn't doubt she would follow through on her ultimatum. In that respect she was very like her father. "Very well. Be seated," Compton said as he laid a map of Europe upon the table and began imparting instructions to her. Laurel's willfulness would be taken care of later. Thomas' too.

"Then I go to Calais?" she concluded with a question.

"*Oui*," said Compton. "We've gotten wind of Prussian, Austrian, and Spanish agents passing very damaging information to an agent here in France who will be taking the information to England. Needless to say, this information jeopardizes the kingdom and sabotages our war effort; if it were to reach England, the effects would be devastating. Their plans must be brought from Calais and returned to his *majesté*. We cannot afford to have traitors at the very heart of France."

"Have you no further information about who the traitor, and spy, is?"

"I'm afraid we haven't much more. Your father's the one who has been tracking him for eight and a half years." Compton expelled a breath. "The most I can tell you is that he's a man with a great deal of power, influence, and access. Obviously, we can't afford to waste any time when tracking this man." He handed the marquis' daughter a packet with some further instructions. "Get going." Before he changed his mind regardless of the potential consequences. Did Thomas ever have a lot to answer for! Especially if Laurel was anywhere near as good as Thomas at losing men sent to tail him. For some reason he suspected she was.

* * * * * * * * * * * *

Laurel secreted the instructions in her doublet underneath the jerkin and the cloth that tightly bound her breasts. Her soft leather boots, very similar to those musketeers wore, echoed off the cobblestones and blended in with the sounds of the busy port city. She darted around the corner and searched for her horse.

Stopping short, she pressed herself to the wall, flat. How had they found her so soon? Well, the horse was lost. Poor Rebelle, but there was nothing she could do for the faithful animal now. Those men obviously knew Rebelle was from the Marquis de Langeac's estate. She took a fortifying breath and dashed back in the direction from which she had come.

At least she still had a hefty sum of money and one of her father's basket hilts. Hopefully she wasn't too out of practice with the sword, for she had a sinking feeling that she would have to be using it all too soon.

And her other numerous skills too.

Laurel quickly checked her hair and was satisfied to note that the tight braid had stayed pinned underneath her hat. As long as no one looked too closely, no one would ever suspect she was not the lad she pretended to be. The woman stopped short as she caught sight of a merchant talking to several armed swordsmen; hired blades. The merchant looked up and pointed at her, indicating that was the boy who had come in on the horse in question. At first she thought herself paranoid, but then she saw the four fighters weaving their way through the crowd and towards her.

Diantre! The devil!

Her ladyship wasted not so much as an iota more of time. Abruptly, she backpedaled and sprinted away from the men, turning and twisting through the streets in an effort to lose her pursuers. Unfortunately, she didn't know her way around Marseille very well, and these men most obviously did.

"*Saperlipopette*," she exclaimed, and added "drat" for good measure, as she found herself faced with a dead end and saw her pursuers closing in on her inexorably. This couldn't be happening. She wouldn't let this happen.

"Come now, be a good young lad. You wouldn't want us to have to hurt you now would you?" one of them taunted.

Laurel felt the urge to break into hysterical laughter, but squelched it. They'd not take her alive. What a time and way to put her rusty fencing skills to the test. She put her hand to the hilt of her sword, and one of the men scoffed, "Looky here, the boy's got a fancy sword. Best put that away before you hurt yerself."

Her newly drawn blade only wavered an instant at her side before she raised it. As she charged towards them she yelled "en garde" at the top of her lungs. Her sudden attack and the fact she went after them in the left-handed style caught them off guard for a moment, and they stepped back and then drew their swords and approached their prey, circling her.

"You know it seems rather unfair?" someone commented from the sidelines.

"You're right, my young friend, it does hardly seem fair that four big strong men are attacking one young boy."

"Perhaps we should even up the odds a bit," his younger companion suggested.

"One moment," said the older man as he turned to address the nearest of the youth's assailants. "Sir, this young lad is hardly worth your time. Why don't we all leave this place and have a nice drink on me—"

"Why don't you bugger off and mind your own business," the assailant replied and lunged at the youth, who deflected the blade with a graceful parry riposte.

"No need to be rude and vulgar now." He shrugged his shoulders. "Do not say I did not warn you, sir," he countered calmly, and he and his younger companion entered the fray, deflecting sword strokes from Laurel and allowing her precious moments to regroup her defenses and parry the next few slashes that came her way, nearly penetrating her guard.

Laurel twirled away from her assailant and then took a tiny step forward and, dipping the tip of her blade, nicked the man's arm with the tip of her sword. Her own breath came in gasps grating harshly in her ears.

Well, this was what she got for being out of practice, she scolded herself as she jumped away from the slash to her side, but not quite quickly enough. For her attacker's blade drew a very fine line of blood along her rib cage. Laurel stifled her gasp at the stinging pain and backed up a step or two, bumping into one of her rescuers who was driving his sword through the man's gut for the third time and then withdrew it quickly, saying, "Go with God," as the man ceased breathing.

Even as she backed into one of her rescuers she caught sight of another of her rescuers and nearly lost her concentration completely as she recognized D'Artagnan. "Huh, *comment*?" She gasped, jumping away from another of her opponent's lunges.

D'Artagnan parried his own opponent's slash and looked up to see Aramis maim another opponent by encouraging the assailant to rush him and at the last moment side-stepping to reveal the wall. The attacker had no time to alter his course or slow his forward momentum, so he rammed his head into the wall, knocking himself senseless. D'Artagnan smiled. Aramis the tactical genius. D'Artagnan focused his mind on fighting again and taunted his own opponent. "Sloppy, sloppy," he criticized as he made a reckless lunge of his own and speared his enemy up through the ribs piercing his heart.

Half out of breath, D'Artagnan came to Aramis' side and pointed his sword towards the two remaining fighters, Laurel and her attacker. "What do you say? Shall we help him out?"

Right at that moment the youngster in question feinted and lunged upward, and her sword tore through flesh and sinew from gut to neck with more force than she thought she had.

"Actually," Aramis responded, "I think he's got the situation well under control now."

"*Mon Dieu*." Laurel panted after sheathing her sword and leaning over to clutch her knees.

"*Mon Dieu,* indeed," a voice interrupted her chaotic thoughts, calling her politely to account for her irreverence. "There is most certainly a God, and He seems to have looked favorably upon you today. However, I suggest that we do not linger here longer than necessary." Seeing that the boy was bleeding, Aramis reached out to help support him, but he jerked away like he was being stung.

"No," Laurel said, her dark blue eyes flashing. "I'm quite all right. It's not very deep. I can walk without assistance."

Startled, D'Artagnan took a closer look at the boy, unable to stop staring at his face. He could have sworn he knew that face and that voice. By all that was holy! It couldn't be, but he had little doubt of it. It was the lady who had given his party shelter from the storm—the lady who called herself Christophe. "You will at least come with us and have that wound tended?" D'Artagnan addressed Laurel with mounting concern.

For a moment he thought the youth was going to refuse to join them for any reason, refuse to have anyone look at the slash. "How could I turn down such a skilled escort?" Laurel replied as she indicated she would accompany them. Matters could, after all, have been worse. If she weren't doubly careful, those agents sent by her father's enemies would again be upon her.

The mismatched trio entered the inn and mounted the stairs to D'Artagnan's room. "I'll go find a doctor," D'Artagnan said, but before he could, Laurel stubbornly insisted, "No doctors. I don't like them, and I don't trust them. At any rate, it's nothing. Just give me a little privacy, and I can take care of the wound myself."

The young musketeer appeared ready to argue when Aramis broke in. "This is not really an appropriate place to debate the issue." As usual, he was right. Already the trio that had stopped on the stairs was attracting the eyes of other patrons. D'Artagnan continued on the path to his room, and the three entered.

"Well, what do we have here?" Porthos inquired as his friends entered with the stranger in tow, a stranger who did not appear at all pleased to be there. Athos winced at the sound of Porthos' voice as he glanced up to see what Porthos was asking about.

"We found this young lad being set upon by a rather unsavory group, so D'Artagnan and I decided to lend our assistance," Aramis smoothly and succinctly explained.

"A rescue operation I see," Porthos commented as he stood. "Always a musketeer's duty to defend those less fortunate or able than himself. Well done."

"You'll have to excuse our lack of manners, but we were not expecting visitors," Aramis told the boy and then took over Athos' role by performing introductions. He nodded towards the blond-haired man in the corner. "Allow me to present Athos, D'Artagnan, and Porthos. And I am Aramis."

She acknowledged the greetings formally. Athos glanced at the lad and recognition finally dawned in his pounding brain. From Langeac. "I didn't expect to run into you in Marseille," he commented. "Does your father know you're here?" Laurel didn't respond, just blinked her eyes dumbly and remained mute. Blinked again as if trying to clear suddenly befuddled senses.

It was unusually hot in here, and an incessant buzzing started pounding ever more loudly behind her eyeballs. Why was the room spinning? She swayed uneasily on her feet, staggered half sideways. At that moment Athos noticed the crimson streak spreading along her side.

In one lightning-quick motion he leapt to his feet to help.

"I'll be quite all right," Laurel insisted stubbornly. But her body betrayed her, and she lost the last vestiges of her balance. Her last coherent thought was that her wound would have to be more serious than she thought it was.

Athos caught her as she pitched forward, and with Porthos' assistance carefully moved her to the bed. The oldest musketeer stood over the youth and focused his gaze on Porthos for a moment. "Bring me that basin of water and some rags. I'll see what I can do for the boy." Porthos retrieved the items and gave them to his companion. Typical of Athos to take charge even when he was not feeling well.

D'Artagnan stood frozen, indecision racking him. He had to say something before the situation spiraled completely out of control. "Athos," he finally said, and the musketeer stopped his preparations to look at D'Artagnan. "I really don't think it is wise for such a crowd to be here. I could take care of him."

"D'Artagnan, I have no time to argue with you. This boy needs attention, and you don't know anything about treating sword wounds. Not enough, at any rate," Athos responded curtly and returned his attention to Laurel.

D'Artagnan took a step towards the bed and the still form upon it. His brow wrinkled in an outer reflection of inner turmoil. "Athos, you don't understand."

"I understand that this boy needs help now and not five minutes from now," Athos stated as he began to tear fabric away from the wound.

"That's just it," D'Artagnan replied, despite himself. "That's no boy you're dealing with. Christophe is a woman. A lady."

"What?" Athos shot a stunned look at the young man and saw that he was completely serious. "Porthos, Aramis, perhaps you should leave. D'Artagnan and I will take care of this." Porthos and Aramis wasted no time debating the issue but simply left their companions to tend the wounded person.

"Grab some more rags, and get over here and lend me a hand. I've got to stop the bleeding," Athos instructed as he tore the last of the fabric away from the wound. Woman better not have a fit of modesty when she woke. By her very masquerade the lady wasn't much for conventions, so she had no right to go into hysterics over a strange man seeing her unclothed body when he was tending a wound. And Athos really wasn't in the mood for it.

"Water, please," the patient croaked as she awoke. Promptly a glass was placed in her hand, and she drank it down, and her eyes met Athos'. "I suppose I owe you all an explanation."

"That could be very helpful," Athos replied. No fit of modesty at least. No mention of who had tended her even. "Whenever you feel up to it, we're all waiting to hear."

Laurel tried to sit up and her head swirled. "Easy," Athos said as he helped her prop herself up against the bedpost.

"How long have I been here?" she asked suddenly and was informed that it had been two days. "I've got to get going."

"*Madame*," Athos told her using the most formal form of address at his disposal. "You're not going anywhere for at least several days. In any case, you're not leaving until you explain what brings you to Marseille and why the deception." They both looked up as the door opened, and Porthos, Aramis, and D'Artagnan entered. "Perhaps," Athos suggested, "you could start by telling us who you really are."

She took a deep breath and closed her eyes in resignation. She opened them again and looked from one man to the next. "My name is Laurel Christophe d'Anlass, daughter and heir, more or less, to the Marquis de Langeac. As to why I'm in Marseille, well suffice it to say that my home was no longer safe for me."

"I guess you'll have to pardon me then," Porthos informed Laurel. "But it doesn't seem that you are any safer in Marseille than at Langeac."

"That was just unlucky chance," she countered with surprising energy. "Those men just happened to stumble upon my horse and identified it as the property of the Marquis de Langeac when a merchant pointed me out as the youth who he had last seen riding the animal. And, well, you know the rest." Hopefully, Rebelle was still secure where the assailants had left him. Another thing to check on when she was able to get out and about.

"With all due respect, *madame*, how do we know that you're telling us the truth now?" D'Artagnan asked, doing his best not to insult the lady, though she was making that goal rather difficult.

"You don't," Laurel admitted, adding absently that *madame* was not her proper title as she was not married. "There's no possible way I could convince you that I am who I claim to be. I do assure you that falsely claiming to be Laurel d'Anlass would be suicidal. So I put my life in your hands; you've already saved my life twice by my reckoning, so I would hope that you would not get me killed now by trying to confirm my identity," she told the musketeers, particularly D'Artagnan.

Athos waved his three companions back and sat down beside the woman whose injury he had recently treated. "How would trying to confirm your identity get you killed?"

She lowered her eyes and winced as she almost pulled her wound open again. Silence encompassed the room, and no one moved for moments that seemed to drag on to infinity.

"Promise me what I tell you will go no further than you four. It's not just my life that depends on secrecy, but also many others, including the king's." Somehow their instincts favored believing her claim. One by one they gave her their words, and she proceeded to tell them about her past. Told them how her mother had died in childbirth and how her baby brother had died a week later, and then she explained that her father decided the best way to protect his only living child was to take her with him on his missions for the king.

Laurel went on to further explain that it was her father who'd first had her pretend to be a boy named Christophe in order to protect her and to make it easier to take her with him on his spy missions. Then she told of her father's recent return and the agents that were after them both. "And now," she paused, imprisoned within her own thoughts, "I must get to Calais and intercept the transmission of war plans and stolen government documents to England. Which means I also have to expose a traitor to France. So, obviously, the traitor will have his own agents looking for me as well as my father."

The room was so silent that even the whispers of the kitchen wenches from below-stairs could be heard in the room. Athos stood and surveyed his companions, his decision clear. "How do you feel about going to Calais?".

"Better than going back to Paris and being bored. Could use a good adventure," Porthos spoke, and D'Artagnan seconded him heartily, pushing his concerns for Constance aside in favor of the lure of a good adventure.

They all looked at Aramis. With complete calm he said, "You'll hear no objection from me. I say we go to Calais."

"*Madame,*" Athos addressed Laurel with careful politeness despite her claims to the title of *mademoiselle,* "allow us to fulfill your mission in Calais and then see to it that all the information gets back to the king. We will get you to Paris and put you under the protection of *Monsieur de* Treville."

"No." She stopped him before he went any further. "I will not be left behind. I know this job, and you do not. I've grown up with the danger and the intrigue, and I'm the only one who can contact my father." Athos' face remained implacable, and Laurel wanted to howl in frustration, but she didn't have the energy left to spare. Why did every man want to lock her away and try to protect her? Did they really think she was so delicate that she would break any easier than a man? "If you leave without me," she warned, "I will follow you." When she had recovered adequately.

However, the musketeers did not know her, nor did they take her warning seriously. When they left for Calais three days later, they left her behind with an escort standing ready to take her to Paris. It was an escort she'd make sure she avoided.

* * * * * * * * * * *

The hot, wet wax pooled on the letter and the man pressed his ring to it, sealing the letter tightly. He set the missive aside and turned his attention to more pressing matters such as who he could find to replace Rochefort.

Pursing his lips, he stopped staring at the ceiling and looked back to the reports laid upon his desk. One, an old one, regarding the death of Milady de Winter, another the relatively recent escape of Thomas d'Anlass from a Prussian prison, and another regarding the war effort against England. Another yet informing him that four musketeers had executed their mission to Marseille, but instead of returning to Paris they had headed in a direction too far west to reach Paris. He did not like unknown factors, especially when it concerned those meddlesome musketeers—Athos, Porthos, and Aramis and that new musketeer: D'Artagnan. That one especially. He had been a major reason the cardinal's plans had been foiled and had made Richelieu look the fool.

"Your eminence." A guard entered the study, and Cardinal Richelieu acknowledged him, requesting what his business was. "There is a lady here who requests to be admitted into your presence. She would not leave her name." As if greatly fatigued by the endless drudgery, he instructed his personal guard to send her in, and he would take care of the situation. He always had to take care of everything eventually.

The lady sketched a perfect curtsy to the cardinal, and he ever so gently kissed the tips of her fingers. "And what can I do for you?" Richelieu inquired.

"It's what I can do for you," she said, pushing back her cloak. "Milady de Winter."

"I can see you must have been informed of my demise. However, that information was a bit premature. I survived my plunge off the cliffs, and those musketeers never bothered to check and find my body to make sure that I was dead." She paused as if reconsidering for the briefest of moments. "I believe I could be quite an assistance to you."

"What makes you think that I require your unique talents, Milady? You failed in your last mission. One would not like to see you suffer the consequences of another failure."

So considerate of the man to be thinking of her well-being. As if he ever truly cared. Milady made a careful circuit around the room, wary of reaggravating her newly healed injuries. "So you deny that you're searching for information on the Marquis d'Anlass or on Athos, Porthos, Aramis, and D'Artagnan?"

"What can you offer me that my other agents cannot?" His eminence challenged the lady, his mind already at work considering and discarding the possibilities.

"I can deliver to you the only daughter of the marquis, and I can find the musketeers in question. They will not expect a dead woman to be pursuing them and will not be watching for a lady. Plus, when I find them I can very easily disrupt any task which may not, shall we say, be beneficial to your best interests."

"Ah," said Richelieu as he reseated himself and indicated that the blond-haired aristocrat be seated. "Perhaps we can come to a mutually beneficial arrangement."

* * * * * * * * * * * *

"Did we lose them?"

D'Artagnan gasped as Athos pulled his mount even with the young man's. "Hard to tell," D'Artagnan responded as he wiped away the streams of rain that continued to fall, trying to obscure his vision. Ridiculous, really. He couldn't remember a rainier summer. "Aramis thinks we've lost the contingent of the Cardinal's guard that was following us."

The four mounted men guided their horses through the sludge of the road towards an inn and tavern. The horses wheezed and shook their tails as if trying to dash off the cold of the falling water. With each step closer to shelter, the steeds snorted and phlegm blew from their noses. Nor were their riders in much better shape than the animals after their long haul and their near-frantic attempt to elude the guards who'd been attempting to follow them.

As the musketeers dismounted, a young lad came rushing forward from the stable to help them settle their mounts, unsaddle them, and brush them down before the men took shelter themselves from the harsh elements.

The drenched men entered the warmth of the main hall, and it enclosed them, making their wet clothes cling more closely to their bodies. Aramis, with his customary aplomb, procured chambers where they changed from their wet clothes into fresh breeches, tunics, and doublets. They hid away their musketeer mantles deeply in their packs. The decision had been unanimous: keep their true identities concealed as well as they possibly could. No further advertising that they were musketeers.

"Looks like our good mutual friend has been spotted," Porthos commented as he downed a swig of his drink, and both Athos and D'Artagnan glanced up to see the tall, well-groomed, dark-haired man enter the room. Aramis' dark, gold-flecked eyes surveyed his surroundings as if searching. One of the barmaids approached Aramis even as Porthos commented upon Aramis' arrival. She offered the man a wink and a smile as she came alongside him and sized him up appreciatively for a long moment.

"Can I get you something?" she inquired with a cute little pout. "Perhaps a tumbler of our best ale for starters."

"Non. Merci, mams'elle. I was looking for someone," he replied with charming politeness that was unique to him.

The wench leaned closer to him, permitting him a perfect view of creamy bosom exposed by a low-cut bodice. Momentarily he lost his train of thought as the tantalizing sight of a well-formed woman caught his attention. With one of her slender hands she fingered the crucifix that dangled from his neck. With another practiced pout she asked, "Are you a priest?"

"Ah, no," he finally responded. "I've not yet gone back to the seminary to complete my vows." He grasped her small hand and gently extracted the crucifix from it. Still her hand remained enclosed in his as he struggled to find a graceful way out of the situation. Wenching was rapidly losing its allure; there was no thrill in it anymore. No sense of accomplishment or purpose. Nor was he in the mood for it now. Hunger and fatigue weighed too heavily upon him this night.

"Well, that's Aramis for you. Always attracting the beautiful women without even trying," Porthos commented dryly before setting aside his drink and jumping to his feet at the sound of the fast-paced music drifting through the air. Lustily, he grabbed one of the barmaids around the waist and set off dancing with her.

Kissing her soundly, he twirled her around the room, enjoying being the center of much attention.

"It looks like you and I are to be left out of the festivities tonight. Or perhaps you'd like to follow their example." Athos made an encompassing gesture as he addressed D'Artagnan.

D'Artagnan cast a wary look upon his remaining companion. "How much have you had to drink?"

"Another nursemaid for me, huh. I suppose someone must take up after Aramis since he has been detained." Athos halted his friend's further words with a firm shake of his head. "Not to worry, *mon ami*, I've limited myself to one small bottle of wine tonight. I'm in no danger of drinking myself senseless or even getting drunk."

"That's nice to know," a strange voice intruded on the conversation, and both men turned their attention to the youth who was perched on a nearby chair. "For I do believe your friend might need your assistance," the youth told them, pointing towards Aramis. "I think maybe he needs some help extracting himself from that pretty little wench who has become rather clingy."

"We would not really want to interrupt our friend without his consent," Athos commented in a voice carefully calculated to turn the intruder away. Nearly rude, though none would have dared tell Athos to his face, except maybe Porthos or Aramis, and D'Artagnan, given some time.

"Well, I think it would be to your benefit to gather your friends before I make a nasty little scene that I'm sure we'd all rather avoid." The youngster was not at all put off by Athos' hint.

"*Mince alors*, good grief, Christophe," D'Artagnan said in a low voice, barely stopping himself from addressing the disguised woman as Laurel. "What are you doing here?"

"I cannot think that's a conversation we want to be having in this room. It would be kind of hard to explain things to the satisfaction of all onlookers, now, wouldn't it?"

Athos turned his attention to D'Artagnan and told him to go extract Porthos. After D'Artagnan had escaped from his chair and braved the crowd surrounding the large musketeer, Athos permitted himself a moment to take stock of the woman who called herself Laurel.

He'd be—she'd actually tracked them, and they never even noticed. Which could well mean they hadn't eluded the cardinal's Guard. Then again the cardinal's guards were rather inept. Laurel forestalled further action on Athos' part by jumping to her feet and proceeding to inform him that since he was so reluctant, she would have to go retrieve Aramis herself. "Not to worry. I'll be back for you," she decreed and danced off to "rescue" Aramis.

Before he could stop her, she had inserted her body in the small space between the couple and forced Aramis' attention to her. "Your friends have sent me to fetch you. It's important, and I'm afraid it is a matter that must be discussed now and in private," Laurel said, fending off the barmaid with ease, and unbeknownst to her, saving Aramis the problem of figuring out how to get rid of the girl.

"You are supposed to be in Paris under the protection of *Monsieur de* Treville," Athos scolded Laurel almost as if she were a recalcitrant child, and his three companions looked on, disapproval plain in their stiff stances.

"I told you before that I am the only one who has the ability to contact my father, and that is a vital part of this mission. And," she said raising her voice so that the men could not shut her out, patronizing sons of . . . "I did tell you that I had a great deal of experience in the field of espionage and that I would not be left behind. Nor will I be left behind again."

"Please, Lady Laurel," D'Artagnan broke in, "we would not have you destroy your life and reputation. We would not see you killed on a dangerous mission. Can you not go where it is safer?"

With those words Laurel lost her composure and ripped into the young man and his friends. "Perhaps all of you should let me be the judge of what is and what is not safe and proper for me. Who are you three to tell me that I am safer in Paris, near the cardinal whom both my father and I not only despise but also mistrust? Knowing that, you still have the gall to tell me what's safe for me." She paused to catch her breath, her eyes flashing in challenge. "I can quite well take care of myself, as well as any one of you. I am a very good rider and an excellent fencer, not to mention that you were able to lose the cardinal's guard, but were unable to lose me."

Porthos leaned over towards the man closest to his height and commented, "Nasty little temper there." Aramis nodded. Almost as an afterthought the big man added, "Is she really any good at fencing?"

"She held her own in Marseille when D'Artagnan and I were fighting alongside her," the would-be-priest admitted, a bit grudgingly.

Laurel pivoted on her heel and turned to glare at Porthos and Aramis. "By all means, if you gentlemen have something to say, please allow us all to hear." In frustration she expelled a breath of pent-up air and sank into the nearby chair. "Why do I even bother?" she mumbled, her words unclear to the musketeers. Why did she always seem to lose her cool at the worst times? Uneasy silence settled on the awkward situation.

"*Madame*, you have a lousy temper," Aramis said, but in his own singular way which conveyed no insult, and Laurel shrugged her shoulders, saying that men weren't exclusively entitled to the right to lose their tempers.

"Is it really so hard for you four big strong men to listen to a woman's point of view on anything, or would that be some affront to your masculinity?" she asked, softly massaging her temples in an effort to ward off an impending headache. She'd been suffering from many of those recently.

Ooh. Porthos flinched inwardly at the lady's words. Barbs more like it. Independent, feisty thing, and stubborn. The lady knew how to fence verbally; that was definitely not debatable. Of course involvement in international intrigue had a way of making people perfect the skill. "I'm sorry, *madame*. We cannot take the risk or put you in further danger," Athos responded, and he truly did seem to regret turning her away.

Her jaw worked in consternation and she closed her eyes, taking deep breaths to steady and calm herself. So Athos was the leader, and it was him she would have to convince. A losing proposition—or so it appeared. "If I were a man . . ."

"If you were a man, we'd still be reluctant to take along someone who's fighting ability and loyalty we were unsure of." Athos anticipated the course of her question.

"But you would not turn him away out of hand, would you?" Athos' steady look confirmed the truth of her assessment. "Yet you'll turn me away without even giving me a chance to prove myself. Are men really so afraid of a woman who could be their equal in intelligence, ability, ambition, and fighting skills?"

"A musketeer fears nothing," D'Artagnan insisted.

"Really, is that so? I thought only fools feared nothing," Laurel riposted, as she made her exit from the room.

For a moment there was confused silence in the room and then D'Artagnan approached Athos. "We can't just let her walk out there. This is a very dangerous place for a lone woman."

Athos forbore telling the young man that Laurel had already likely survived many such unsavory places in her pursuit of them. "What do you propose I do? Do you think I can stop her without making the very scene we would like to avoid at all costs? No. I'm afraid in this we can do nothing but leave her to follow her own path right now," Athos concluded and then changed the subject. "Porthos, Aramis, are either of you acquainted with Thomas d'Anlass or do you know anyone who is acquainted with him?"

"Ah, the great and noble Marquis de Langeac and our erstwhile lady's father," Porthos said loudly, leaning back in a chair and propping his feet on a nearby table. "Can't say as we've ever met. Man's a little beyond my age. Must be in his mid to late forties by now." His friends directed him disgusted looks for wasting valuable time with a brief run down on the man's age. "No sense of humor and always in a hurry," he mumbled and then looked to his companions. "Well then, best I can do for you is that I'm a distant cousin to the man on my mother's side and the family is very old and well established." Aramis lifted his palms upward in a silent gesture that told Athos he had even less connection to the marquis. "I don't suppose you know much about the marquis." Porthos shot a look at D'Artagnan.

"Sorry. Never even really heard of him until recently." D'Artagnan stifled a humorless chuckle. "So it looks as if we're going to have a very hard time finding a man who's not been seen or heard from in almost two years. And Lady Laurel d'Anlass really is the only one who might know how to contact her father."

* * * * * * * * * * *

"No, behind the hovel," Guillaume ordered in a harsh whisper, and Joseph quickly complied.

Joseph began to speak, and Guillaume waved his hand, stopping him in mid word as he listened at the wall of the small dwelling. Low voices caught his attention, and he strained his ears to hear each word.

Guillaume pulled away from the hovel, and Joseph signaled that all was clear as far as he could see. Cautiously the two men retreated from the building into the sheltering copse of trees. "What'd you learn?" Joseph asked impatiently.

"A man answering to the name of Antoine Françoise passed through here about a day and a half ago. He was headed towards the Pyrénées."

"Did they mention anything about what Antoine looked like?" Joseph questioned, and Guillaume sketched the brief description that he had overheard. The brush rustled, and both men ceased conversation, straining to be sure that no one had stumbled upon them.

When they had assured themselves that they were alone, Joseph continued, "Sounds like one of the identities the marquis appropriated on a mission to Corsica. I think splitting up and coming into the Luz area by two different directions might be the best plan." Guillaume nodded his head, and the agents went over the last details of the plan before disappearing into descending dusk.

Section Two

Milady de Winter restrained herself from raising her voice, unwilling to reveal her vexation to either of her bodyguards. Already Richelieu was attempting to limit her access to the funds she required to carry off the tasks his eminence had entrusted to her. In addition it was beginning to appear that after the successful completion of this last job the cardinal would relinquish the major reasons for his hold over the *comtesse* if she kept a close eye on things. Of course, there was always that one influence she wasn't sure how to remove from his hands.

Almost imperceptibly, she winced as a shot of pain struck her, reminding her that her ribs were still tender. Well, she would not be dancing to the cardinal's tune, not after she visited her first stepfather's estate and claimed the money she had secreted and never had the opportunity to retrieve. Until then her leverage was very limited, considering . . .

Gracefully, she took the proffered hand and entered her carriage, informing the driver to head towards the Loire River Valley. The door closed behind her and the carriage rumbled off towards its destination, and away from Moulins, as Milady stashed the ornate but highly functional dagger in the sheath between her breasts.

Where to find Laurel? That was the question. She had obviously fled the estate, but to where? Where had Thomas told her to seek refuge when she thought that she was in danger? *Monsieur de* Treville. No. The marquis' dislike of the cardinal and anywhere near Richelieu had surely infected his daughter. Milord Compton, however, was a possibility, and Compton was in Marseille; it appeared she would be headed to Marseille after the stop at her stepfather's estate—logically speaking.

"Marseille," she spoke aloud. "Of course! That was where Athos, Porthos, Aramis, and D'Artagnan had escorted a caravan of merchants several days back." According to Richelieu the musketeers had not yet returned. If Laurel went to Marseille she might have contacted the musketeers. Dear old Thomas had adored the musketeers, as had his daughter. Which could mean that if she found the four musketeers, she would also locate Laurel d'Anlass at the same time. Now where had the cardinal's men lost sight of those musketeers?

Milady rapped upon the screen, and one of the drivers opened it. "There's been a change of plans," she said brusquely. "Head towards Aurillac as quickly as you can." She closed her side of the screen and leaned back. Her instincts had not been wrong before, and she saw no need to doubt them now. Besides, her money had waited this long. It could wait a little longer.

As the carriage rumbled through streets that were badly in need of servicing. Milady pushed aside the curtain and peered into the bustling street scene, carefully committing each detail to memory. Her life could depend on it.

Just as she was about to let the curtain fall back into place, she caught sight of a man striding purposefully away from the market. Taller than average, with shapely legs that matched the rest of his well-toned body. Blond hair and commanding carriage and confident stride. She knew that man. He turned around for just a moment before he disappeared from her sight. She let the curtain fall back and whispered under her breath, "Athos." Swiftly, she instructed one of her bodyguards to follow the man who had just vanished and not to come back until he knew where the man was staying.

As Milady de Winter was completing her task of getting settled in her recently procured chamber, her bodyguard entered and bowed. At her bidding he informed the lady of the name and location of where Athos was staying. "*Merci*," she said without an audible change in the tone of her voice and dismissed the guard.

The noblewoman double-checked to be sure that her dagger was in place between her breasts and another in her hair comb. Satisfied, she donned her hooded cloak and slipped from her room to the darkened alley below. She stopped short as three men sporting sabers by their sides approached the door-jamb of the derelict building.

A tall man with a crescent-shaped scar from ear to chin and an eye patch swept his hat off and addressed her. "What can we be doing for you, *madame*?"

Milady ignored the lapse, the fact the man had not accorded her fully qualified proper title. She would rather they not know anything about her identity. She extracted a sack full of pistoles and several gold pieces from her purse and put them in the scarred man's hands. "That is the first half of your payment. If you carry out the task successfully then you will get an equal sum when you report back here tomorrow night."

The man undid the drawstring of the little bag and ran the coins through his fingers. She was offering them what these men considered a small fortune. "What would you have us do?"

"Tonight I want you to kill a man, and I'd best not be disappointed," she responded with a disturbing lack of emotion. Emotions would not be permitted to interfere with revenge, not this time as they had before. She simply could not permit it. Besides, it was too late to save her blighted soul. Far too late.

* * * * * * * * * * *

She awoke to the sound of rustling straw and propped herself up on her elbows. A moment later she eased her hand to the hilt of her sword and glanced around the interior of the stables. Gulped for several breaths as she calmed her thudding heart.

There it was again. That was no horse. Those were the steps of men trying to hide their approach. Easy, Laurel instructed herself as she gained her feet without a sound.

Laurel took several stealthy steps and peered around the corner to see the shadowy silhouette of three men. One turned to glance back, and she pressed herself against the wall, biting her lip to prevent a loud intake of air that would reveal her presence.

When she was sure that the men were once again focused on entering the inn, she fumbled inside her vest and extracted the small pistol that had once belonged to her mother. Reached inside her cloak again and took out a ball and powderhorn. Carefully, she primed the weapon and set off, without making a sound, in pursuit of the three uninvited visitors. Her mouth fell open dumbly as she saw them lean a ladder against the side of the building and next to the window. That was Athos' room, wasn't it?

Laurel awkwardly held the gun in her mouth and sent a quick prayer to the Almighty before she tested her ability or lack thereof to scale walls, especially with a gun in her mouth. Beads of sweat trickled down her forehead, and she did not dare flick them away but had to allow them to sting her eyes. Her arms shook under the strain and her mouth trembled. *Parbleu*, the gun was heavier and bigger than it looked, and she couldn't afford to lose it and have it go off.

Finally she dropped in through the window of the second story, and snatched the gun from her mouth, panting for breath. Her hands were still shaking as she re-primed the gun and searched for the servants' entrance to Athos' room, hoping that he would not have thought to lock it. She had a bad feeling about this. Really bad.

As she opened the servants' entrance she heard the tell-tale spanning of a wheel lock, and she propelled herself headlong into the chamber, yelling, "Athos," at the top of her lungs.

Athos roused just in time to see a man pointing a loaded gun at his head, and he rolled away as the gun shattered the tranquility of the night. He was quick enough to save his life, but not quick enough to avoid the bullet as it impacted with the flesh of his right shoulder, narrowly missing the bone. He howled in agony even as he grabbed his sword with his left hand.

Seeing that another assailant who had just entered the room was preparing to fire on the injured and defenseless man, Laurel took aim, cocked her own weapon and pulled the trigger.

This was one time she was grateful her mother had owned one of the first flintlocks. The man fell back with one scream of agony, clutching what remained of his face before he died. She threw aside the empty gun and drew her sword, quickly deflecting a second blade away from Athos.

Athos stepped back and twirled to meet his opponent's attack, wincing as the impact jarred his useless and bleeding shoulder. He was not prepared to meet his maker tonight, he informed himself as he shoved his opponent away with a mighty push. He swiveled and lunged, parrying and dodging as he fought against nausea and the buzzing in his own head. Sloppily, he deflected another blow, cursing the injury that prevented him from fighting with his normal brutal effectiveness.

Nevertheless, he had to end it quickly before the man wore him out and killed him. Desperately, he gasped for air and sent a prayer to God, hoping that as Aramis had once claimed in a similar situation, "You see there is a God."

Athos screamed and charged towards his opponent, catching him off guard, and he felt the blade impale the man who sank to his knees, shaking as blood poured from his opened guts. Mercifully, he lost consciousness before blood loss killed him.

It was then that Athos turned to see his rescuer cut down the final assassin and clean the sword before sheathing it. Athos made a clumsy attempt to retrieve his own blade from the dead man's body but only staggered.

Laurel's head shot up as she heard the musketeer stumble, and she rushed to his side, thrusting her arm under his good shoulder and guiding him back towards the bed. "Come on, Athos, help me," she said, her words coming between gulps of air. "I've got to get you to this bed before you collapse. I'm not quite strong enough to do it on my own. Come on, help me, man. *Aidez-moi!* You're too heavy for me to lug on my own." At least when she was tired as she was now.

From out in the corridor a loud voice called, "Athos, are you all right? Answer me, are you all right? Open the door." The door rattled but hardly budged against the lock.

Laurel looked over her shoulder as she laid Athos on the bed, and Porthos came hurling through what remained of the broken door, Aramis and D'Artagnan following closely behind him.

The musketeers stopped short as they took in the three dead bodies and the young person standing over Athos' still form. "Don't just stand there," Laurel commanded as she tore the fabric away from Athos' shoulder to reveal the nasty bullet wound. "Help me save his life or at the very least his arm."

Aramis hurried to the bed and helped get Athos positioned completely upon it as Porthos left the room in search of lots of fresh bandages. Of course, first he decided to dispose of the bodies where no one would readily ask questions.

D'Artagnan filled a basin with water and hauled it over to the bed, placing it just out of Athos' reach and beside Laurel. Laurel lifted her bloodstained face. "Do either of you have a small, very sharp knife?"

"In my room," D'Artagnan replied, and he dashed out to get it before the woman had a chance to ask.

Athos grunted and struggled as Laurel and Aramis attempted to staunch the bleeding. "The ball's still in there, isn't it?" Aramis said with an unearthly calm even as he tied a loose tourniquet and got up to light several tapers for them to better see by.

Laurel nodded tersely. An instant later, Porthos re-entered the room; his arms were laden with fresh linen, and he was carrying a bottle of cognac—the strongest he could procure—in each hand. It had taken him a while, but apparently he'd been successful Laurel noted as he dropped the linens at the bedside and pulled a cork out with his teeth and then proffered the bottle to Laurel. She snatched it with a word of thanks, diverting her attention to preparing to perform emergency surgery by scrubbing her hands in the water.

Athos thrashed again and his clouded, pain-filled eyes focused on Aramis and Porthos. "Is he dead?" Athos demanded in a weak voice.

"Yes, they're all dead, *mon ami*," Aramis assured him, his voice soothing, as D'Artagnan entered the room, knife in hand, and offered it to Laurel, who took it with a nod. "We are going to see to it that you are all right. We have seen you through worse wounds than this one. We are not about to lose you now."

"Athos," Laurel said softly as she poured another swig of the brandy on the cloth. "The ball is still in your shoulder, probably at the joint. We have to get it out. I do have some skills in treating wounds such as this. Will you trust me, or do you want us to send for a sawbones?" Athos' pain filled eyes met hers, and he told her that his life was in her hands.

"In that case, brace yourself. This is going to hurt." Laurel shifted her grasp on the knife. "Aramis, Porthos if you'd be so kind as to see that he doesn't thrash about," she commanded as she cleaned the wound with the brandy-soaked rag.

Athos winced as the alcohol stung and set the bloody injury on fire. He clenched his teeth together as she poured more cognac on the open wound and gently wiped away most of the blood. Laurel, seeing his distress, placed one of the cloths between his teeth to prevent him from biting through his tongue. The woman did have strange medical practices picked up from who knew where, but she seemed completely confident in what she was doing. She better be, because it hurt like the devil. A flinch immediately followed Athos' thought.

Laurel glanced around and her eyes latched on to the unopened bottle of cognac. D'Artagnan lifted it from the table and uncorked it as he was instructed. He brought the open bottle to the bed and Laurel said, "Give it to Aramis."

D'Artagnan did so immediately and backed away, going to the corridor to fend off and explain to the proprietor and other guests who had finally come to see what all the commotion was about. As he invented a plausible explanation for the situation, he was able to prevent the visitors from disturbing Athos and his friends, and he made sure that the bodies Porthos had moved were better disposed of.

"Aramis, help Athos drink the entire bottle. Let's see if we can dull the pain or maybe even knock him out before I do any cutting." If she had to resort to crude methods, crude it would be. That many would not find her methods so crude escaped her in the heat of the moment.

Moments dragged by as Aramis urged his friend to keep drinking until the bottle was drained, every last drop. He set the empty bottle aside and both uninjured musketeers prepared to hold Athos motionless.

Laurel lifted the cognac-soaked blade to the wound and made a deft, deep slice in the flesh of Athos' shoulder. Athos thrashed weakly, and the men held him down until finally he passed into merciful unconsciousness. With her arm, Laurel wiped sweat from her brow and made another careful incision next to the wound.

Suddenly the bleeding started again, and Porthos grabbed a fresh cloth and stanched the flow of blood while Laurel looked around for a forceps of some sort and laid them on the blood-stained bed-cloth. She paused right in the middle of making a third cut, and Aramis and Porthos both looked her straight in the eye. Long, palpably tense moments ticked by. "You can do it," they both encouraged her, and she bent her head and returned to the task at hand. There was no other option.

For one more moment her hand was poised above the wound and then the knife descended. One final, quick incision, and she set aside the sharp blade. Porthos lifted the makeshift forceps and handed them to her with a silent word of luck. She took them. "Try to keep the wound open so I can see as clearly as possible." Absorbed in her task, she bent her head so she could more easily see the open wound.

"Do you see it?" Aramis inquired.

She allowed the question to hover between them as she gently probed the wound for a sign of the ball and was finally rewarded by the hard touch of the lead ball against the makeshift forceps. No bone-chips, and the ball seemed whole. He was extraordinarily lucky. She sincerely hoped pulling this out did not cause more damage than Athos could survive, but she could see no other way than extracting it since leaving it in would more than likely kill him, slowly.

"*Oui*," Laurel finally replied. Taking a deep breath she grasped the ball firmly and pulled it out quickly.

She looked at her bloody hand and the equally bloody instrument and smiled in relief as she saw the ball was whole and it was entirely out. "I got it," she announced, and the other musketeers returned her relieved smile even as D'Artagnan approached with a needle and thread and offered them to the woman, "I thought that these might come in useful."

"*Merci*," she responded and used the last of the brandy on the needle and the open wound. While his three companions looked on, she carefully stitched together the flaps of skin and sealed the wound. Swiftly, she untied the tourniquet, hoping too much damage had not been caused by the desperate measure to stop the bleeding. When it was all over, she sank back on her heels and prepared to face Athos' friends.

Showing the strain of the last long minutes, D'Artagnan asked, "Do you think he'll live, *Mademoiselle* Laurel?"

"He was very lucky. The ball did very little damage overall, and I'd guess he's got a very good chance," she responded honestly. "He's a strong man and in good shape. I think we were able to stop the bleeding and get that ball out in time. As long as we can keep it from festering, he should survive. We should know better tomorrow."

The three musketeers surveyed the exhausted woman, and Aramis offered her his arm. "*Madame*, you look utterly spent. Perhaps I could escort you to someplace where you can clean yourself up and get some sleep." She nodded and clambered wearily to her feet. It dimly registered that this was the first time she really appreciated, even liked, Aramis' cultivated correctness. So very stable and dependable, even if it probably did hide just how dangerous the man could be.

Just before the pair left the room, Laurel informed them, "Oh, and seeing as it would be extremely awkward to explain the presence of a female, I do suggest that you remember to refer to me as Christophe at all times." With the parting reminder, she and Aramis left the room.

"Christophe." A voice called from a great distance, pulling the young woman from a deep and dreamless sleep. She rolled over in the bed, deciding it was only her imagination and that she could go back to sleep. No—on second thought she was not awake at all but dreaming, and an unpleasant one at that. The noise, however, did not diminish, and a hand grasped her shoulder and shook her gently awake. "Christophe."

"I'm awake. I'm awake," she protested, sitting up and opening her eyes to focus blearily on D'Artagnan. "What do you want?" she inquired testily, yawning. The desire to fall back against the pillow was so very enticing. She started to sink back and then shook herself.

"Athos has been calling for you."

She groaned in the back of her throat. "Nice to know I'm so wanted," she grumbled. Rather not be wanted right now, though. Some days she hated mornings more than others. This was one of those days. "I guess that means I'll be getting up now."

D'Artagnan rose, preparing to leave the room and allow her some privacy to get dressed. "Don't bother," Laurel halted him. "I sleep fully clothed. It's safer that way." The woman checked to assure herself that the tightly wound bun was still in place. "If you would just hand me my boots and hat," she said, swinging herself half out of the bed, "I'll accompany you right now."

She tugged one boot on and then the next and placed the hat upon her head. "Well, how do I look?"

"I don't know how you do it," the youngest musketeer addressed her. "You look just like a boy, especially when one can't see your face very clearly or sees you only from a distance."

"I should hope so. My life depends on it, and I've had enough practice that I've quite perfected the outfit and mannerisms. Is there anything wrong with Athos?"

The musketeer quickly shook his head and raised his hands in front of him. "No. Well, other than a nasty headache and fatigue he seems to be fine." D'Artagnan forestalled her next question. "He insists on seeing you. I think he wants to go over what happened last night and find out exactly what he's gotten himself into."

"Hold on a second," Laurel protested as they closed the door behind them. "Those men last night had nothing to do with me. They knew exactly where they were going, and they headed directly for Athos' room. I'm willing to wager that those men were hired to kill Athos, which means there is a new enemy in the picture. Or perhaps even an old one." Old grudges had a way of coming back to haunt the present.

Athos was an incredibly fortunate man, more fortunate than even Laurel had initially thought. Fever only seized him for a day and then he began an extraordinarily swift recovery under the close supervision of his friends.

As each day passed the wound continued to heal, showing no sign of infection or serious scarring. It wasn't very long—less than two weeks—before the oldest musketeer was beginning to get back into his routine, and he became anxious to push on and finish the mission. His country and his king were depending on it, and time was limited. Too much had already been squandered.

After days of his friends' ministrations he sent them away, wrapped the wound himself then dressed himself completely, and on his own. Shortly after that he was even strong enough to take his horse for a brief ride. In fact, he was just coming in from that ride when he nearly ran into Laurel. Hastily he begged her pardon and then drew her aside from the onlookers. "I don't believe I've thanked you yet. I owe you my life and my arm. *Merci*."

"You're welcome," the woman said modestly, as if trying to divert the subject. "Although I do believe we are even now. As I recall, you probably saved my life in Marseille." She started to pull away and head back towards the door that led to the stables when Athos spoke. "Christophe, how did you know exactly what to do to save me?"

Laurel turned and stepped towards Athos. "When my father took me on assignment with him, many times we were around people who were shot or wounded in the line of duty." There was a war going on all over Europe, after all, and she'd been in the thick of it numerous times. "Nor were there many doctors available, and every healthy person was expected to lend a hand."

"Your father didn't try to keep you out of this?"

"It would have drawn undue attention to him to prohibit his own son from helping injured men. Basically from my twelfth year I began doctoring wounded men. I saw first-hand what did and didn't work in a given situation. By the time I was six and ten my father and I had saved more lives than any field doctor had. And do you want to know why?"

"Why?" Athos questioned, sincerely interested, surprising himself at the question.

"Because we were willing to experiment and change our treatments. We rarely amputated, and we listened to advice from all sides, even from Asians. Nor did we ever drink before we went to work. You know what?" Laurel glanced at the musketeer and he told her he didn't know what. "I've come to the conclusion that bloodletting often kills a man, and that more often than not, amputations that are done to try to save a man's life actually kill him." Of course Laurel well understood what could drive a doctor to drink. Those things she had seen in her not too distant youth had caused her none too few a nightmare.

"What other strange notions have you come across in your travels, lad?" Porthos said as he joined them.

"*Oui*, I admit my father and I are very eccentric, but what we did saved men's lives," she defended, taking offense at the suggestion in Porthos' tone that she was most definitely not what she should be. "We learned to use strong alcohol to wash out wounds and to pour that same alcohol on every instrument that we used during surgery. We took to frequently washing our hands and faces with soap and water between patients. Oh don't look so scandalized." She frowned at the two men. "It worked, and it was this knowledge I used to save Athos. If you'll notice, he has recovered very quickly and with very few complications. None that I can think of, to be precise."

"I suppose you also advocate full-body bathing as often as possible," Porthos commented, his tone clearly derogatory. *Madame* was very easy to provoke.

"As a matter of fact, I do. I believe in full-body bathing with soap and water at least once or twice a week when possible." Sometimes more frequently.

"Wherever did you pick up such a strange notion? Don't you know that bathing causes sickness and chills, drains life away?" Porthos informed her, deliberately baiting her further.

"Well, I'll have you know that I've been bathing in this manner all my life, and I am rarely ever sick. And the Asians have been doing so for centuries, and they live significantly longer than most Europeans." Barring war, that is.

"Where did you become such an expert on Asians?" Athos changed the subject before Laurel took it into her head to go after Porthos and do him some mischief.

"Before I was born my father used to frequently travel to the Indies and was an active participant in the spice trade. He made a fortune in it because he adapted to the Asians' way of life. He followed many of their practices and won their respect. Eventually, he hired a half dozen Asians to come back to France with him and serve in his household. So I grew up with an Asian nursemaid and other Asian servants. I cannot think that the Asian traditions I have followed would hurt anyone," she concluded. She was beginning to suspect Porthos might have been baiting her. Would fit perfectly well with the big man's personality.

"No wonder you're such a queer little thing," Porthos interjected, and Laurel looked as if she'd like to shove his words back down his throat no matter how much bigger he was. All thoughts he might have been baiting her fled from Laurel's mind.

"I'm not little, you hulking elephant. And call me queer if you must, *monsieur*," she threw back at him, deliberately slighting his rank as much as possible. "Of course, I think that men are afraid of change, afraid of a woman or anyone for that matter who is proud to be independent and not ashamed of who and what she is." She spat out the last words with all the hurt anger that was pent up inside her being.

"Christophe," Athos tried to break through her tirade, but she was determined not to stop. He grabbed her shoulder and turned her around to face him. "Christophe! Christophe!" he cried, shaking her until she shut up. "You are creating a scene and could well blow what is left of our cover with this tirade. I suggest you finish it in private." Each word became softer so that only she could hear it.

The young woman took several deep breaths and stood up straight, trying to regain her composure. Very quietly, with fiery intensity, she told Porthos, "I am who I am. I will make no apologies for that. I'm an eccentric, just like my father, and I'm very proud of that. I've got every reason for my pride, just like you, or Athos, or Aramis, or D'Artagnan take great pride in the unique people you are." She choked on a word before going on. "But I suppose that makes me a freak who cannot fit into society anywhere, beyond the pale and not a true lady or woman. At least you have somewhere where you belong, *monsieur*. I don't even have that. So at least allow me my pride in myself, my accomplishments, and my heritage," she finished and rushed from the room to the streets and lost herself in the crowd. At least she had gotten the last word.

D'Artagnan joined his two companions after almost being bowled over by Laurel as she stormed out of the room. "What happened with Christophe?"

"Christophe lost his temper again," Athos finally answered, his eyes looking for Laurel's form. Her temper might well end up getting her killed just as his own temper had nearly killed him about eleven years earlier, before he had learned to better control it. That and her penchant for trying to help through direct challenge when other methods other than frontal assault might well have worked better.

"Let me know when Christophe gets back. I want to talk to him immediately," Athos told his companions and then made his way to his room, flinching as he jarred his still tender shoulder.

* * * * * * * * * * * *

Rats scurried along the floor and water dripped from the ceiling, drop by drop. A torch sputtered in the dankness, and a whip cracked once then twice and then too many times to count.

The unremitting stench of urine, feces, and rotting flesh was overpowering as the cardinal passed through the dungeons, followed by several of his personal guards who were close to retching. Yet Richelieu continued on, undisturbed, towards the secret meeting chamber. He signaled for his guards to open the door. They scampered forward and did so. As his eminence entered the room, they held the door open. With a flick of his wrist he imperiously sent his guards out and instructed them to close the door behind them.

"Your eminence." A man stepped to his feet and bowed over the cardinal's outstretched hand ever so slightly.

"*Monsieur*," Richelieu responded, bowing his head in brief acknowledgment of the foreign nobleman. "Shall we make ourselves comfortable?" Both men sat down, and the cardinal poured each of them a glass of his best champagne. His eminence drained the glass and set it aside before addressing the other man. "What of Buckingham?"

"My brother, his grace," the man said, leaning forward, "is prepared to agree to your proposal. However, he will help you overthrow Louis and acknowledge you as the legitimate king only if you can provide detailed battle plans and inside information about the Austrian Empire in addition to the already promised informant."

"I can guarantee his grace, the Duke of Buckingham, half of Europe if he has but a little patience," the cardinal said unflinchingly, thinking of how unfortunate it would be if he would have to lose Anne of Austria as his own queen because he sold her country to England.

"Unfortunately, my brother cannot gamble on helping you with a coup d'état without proof of good faith that he will not be betrayed or undermined. I am afraid that we have wasted our time." The Englishman rose to his feet in preparation to leave.

"Plans outlining Spain and Belgium's defenses are already on their way to England, along with other highly secret documents of state. If, however, Buckingham has lost interest, I could always see to it that those documents never make it out of the country, or I could send them to Prussia instead."

The Englishman turned around to face the cardinal. "As soon as his grace receives the papers in question, we will send you the promised fleet, Cardinal Richelieu. I guarantee it personally." He turned to leave. "And don't forget you promised to deliver the spy, Thomas d'Anlass, to us in exchange for providing certain funds."

"You will not be disappointed. The marquis will be off French soil and in your custody by the end of next month," the cardinal assured him.

Once the man had left, Richelieu turned his attention to the sealed message on his desk. Deftly he broke the seal and read:

> Your eminence,
>
> The final destination of the musketeers in question is Calais. I will receive more information as to their task from my sources in Marseille—soon. Be assured that the information will be forwarded to you immediately.
>
> Milady

* * * * * * * * * * *

"D'Artagnan, you are going to wear a hole through the floor boards of this room if you do not take it a little easier," Aramis addressed the man who was three or so years his junior. He closed his Bible and placed it on the nightstand, then leaned back in his chair, propping his feet up. "What are you so agitated about?"

"Do you know where Athos went? His room is empty and no one's seen him for hours."

"You sure he's not back yet?"

D'Artagnan said he was sure.

"I know that since Christophe did not come back yesterday Athos went in search of Christophe today. However, Athos should have been back by now. Have you asked Porthos?"

"He hasn't a clue," D'Artagnan dismissed the suggestion. "He's been drinking, dancing, and wenching since at least midday. If he's not thoroughly inebriated by now, I'll eat my hat." Porthos and his wenching, he thought. Did the man ever stop or even know when he had gone overboard in that area? Or in any area of his life, for that matter?

Aramis got to his feet and buckled his sword and scabbard around his waist. He then slipped into his overcoat and placed the black hat with its drooping plume upon his head. "I guess we should go look for them then. Together." This so-called mission of utmost importance was turning into a disaster, or at the very least, a comedy of errors.

"Milady, we found this lad snooping around," a bodyguard informed her, gripping the squirming youth even harder—a youth whose hands were bound behind him. She was a match for one boy. Milady de Winter took a closer look at the uninvited visitor and dismissed her bodyguards. "I'll handle this. If I need anything, I'll call you."

The youth stood defiantly in front of her, topping the noble woman by several finger widths. "I see you have nothing to say for yourself," Milady said in a deceptively offhand manner, approaching her guest in mincing steps. Her hand snaked out, and she tore the hat from the boy's head and grasped his chin firmly in her fingers. She chuckled under her breath, "Laurel, still acting the part of Thomas' son I see."

"Sabine." She half gasped, thinking the woman long dead. "But Papa said you had died several years ago."

"My step-father was mistaken in that as he was in a great many other things about me." She turned away from her stepsister, twiddling a letter opener between her fingers.

"Sabine, I tried to explain to Papa that it wasn't you who had killed Philipe, that it was me."

She whirled on her stepsister. "You lied for me?"

"Well, not really. When I heard you screaming and kicking and saw his hands clenching tighter and tighter around your throat I stabbed him."

Milady interrupted her with a deathly calm voice. "Correct me if I'm wrong. But did he or did he not kick you into the wall and return to me?" Laurel didn't correct her. "Then as I recall, I pulled your knife out of his back and desperately stabbed and stabbed until he let me go. Wasn't that the way it happened?"

"*Oui*, but that isn't the point. That story wouldn't have saved you. In a manner of speaking I was responsible for his death. So I tried to tell him that I killed Philipe because he was attacking you, but Stéphane spoke against me. He said you'd murdered Philipe in cold blood." Sabine swirled glaring at her stepsister. "Stéphane, your half-brother," Laurel stuttered, "hated you with an unnatural passion. Sabine, he did it because you refused his offer of marriage, and everyone believed his story rather than mine."

"Still you stood by while I was branded with the fleur-de-lys and convicted for murder, about to be executed?"

"No. I didn't just stand by. Stéphane locked me in my room to prevent me from helping you escape your sentence. Then he told Papa that I was too sick to come down and just wanted to sleep. You don't know how happy I was when I heard you'd been able to escape despite Stéphane."

"Really, do tell me," she urged, seating herself, wondering where Laurel's fast-talking was leading her.

"I even told Stéphane that I was thrilled that you had escaped, that his plan had failed. In fact I lost my temper and cut into him." Milady de Winter suppressed a quick smile. Laurel and her fiery temper. One day she'd control it or suffer the consequences. "He began hitting me and kicking me, screaming at me to shut up, using language even cruder than I care to reproduce."

Laurel's voice wavered, and she closed her eyes against unwelcome tears, stopping them before they fell. "So I ran to mother's room and found her pistol. I warned him. I swear with God as my witness that I warned him not to touch me. He didn't listen, so I shot him. Stéphane died a week later."

Both women were silent. "What did Thomas do to you?"

"He believed every word I said about my step-brother and almost ended Stéphane's life then and there for beating me. As it was, the doctor tried to save him, but he ended up dying later."

"I won't say I'm sorry to hear that my half-brother died. I wish I had found out before tonight."

Laurel glanced at Sabine. "Papa kept it quiet. He had Stéphane buried without ceremony. Only he, myself, and the priest were present. Papa wanted no further scandal about his stepchildren. He loved your mother enough that he couldn't stand that the children of her earlier marriages would both be discredited and shamed."

"Still he never had me called back," Milady accused.

"That's the biggest mistake he has ever made, but in his pride he could not admit that he had accused an innocent woman who had only acted in her own defense. He couldn't face the fact that he condemned her to death, and he refused to listen to any mention of it. He ignored me when I pleaded with him to please find you and bring you back."

Sabine surveyed the only surviving child of Thomas' second marriage. Laurel had been like her own little sister. It hadn't mattered that they had no blood ties. Laurel had always been her sister. Never had she wanted to believe that Laurel had betrayed her, and now she was in a no-win situation. Her sister was back, but she'd promised to turn Laurel over to Richelieu, and to renege on that promise was to bear the brunt of the cardinal's wrath.

"A year later," Laurel continued, "I heard that a woman answering your description was engaged to marry a rich *comte* who was very much in love with her. I prayed so hard that it was you and that you would be happy with him . . ."

Sabine interrupted her, "You were there, weren't you? You were the unknown young lady in green who attended my wedding. You were the one who disappeared without a trace after leaving a silver place setting as a wedding gift."

Laurel nodded. As if coming out of a trance, she remembered that the woman she was facing was now five and twenty and the *Comtesse de* Winter and that almost seven years had passed since that first wedding. Something was wrong here. What was Sabine playing at?

"Sabine, what happened?" Milady blinked several times and left the room. No sense in getting reattached to Laurel when she would only lose her sister very soon. All Sabine thought of saying was that Richelieu had better keep his end of their bargain. She was not so good as to voice that opinion to Laurel. Nothing this young woman could say could save the damned. But . . .

Athos sat up rubbing his head, looking at the two men who supported him. "Well, *mon ami,*" Aramis commented softly, "it looks like someone really does not like you. What are we going to do with you if you keep insisting on getting yourself nearly killed?" Athos groaned as D'Artagnan and Aramis helped the musketeer to his feet.

Athos rubbed his sore head again. It wasn't in him to try to cross words with Aramis, particularly now. "It was no one with a personal vendetta against me this time. I was surprised by several bandits who were so kind as to bludgeon me senseless and relieve me of my purse."

"How are you, really?" D'Artagnan asked in concern.

Experimentally, Athos rolled his shoulder and stretched his arm in several different directions. No blood. No tearing. Only some residual soreness and a nasty bump on his head. "My shoulder's fine; no other real complaints. Has Christophe returned yet?" Decisively he changed the topic. Both of his companions shook their heads. One fine disappearing act the woman could pull. Or she was in trouble.

"D'Artagnan and I can go look for the little hoyden after we get you back to the inn." Athos rolled his eyes at his would-be nursemaid and longtime companion who he'd never seen at a loss for words. "Come now, Athos, do you really think you would be any good in a fight right now? *Bon,* I see we're all agreed. Back we go. Let's go."

The musketeers returned to the inn; taking advantage of their numbers, they extracted Porthos from his activities. As they proceeded to Athos' room, Porthos was filled in on all the details of what he had missed. They entered the room and closed the recently repaired door behind them.

Simultaneously the musketeers looked at the person sitting in a chair, calmly reading Aramis' Bible, or feigning to. "*Her majesté* finally returns," Porthos teased in his brusque, affectionate way.

This time Laurel ignored Porthos' comments. He was more show than action, more bark than bite. Liked the attention his remarks drew to him. He'd not provoke her temper this time.

"I'm sorry if I worried you," Laurel apologized. Weak words she knew, but perhaps better than nothing. "I would have been

back sooner, but I ran into my stepsister." The woman set Aramis'
Bible down and announced, "I'm leaving for Calais tonight. I'd
prefer if you'd return my papers to me, or it'd be even better if you
would agree to accompany me."

"Why tonight?" D'Artagnan asked her.

"Richelieu's after me. I think he's the one that is responsible
for feeding information to the spy we are chasing. Anyway, the
longer I stay here, the more danger of being caught I'm in."

"You are a lot of trouble," Athos remarked. "But you do have
a lot of talent."

She almost jumped in surprise at the acknowledgement of her
skill combined with the setdown. "What exactly does that mean?"

"It means," Athos explained, leaning towards her, "I'd much
rather be working with you than have you compete against us. I'm
telling you that you've proven yourself as a resourceful person to
have around. I'd like to have you working with us." That and he
would like to make sure her temper didn't get her killed. He owed
her that much.

Laurel looked at each musketeer's face, one after the other.
So she was right in her assumption: convince Athos to take her on,
and the other three would follow suit, no matter what their
personal convictions.

"Do we have an agreement?" the unofficial leader of the
group asked.

Laurel nodded her head and asked, "Can we be ready to go
before dusk?"

Athos smiled, breaking the image she had formed of him as a
sober, no-nonsense man. Porthos spoke for his friend, "We can be
ready to go sooner than that, *chérie*. Do you have a horse?" The
woman nodded. She'd managed to get herself and Rebelle out of
Marseille and this far, although she still wasn't sure how she'd
done it. "In that case, how about we meet in the stable and be
ready to go" he glanced at each of his fellow musketeers as if
silently confirming the time of departure with them before
clapping his hands together, "shortly before four this afternoon?"

"I'll be there," Laurel responded moments before she excused
herself and left the room.

Aramis looked up from cleaning his sword and asked,
without conveying any insult, "Is it really wise to have her join
us?" One did not show one's dissensions in front of a stranger or
an enemy. Sometimes not even in front of friends.

"Is she or is she not a highly talented swordfighter?" Athos asked pointedly.

"She's very good," D'Artagnan said softly, almost reluctantly. "Probably good enough to be a musketeer . . . if she were a man."

Aramis shrugged his shoulders. "She also saved your life."

"And the little she devil tracked us even after we lost the cardinal's Guard," Porthos added. "Still she's reckless, and that temper of hers . . ." Not to mention the prickly pride.

"No more reckless than any of us were when we were about her age. In fact she's probably less reckless than D'Artagnan," Athos confessed. "As for her temper, we'll just have to see to it that it isn't provoked."

"No offense, Athos," Aramis addressed the man, "but Laurel, Christophe, has a very short temper that takes very little provocation."

"Then we teach her to control it," Athos concluded.

For a moment no one said anything. "We aren't very good at being discreet, are we?" D'Artagnan observed aloud, and no one contradicted him. At least it got away from the point of contention.

"I guess that's something we're all going to have to work on," the oldest musketeer confirmed. "That means no wenching for any of us. And for you, Porthos, do try not to draw attention to yourself any more than you must. Bragging has its place, but not here. No duels for you, D'Artagnan. And for you Aramis, no instructing ladies in theology, not even if you do it discreetly."

D'Artagnan met the blond-haired man's eyes and did not flinch away. "And no drinking for you."

"I won't drink any more than you or Aramis. My word on it," Athos assured the youngest musketeer.

"Oh great leaders," Porthos said sarcastically, and all attention was directed to him. "We've forgotten one small detail. How are we going to explain the presence of a young boy in the company of four grown fighting men?"

"Christophe's my little brother," D'Artagnan offered, "and he ran away from home, so we've been forced to escort him back."

"Ah, *oui*, the mischievous pranks of youth." Porthos kicked back in a chair. "You're still a cocky young pup, D'Artagnan. Yet—I do like your style, quite like my own."

"Let's do it then," D'Artagnan challenged his companions to successfully complete this mission even as he stretched his hand out. Three other hands joined his, and the musketeers quietly but forcefully said, "All for one and one for all."

Shortly before four, five riders left a trail of dust behind them and headed north.

* * * * * * * * * * * *

Milady sealed the missive and sent for her messenger. She was still not sure she liked the efficiency of Richelieu's relay method, but it did get messages back and forth between them quickly. "Get this to Richelieu immediately. And, prepare my carriage for departure." The man left the room, and Sabine twirled the ornate dagger between her fingers. Those musketeers must be found, as must Laurel. Why Sabine had let the young woman go still remained a small mystery, even to her.

On the heels of that uneasy sentiment, she sheathed the dagger as she stared, mesmerized by nothingness. She allowed her eyelids to slip closed, and the picture of a young man with light brown curly hair and blue eyes took shape.

"D'Artagnan." The youngest of the musketeers (less than a year of service), the most naive and reckless. How to exploit his vulnerability to her advantage. She smiled; the smile did not reach her eyes. Constance Bonacieux. The young woman he had taken a fancy to. But how to get access to the queen's ladies in waiting. She would think on it. Perhaps she would ask his eminence.

She placed her fingers to her lips. As for the others, what were their weaknesses? What would give them away even if they were traveling incognito? According to her sources, Athos was recovering from a bullet wound to his right shoulder, so he was handicapped. Noble to a fault, loyal, and bound by honor. God, king, country, justice, and then, and only then, love. He had a habit of being abrupt and uncommunicative, liked to be left to himself.

Then there was Aramis. He'd been a student of Richelieu himself up until he was nearly ten and eight. That would be some five years ago. Claimed he was going to become a priest soon, but he had a great weakness for pretty women. Other than that he was remarkably straight and very cunning. On the other hand it could be deceptive. Not much was known about his past; that one was very secretive. And more dangerous than she liked to contemplate.

Finally Porthos—the big man, a braggart. He'd been a musketeer since he was a little over twenty. Five and a half years of service to the king with a habit of telling tall tales. He liked to be at the center of attention, which could account for the reason he had been a pirate for two years before his parents had gotten wind of the scandal and used their influence to have him shipped off to *Monsieur de* Treville for a little discipline. Of course he ended up not returning home and joined the musketeers. A man who loved his work, indeed. He frankly reveled in his reputation as a pirate and a great musketeer.

The cardinal broke the seal on the letter. What did the *Comtesse de* Winter have to report to him this time?

> Your eminence,
>
>> Laurel d'Anlass met with the *Comte de* Compton in Marseille. She delivered some large bundle of documents of unknown origin. From him she received a packet of information. *Mademoiselle* Laurel was rescued by two of the musketeers when she ran into trouble. It is safe to assume that the musketeers are helping *Mademoiselle* Laurel do whatever the *Comte de* Compton requested of her.
>
> Milady

Richelieu set the letter aside. Meddlesome musketeers. Perhaps an accident should be arranged for them, an unfortunate accident. As for Compton, he was untouchable at the moment. Too much power and influence in his province. He was a well-loved and respected man and Thomas d'Anlass' contact as well as go between to Louis XIII. Which could well mean that Lady Laurel was the one entrusted with the mission to stop documents from going to England to stop the spy and traitor to France. That could explain her sudden disappearance: she had become a spy in the service of Louis XIII, like her father.

* * * * * * * * * * *

He spurred his horse, and the chestnut mare sprinted forward. As he gained on his companions, the sash tied around his head snaked out from beneath his hat and whipped in the wind. He reined back on the horse as he drew alongside D'Artagnan, Aramis, and Athos. "Gentlemen, I do believe that we have a problem."

"Come now, Porthos, tell us something that we do not know?" Aramis said.

"We're being followed and not by the cardinal's men. These people are good." As if anticipating the next question, he suddenly became serious. "They've been following us for several leagues. Christophe and I have tried losing them without success."

Athos ran his gloved hand through his beard. "We split up. D'Artagnan rides with me. Aramis, Porthos, you ride with Christophe. With any luck, we'll lose them and then meet up in Boussac." The musketeers nodded, and Athos and D'Artagnan split off while Aramis and Porthos went back to join Christophe.

"What's going on?" Laurel inquired as she met the riders half-way.

"We're losing our pursuers," Porthos declared with a lusty grin. He spurred his horse, and the animal took off as he was yelling, "*Sapristi*, I love my job."

"What's the plan?" she asked the remaining musketeer.

"We catch Porthos, cover our tracks, and hopefully lose our pursuers. Then we *rendez-vous* in Boussac," Aramis enlightened her succinctly and translated for Porthos at the same time.

"Is he always so loud?" Laurel questioned, cringing inwardly at the attention the large man was drawing to himself.

"That is why I get paired with Porthos whenever we have to split up. I am the expert at being inconspicuous and making Porthos be inconspicuous. I suggest we catch him before he draws any more attention to himself."

"Certainly," she replied in the affirmative as they took off in pursuit of the large musketeer. Deeper and deeper. Would be nice to know the rules of the game.

"*Mes amis*." Porthos broke the silence of their slow pace. He took his gloves off and then grasped the reins again. "What's the best way to Boussac from here?"

There was no response for a moment. "Let's be sure we lost them. I have no intention of bringing them down on my father."

"Your father is not with us . . ."

"Porthos, do think a moment," she interrupted. "I have to contact my father in Boussac by tomorrow and then send a missive to Brussels. I can't chance leading his enemies right to him."

"Shh," Aramis said, raising his hand, and they all strained their ears, trying to identify the sounds Aramis had heard seconds before.

Five mounted sword fighters burst from the trees. One raised a pistol and fired, bringing Porthos' horse down. "We did not lose them," Aramis observed unecessarily as he raised his loaded pistol and shot a man in the shoulder before he could shoot the distracted Porthos who was still struggling to free himself from his downed mount. "Go with God," he said as the enemy rider fell.

From inside his saddlebags Porthos grabbed his own gun and bolas before he dove for cover. He bounded to his feet swiftly and whipped the bolas in a circle around his head, releasing them as the horse charged at him.

They soared through the air and found their mark twining around the rider's neck several times before smashing into his face with a crunch of shattered bones. The rider fell from the horse, and Porthos leapt from his cover, drawing his sword as he did so. He took a deep satisfied breath and charged at a man that Christophe had dismounted and maimed. "*Dites donc*, do I love my work," he declared as he taunted his opponent. Almost as an afterthought he signaled Aramis with his closed left fist.

Aramis grabbed the reins of Laurel's steed and ordered, "We are out of here. Quickly. Porthos can handle the rest of this and meet us later. We have got to get you to Boussac."

He released the reins of her horse before she could respond, and all she could do if she wanted to make herself heard to the man was to follow him. Arrogant, annoying man. Always thought he was right, but what was more annoying was that he so often was right. Laurel leaned down over the cream-colored gelding and pressed her heels to its flanks, setting off in a gallop after Aramis. At least she could ride as well as he could.

Laurel and Aramis caught their breaths as they maneuvered their mounts through the underbrush. Aramis glanced back over his shoulder and saw nothing. Hopefully, no one would find his hat, but that did mean that he'd have to acquire another. "Those were *not* Richelieu's men following us," Aramis apprised his companion without looking her way or losing his concentration.

"I know," she acknowledged.

"You know," he repeated and then rapidly jumped to the only logical conclusion he could think of. "Just who's after you?"

"Those were Milady de Winter's men," she announced casually. Already Sabine had turned the tables. Apparently, it had all been a setup, letting her go.

"Excuse me." He brought his horse to a stand still, slightly disconcerted. "She's dead. I saw her jump from a cliff. No one could have survived the fall."

"You obviously didn't find her body. She survived." Laurel barely stopped herself from showing unseemly irritation with the man. He was being perfectly polite, after all.

Aramis' eyes narrowed, yet he did not contradict her. "How do you know Milady?"

"She's my stepsister. I escaped from her custody two days ago . . . kind of." Aramis was too shocked to respond for a moment. He couldn't find the proper words that a gentleman could use to address the topic.

"You know she works for Richelieu," Aramis told her with detached calm.

"I know," she snapped. Even now the sting of betrayal and disappointment was strong, curdling her senses.

"And you did not deign to tell us until now?"

"She's my stepsister, Aramis; I didn't want to get you involved in a private family matter. Look, all I heard her say was that she had to turn me over to Richelieu or she'd be punished." She stopped and regrouped her thoughts, trying to make them more lucid. Only way she stood any chance of convincing the all-too-bright musketeer. "I thought if I disappeared you would be safe. It didn't occur to me that she might be after you too."

"Nor did it occur to you that she might be responsible for the attack on Athos?" he countered, somehow managing not to sound like he was accusing her.

"No," she stuttered, taken aback. "Why should that have occurred to me?"

"She is Athos' wife, and he has condemned her to death twice," Aramis revealed. Laurel closed her eyes in denial and then asked what had happened. Knowledge was better than ignorance no matter how shocking it was in this instance.

Aramis explained how Athos had discovered the brand of the fleur-de-lys on Milady and believed her a murderer, so he turned her over to the constable. He went on to tell her how about ten, maybe nine, months ago they had caught her while she was trying to smuggle a treaty to England, and Athos condemned her again because she truly had become the monster he had thought she was when he first turned her out.

"I'm sorry. I didn't know," Laurel said, very conscious of the inadequacy of the words, of the empty aching in her soul. Almost, she began to understand the emotions her father had felt upon the deaths of his wives.

"Neither did I until roughly ten, nine months ago." Aramis cocked his head. "Nonetheless, let's get to Boussac." Recriminations later when there would be more time for them.

D'Artagnan was on hand to help when Laurel and Aramis arrived. He hefted one of the saddlebags and helped take the saddles from the horses. Huffing for breath, he asked, "Where's Porthos?"

Laurel lowered her eyes, not knowing what to say. There was no kind way to say she had abandoned the man, a man whom she should have stayed and fought beside.

"We ran into several bounty hunters." Aramis finally broke the tension. "Porthos stayed to finish them off. He signaled me to get Christophe to Boussac so that he," Aramis paused, still finding it hard to speak of Christophe as a male when she wasn't, "could make contact with his father before the marquis left. By tomorrow he should meet up with us."

"What if he doesn't?" D'Artagnan asked.

"Then I'll go back and find him myself while you, Athos, and Christophe go on ahead."

"And leave you behind? No way."

"Duty to France and the king comes before duty to a fellow musketeer, D'Artagnan. We must stop those plans from getting to the Duke of Buckingham."

D'Artagnan cast Aramis a disgusted look, but did not argue. In this case Athos would only agree with the man, and he hardly could take on Athos as well. The man might well decide to shoot him if he did so. Athos didn't permit brooked discipline even though he accepted input. The young man glanced at Laurel's saddlebags and saw a yellowed slip of paper peeping out. Pointing, he inquired, "What's that?"

Laurel reached down and plucked the paper out. Her eyes quickly scanned it and then she tore it to shreds and consigned it to the little fire that a stable hand had been cooking his meal over. "My father is still here. He wants me to talk to him personally, tonight," she announced and headed inside, her brow furled in preoccupation.

Laurel wrinkled her forehead in consternation, pacing back and forth across the room. What was she going to do? She stopped short when D'Artagnan hailed her. "Are you going to come down and join us for dinner, Christophe? Christophe, did you hear me?"

"*Désolée*, sorry," the woman apologized, dimly aware that she had been apologizing a lot recently. "I guess I'm a little preoccupied. About dinner . . . well, I don't know that I'm up to it tonight. You go on down without me. If I'm hungry I'll grab a little something later."

Reluctantly, the young man left her and headed downstairs to join his two friends. From a nearby barmaid he grabbed a mug of ale and sat himself next to Aramis and across from Athos. The youngest musketeer swirled the contents of his mug and took a sip. Set the vessel down and pushed away from the table. "Look, I hope you two'll excuse me. Something's wrong with Christophe. I think I'd better go up and find out what's worrying him."

Aramis held him back, firmly grasping the man's arm. "I will go talk to him. I think I might have a good idea of what's bothering him."

"Sit down, both of you," Athos commanded. "Unless this is an emergency, we should all eat and then go back and find out what's going on. What do you think, D'Artagnan, was the situation that critical?" He shook his head, and the men ate a hasty meal and then, as one, converged on Laurel's room.

A firm knock echoed through the room and a contralto voice called, "Who is it?" At the muffled reply of Athos, Laurel unlocked the door and opened it. An eyebrow shot up in mild surprise as not only Athos but also Aramis and D'Artagnan entered the room. "I thought we had already filled everyone in on the details of what has happened so far today?"

D'Artagnan shifted on the balls of his feet, back and forth. Clearly, she was still preoccupied as she was trying valiantly to hurry them out of her presence, and the tone of her voice was eerily distant.

"That's not why we're here," Athos informed her, forestalling any pussyfooting around. "D'Artagnan was pointing out that you were unusually preoccupied. Seeing you now, I'm inclined to believe him. So, I was wondering if you could perhaps share with us what you're worrying about as it could well affect us too."

"*Chantage,*" blackmail, she grumbled under her breath, but she knew they might be able to help her. Just as she knew that not telling them about what was going on could conceivably endanger them, and she already felt guilty enough on that score.

Then add to that the very recent Milady event, and she knew what she should do. Trust her companions with anything, even if it seemed downright ridiculous. "I don't suppose any of you can get a hold of a dress in the next three or so hours?"

"Come again?" D'Artagnan shook his head as if trying to convince himself he had heard right. "Did you say a dress?"

"*Oui.* My father cannot risk meeting me here. There is, however, a town dance going on tonight. My father is expecting to talk to me there. I can't very well attend as Christophe or without a dress, so I sort of am in need of a dress," she concluded, lamely, painfully self-conscious for the first time in ages. Athos cast a look at Aramis, and the man shrugged his shoulders eloquently.

Athos smiled. There was a feminine uncertain side to her. He said, "I think we can handle that. Why don't D'Artagnan and I leave you with Aramis for a few minutes?" His words were immediately followed by action.

"*Madame*, if you would please stand and remove that vest and hat?" Aramis lazily pushed away from the wall after Athos and D'Artagnan departed.

"Why?"

"I will have to estimate what size dress you wear before I can procure the proper garment for you, *madame*," Aramis said, even as he noticed a slight blush tinge her cheeks, a blush which was quickly banished. Swiftly, she did as the musketeer instructed, conscious the entire time of the fact that it was inappropriate to have a man buy a dress for her, but for some reason she did not think that Aramis would allow her to give him money to buy the dress, and she'd really rather not press her luck.

After carefully sizing her up, he asked her to undo her hair. Wordlessly she did so. Gently he grasped her chin in his right hand. He turned her head first one way and then another, debating what color would best suit her. He dropped his hand, and she asked with a surprising amount of equanimity, "Finished?"

He nodded, and before she could ask another question he said, "And if I might be so bold as to inquire, whom are you going to this dance with?"

"As in escort?"

"As in who is escorting you?" he confirmed, and she nibbled her lip and shrugged her shoulders, saying she hadn't gotten around to asking anyone yet. To be honest the consideration had slipped her mind. It'd been so long since she'd played a woman's role in front of society. "I'll get that dress for you and take you there myself if that is agreeable to you."

"Sure, that's fine," she said as he left the room, trying not to dwell on the fact that she would soon have to be the model of a perfect lady. This was not going to fun.

It was the sound of hoofs crunching against dirt he concluded as he stared into the evening lit by an expanse of full moon. Was it truly possible that there were still more men pursuing him that he had neither lost nor disposed of? Without hesitation, he jammed a stick into this mouth and bit down upon it, breaking it in half as the wave of pain passed. No screaming; that could wait for later, when he couldn't be heard. He scanned the ground and found another stick: thick and sturdy, hopefully, and bit it tightly.

Stealthily, he crawled upon the ground, one quick burst after the next until he reached a tree. Closing his eyes, he bit down more firmly on the stick and hit his left shoulder upon the trunk of the tree. Once, then twice, then a third time.

Shots of pain flooded his brain, and he bit harder on the stick his eyes watering as he hit his shoulder against the tree one more time, and it finally slipped back into place. Panting, he let the stick fall from his mouth, and he leaned against the tree, listening for the sound of hooves. Bloody little cretin had dislocated his shoulder. Of course the cretin had not lived long enough to take advantage of the injury.

More hoofbeats, off at a distance this time. Sounded like one horse and followed by a group of horses. A chase! Not unlikely.

Porthos peered around the tree and saw in the distance the galloping gait of a horse. That was the way D'Artagnan's horse galloped. Impetuous young pup. Probably hadn't listened to

Aramis and Athos. Porthos dug through the saddlebags he had retrieved from his fallen horse and took out a length of rope. Quickly he knotted it around the trunk and dashed across the path with the other end of it. Gritting his teeth, he twined the rope around the tree, knotting it firmly. He glanced up.

D'Artagnan's horse was almost upon him. The large man dove for cover as the musketeer galloped by. Seconds later three other riders, all abreast, came galloping on his heels.

"Showtime," he announced under his breath and pulled the rope taut so that it extended across the path, tangling in the galloping horses' legs.

Horses bucked and whinnied as the riders flew over the animals' heads, hitting the ground with impacts that Porthos almost felt from where he hid. "Lovely," he praised himself as he stood and surveyed the road. Two men lay at unnatural angles, their necks broken from the fall. The other appeared to have been knocked senseless, and two of the horses seemed to have bolted.

Porthos glanced to his left as he saw D'Artagnan's horse approaching him again. As soon as the man was close enough to see, Porthos confirmed that it was indeed his fellow musketeer. He stepped from the shadows and called to the man who had just stopped his horse and was surveying the scene.

"I absolutely love sweeping people off their feet. Perhaps I should try it more often. What do you think D'Artagnan?"

"Porthos," he said, relieved, and jumped from his horse to brusquely hug the man.

"*Tiens, tiens,*" he commented in an offhand manner. "If I'd known you were that hard up for company, I would have brought a courtesan along with me."

D'Artagnan expelled a pent-up burst of air between his teeth and slugged the large man in the left shoulder. "Bad choice." Porthos gasped and D'Artagnan quickly apologized.

"Porthos, *sapristi,* man, I was worried about what had become of you. I'm glad to see you're all right is all. You are all right, aren't you?"

"A few cuts and bruises. The most serious thing was a dislocated shoulder that I had to put back in place," Porthos responded as he inspected the only spooked horse that had not yet escaped the tangled rope. He calmly stroked the animal after freeing it and inspecting it to make sure there was no damage. Remarkably enough, the animal was well, except for fright.

D'Artagnan remounted his horse and looked at his companion. "You ready to head back to Boussac then? I'm sure Athos and Aramis will like to see that you're okay and find out what you have been up to too."

"Lead on oh fearless master," Porthos said, flourishing his beaten hat, and they rode towards Boussac.

Fast-paced music echoed through the hall. Violins, cellos, violas and a plethora of other stringed instruments. Heads turned as a new couple entered the festivities. He was tall, well toned, and darkly handsome. His partner was a tall blond beauty sporting a light blue dress with a somewhat fashionable décollcté. It set off her skin tone and breathtaking figure perfectly, despite its relative simplicity. There were whispers about the pair as they joined the reel. Obviously nobles, but strangers still.

"Do you see anyone that might be him?" the dark-haired gentleman asked his partner in a soft voice.

"He'll find me and make his way over here when he gets a chance. He can't miss us, considering we have become the center of attention," Laurel said for Aramis' ears only. She should have known that even dressed in simple but well-cut clothes Aramis would make a stir, but it was too late now to try to blend in with the crowd. Hopefully no one but Thomas would recognize them. "In the meantime, we dance."

"Of course, my lady," he quipped gently and leaned forward to whisper in her ear. "You are a terrific disguise artist. The way you look tonight no one would ever believe you could be mistaken for a boy or anything but the beautiful woman you are." Laurel scowled. Flatterer. Did he ever act differently than the consummate gentleman?

Laurel was not permitted a chance to respond, for the music broke off, and an old man with an eyepatch and wrinkled face caught Aramis' attention. "Lad, perhaps you would be so kind as to lend your lovely lady to an old man for one dance. It's so very rare that an old man like me gets the company of a beautiful woman for even a short time."

Aramis bowed slightly and stepped away, allowing the older gentleman to lead Laurel in the set. He was not left alone very long. Almost immediately several young women were introduced to him by their mothers or duennas.

"All is well with you, Laurel?" the old man said, and her smile answered him. "So who is your dashing escort? You do know that you have made many of the ladies here envious tonight, *ma petite*?"

"Thomas," she warned quietly. "His name is Aramis. He and three of his friends are helping me with the mission to Calais and the effort to apprehend the traitor to France. Don't worry, Thomas. They are musketeers, and they have no fondness for the cardinal." Thomas gracefully led his daughter through another turn. "How did it go in Luz?"

Thomas smiled as if she had said something extremely entertaining and waited for the eyes to turn away from them again. "I got the missive, but I barely eluded two Prussian agents. You got the papers to Compton?" She nodded. "Don't forget to write Brussels, *mademoiselle*," he concluded as the song ended. He bowed over her hand and deftly slipped a small packet of papers into her palm. As she curtsied she slipped the packet inside her bodice and watched her father depart. She danced two more sets, and then she and Aramis slipped from the festivities into the dark streets of Boussac.

Aramis opened the door and hurried a woman shrouded in a black cloak inside. He carefully led her through the crowded room, being sure that the woman's face was hidden from curious onlookers. The pair hurried up the stairs and down the hall to Athos' room and the unofficial meeting place of the musketeers for this leg of the trip. Aramis looked both ways. He saw no one in the corridor. Nor was anyone coming up the stairs behind them. Once again, he opened the door, and the couple slipped stealthily inside the warm room.

Laurel pushed the hood from her head, breathing normally for the first time all night. She almost jumped at Porthos' booming voice greeting Aramis. As it was she overheard how D'Artagnan had gone after Porthos and how Porthos polished off the young man's pursuers. They had only just arrived back minutes earlier.

At that moment Porthos took notice of the woman Aramis had entered with. Both eyebrows went up as the large man surveyed the woman. He whistled softly. Aramis always did have exquisite taste. No doubt about it. "I thought you had agreed no ladies so that we wouldn't draw undue attention to ourselves."

"Lay off, Porthos," Laurel ordered. "I'm not one of Aramis' ladies."

"Christophe," Porthos said in disbelief after he could get his slack jaw to work. The lad made one fine-looking woman.

"I wasn't Christophe tonight. Tonight it was the belle of the ball," she said in an offhand manner that belied her own concern about getting out of Boussac before someone remembered the stir she and Aramis had created and became a little too curious. She directed her attention to Athos. "I got the information. We need to leave no later than tomorrow afternoon."

"We leave an hour after dawn," Athos decided, and the group dispersed to gain several hours of much-needed sleep—that was after Aramis disposed of the dress Laurel returned to him, naturally.

Section Three

Another pigeon burst from the cardinal's hand into the crisp morning air, disappearing in a flurry of wings illuminated by the rising sun.

Dispassionately he watched a second bird make its way across the sky and another until not a single bird remained in the cage. It was done exactly as Milady de Winter had requested, a thousand gold pieces for each. Porthos, Athos, Aramis, and D'Artagnan, dead or alive (dead preferably, of course). One thousand five hundred for *Mademoiselle* Laurel d'Anlass, alive. One way or another he would get his hands on that woman.

At the window ledge, he stood several moments longer, his strong hands, and long fingers curled around the stone rail. Without further ado, Richelieu turned his back on the balcony and strode back indoors. From inside the folds of his robe he withdrew Milady's latest letter. He tapped the open letter against his left palm. Suddenly he stopped and glanced back towards the balcony, mentally reviewing the contents of the *comtesse's* letter.

Athos was injured, one plus for him. If Athos could be put out of the way the effectiveness of the entire group would be significantly reduced, seeing as he was their undeclared leader. Laurel had definitely teamed up with the four musketeers in question. Not a favorable state of affairs. Richelieu glanced at the note again and reread a passage:

> . . . seven men were lost to the musketeers. . . . More recently, my sources could only confirm the presence of Aramis and *Mademoiselle* Laurel d'Anlass in Boussac. It seems that they made quite a stir at a local dance and then disappeared by the next morning. It is quite possible that Aramis or Laurel met someone at this dance, but my agents have been unable to confirm who. I expect to learn more when I question

> them myself. As to the other three, I find
> it very unlikely that Aramis and Laurel
> would have abandoned them. More likely
> they were traveling incognito and fled
> Boussac along with Aramis and
> *Mademoiselle* Laurel. . . .

Nor had he received any further information about Thomas D'Anlass. Apparently France's premier spy had vanished from Luz without a trace. Of course with Thomas' daughter in his hands he could easily flush the marquis out, and from all indications Milady was very close to apprehending the young woman in question. Not too much longer, and he would be able to secure the Duke of Buckingham's backing for his coup d'état.

Decision made, he called in his sergeant and instructed the man to send a small contingent of his best men to Milady de Winter in Boussac immediately and to change horses as many times as necessary to ensure that swiftness. No unnecessary chances. Those musketeers must not be allowed to succeed. His red robes swirled around his legs as he marched from the room to the church to lead the Sunday morning mass.

In the meantime, it was time for Louis to be made aware that four gentlemen seemed to have deserted the King's Musketeers after their mission to Marseille. Conduct unbecoming a musketeer at the very least.

Louis XIII, followed by several guards, burst into *Monsieur de* Treville's office unannounced. *Monsieur de* Treville clambered to his feet and bowed low before his *majesté*. "*Votre majesté*," he said with well-polished courtesy.

"Oh, sit down, be at ease. We are friends here," Louis stated as he straightened his ornate green vest. "And of course friends are allowed to visit one another, are they not?"

"Absolutely correct, *votre majesté*. May I offer you something to drink, perhaps?" The king shook his head and motioned for his guards to step outside so that he could converse privately with the *capitaine* of his musketeers. "Is there some problem, *Votre Majesté*?"

"Not that I'm aware of currently," Louis said almost as if he were hinting at something. "Actually I was wanting to engage the services of your four best musketeers again. D'Artagnan, Athos, Porthos, and Aramis I believe."

"Well of course, *votre majesté*, but . . ."

Louis interrupted the man. "But what *Monsieur de* Treville? They did return safely from Marseille, did they not?"

Treville hid his irritation. Richelieu again. He'd bet his not insubstantial fortune on it. Only Richelieu could have sent Louis to him to ask for the services of several musketeers who had not returned to Paris in more than six weeks. What was his game? Could there be something more to it than the fact that he held a grudge against the four men in question and wanted to see them dishonored and discredited? "They successfully discharged their task in Marseille," he said while his mind ran through possible options and scenarios.

"Perfect." Louis clapped his hands together. "Then there will be no problem engaging these men straight away."

Treville said nothing for several moments as his thoughts raced about in his head. He hadn't heard from the musketeers in question since D'Artagnan had written to request that *Monsieur de* Treville take in the daughter of the talented French spy, Thomas d'Anlass, while they headed to Calais. No explanation why they were going to the opposite coast, just that they were going there. Then, the woman had never arrived, and he'd still heard nothing. Quickly he decided: no flagrant lying, but maybe he could buy them some time. "*Votre majesté*, I'm afraid that's not possible right now. I sent them to Calais on a special errand."

"But they will be back shortly, my friend, right?" Louis pushed for a full response.

"I expect them back in Paris within the fortnight, give or take a day," he said, hoping that the musketeers contacted him soon so that he could get in touch with them and inform them of the situation in Paris. Louis was not known for his equanimity or his mercy. And hoping for his indulgence or patience could be asking for a miracle.

"Good," Louis said as he got back to his feet. "I'll expect to see them then." He turned to face the standing man and asked, "Oh, and Treville, would you care to accompany me on a hunting expedition today?"

"I'd be honored, *votre majesté*," the *capitaine* replied and added that he would be along as soon as he had prepared his horse. Worse and worse. He hated hunting. He was getting too old for all of this. Truly the political scrabbling and backbiting was a younger or more unscrupulous man's game.

* * * * * * * * * * *

Aramis came galloping back towards the copse of trees where four horses, tethered, were grazing contentedly. He reined back on his horse and dismounted in a fluid motion, quieting the animal as he searched for his companions.

"Hold," a voice commanded, leveling a sword at Aramis' throat. Aramis met the eyes of the speaker and recognized D'Artagnan.

"Easy, D'Artagnan, it is I—Aramis. I have just finished my scouting expedition."

D'Artagnan edged closer, still on his guard, and surveyed the man. The new arrival wore plain, patched clothes of various shades of browns, and a beaten hat, and his dusty horse was saddled with frayed blankets. The man's entire face was covered with a bristly, black, badly tended beard. From behind the beard, dark brown eyes flecked with gold stared back steadily.

D'Artagnan sheathed his sword. Recognition flared through him. "*Parbleu*, Aramis. You look like . . . well, like something that was just released from prison." Smelled very like it too.

"I could not afford to look well off while scouting. I would have been remarked upon. Where are the others?" he inquired, scratching his chin through the thick, ill-trimmed growth of beard. He had a sinking suspicion that lice found him mighty attractive about now. He'd have to do something about that.

"They're down at the stream, fishing. They claim it's going to be lunch. As for when they'll be back—should be back about midday." Aramis nodded slowly and set about making his horse more presentable, brushing the tangles and dust from the animal in an effort to transform his mount back into looking like the noble and well-trained steed it was. After getting out the worst of the visible tangles, he lifted and disposed of tattered blankets and brushed out the ground-in dirt and tangles hidden underneath.

"Aramis, what did you find out?" D'Artagnan queried as the man lifted the saddle from his horse and set about scrubbing it clean, or trying to. Aramis was so efficient and diligent that sometimes D'Artagnan wondered how his friend did it. After all, sometimes he had so much energy, it made him restless, and consequently he couldn't even try to project that same aura of cool competence.

Aramis looked up from his work, his chest heaving and drops of sweat dribbling down his brow. He wiped the sweat from his face and looked directly at the younger man. He could feel the scarcely reined impatience emanating from D'Artagnan. "Someone has sent bounty hunters on our trail. A thousand gold pieces for each one of us alive or dead and fifteen hundred for Laurel d'Anlass, alive." The woman had been right. Someone would have to have a death wish or be a masochist to misappropriate her identity.

D'Artagnan slapped the innocent tree and glared at the expanse of blue sky through the tree limbs. The tip of his tongue traced his teeth and clucked against the roof of his mouth. Great! Not what he needed to hear. Meant more sneaking around, more waiting, more restrictions on his activities and his already limited ability to communicate with Constance. This was beginning to become a lot like the first time he had journeyed to Calais with the last of the musketeers after Rochefort and Richelieu had tried to disband them. For the second, or was it third, time in a year and a half, and in his close to twenty–one years, he had a price upon his head. "Did Richelieu put the price on us?"

"Always possible and not at all unlikely, though he'd have to have come up with a plausible reason to get pigeons from the king unless he took them and framed someone else for their disappearance. Still it could be hard, considering Louis has been slowly restricting the cardinal's power," Aramis said, grunting as he dug the encrusted dirt from around the saddlehorn and flung the gritty substance to the ground. Not that Louis was ever going to seriously check the cardinal's power unless Richelieu were to do something patently stupid and out of character.

"Then he did put the price on us," D'Artagnan told himself. "How much information have the bounty hunters been given and about how wide of an area have the messages reached?"

"As far as I can tell," Aramis grunted, straining to work out a matted wad of hair, "messages have been sent all over France. There are relatively complete descriptions of each of us, including names. Laurel's in the best shape in that department; they have only a cursory description of what she looked like two years ago and in the role of lady of the manor." Aramis grimaced in distaste as his thick scraggly beard scratched against his exposed forearms.

He hated being in such a state of disrepair, although he had resigned himself to the necessity of it.

"Aramis"—D'Artagnan knelt by his friend—"your spare change of clothes is in my pack if you want them, and if you want to get that beard and hair back under control, you're welcome to use the razor. It's in Porthos' pack."

"Did I hear my name called? Ask and ye shall receive." Porthos' loud voice boomed out as he swaggered into the small clearing. The large man cast a quizzical look at Aramis and took a slow circuit around the working man. "Could this possibly be our . . . NO," he said with exaggerated emphasis and a healthy dose of sarcasm, "it can't possibly be our fastidious Aramis."

The scraggly man stopped scrubbing at his saddle and looked Porthos over from head to foot. Beads of water dripped from wet hair and sash. Porthos held boots stuffed with stockings in one hand, and his weather-worn hat in the other. Aramis studiously ignored Porthos' jibe, instead saying dryly, "What happened to you? Did you fall in?" D'Artagnan was unable to hide his grin at the exchange the two men had started to carry on, and he settled back to watch the brief show. He needed the entertainment. Camping out for the past few days had been rather dull and · monotonous. One thing he had never been good at: monotony.

"No, I did not fall in," Porthos said, implying that any reasonable person would not think the great Porthos fell in any stream. Completely beneath his dignity.

"Pushed then," D'Artagnan couldn't resist adding.

"No," he repeated in the same tone. "Since you two obviously can't control your rampant curiosity, be prepared to be enlightened."

"I'm waiting," D'Artagnan prompted when Porthos remained silent for several moments.

"This," the big man gestured to his wet state as he dropped his boots to the ground, "was Christophe's idea. Lad got it in his head that it'd been far too long since his last bath and that Athos and I were both just as in need, 'more so,' to quote him, of a bath as he was. . . ."

"Of course." D'Artagnan snapped his fingers, and this time it was Aramis who couldn't hide his grin. "I understand now, Christophe pulled you in after him, and you got drenched."

"Not quite," Porthos said in a disgusted tone. "He kind of dared me to do it. Said no big, strong, brave man could possibly be afraid of a little water. And," Porthos waved his finger at both his companions, "he had to go and add that I probably couldn't even swim, so of course I was afraid of the water. Me, a pirate who has sailed the seas."

"So you went in." Aramis slung a compassionate arm over his friend's shoulders and found he didn't have to reach as high as usual. He could get to liking this; perhaps Porthos could go bootless more often. Maybe, just maybe, Laurel, Christophe, might prove a good companion; was still going to reserve judgment on that one. "I understand," he continued, and Porthos was not quite sure whether he was being mocked or not. For that matter, neither was D'Artagnan. Sometimes you couldn't tell with Aramis.

Just in case he was being mocked, he felt justified in adding, "For the record, Christophe challenged Athos too, and he went right on in with me. Just you wait, my young cocky friend," he told D'Artagnan. "She'll, he'll, whatever—he'll have you in there too. And he'll certainly waste no time in getting Aramis into the stream considering the state Aramis is in now."

Thoughtfully, D'Artagnan nodded. Porthos could well be right on that one. When Laurel really set her mind to something, she could manage to get it done without your quite realizing it. However, he decided it was a good time to change the subject. "Out of curiosity, are we going to be having lunch today?"

"Of course, lad," Porthos said as he reached behind a tree and retrieved several fish. "And Athos and Christophe will be bringing more shortly. Oh, and it's your turn to cook tonight," Porthos informed him.

"Look, just because I'm the youngest, other than our guest, doesn't mean I should always get stuck with the dirty work. Why don't you have Laurel—Christophe," he corrected himself, "do it? He hasn't had to cook in a couple days."

"D'Artagnan, as much as I would like to tell you we'll put Christophe in charge of this detail, I don't think it will happen. You see Christophe has this little idea that since he fished, he doesn't have to cook. And he also has the notion that every person should cook; he refuses to be stuck cooking again until each one of us has had our turn," Porthos enlightened the young man. "I think if we push the issue Christophe could well burn the food out of spite." Would coincide with the feisty woman's style.

D'Artagnan rolled his eyes and shot a decidedly displeased look at Porthos and Aramis but said nothing. He grabbed the fish and went off to get the fire ready and start preparing dinner.

Five people sat around the evening fire, just outside of its circle of warmth. A gentle breeze laughed through the trees and crickets chirped, adding their music to the warm summer night. The remains of yet another meal of fish and wild fruit were scattered about.

Porthos sat, legs crossed, nibbling on a root, his eyes fixed on nothing in particular. Aramis lay stretched out, propped on a single elbow; he still managed to look like a gentleman, though his clothes and hair in disarray should have led one to conclude otherwise.

D'Artagnan sprawled backward, looking up at the stars that were dotting the sky and winking at him playfully. He had the distinct urge to wink back at them. Laurel remained in her complete guise as Christophe; she had not even taken off her hat or her vest, despite the warmth of the day and the evening.

Athos leaned forward, crouching over an expanse of open dirt. He toyed with D'Artagnan's small knife for an instant before interrupting the moment of relaxed pleasure. "Gentlemen," he called for their attention, and they all came closer and seated themselves around the open expanse of ground. "As you all know, we have a price on our heads. First off, that means we need to find a safer route to Calais, something that avoids as many populous places as possible. Now," Athos drew an X in the ground with the knife, "we're north of Issoudûn. We know we must avoid Paris, and we still also must be able to get supplies."

"We could go towards Vendôme. I believe Porthos' family has a home, a bit removed from the beaten track, near there," Aramis suggested, taking the proffered knife from Athos and continuing to draw a rough map. "Then from Vendôme we could make our way around Paris and towards Rouen. Then on to Calais."

D'Artagnan, Porthos, and Athos all mulled over the possibility and thought that could work very well. Athos was about to call that the plan when Laurel broke in. "I need to post a letter to my father very soon so I can find out if he has completed his task in Belgium. It's vital."

Athos fixed his eyes on her eyes. "So what problem are you seeing?"

Laurel did not back down from the challenge in the musketeer's gaze. "I need to get to a town where I can get a letter taken to Belgium very quickly. Vendôme, unfortunately, gets mail only once every fortnight." If memory served her correctly.

"We're open to suggestions," Athos said, forestalling any complaints his companions might have made. Other than Laurel, he alone knew the content of the packet Thomas had slipped her in Boussac. Thus they were also the only ones who knew how vital it was that they get the information from Belgium.

"May I?" she inquired, and Aramis yielded the blade to her. She heaved a deep breath and etched a line in the dirt and an X. "Starting at slightly after dawn tomorrow, we could ride our mounts hard towards Meung and make it there by nightfall. Then as Christophe, I could go into Meung and post the letter. I could meet you the next morning several leagues north of Meung."

"Wait a second," D'Artagnan interrupted. "You want us to leave you alone for the entire night in a place that is probably crawling with mercenaries that are out to get you for the price on your head. You can't do that." .

"There is no other choice." She defended her conclusion. "Of the five of us, I'm the one who stands the least chance of being recognized. And even if I was recognized I am wanted alive. You are wanted dead or alive, which means they probably won't bother to see to it you keep breathing."

"She's right." Athos quelled any further argument. "The letter must be posted immediately, and she's the only one who has a good chance of getting in and out of Meung unnoticed. Go on," he instructed Laurel. *Mince*, if it wasn't hard to keep from being very over-protective of Laurel! Despite it all, she was still a lady, the only child of a well-endowed, albeit eccentric, marquis.

"From Meung we could veer towards Beauvais and then on to Calais," she concluded.

"Any problems with that other than the one D'Artagnan pointed out?" Athos inquired. No one brought up any, and Athos dismissed them, declaring that was the plan.

"Wait," D'Artagnan suddenly cried, recalling a certain letter he'd written more than a week back. "I don't know what we were thinking. Did anyone write *Monsieur* de Treville and tell him that Laurel wouldn't be coming after all?" All the responses were negative. D'Artagnan had the writing supplies, and no one barring Laurel had touched them in days.

"D'Artagnan, why don't you write him a letter tonight and let him know? We can have Christophe post it too," Athos half suggested, half commanded, and D'Artagnan said he would. Business concluded, Athos, Porthos, and Aramis all withdrew from the fire, heading towards the nearby horses.

Laurel put a hand on D'Artagnan's arm as he crouched over the letter he was composing. He had just dipped the quill in the small ink-bottle when Laurel's hand touched him. "Why don't you also tell *Monsieur de* Treville he can post a letter to Christophe Moulins in Beauvais. That way he can confirm he got your letter. I'm already going to need to pick up a message from my father there," she admitted.

"Good idea," D'Artagnan replied and wrote hastily to the *capitaine*. He blew over the ink, encouraging it to dry before handing it to Laurel. She slipped it inside her doublet alongside the one to her father.

D'Artagnan sealed the ink-bottle and put it away. Reluctantly he returned to the fire and began cleaning up the mess. Laurel distracted him again. "I'll make a deal with you."

"What's that?" he said dropping a bone in the fire.

"I'll clean up all this," she pointed around the fire at the scattered mess from the last meal, "if you take a bath in the stream tonight." Not that D'Artagnan, or for that matter all the musketeers, didn't bathe, but then again no one could bathe frequently enough for *Mademoiselle* Laurel.

The young man guffawed, and Laurel stared at him as if he had lost his mind. Getting his laughter back under control, he mumbled, "Sorry. Porthos did warn me that I'd be next. Still, you drive a hard bargain. You've got yourself a deal. My word on it," he said and left Laurel to the cleaning without protest. Three down, one to go, she thought with near elation. The job was almost done. Perhaps she wouldn't have to deal with the stench of unwashed humanity for at least a short while. Right now she would take whatever small victories she could get.

Restless. The man tossed and turned in an unfulfilling sleep. With a start he woke fully and stared at the stars. Not dawn yet, and he was unable to get back to sleep. He continued staring at the sky, and the clouds drifted away from the moon, the nearly full

moon that was now able to pour its light downward. Grabbing his
sword, he got to his feet and slipped into his boots. His soiled,
untucked tunic hung from his shoulders. Breeches, frayed and
worn, covered his legs, but would be sadly inadequate for any sort
of warmth or protection. Soon they wouldn't even be good enough
to conceal anything. Modest decency ought be satisfied.

He picked his way through underbrush led by the moonlight
to the edge of a deep and languid stream. His boots crunched upon
crisp leaves from the past fall and a stooped-over figure shot a
glance directly his way. "Couldn't sleep either, Aramis, huh?"
Laurel spoke softly without disturbing the peace of early morning.
She watched silently as he set his sword on the bank a hand's
reach away.

"I need a drink," Aramis said scooping some of the fresh
water in his cupped hands and lifting it to his mouth and downing
the soothing liquid.

Laurel frowned at her feet. That perfect correctness of his was
really getting on her last nerves. Never mind that he seemed to be
gifted at annoying her; she wasn't prepared to deal with it right
now, and yet here it was again come to haunt her. She had the
sneaky feeling that this time she had failed to cover up her
irritation at his behavior. Well then, no sense in trying to cover it
up any longer. Besides she hated all this false politeness and not
speaking one's mind. "Aramis, do you never let go of that
composure of yours?"

"I am sorry." He directed a piercing gaze at her. He was very
well aware that his composure often rubbed Laurel the wrong way.
Not that he was about to lose his composure simply to please her.

"Do you have any idea how annoying that perfect composure,
never losing your cool, and cultivated charm can be? It'd be nice
to see that you too have some human imperfections like the rest of
us mere mortals." She stopped. "Like now, you avoided my
question? Is it really that bad to answer me, to tell me, yes I
couldn't sleep?"

"It is irrelevant," Aramis replied, unruffled despite his
scraggly appearance. "I did not mean to disturb your peace or
startle you." He stood up and looked as if he was about to leave.

Laurel threw her hands in the air. "There you go being
completely polite to me again. You didn't even bother to ask if I
minded if you stayed. Plus, you still haven't even answered my
simple question, and it is simple."

Aramis crouched down beside her again and leveled a serious look on the unorthodox young woman. "I was under the impression that you liked to be treated with courtesy, politeness, and respect. Was I wrong?"

"Stop it. Stop it you hear," she snapped. "Stop treating me with that practiced correctness of yours. Tell me to leave you alone, or to shut up, or that it is none of my god d—"

"Thou shalt not use the name of the Lord thy God in vain, and it is unbecoming a lady of your stature to resort to such crude language," Aramis reminded her, ignoring her scowl. "At any rate, why are you encouraging me to be rude to you like Porthos is?"

"Okay, so maybe Porthos needs to learn a little tact, but you need to learn how to let people know how you're feeling, to come out from behind that facade of yours once in a while. At least Porthos is being honest about how he feels about me and the things I do. A little bluntness wouldn't hurt you every once in a while."

"So that is what you choose to call a tirade? Bluntness. More like rudeness," Aramis countered without losing that disputed composure.

She shook her head, uttering a humorless chuckle. "You just don't get it." Aramis didn't notice the gleam in her eye until it was too late, and with a mighty leap she shoved him into the stream, drenching the man from head to toe. Served him right.

From inside laughter bubbled up. Finally, she couldn't hold it in any longer.

"Funny is it?"

"Oh, Aramis, you should see the way you look." Another giggle slipped out.

"On the contrary, you should," he said, tugging her struggling form into the stream with him. "Now we are even."

"Well, I guess I'll be getting a second bath," she said with unusually good humor. "And now I've assured that all four of my ever-so-strong and brave escorts have overcome their fear of being wet all over," she teased and was nonplussed when Aramis slammed his open palm against the water, splashing her full in the face. "Laurel, shut up," he ordered forgetting almost all trace of politeness and formality for an instant.

"*Oui, monseigneur,*" she said, not even a shade contrite.

Perverse little thing. "Forget it. Would you be so kind as to allow me some measure of privacy so I can finish this little bath you have so kindly encouraged me into starting?"

Without replying, she scrambled from the water and picked up her boots from the side of the stream, glad she hadn't put them on or they'd have been soaked. Come to think of it, she'd no desire to be around the man when he tried to make do with water-soaked boots.

Quietly she slipped back to the camp while Aramis took full advantage of the remaining time before dawn to wash, trim his beard back to a respectable goatee, and change into clothes that were in better repair.

Only half-awake, she climbed upon the horse, almost falling as her boot tangled in the stirrup. However, she caught herself before she fell and wiggled her foot from the stirrup without further incident. Athos handed her the ratted blankets and the doublet and vest Aramis had recently used on his own scouting expedition.

Over the thin linen tunic she slipped on the doublet, cinching it with a sash so that it wouldn't be too unruly—the vest she handed back. It was too large, and she didn't need another layer in this infernal heat. So hard to find clothes close to her size when she was traveling with four relatively large men. Porthos aided her in disguising her mount, and she sighed regretfully at the mangy state they ended up achieving. Athos rubbed his hands together and glanced at Laurel. "You ready to head to Meung?"

She nodded. "I'll meet you tomorrow morning."

"Be very careful," the oldest musketeer warned, and she nodded once more as she headed towards Meung and away from the protection of her four companions.

"Athos, let me follow Christophe," D'Artagnan implored. "If something happens I might be able to help."

"Not if you're recognized by those bounty hunters," Athos countered, not liking the idea of sending anyone off alone when there was a reward on the person's head. And he liked even less that Laurel was going off alone. As much as she might try to deny it, it was more dangerous for a woman than a man, and if she was discovered in her masquerade . . .

Aramis leaned over the saddlehorn, crossing his arms in front of him. "You know, Athos, D'Artagnan's description was not as complete as ours, and with that beard that has finally started growing, we might be able to disguise him enough to throw the bounty hunters off."

D'Artagnan watched Athos intently, looking for some sign of what was going on in the man's mind, hoping that Athos would follow Aramis' suggestion. "Dismount," Athos commanded preemptively, and D'Artagnan complied quickly. The older man turned to fix his gaze on Aramis. "See to it that he can't be recognized, and you'd best hurry before Christophe gets much of a head start."

"I'll meet you later then. And yes, I'll be careful, very careful," D'Artagnan insisted when Porthos and Athos brought up his past recklessness and his penchant for getting involved in duels. Athos and Aramis maneuvered their horses and set off in a westward direction.

Porthos lagged behind a moment. "Lad," he called, "you keep yourself out of sight, and don't let Christophe see you, or you'll live to regret it."

As if he needed any reminding of that. "Absolutely," he replied and firmly shook the man's outstretched hand before heading off in the direction Laurel had recently taken.

* * * * * * * * * * *

Milady was not in a good mood. She had been unable to find any trace of where Athos, Porthos, and D'Artagnan might be or might have gone. It was beginning to look like they had never even gone into Boussac. She winced as the wheel of her carriage rumbled over the uneven turf, bouncing and gyrating as it kicked up pebbles and clumps of dirt. Nor had she been able to confirm anything unusual about Laurel's appearance at the dance other than the fact she had made herself so obvious that Laurel must have known she'd be remarked upon.

Her long, thin finger tapped against her lips. There had to be a reason for the fact she had decided to draw attention to herself. Unlikely she would have gotten a dress without good reason, since she obviously was still traveling as a boy and not as a woman.

Milady stared at the missive she held in her hands, reviewing its contents in her mind. Still, she concluded that there was no need to let the cardinal know Laurel was traveling as a lad; Milady could handle her sister on her own. Nor, she decided, could she really tell the cardinal more than she had imparted. Obviously, they had been avoiding populated areas and resorted to camping, but their supplies had to be getting low. Time to follow her intuition and hope that they stopped at some populated area for supplies or to try to contact Thomas d'Anlass.

That was it! Her hand fell to her side. Laurel must have passed a message to someone at that dance, either her father or someone who could get to her father. She was sure Thomas had to contact his daughter; after his successful escape from Luz, it was plain he had gotten what he had come for. Which meant that he had to head for Belgium or the Netherlands in order to get the documents that would help his daughter capture Richelieu's man in Calais. So Laurel obviously had to send a letter north very soon if she hoped to get the proof before the spy made his delivery to Buckingham. Obviously, she'd have to go somewhere where she could hire someone to deliver a letter quickly or post one quickly, which meant a place like Chartres or Meung.

Tapping on the grating, she signaled the coachman. The wooden panel slid open. Without preamble she instructed the coachman and bodyguard, Jacques, to send up the sergeant Richelieu had sent to her. The driver responded quickly in the affirmative, and Milady de Winter closed the panel firmly. The carriage drew to a halt, and a sergeant of the Cardinal's Guard bowed and entered the vehicle, leaving his horse to be brought along by one of the men in his command.

"Milady de Winter," he spoke humbly, and she acknowledged his greeting with the expected, rather curt, response.

Shrewdly, she assessed the commander before her. Handpicked by Richelieu to lead the cardinal's most skilled fighters: obviously a man who would report back to Richelieu every move she made—were he so inclined. She wondered how the cardinal kept this hard man's loyalty. Man of God, not. Ruthless conniver, and that was a far-too-flattering epithet.

None of these thoughts were revealed in her face as she requested the man's report and listened closely to the details. Details, even seemingly insignificant ones, could make a tremendous difference.

When he had concluded the report, she came to her decision. "I have reason to believe our group may have split up," she told the sergeant, and he dipped his head minutely. "Therefore I want you to take half your men and Jacques to Chartres and see what you can find of the musketeers in question. I travel to Meung." The woman paused to make sure that the sergeant understood not only the instructions but also the unspoken warning not to cross her. "I will contact you from Meung with any further instructions. And I expect you to post a report to me immediately after you have arrived," the *comtesse* finished and instructed Jacques to stop and let the sergeant out.

The sergeant descended from the carriage and went to gather five of his men and Jacques and then head quickly to Chartres. Somewhat satisfied, the *Comtesse de* Winter leaned back against the seat as her other bodyguard took the reins of the coach and urged the horses to get going again at as swift of pace as he could manage the beasts. She closed her eyes in quiet contemplation as the coach rumbled forward towards Meung. Time to be on the lookout for a thin lad with unusual dark blue eyes and an almost effeminate face.

The billow of smoke rose from the barrel of the gun. Content, the man slipped the weapon back into its holster. He stepped forward over sprawling legs and leaned over the hunched-over figure. Grasping the wrist, he felt for a pulse. None. Good, the man was dead.

For a moment he remained suspended, surveying each and every direction. He saw no one. He heard no one. So much for the Spanish spy who had been sent after him to reclaim certain very valuable government documents. He frisked the corpse, and from inside the pocket sewn in the dead man's vest, he took a pouch of coins and a bundle of papers.

Through the papers he flipped and smiled in satisfaction.

Everything was in order; every one of the documents was now back in his possession. Standing, he kicked the body aside. It'd be discovered by some vagrant later. In the meantime, he was off to Calais, the last of the papers he needed to deliver to England now in his possession. Sometimes he very much enjoyed his chosen occupation.

* * * * * * * * * * *

Laurel tethered her horse and glanced about her. What remained of the setting sun beat down on her, and she rested against the post for a moment, looking about her at the people who bustled through the streets about their daily business. The sooner she got out of here, the better; she had a bad feeling about this place. Too many people—too many people that might be looking for her—could possibly recognize her, despite all her precautions.

The woman pushed away from the post and ambled down the street towards a tavern. Only for a brief moment did she pause to make sure that her disguise was still in place, hat pulled down low to hide her face, before she continued towards her chosen destination.

Hopefully, one of the men her father frequently hired as a messenger was here. Truly foul. Laurel ducked inside the smoky room, almost gagging at the stench of unwashed bodies mingled with melted wax, smoke, and ale. Several eyes turned towards her and she studiously ignored them. Even a dirty lad drew an uncomfortable amount of attention here. Just find the man and get the letters sent, she reminded herself.

Relief flitted through her eyes as she caught sight of the messenger and sat down across from him. She called for two mugs of ale, one for her, one for him, and introduced her task by placing the two sealed scrolls on the table, several gold coins hidden underneath them. The woman took a sip of the alcohol and almost shuddered. Ale was a truly vile brew. She'd take bourbon, cognac, or champagne over it any day.

"This letter," she said softly, "goes to Brussels and this one goes to Paris as quickly as humanly possible. I believe you should find the proper inducement under them."

The man casually lifted the letters and tucked them inside his tunic. Briefly he counted the coins and smiled, raising the mug of ale to his lips and drinking it down in one chug. "It will be done," he replied and setting the empty mug aside vanished into the darkening streets. Laurel remained a few more minutes and took one last sip of the bitter brew.

Setting the nearly full mug aside, she left exactly enough to cover the drinks and made her way back to the streets. Time to get out of here; she shivered as a cool breeze nipped against her skin. She picked up her pace again, striding towards her horse. Couldn't wait to be away from this place, and the sooner the better.

From the corner of her eye she glimpsed a movement, and she felt her heart thud and blood pound. Could someone be following her?

She picked up the pace just slightly and glimpsed another movement out of the corner of her eye. Laurel's eyes darted this way and that and caught sight of a woman strolling down the street. *Non!* She turned to go back the other way but was too late as a blow caught her off guard, and she crumpled to the ground unconscious; her last thought was one of dismay that her own sister could well end up betraying her and France.

"*Sacrebleu,*" the young man cursed mildly under his breath and flattened himself behind the corner of the nearest building. Milady de Winter back from the dead, exactly as Laurel had told them after leaving Boussac. Now, from what he had just witnessed, the *comtesse* had captured her stepsister. Nor did he have any doubt that Milady was well aware that the lad her men had apprehended really was Laurel d'Anlass.

Now what was it that Aramis had said about blending in with the rest of the crowd and being able to follow someone without them noticing you? Ah, yes, don't hurry. Stay at a distance, and stop and mingle with the crowd every so often, but never let the person out of sight.

Stealthily he crept from behind his hiding place and caught sight of the woman and two men, one carrying an unconscious young boy, or so it appeared. Well, no time like the present to test his skills and Aramis' advice. D'Artagnan concluded as he followed the small group through the streets of Meung.

D'Artagnan crouched behind an abandoned pile of refuse as Milady rapped on a door in a back alley. She was admitted promptly, and the two men followed her in. The door fell closed behind the group, and the young man crept towards the entrance. To one side there was a window which he crouched down under and looked in. His clear, striking blue eyes took in the scene being played out in the interior. He watched as Milady swept from the room and several men came in and out.

Several minutes passed in agonizing slowness, and D'Artagnan crawled around the corner and sat down, pondering the situation. Five to seven men and then the *Comtesse de* Winter herself. Not the greatest of odds. Nor was there anywhere he could go for help. He couldn't exactly get in touch with Athos, Porthos, and Aramis, considering they wouldn't yet be at the rendezvous point. Maybe he'd better start praying, he remarked. Or maybe he better start using some cunning, as Aramis had called it, preferring not to call it guile.

One more time he went back and peered in the window. Laurel was seated in a chair, her hands tied behind her, still unconscious, or it appeared so from the angle her head lolled. There were three men in the room with her. As he watched he heard her low moan and saw her head swing slowly from side to side. Well, she was waking up, the man concluded. Maybe she could prove resourceful then. She had proven quite resourceful in the past, but still he had to get her out of there. He needed a distraction, but what?

Athos drank a swig of water, wishing it were something stronger, and looked up at his horse. Perhaps it wasn't exactly the wisest of ideas to be sitting so close to the hooves of the animal, he decided, as he got up and came over to where Aramis and Porthos sat playing a game of their own devising. He never asked what game they got so involved in; it was better to remain in ignorance on that front.

Athos glanced at the sky. The sun was rising higher. Definitely was going to be a very hot day. He seated himself next to his companions. It was already very warm and uncomfortably so. He fingered the little packet that Laurel had presented to him, the one Thomas had delivered in Boussac. Laurel. This was not a good sign. Well past dawn, and approaching midday without a sign of either Laurel or D'Artagnan.

Porthos suddenly stopped his blustering as if he felt Athos' brooding, and Aramis met the oldest musketeer's gaze. "Christophe obviously ran into trouble," Aramis said before Athos could say it. "I know. However, how much we can do about it is debatable."

"Without the . . . lad," Athos said, "this mission fails. Christophe's the only one who can possibly get a hold of the last of the information from Thomas D'Anlass in Beauvais, information critical to apprehending the traitor."

"We could go back to Meung and see if we could find her, him, them," Porthos suggested in a much-subdued tone.

"It may come to that, but I'd rather leave that as an absolute last resort. If Christophe ran into trouble in Meung, we'd probably only run into more. If the lad was recognized, we'd most likely be recognized, and I'm not quite prepared to take that risk yet." Athos scowled more deeply than usual.

Porthos could find no words, and no ideas came to mind. Things looked pretty dismal as far as he could tell. Ideas were not his strong point. Come on Aramis, think of something, say something, he urged silently. The large man was not disappointed.

"Athos, Laurel," Aramis said deliberately, using the woman's real identity, "is a very cunning, resourceful woman. She has escaped from very perilous situations before. Plus, we can probably assume D'Artagnan is with her. They may be a bit headstrong and reckless, but I think between the two of them they can prove a match for almost any situation, especially once they realize how important it is."

"I hope you're right, Aramis," Athos said aloud. "I hope to God you're right." Regardless, he was only going to wait so long.

Laurel rolled her eyes heavenward and closed them, hanging her head and still trying to deny the sight of the man who lay trussed at her feet. D'Artagnan. She was sure despite his ragged and scruffy appearance. And people called her reckless. Impetuous little fool.

Casse-cou! Reckless! Opening her eyes, Laurel glanced around the room: one guard with his back to them.

D'Artagnan moaned and came to. "What were you thinking?" Laurel chastised the musketeer. That's right; he wasn't thinking.

"Give me a second, Christophe," he complained as he blinked his eyes and restored his befuddled thoughts to some semblance of order. "Things really aren't as bad as they seem. I've got a plan."

"Oh really, is that so?"

"*Oui*," the young man replied as the guard momentarily vacated the room. Quickly D'Artagnan jumped to his feet, awkwardly, but he made it and stooped over. "Quick." He gasped. "My knife's hidden in my collar. See if you can grab it somehow."

Sheer luck that they hadn't found that blade then. Laurel stared at him in amazement, but her agile mind went straight to work on the problem. She leaned forward, and with her chin scooted his collar aside, catching sight of the very small blade. With a dexterity that was extraordinary even for her, she grasped the knife in her teeth and bent down to place it under her leg and barely within reach of her tied hand.

"What next?" she said to him, and he told her they were waiting for a distraction as he collapsed back to the floor.

Before she had the chance to ask what distraction, two guards entered the room. The musketeer surveyed the two men. It was now or never he thought, and let out a loud shrill whistle. The guards swirled to glare at him, and suddenly the stomping of hooves overwhelmed them, and a horse came charging through the broken door. The guards jumped back as the animal careened straight towards them, and Laurel grasped the knife in her hands and desperately sawed at her bonds. Distraction indeed. Maybe she had underestimated him a bit. He was resourceful at least.

Ropes fell from her wrists, and she bent and hacked the bonds from her feet. Immediately, she lunged to D'Artagnan's side, glancing to see that the guards were still occupied, but only just. Desperately, she sawed at his bonds.

Finally! He was free. They leapt to their feet as two more guards burst into the room. Thinking quickly, D'Artagnan hurled Laurel out the broken door and followed a few steps behind. She wasted no time in sprinting down the alley and as far away as possible, and the musketeer took off after her. Quick little thing. Or not so little.

D'Artagnan glanced back, stopping for a second, and whistled one more time, praying that his horse would hear him and come on his command and that the animal hadn't yet been shot. God must have been watching or listening, for his horse came charging towards him and stopped. Quickly he mounted the animal and urged the horse in pursuit of Laurel. Already he heard the guards gaining on him.

There she was, D'Artagnan noted as he closed on his companion and leaned low off the left side of his horse. He let go the reins and grasped her around the waist, swinging her up and onto the horse with him. Luckily she was light and didn't struggle except to right herself in the saddle. "Do they have your horse?" he asked and she shook her head. "Where is he?" Laurel directed him to the post where she had left the spirited gelding.

He reined the horse to a stop, and his passenger jumped off. "How close are they?" she cried as she checked her mount very quickly.

"You've got a little time," he replied, "but you'd better hurry. Correction. Make that—they're coming right now."

Without further ado, she hurled herself into the saddle, spurred Rebelle forward. In a flurry they were off, Laurel and D'Artagnan careening through the streets of Meung as fast as they dared.

They reached the town border before their pursuers, who were much delayed by the bustling traffic. Only just, though. Not even glancing back, they took off at a gallop.

For long minutes they galloped. Muscles rippling beneath their legs, the sound of their breathing at least as harsh as the wind battering their ears. Only when Laurel was finally reasonably sure of their escape did she slow, and the musketeer followed suit.

They really had made it. By some miracle.

At that moment it hit her that she had lost both her mother's gun and her hat during the fray, but at least she hadn't lost her sword, which she had left with Athos. And she had another hat in Athos' saddlepacks. With new respect she looked at the young man. "Well done. How did you manage that?" Other than a good deal of luck.

He puffed with some pride and informed her he had hired an urchin that his horse actually liked. And it had taken a long time to find an urchin his extremely well-trained horse—almost too well-trained—liked. Anyway, he told her that he hired the urchin to release his horse when he heard D'Artagnan's shrill whistle and to see to it that the mare was running all out in time to break down the door. "And it worked," he concluded, despite the fact it had been a rather rash gamble.

"I noticed," she responded. "But what are we going to do about defending ourselves?"

D'Artagnan smiled and slowed his mount enough to open his saddle-pack and dig out the rapier he had wrapped inside a cloak and hidden there. He unwrapped the sword and sheath and strapped it around him, saying, "I have my sword." Laurel just shook her head and laughed. He was learning. Still had a ways to go, but he was learning. Pointless to argue with favorable results anyhow. Athos could, and probably would, do that for her and in a far more effective manner.

"Porthos, where are you going?" Aramis respectfully demanded, but demanded nonetheless.

"Just out for a little ride, my good friend," he shot back.

"That ride had better not be for Meung," Aramis informed him. "It would be suicidal for us to go riding into the place one person at a time and let them cut us down one person at a time."

"Spoilsport," the large man grumbled. "You would have to be absolutely sensible. Fear not, my noble friend. This time I am not heading back to Meung. I am simply taking a wee little ride," he assured Aramis as he left the man behind.

For a league or so Porthos rode, enjoying the wind running through his hair and against his face, cooling him. Too bad the ride couldn't make him forget about the waiting game he was forced to play. He'd have to go back to camp soon if he didn't want to miss what passed for dinner. His horse began to fidget. The large man slowed the mare and patted her neck to reassure her. "What do you smell, girl?" he asked as he scanned the territory.

The horse, however, was not forced to respond, for Porthos saw it himself. Two riders coming towards him at a semi-leisurely pace. For an instant he studied the gaits. Well he'd be darned, it was definitely D'Artagnan, and the rider beside him was probably the lovely Lady Laurel. He spurred his horse forward to greet them, knowing that D'Artagnan should be able to recognize him, counting on it, in fact.

As he joined the two disheveled young people he cried jovially, "So the kiddies have finally made it back."

"Glad to see you too, Porthos," Laurel quipped, her humor far better than reason seemed to dictate. "However, you see Hero here,"—she pointed to D'Artagnan—"and I have kind of had a trying day and have spent quite some time searching for you three. So anyway, if we could please forgo these long greetings and reminiscences, I'd much appreciate it."

"Of course, milady," Porthos responded, flourishing his hat and making use of an English phrase, "Your wish, as always, is my command. To camp it is then. Follow me."

"Athos, Aramis," Porthos announced as he rode up with D'Artagnan and Laurel in tow. "Look at what I found. Sheep who had lost their way."

"And of course you are an excellent shepherd for God's flock, are you not, Porthos?" Aramis teased, and Porthos was pretty sure that the man was teasing this time.

Aramis turned to the young woman and young musketeer. "Welcome back to the fold, my children; you look in need of some rest and some sustenance, I mean fish. Could I perhaps suggest some water? I know it is not wine, but we will have to make do," he added for Porthos' benefit.

Laurel climbed down from her horse and frowned as she took in the gelding's pathetic state. She had her work cut out for her indeed. "Actually, nothing for me right now," she said. "I've got to get Rebelle taken care of first."

The woman uncinched the saddle and hefted it from the horse to the ground, her muscles straining as she did so. Thank goodness she hadn't overbalanced and ended up with the saddle atop her. A few broken ribs were not in her plan. She searched the pack for a brush and after several seconds found it. In resignation, she set about brushing down the sadly disheveled animal while D'Artagnan followed suit with his own horse.

Her arms ached with a vengeance, telling her that she was being unreasonably demanding, and even her finger bones and muscles screamed for respite that was unlikely to come soon. She had done too good of a job making her horse look neglected. And it was hot out here, despite the fact it was getting close to evening. Her chest heaving and sweat dripping, sliding, down her back and causing her shirt to stick and then wrap around her breasts constricting her, she paused with the brush suspended in midair.

In fatigue, she stood, trying to recover her wind when Porthos plucked the brush from her hand not allowing her to protest. "Come now *votre majesté,*" he teased, "you're quite tired. Allow me to be your humble servant and finish this task for you."

Despite her mild annoyance and fatigue, she chuckled and then reluctantly decided to turn the job over to Porthos. Not that she really had the energy to argue with him. With the back of her hand she pushed a strand of her bangs from her eyes and checked to assure herself her hair was still bound tightly. It was, except for a few windblown strands. "You better be careful with Rebelle, Porthos, you hear, or you'll have me to answer to." What she failed to mention was that Rebelle had never been very fond of anyone other than herself.

"Quite right. As always, I am devotedly at your command," he assured her, and she stepped away from her mount, glancing over to D'Artagnan to see that Aramis was relieving him of his task, and the young musketeer headed off in what appeared to be Athos' direction. What in the world was the man up to, she thought in confusion as she stared at Aramis even after

D'Artagnan's departure—long after the youngest musketeer's departure in fact.

Aramis caught Laurel's glance, and she could almost have sworn he winked at her before she dismissed the outrageous notion. As the raven-haired man set about grooming D'Artagnan's horse, Porthos said, "How bout some water and sustenance now?"

"Actually," she pondered thoughtfully, "if you would just point me to the nearest stream, I'll be quite all right." She felt so incredibly tired, filthy, and hot that a cold bath sounded heavenly.

"You're not seriously going to take another bath so soon?" Porthos asked her, pretending to be scandalized.

"Oh don't worry, Porthos, I'm not going to drag any of you in with me, at least not today. I just can't think of anything more lovely on a day like this than a nice cold bath and soaking these aching muscles," she retorted, and asked Aramis to point her to the stream again. He did so, and she beat a hasty retreat before Aramis could make one of his tantalizing and cryptic remarks. Or, before Porthos could make an undiginified one.

"You wanted to see me?" D'Artagnan addressed Athos with mild confusion and pronounced fatigue in his voice.

"Have a seat," Athos told him. Aramis had done his job well, although he hadn't counted on Aramis finishing D'Artagnan's horse tending task for him. Not that D'Artagnan didn't look nearly dead with fatigue, and he deserved a bit of a break. "Why don't you let me know what happened in Meung?"

Falteringly he began to relate his story and then became more clear in his narration. He outlined Laurel's capture and his plan to get her out and then he told Athos of their escape.

A wry half smile touched Athos' lips. "You're still reckless, D'Artagnan and a very lucky young man. Lucky that they didn't find that knife and lucky that your horse performed as expected. And lucky Christophe is a quick thinker." He put a hand up, stopping D'Artagnan from speaking in his defense. "I am not criticizing, D'Artagnan. I'm pointing out what you still need to work on. Next time you may not be so lucky, so you'll have to be more careful and cunning."

D'Artagnan mumbled his thanks, and Athos accepted them mutely. For a moment both men were silent. "Did Christophe get the letters sent off?"

"As far as I could tell it was after he delivered the letters that Milady and her men captured him."

"I'll confirm it with the lad," Athos concluded. "Why don't you get some rest? We'll stay here tonight, and you look as if you could use the nap."

D'Artagnan scowled half-heartedly. "As long as I don't have to prepare dinner, and you remember to wake me up for it."

"Will do," Athos replied, and the youngest musketeer wandered off and found himself a nice patch of ground to take a nap upon.

Athos had another distinct urge for a drink: a good stiff one. It'd been too long since he'd last had one. Sabine. Sabine, Milady again. He knew he hadn't heard the last of her since Laurel had told them all the truth of what had really happened the day she lost her temper and disappeared for a good day or so. Was she really so warped that she would sacrifice her sister for some sinister agenda, even though Laurel was probably right in believing that Sabine still loved her?

Sabine apparently still loved him too, even after he had cast her out for deceiving him and then refused to listen to anything she had to say in her defense. Yet she was bitter towards him, so very bitter that she'd tried to have him killed. "Oh, Sabine," he whispered very softly to himself. "Sabine, I'm sorry. Can you not forgive me even now?" He'd had to do it, had to let her die the second time, for by her own admission she was guilty of murder and more. But there was no solace in the words.

He snorted in what might have been taken for humor, only it wasn't. "What have we done, Sabine? What have we become?"

Athos jerked himself from his brooding as a freshly washed Laurel walked by, her long hair undone and falling to her waist, dripping wet; once again she was in her male attire, and clean attire at that. Another reason to teach Laurel to control her temper; if she didn't she could mess up her life as badly as he had screwed his up. At least she didn't believe in love, didn't even really hold out much chance of marrying let alone finding a love match. At least that's what she had once told him. "Laurel, I mean, Christophe." He crooked a finger and she came.

"*Oui*," she said concern evident in her tone and eyes. Tentatively she reached forward and touched his arm. "Athos, are you all right?"

"Nothing a good drink won't take care of," he told her grimly, knowing that a drink was not an option. He'd given his word. "I'll be fine," he added, and she reluctantly withdrew her hand. "Were you able to get the letters posted?"

She nodded. "The man has been paid well to do his job, and he has run messages for my father before, so he knows that it's worth his while to be swift and reliable. If he isn't, he'll lose the bonus my father will give him." With these words she paused and decided it was time to face the music and let Athos know the entire story of what had happened in Meung. "About Meung . . ."

"D'Artagnan already told me," he said with uncustomary gentleness. "I think maybe you should get some rest too before dinner." At her narrowed eyes, he elaborated. "D'Artagnan's already taking a nap. I'll make sure I wake both of you up in time to get a meal, even if that means I have to make it myself. We'll try to leave an hour or two after dawn tomorrow."

She smiled sheepishly, but there were thanks and a bit of relief in her eyes as she retreated to fall into the welcome arms of sleep. Laurel and her prickly pride. Athos shook his head as he watched her sleeping.

* * * * * * * * * * *

The unsealed letter sat atop the empty desk as a soldier walked by the open door. Taken by surprise, he stopped and stared at it. Could be important. But could he get to it before *Monsieur de* Treville got back? The man was never gone long if he left something out.

His decision made, he dashed into the office and scanned through the contents of the letter:

> *Capitaine*:
>
> We must humbly beg your pardon and beg your forgiveness, *s'il vous plaît*, for not informing sooner about our change of plans. By now you must wonder where Laurel d'Anlass is. We have decided it is safer for her not to return to Paris and be put under your protection since we are fairly sure the cardinal is after her. We regret the inconvenience. We are still on

our way to Calais and will return to Paris when we are able. Also, should you need to confirm receipt of this letter, please write Christophe Moulins in Beauvais, with all due haste.

Vive la France. Vive le roi.
D'Artagnan

The sound of boot heels clicking upon the floor and coming closer startled the man, and he jumped.

He could not afford to be caught in Treville's office reading his private correspondence.

With little semblance of grace, he stepped back and bumped into a window ledge. Quickly he stepped out the window onto the ledge and made his way away from the room, refusing to look down from his three-story height.

All he had to do was make it to the next balcony and he was safe, home free. Reaching out with his left hand, he grabbed the rail of the balcony in a death grip. He heaved and swung himself over the rail onto the balcony. Calmly he walked into the hall and back towards the stairs. Richelieu would want to know about this.

Monsieur de Treville picked the brief letter up from his desk and rolled it. Swiftly he tucked the roll inside his doublet and underneath the musketeer mantle. So Thomas d'Anlass' daughter would not be showing; if she despised and feared the cardinal like her father then it was understandable she'd want to avoid Paris. Plus, if D'Artagnan was right about Richelieu being after her . . .

Still, D'Artagnan had failed to inform him of her whereabouts. That could be just as well that he hadn't. Then again, it could very well mean they had the lady with them. If that was the case there was definitely something going on, something that could easily involve the security of king and country.

Curse Richelieu and his plotting. Unless his men returned in about ten or eleven days, the king himself would send out a warrant for their arrest. The charge being dishonor, disloyalty, and desertion. In short, conduct unbecoming a musketeer. There was simply no alternative except to hope the letter, recently written and dated, which he was about to post to urge them to be more quickly on their way, would be of some aid.

"Your eminence." The man bowed deeply over the cardinal's outstretched hand, kissing the ring that was the signet of his office. "I have news I thought might interest you."

"You are aware I am a very busy man with many demands on my time." The cardinal warned that he'd best not be wasting valuable time.

The soldier hastened to prove to the hawknosed man that he was not wasting the cardinal's time. "Your eminence, I thought you might be interested in information about D'Artagnan."

"Indeed, go on. I'm listening." The soldier scrambled to reveal all the details he had read in the letter to Treville adding that he thought the *capitaine* was mailing or already had mailed a letter in response. "I am quite pleased. You have earned my gratitude," he informed the young soldier, presenting him with a gold coin. "If you do happen to see anything else suspicious in the future, do remember to come to me, and as the good Lord has instructed me, I will relieve your burden."

The young soldier left, murmuring his undying thanks and loyalty, and the cardinal smiled deviously. Quite a turn of luck. Time to inform Milady that their prey was likely heading to Beauvais. Dipping the quill, he scribbled a brief note about what he had just learned and reminded her that if she did not soon deliver Laurel d'Anlass to him, the consequences could be unfortunately grave. In the meantime, he hoped the *comtesse* was making the best use possible of Constance Bonacieux, whom he had recently sent to her. Although, he did have to admit, that was one thorn out of his side. With Constance gone, access to the lovely Anne was much easier. The other ladies in waiting weren't nearly so protective or so suspicious of him.

He blotted the ink and sealed the paper, pressing his signet into the wet wax. He tied the message on to the pigeon and released it. Taking a deep breath, he smiled again. Soon, very soon, the royal treasury would be completely at his disposal, and all of France would look to their devoted spiritual leader for guidance. Come to think of it, soon enough half of Europe would also be at his feet. Ah, the works of a servant of God were never done. He turned from the window and went back to his desk.

He pulled the drawer open and grasped a ring in his hand, the ring he had intercepted before it had found its way to *Monsieur de* Treville. How sad that Aramis' father had taken typhoid and about a fortnight earlier died, leaving Aramis with a year to claim his father's title and estate before the property became part of the Church's holdings. Also quite sad he might never know that he was now a *duc*, the *Duc de* Rouen, should he step forward. But then the world was so often an unfair and cruel place.

* * * * * * * * * * *

"We need supplies, and the horses need better feed than they have been having in order to maintain their strength," Aramis told his four companions after checking his mount's teeth, flanks, and legs. Already the horses were showing the strain of the journey and inadequate food.

"Then it looks like we'll have to stop in the village." Laurel was resigned to the less than favorable situation.

"Probably," Athos agreed grimly. "But first let's figure out exactly where we are. Aramis, how many leagues have we traveled from Meung?"

"From Meung? Too many. I would place us right about a good day and a half's ride from Beauvais. Actually, I believe we have veered a little farther west than we intended."

"How far west?" Athos pressed.

"I would say about three leagues, maybe two and a half."

Porthos sighed and all eyes turned to him. In an oddly subdued voice he said, "You know there is another choice other than going to a village?" They all waited anxiously as Porthos took his dear sweet time. "My family's main home is probably just about a little more than a two-hour ride northwest from here. They would probably take us in. My father does have a great fondness for horses. Raises them, in fact."

"Why Porthos, you don't at all sound happy about the prospect of going home to the bosom of your loving mother and father," Laurel teased, and he glared at her.

"Loving as a pack of barracudas during a feeding frenzy," he countered. "Just don't say I didn't warn you. So consider yourself warned. I've got three younger and eligible sisters, two of them hellions or close enough, and a very managing mother. Plus, there's a handful of cousins my mother's trying to find wives for."

"We've been warned," Athos said. "However, it's still the best choice we have. Let's move out. You too, D'Artagnan," he said, calling the young man from his preoccupation.

The stiff and proper butler raised his eyebrow in disapproval at the ragtag bunch that was standing in the open doorway. Four men and one lad, and all carrying swords. One tall and darkly handsome man, alluring, dangerous even. Another, a blond with a refined but rugged air and broad shoulders. Another yet who appeared to have just entered manhood, and a handsome young devil as well. Finally, there stood the frowning heir apparent to the *comte*.

"Please inform my mother that I am here," Porthos spoke.

"As you command, *monseigneur*," the butler said chillingly, ushering the small party into the entry hall. The butler disappeared through a massive oak door.

Moments later a dainty older matron, sporting a dress that was low-cut even for the standards of a married woman, floated out into the hall, her small slippers clicking ever so lightly on the marble floor. She cast a quelling glance on the large man with a sash tied around his head. So her son had finally decided to show his face again after the terrible way he had abandoned the lovely wife his father had found him, and he hadn't even bothered to return when she had died in childbirth. Rather, he'd decided to keep himself fully occupied with building his reputation as a dashing and daring musketeer. "Well, Jean-Paul . . ."

"It's Porthos, Mother," he corrected, but she paid him no heed. Some things never changed.

"You have finally decided to return home. It is about time. Come now, don't just stand there. Don't you have a kiss for your mother?"

"*Oui, Maman*," he replied as if compelled against his will, and he bent down and kissed her dutifully on both cheeks.

"Much better." She patted his arm, and Porthos cast her a highly annoyed look that she ignored. Suddenly she acknowledged his three gentlemen companions. "Come now, introduce me to your friends."

Porthos pointed out Athos first, then D'Artagnan, and Aramis. "And the lad, Christophe," he said, "is D'Artagnan's younger brother. Bit of a trouble-maker. Seems he was causing a few problems by running away from home to follow his big brother, so now he's kind of tagging along with us." Each man acknowledged the lady of the house, by bowing over her hand and kissing it, even Christophe.

"Delighted," she murmured sizing Aramis and D'Artagnan up and preparing to move on to Athos. All very nice specimens of manhood and with an unmistakable air of refinement that bespoke money and rank. There were several young ladies she had in mind for introductions, the sooner the better.

Porthos leaned over and whispered in his mother's ear. "Don't even think of it, *Maman*. Athos is already married." He stood straight again and addressed his mother. "Actually, Mother my friends and I were in need of a place to stay tonight and a place to stable and feed our horses."

"Don't be silly," she said. "You'll all be staying more than a night. David, please show each of these gentlemen a room," she instructed a servant.

"*Maman*, we have to leave tomorrow."

"Of course, son," she agreed, patronizing him with a pinch on the cheek, and she then swept from the room to see to it that a dinner of proper elegance would be served tonight. She was going to be quite busy over the next few hours, preparing the proper environment for some match making. Aramis, D'Artagnan, and Laurel couldn't help but laugh at Porthos' predicament, and even sober Athos let loose long enough to smile. They'd been warned.

Once she had gotten her giggles under control, Laurel addressed the large musketeer. "I assume your mother is a stickler for proper etiquette?" He informed Laurel that conjecture was correct, except if it hurt her match making schemes. "Then please extend my apologies to your mother. Seeing as I am too young and undisciplined to join you at the dinner table, I must take dinner on my own in my room."

The devious, little, conniving . . . Well, so Laurel would get out of dinner with the family, but not out of the after-dinner entertainment, not by a long shot. "You will of course be joining us in the music room after dinner?" He smiled, and she conceded him the point before docilely traipsing off to follow the servant to her appointed chamber.

The servant opened the doors to the music room and ushered the now more presentable tall lad of what appeared to be about twelve years into the room. Still couldn't convince him to give up the hat, but the servant was pleased overall with the feisty boy's transformation, and, besides, it was not his duty to train the lad in manners and decorum.

Calmly Laurel surveyed the little scene set out in front of her. There were Porthos' three sisters, all with dark brown hair and between five and ten and eight and ten. Actually, two appeared to be twins of roughly ten and five, the other a young woman of eight and ten. They were all clustered around Aramis and D'Artagnan, who had cleaned up even more nicely than Laurel; the twins were flirting outrageously with Aramis. Athos sat off to himself every so often talking with Porthos' father and overall enjoying himself, without even touching a drink. The man really knew his horses and had seen to it that theirs were well cared for. Now she could see where Porthos had gotten his height and build.

It looked like Aramis and D'Artagnan did not hold the eldest girl's attention; it seemed she was glancing at Athos. Or was it at her father? Ah, well, it mattered little to her.

Speaking of Porthos, where was the hulk?

"So glad you could make it," Porthos cried as if she had summoned him by mere thought. Dismissing the servant, Porthos lifted her with her elbows, escorting her farther into the room and left her facing his mother while he went off to join his cousins. She was not happy about that. Not at all. Here was hardly the place to vent her temper, though, so she stewed while his mother set about tutoring proper behavior to the lad who would soon be growing to manhood. Porthos' mother ploughed ahead with lectures on etiquette and protocol, and now Christophe remembered why she had hated those lessons.

One of Porthos' cousins detached himself from the group and joined D'Artagnan and Aramis. He shook each man's hand, introducing himself as Georges. "So, you're friends of Porthos."

"We've been charged with that before," Aramis replied lightly, and the man nodded as if a bit confused by the unexpected reply. D'Artagnan simply took it in stride; that was simply Aramis for you. Aramis nodded and turned his attention back to the ladies while Georges turned his attention to D'Artagnan.

In a voice like that of the cat who has just eaten cream, Georges said, "Have you heard about the terrible tragedy?" Imparting the latest morsel of gossip was something he always enjoyed doing.

"Sorry, I don't think so. I've been on the road a lot lately."

"Well," Georges said as if imparting a great secret. "It seems the old *Duc de* Rouen recently died of the typhoid, and his heir has yet to step forward and claim the title. There's even rumors that the heir has left the country and has not returned, due to a falling out with his father years ago."

"Oh," D'Artagnan responded and glanced at Aramis who abruptly seemed to grow weary of Porthos' sisters and their attempts to lead him into revealing more of himself than he cared to or to wheedle a proposal of marriage from him.

"Excuse me, please, *mesdemoiselles*," Aramis said politely. "It is time I turned in for the night. I am quite tired and must be up early." He bowed and exited with a little more haste than was really proper.

Laurel glanced away from Porthos' mother, watching Aramis as he excused himself from the room. A strange feeling crept over her. Why did something feel distinctly odd about Aramis' departure? Her eyebrows furrowed, and she failed to respond to one of the older woman's queries, only to be called to account for it. Every so often, she glanced back at the door, but the musketeer did not return.

There had to be a way out of this. Slowly she began slouching as if her stomach were in pain. Then as if the pain could no longer be ignored, she clutched her stomach and moaned under her breath in perfect imitation of a boy who was struck with a nasty stomachache, perhaps caused by overindulgence in food. "Please, my lady," she pleaded. "I feel very unwell. Could I please beg your pardon and be excused?"

"Of course, lad," the old woman said with skeptical concern and watched the lad exit from the room, clutching at his stomach. She was already planning the lessons for tomorrow. As the door closed behind her, Laurel dropped her hand from her stomach and took the stairs two at a time, pushing down her guilt at deceiving Porthos' mother and causing her such concern. The deception was for the best.

Laurel was scarcely out of breath when she reached the top of the stairs and made her way down the corridor. Now, which way was the room David had put Aramis in? Ah, yes, third on the left. Outside the third door she was brought up short. It was cracked open a bit, and she could see the dim glow of several candles coming from the room.

"Aramis." She knocked on the open door. When she heard no response, she pushed it farther open and entered, closing the door behind her with a soft click.

"I said," he commanded, his voice sounding curt and abrupt in his own ears, "go away. Your presence was not requested here, nor is it welcome." He sat in a dark corner in a chair, head stooped over his knees and glaring at her.

"Aramis," she repeated, and he lifted a bottle of wine to his lips and drank deeply from it. The woman grasped the bottle immediately after he had briefly set it on the bed table. It was nearly empty and who knows what else he had already had to drink earlier. "How much have you been drinking?"

In a very clipped voice, he reiterated, "I said, Lady Laurel, get out of my room. Unless . . ." He paused and cast her a look that left even Laurel little doubt as to his meaning. Then as if his drink-befuddled mind suddenly realized the inappropriateness of trying to bed a single lady, he said, "Forget it. Listen I want to be alone, or can't your feeble intellectual powers comprehend that there are a few times that even I, perfect gentleman that I am, want to get smashed out of my mind?"

"It's not like you," she protested. Right now was no time for her to be timid. Time to be blunt.

Aramis chuckled, and she shivered at the eerie sound. He tugged the bottle from her suddenly limp fingers and drank another chug of the contents down. "Not like me. Really? Is that a fact? And I guess you know me so well. *Parbleu*, you know everyone and so perfectly. Papa's little angel, I believe; sees everything so clearly, gets everything she wants or loses her temper and throws a fit. Doesn't even know where she's not wanted. When it's better not to stick around."

With repressed anger under tight control, she stalked a step towards the drunken man, her voice harsh and biting. "*Oui,* Aramis. I do know you. I know you as much as any of your friends, probably better. 'Cause you see, Aramis, I'm smart, maybe even as smart as you are, and that frightens you because I have the ability to match wits with you and actually win. It frightens you because I'm observant, and I just might start to see things that you'd rather not have seen. Like the fact that I was the one that noticed something was wrong and followed you tonight. It scares you to think that I could see you in this state, doesn't it, or in any state where you aren't perfectly in control?" Her chest heaved up and down, and she hit the bottle out of his hand.

The bottle exploded into dozens of fragments, skittering across the floorboards, and the last of the wine stained the floor. "No more drinking. It's not what you do."

"Look, *mam'selle*." He grasped her wrist tightly. "You don't know me. I don't even know myself. Maybe I never knew myself. So don't presume to lecture me on my fears and aspirations and what I'm like." His fingers clenched tighter around her wrist, and she yelped in pain, unable to stop herself as the pricks of agony became more intense.

As if she had become poisonous, he dropped her arm and dropped his face into his hands. His shoulders slumped, and he seized control of himself long enough to look up at her with bloodshot eyes and say, "I'm sorry, Laurel. *Vraiment désolé*." His head fell back in his hands.

Laurel came closer, anger abruptly gone, and knelt in front of him. She placed her hands one on each side of his face and lifted it so that he looked her in the eyes. "Aramis, what happened in there tonight?" she coaxed, urging him to let her try to help.

His gold-flecked eyes were intense and unreadable, but he didn't draw away from her gaze. Excruciatingly long seconds ticked by, and he was silent, daring her to go, thinking she would give up. She did not surrender, and he said hoarsely, "According to Porthos' cousin, my father just died of the typhoid within the last month. I haven't even seen him in the past two and a half or three years. Not ever since I declared I'd be a priest, no matter what, despite the fact that my older brother had died and I was no longer a mere second son, but his heir and only surviving child."

Laurel brushed a single tear away from his eye, saying nothing. "I can't tell you how many times I wrote my father, begging him to forgive me for not wanting the title, to please give me his blessing to follow my own path."

"And he wouldn't give it?" she said softly, and Aramis lowered his eyes.

His voice and eyes were far away. "He invited me home after I got back from Marseille. Only now he's dead, and I'll never get the blessing that he was finally prepared to give. The blessing to become a priest."

Sympathy filled her eyes, and she put her arms around his shoulders, hugging him tightly like his mother had done when he was a child frightened by a nightmare. "And now," she urged, "what will you do?"

"I don't know. I honestly don't know," he confessed. "You know, I'd be a *duc*. I never wanted to be a *duc*, but I have a responsibility, and if I don't claim the property, the people I love will be turned off the land, away from the only homes they've ever known, when the Church claims the land." No one else was left to inherit, and this property would not go to the king.

He sounded so alone and lost, and she desperately wanted to say the right thing, but there was nothing. Except, . . . maybe? "Is there any chance that Porthos' cousins may be wrong?"

"*Non*," he responded. "I heard Porthos' parents say it too, and Porthos' mother never gossips about death unless she knows that a person is truly dead. I know because it's one positive thing Porthos will say about his mother. I just didn't want to believe that, but then Porthos' father and cousin confirmed what the lady had said." He halted, saying no more.

A silent tear of grief fell down his face, and he let Laurel hold him, just rocking him back and forth and stroking his hair until he gave up to an exhausted sleep, and then long after that too.

Tenderly she brushed the hair from Aramis' eyes and extracted her arms from about him, and eased him back in the chair. Fortunately, he remained asleep. She rose to her feet and headed towards the door.

Laurel turned. He was going to have the most annoying, unpleasant cramps in his back and neck from sleeping in that position. Without another backward glance, she stole from the room to the corridor, easing the door shut behind her.

"Christophe what are you doing?" Laurel started as she heard Athos' voice come from nowhere.

"I . . ." she shut her mouth. How did she get herself in these awkward situations?

"Oh." Athos sounded surprised. He never would have figured Laurel for a woman who would give herself to Aramis or to any man without marriage. But what other explanation was there for her having disappeared at around eleven–thirty and only now emerging from Aramis' room at nearly three in the morning? Plus, she was standing there shuffling her feet. Looking guilty. She wasn't even looking at him. "Never mind. What you do is your own business." he replied curtly. "I haven't the right to demand explanations from you."

"Athos," she touched his shoulder, "it's not like that. Aramis really needed someone to talk to. *Mince*, this sounds all wrong, but it's not my story to tell you," she declared, more exasperated at herself than anyone else. "Just believe me when I say, Aramis and I are not lovers. Aramis is too honorable a gentleman to take an unwed lady's virginity. And I do not believe in love or passion. Sometimes I even doubt I believe in the institution of marriage."

"Good night, Christophe," he said, giving her a graceful out. This had never happened, as far as he was concerned.

Section Four

The blond-haired man stood watching as the groom brought out each of the five horses, one after the next. Each animal had been meticulously groomed and rubbed down so that its coat shined. Even the saddles and bridles had been carefully cleaned. No, Porthos had not been exaggerating when he said his father loved horses and had very well-appointed stables. The horses lived as well as Porthos' family, as far as Athos could tell. Perhaps better. He thanked the groom and stroked his own mount several times as he walked beside the mare.

He glanced towards the château. The pressure he had to bring to bear to get Porthos' mother to allow them to leave. Definitely a managing mother and matchmaker to boot. Never in his life would he make an effective diplomat.

For a moment, his attention was diverted by the swirl of skirts in the periphery of his vision. For one startled instant, blue eyes met frightened brown ones.

Another moment, the plain brown-haired girl stood transfixed—her heart beating wildly. What had she done? Her eyes fixed on her hands, fingers that she tried not to wring. She was sure it was patently obvious what she had been doing out here. The dirt stains on her skirts and hands which matched the ones on her face told a story. That, and the horse that stood behind her, a man's saddle on it. Her father was going to kill her, or near enough, and she'd never hear the end of it from her mother. Normally she was a good obedient daughter, but that would make little difference, considering the circumstances.

Mortified, she cringed. Dared to glance back up at the blond-haired man, only to immediately glance away again.

Athos gently stroked the horse one more time, trying to settle the animal. The animal knew fear when it smelled it. But in this case, Athos didn't need the horse's keen senses to tell him that the young woman paralyzed in front of him was terrified.

As unobtrusively as possible, Athos surveyed the dark-haired woman. Yvette, Porthos' eldest sister, if he recalled correctly. She hadn't spoken more than a few words during his stay.

"*Mademoiselle*." His voice was low, soothing, in a manner very similar to the way he was soothing his mount. He opted to be slightly less formal than strictly called for. "My apologies. I did not mean to disturb you."

Her heart slowed. Maybe he wasn't going to get her in trouble. He was Porthos' friend, and she and Porthos had always looked out for one another. Yvette opened her mouth to say something and found her tongue worked soundlessly.

"Is there some way I can assist you?" Athos offered when he realized the woman had not yet gotten a hold on her emotions.

A breath left her in a rush and she found herself blurting, "*S'il vous plaît*, please, don't tell my father. I meant no harm."

The musketeer's eyes drifted over the woman and to the horse. So she had been riding astride. A rather minor offense, especially on her own estate. "No harm done. Your father won't hear a word of this. You have my word."

Compelled by the sincerity of his voice, she met his eyes another instant, whispered her thanks, and then scurried off.

Her retreat the man watched. Wondered for a moment why a woman would fear her father so thoroughly. Athos had not seen any evidence that Porthos' father was like his own had been—a man who beat women . . . and young boys. No further time had he to contemplate the puzzle.

"Athos." The man looked in the direction of the call and saw D'Artagnan coming towards him. The young man took in the sight of the five horses and whistled lowly. Fine job. Made him almost homesick for his own well-appointed stables and even his pack of younger siblings. Which in turn made him think of Constance. What must she think of her absent suitor? "We are leaving soon?"

"As soon as the others come out to join us," he replied. "The sooner we leave, the better. This day is only going to get hotter the later it gets. Then also we don't have very much time to waste. Each second we delay is another second closer the traitor gets to England."

D'Artagnan nodded and offered to go in and fetch the other three. Athos offered no argument, and the young man hurried back into the manor in search of his friends. Triumphant, he emerged with his friends and a dainty lady tagging along. "*Madame la Comtesse,*" Athos bowed over the older woman's hand. "We thank you very much for taking us in and taking such good care of us and our horses."

"But," she prompted.

"However, as I said before, we are on an urgent mission for the king. It's a matter of national security, and as much as we might want to linger here longer, we cannot afford to." The woman nodded her understanding and simply insisted that he be sure to remind her son to return shortly for a lengthier visit. Without looking at Porthos, Athos assured the woman he'd remind his friend. Of course if he didn't, D'Artagnan or Aramis or Laurel would surely take it upon themselves to bring the subject up every so often.

Each of the men sketched her a courteous bow and mounted his animal. The lady stepped back, giving them a wide berth as they directed their mounts off the estate and towards the north. Next stop: Beauvais.

* * * * * * * * * * *

So it was Belgium. He abandoned his horse and stole another. There was simply no faster way to get to Belgium than to run his horse into the ground and then procure a new one and do the same thing until his destination was reached. One way or another, he would make it to Belgium in time to find Thomas d'Anlass. The man would not slip through his fingers this time.

That marquis had had a long and fruitful career as a spy— twenty–one years, maybe more. And in those years, he had passed numerous Prussian secrets to his king. No more. Justice would be done, Joseph swore, retribution exacted. Not only was it his own duty to kill the spy who had almost brought the struggling Prussia to its knees, but it was also his duty to avenge Guillaume's death at the marquis' hands. Richelieu be damned. Thomas d'Anlass would not be turned over to his eminence alive. The cardinal had no sway over him anymore. He no longer cared about becoming a French *duc* when Richelieu came to the throne. Tired, he was tired of being a double agent, traitor to his own people, and would no longer tolerate it. His first loyalty was to Prussia, and Thomas' death would prevent more secrets from being smuggled from Prussia and punish the man responsible for much damage to his state. Even if it meant his own death, the marquis would be eliminated and Joseph's honor would be restored.

Joseph grimaced as the rain pelted him. Mud slurped at the horse's hooves, greedily trying to claim them as its own. Thunder rumbled in the sky and a streak of lightning electrified the atmosphere. He would almost be grateful for summer storms if those same storms didn't render the roads nearly impassable, slick with muck and churned, delaying his passage to Belgium longer than he could reasonably tolerate.

Wheezing and snorting, the beast pushed on, and Joseph did not permit it any rest. What did he care if it lived or died? There were more important things. He must make the border long before nightfall. Grimly, with purpose, he turned his thoughts away from emotion and to business. Now what was the name that Guillaume had discovered and imparted to him moments before his death? *Oui.* That was it. Jacques Devré, a merchant in Brussels, theoretically.

Rain stopped falling and the clouds cleared from the sky, ending the brief summer storm. Joseph did not notice. Rather, all his attention was focused on crossing the border to Belgium without being seen, as being seen would cause undesired delay. Delay would only allow Thomas more time in which to successfully complete his task and escape. Then he would have to track the man again, and he would have no idea where to start looking if Thomas were to slip through his fingers here.

Without incident he crossed the border and traded his horse in for a fresh mount. From the horse dealer he made his way to a tailor and purchased a new set of tunic and breeches that he donned, chucking the old ones into the fire. Now he looked like a respectable man who would reasonably have business with a well-to-do merchant. From the tailor's shop he headed to the blacksmith. "Excuse me?" he asked the man who was furiously pumping the bellows, large muscles bulging, and coated with sweat and soot.

The blacksmith stepped away from the blistering heat of the forge, task temporarily set aside. He wiped his hands on his apron and asked, "And what can I help you with today, *monsieur?*"

"I'm in need of information that is necessary for a very important business transaction. And since I understand that I will be using your valuable time, I will compensate you for the lost work time. Will two gold pieces be adequate compensation?"

"It'll be sufficient," the smith said, taking the coins and asking what information the gentleman sought.

"Tell me all you know about a merchant by the name of Jacques Devré, including directions on how I can find him,"

Joseph instructed, and the smith did so with a shrug of his massive shoulders. It was none of his business.

* * * * * * * * * * *

"Good day, *madame*." The man doffed his hat and proceeded down the road, apparently oblivious to the crowds briskly walking the streets, carriages rumbling by, and riders kicking up billows of dust. The smell of horse droppings and the flies that buzzed around them failed to distract him from his reverie. However, he noticed all. Each person as he or she walked by. If they shuffled their feet, laughed with a high-pitched whine, or looked cross-eyed, he noted it. He could even describe every parcel that the valet or lady's maid clutched as he or she followed after his or her master.

More than that, however, he noticed he was old. He felt it in his bones today. The weariness of the hectic life he had entered almost twenty–two years ago. Today he felt every bit of his seven and forty years and more. He'd buried three wives and four children, including those from his first arranged marriage. Only he and his daughter were still living. Laurel. He had a letter from her to pick up according to the message he had received upon arriving at the office of Jacques Devré this morning. Thus, he had discovered that the messenger had asked to meet him this afternoon at a fountain that lay on the southwest side of Brussels.

He raised his hat in salute at the lovely young Belgian as she passed by, and the girl batted her eyelashes and giggled as her escort urged her on with a few quelling words.

Society was so silly, and they didn't even realize it, Thomas remarked. So silly about what it tolerated and what it didn't, always out for scandal and very fickle. No tolerance for individuals and harmless differences and things such as playful flirting. Perhaps that's why he had never been much for following its demands and had become a spy. One of the best spies that France had ever known and a man wanted by more governments than he cared to think of. Sometimes, still, he wondered if he had chosen the right path in being a secret agent.

"Good day," he addressed a man who appeared to be lost, just wandering in absent circles to and fro, around the fountain. "Come, let us sit," Thomas suggested as he led the man to the fountain's edge and perched on the wall, saying, "Are you lost, my good young man?"

"I ain't never been to Brussels before," the other man said for the benefit of curious onlookers, and they passed by, losing all interest in the two men by the fountain. "Me young master sent me to find Jacques Devré, but I seem to have made a wrong turn and missed his shop. Now's I'm going to be late and may miss the merchant. And me master wouldn't be none too pleased with me."

"Jacques, the spice merchant. *Oui*, I know him. I believe he was expecting a message from Christophe Moulins or some other important business missive," the marquis said in full acting mode and heaved a disappointed sigh. "I'm afraid he's out for the day. Perhaps you could give me a message, and I'll pass it on to him."

"Oh would you?" He handed the letter to the marquis. "You just see to it that he gets that, you will? I wouldn't want to fail my master."

"Absolutely, my good man. He will get it. That I guarantee," he said, extending his hand for what appeared to be a handshake to onlookers, but rather was Thomas passing several gold coins to the man. "Will you be in town long? Devré may well wish to send a message back to the young lad quickly."

"I'll meet you here late tonight if you have anything. Otherwise I'm back for French soil," the man said quickly and wandered off, never once giving Thomas d'Anlass away. He was not a man who fancied losing a good living or sacrificing a lucrative income.

The marquis remained perched by the fountain and broke open the message with a deft slip of his hand. Laurel's unpretentious handwriting greeted him, and he read her brief message. It seemed that several government documents had suddenly mysteriously vanished, and that Laurel had every reason to assume the spy and traitor had gotten nearly the last of the papers he needed and soon would be on the way to Calais.

So his daughter needed more information on the spy if she and the musketeers were to apprehend him. If his source from the Belgian secret police came through this evening he should have the last of the information that would peg the traitor. Which reminded him, he had to find a way into the governor's house to talk to the Belgian agent Mazin had instructed him to contact.

Rapidly, he stood and folded the letter, inserting it in a pocket. There was no time like the present, and there was not much time before he had to get the information back so that Laurel would receive it in Beauvais.

There was a persistent, loud rap upon the mahogany door of the governor's residence. The butler opened the door and saw no one. Confused, he looked side to side for a sign of the caller and saw no one. As he turned to go back inside, a young vagrant ran up to him and clung to his feet, begging him tearfully to please forgive him and calling him father. The poor man tried desperately to disengage the little vermin; he had no bastard children. His efforts began attracting a substantial crowd and, unseen in the hubbub, a man slipped inside the open doors and made his way through the corridors without encountering a single person.

He rounded the corner and exited through a door that led to the well-tended gardens. The man took the closest pathway to the right and strolled down it until he saw the gardener pruning back several hedges. Here he stopped and spoke the coded response, "*Mon fils arpète.*"

The gardener stopped his pruning and glanced at the tall man. Thomas d'Anlass' reputation had not been exaggerated. The man was good, very good. He'd arrived sooner than expected. "*Mon père bouc,*" the gardener gave the expected response and turned his attention to taking off the thick dirt-encrusted gloves.

"Do you have the information?"

The gardener nodded his head ever so slightly. "It cost us two good agents. The man you're after is very crafty. He's got connections very high up in not only your government, but also in our own."

So that was why Mazin was using such stealth to convey the intelligence to him. He didn't know who in his own government could even be trusted. The marquis took the proffered packet and ruffled through the damning documents. With this in her hands Laurel would have all the information there was about the traitor to France and the arrangements he had made with Buckingham and the Prussians. Added with her knowledge of the secret state documents that had been smuggled out of Spain to this spy, the puzzle would be complete.

God willing, Laurel and the musketeers would be able to apprehend this spy where he had failed before. True, he'd come close enough to see the man's eyes, but had been unable to get closer. With this information his daughter and the musketeers could well succeed.

"Send my warmest regards to Mazin," Thomas remarked, quickly concealing the packet. "The spy will be put out of commission, and Compton should contact Mazin with a list of who the spy's contacts were in your government." The gardener assured Thomas the message would be passed on as he escorted the marquis to the old servants' entrance and watched him melt away into the streets, vanishing before even the gardener's sharp and observant eyes.

Thomas slinked through the dark streets as quickly as possible, temporarily losing the man who had been tracking him. The fountain. At last. Now the messenger had better show before his shadow picked up his trail. From behind a tree a man moved, the messenger, and approached the marquis. Wordlessly, the man accepted the wrapped and resealed packet from Thomas d'Anlass.

"See to it that this arrives in Beauvais within two days. To Christophe Moulins and unopened," were his final instructions, and more money, hefty sums of it, exchanged hands. The messenger turned and melted back into the trees.

Thomas shivered and walked quickly away from the fountain. His shadow was close. His hand went to his sword, and he walked more briskly, staying close to the shelter of the buildings in an attempt to shield himself as much as possible.

A shot rang out in the night.

Wood spat from the post next to him where the ball buried itself. Thomas ducked and lunged for cover, grabbing for his own pistol. As he grasped the cold metal handle, another shot rang out, and his shoulder exploded in excruciating pain. Down he bit on his lip to silence any outburst. He scrambled to a nearby door, blood pouring from the wound, and crawled under the doorjamb. His breath came in ragged pain-filled gasps that he did his best to stiffle. Now where were those shots coming from?

Silence, eerie and tension-filled. His shadow assailant wasn't gone, and he was trapped. Priming and cocking his own gun, he leaned back, waiting. Time was running short, and his thoughts were already losing touch with reality. Calmly as he could, the marquis fired his own weapon.

Unnoticed, a third man apparently independent of the shooter drew himself further into the shadows. Stepped carefully. Silently, with the utmost stealth towards Thomas' shadow pursuer.

The third man crouched. Nimble fingers felt for a pulse on the vengeance seeker. Nothing. Well, the Prussian agent who had been shadowing Thomas was dead then. Personal vengeance had a way of doing that to one. In one swift movement, the unidentified dark-haired man removed the pistol from the limp fingers.

Quickly he examined it. Flintlock. Pricey and more than likely stolen. With equal swiftness the man retrieved the powder and the balls. Loaded the weapon. Slowly rose to his feet. He thought he could still hear the heavy breathing of the Marquis de Langeac if he concentrated.

Without a look back, the man moved. No sound echoed from his boots. A moment he paused, straining, listening. Waited an instant and then moved forward. Forward again. There. A movement caught his peripheral vision. The doorjamb.

No hesitation in his actions, the dark-haired man leveled the gun. Finger pulled back on the trigger. The report echoed in his ears and, a moment later, a loud grunt. "Impact," the shooter said to himself.

Paused another moment and was about to go forward when the scuffling of feet brought him up short. Figured. The watch. Quickly he changed directions, melting back into the shadows. He had other things to do. Later he could check on the old spy and find out how true his last shot had been.

* * * * * * * * * * *

Sabine turned her back on the woman, leaving her to her chaotic thoughts and gnawing fear. Constance Bonacieux had nothing to worry about for the moment, nor was she hysterical, so she needed no extra supervision. Nothing for the hostage to worry about until D'Artagnan and his friends tried to sneak into Beauvais and retrieve a message for one Christophe Moulins, according to Richelieu's latest message, that was.

Still, things did not quite mesh. The musketeers and her sister would have had to stop in a village to get supplies for their horses, if not supplies for themselves. No horse, no matter how good, could continue for weeks of intense riding without getting good fodder, and the countryside was hardly abounding with that.

They had to have found refuge at some local lord's holding, some local lord who had the money to keep horses. Yet she didn't have the power to send the cardinal's men to search the estates of all the local lords that could care for horses. They had too much power, and they wouldn't stand for the privacy of their own homes being invaded, short of a direct order from the king or a war on their own turf.

As for the cardinal, something had to be done. His threat to her needed to be neutralized. For Sabine was still not quite sure she could turn her sister over to that man. Apparently, a small grain of honor still lived in her atrophied soul. *Oui*, she would detain Laurel and prevent her from completing her mission, but as for more she wasn't sure, and she did not enjoy being pushed. Never had. A character failing?

"*Comtesse de* Winter," Constance addressed the woman, and Milady approached her, fixing a sympathetic look on her features. It would not do for the young woman to discover that she was the enemy, and not another guileless victim. As it was, she had been able to obtain the woman's sympathy. Of course it had required some carefully crafted lies, intermingled with a touch of truth here and there. Overall, she'd given a quite convincing performance. "What are they going to do with us?"

Sabine grasped the other woman's hand in a gesture of wordless comfort. "We are Richelieu's political hostages. Until he gets what he wants from our families and close friends, we will not be returned. Still, we are too valuable a commodity to get rid of. Therefore, we must be kept away and remain undiscovered."

Constance scowled at her feet. Court machinations and the struggle for influence over the king were too much for her. Already, in her years, nearly two of her contracted three, of serving the queen, she had seen how dangerous those machinations were. It was enough to make her want to forsake the court life all together and marry immediately. She was old enough, ten and seven. More than old enough, if truth be told.

But there was Anne, and the queen was her friend. Plus, if she returned home she would be unable to readily see the handsome young D'Artagnan. D'Artagnan. If only he knew where she was now, she'd feel much safer. He and his friends were musketeers, and they could rescue her from the cardinal's grasp. But they didn't know what was going on, and there was no way to let them know. "So we are kept moving?"

Sabine nodded. The woman was young, but she was by no means stupid, just a little naive. If she was not careful, Constance might realize that she was not being told the entire truth, and she didn't want the woman suspicious of her yet; her confidence would be so much better, for then the woman would tell her anything. "Is there no chance someone could rescue us, find us and foil his eminence?"

"There is a chance," Milady admitted, "but only if we could get a message to someone that could help, and I know no one in this area that could help me."

Constance folded her arms in front of her and stared around the room. "If only I could contact D'Artagnan, I know he would help us. He's a musketeer, and he and his friends saved the king once already. There has to be a way. Please help me find out how to contact them," the young woman implored.

The *comtesse* smiled inwardly. It was the invitation she had been looking for. However, the role must be played. Milady allowed conflicting emotions of fear, resignation, and excitement to flit through her eyes before she said, "I will help you with what I can. But you must trust me no matter what happens. I will try to use my experience for our benefit."

The other woman offered a hesitant smile and nodded in understanding. "I'll do my best. I won't let you down."

"I'm sure you won't," the *comtesse* remarked to herself. Regardless of what happened, Constance Bonacieux would provide a great deal of leverage over the youngest musketeer, and consequently, his friends as well. Romantic young fool.

* * * * * * * * * * *

D'Artagnan rode up front with Athos, searching for a sheltered place to stop for the night and a chance to eat some of the dried meat and fruit, nuts, and bread that Porthos' mother had provided for them. The man was taciturn and not very talkative. Not that the behavior was particularly unusual for Athos.

Something was unusual, though. He was sure of it. He just hadn't quite been able to put his finger on it. There was this nameless tension about them all, and it was more than fatigue brought on by a long, stressful journey. More than nervousness and anxiousness to successfully outwit several crafty opponents and save France from a traitor. And more than the now familiar tension of having a woman traveling incognito with them.

Someone else had to be feeling the same discomfort as he was, D'Artagnan reasoned. What he really needed was someone to talk to. Get his mind off his worries and all these morbid thoughts that were running around in his head. Maybe one of Porthos' jokes to cheer him up, but the man was still a bit grumpy about the visit with his family. Even Aramis' subtle and amusing talk would be better than dwelling like this, but Aramis didn't seem to be quite himself. He was still a perfect gentleman and shared the burden of decision and suggestion making, but something was decidedly off. Perhaps he was making a big deal out of nothing, out of the fact Laurel appeared to be watching Aramis much more closely than she had previously in the past days. Foolish to think she was, but the woman was carefully watching Aramis, every time he wasn't looking her way.

"Athos." The oldest musketeer reined back a fraction to ride side by side with the young man. D'Artagnan pointed in the distance and off to his right. "I think there might be something there that could give us some cover. I'd like to go on ahead and check. I promise I'll be careful. No rushing in without looking to see what's about."

Athos mulled it over for a bit, a bit by his standards. Others would have called his decision near instantaneous. "Go for it. Don't take too long to report back to us. We'd rather not backtrack to find a campsite."

"Understood," the young man said smartly. "See you soon."

A quarter of an hour, maybe twenty–five minutes later a much refreshed and less solemn D'Artagnan rejoined his companions, happily informing Athos that he had found what appeared to be an almost ideal place to stay the night. The young man seized his opportunity and led his fellows to the site at a brisk pace. It was getting dark, and soon it would be dangerously difficult to see, even with the light of the moon and stars.

The men and Laurel didn't bother to light a fire. The night was plenty warm and nothing needed any cooking or drying. In addition, a fire could be spotted since they were relatively close to a pretty large village. D'Artagnan almost regretted that state of affairs because either Porthos or Aramis would have had to cook the meal and clean up afterward. Way this trip was going it looked like they might almost worm their way out of the job that he had gotten stuck with nearly every time since Laurel had delivered her ultimatum. Okay, so Athos had taken care of the duty a handful of times, but Aramis almost always managed to be gone when his turn came, and Porthos almost always managed to shift the undesirable duty off on someone else, mostly him.

Instead, he dug into his pack and plucked a salted piece of jerky from it, followed by one of the last pieces of bread. He bit into it, chewed, and swallowed. So what if it was getting slightly old. On an empty stomach after a hard day's riding it tasted heavenly. And it wasn't fish! He made short work of the rest of the bread and consumed the strip of salted beef at a slower rate. He'd like to have eaten a bit more. Unfortunately, the food needed to last for two to four more meals and he couldn't in good conscience expect his friends to give him what was left of the fruit and nuts Porthos' mother had provided. Yeah, life of adventure.

After licking the last of the salt from the tips of his fingers, he laid his sword over his crossed legs. He stared at the delicate-appearing gold hilt, the hilt that his father had once held. The very same sword that his father had used to defend king and country. Now it was his, and he'd proven himself with it well enough that he had fulfilled his dream and become one of the king's musketeers like his father before him.

Zut alors! Or blast, as Porthos or Athos might say. This was getting to be more than absurd. It was downright ridiculous. So he and his friends weren't generally the most talkative bunch after a long, hard day, but they usually talked a little. As it was he couldn't remember the last time anyone had said a word other than when he had gotten Athos' approval to scout. "No offense," D'Artagnan broke the brooding silence, "but is there something wrong here that everyone is worrying about and no one has yet seen fit to tell me about?"

"Lad." Porthos took a hefty sigh and responded. "I'm afraid to tell you that we really aren't worrying about much that we haven't already been worrying about. You know? That's it, my young friend, you've dragged it out of me. We've all made a pact to not talk so that we could see how long it took to annoy you. I said it would surely be before we stopped for dinner, but Christophe disagreed. Said you wouldn't break down until at least dinner, probably later."

"Porthos," Laurel cut him off. She was not in the mood for Porthos' jokes. Life could not always be laughed at. "Stop confusing him. Truth is, D'Artagnan, that I don't think that any of us have much been in the mood for conversation. I know the story's not as flashy and entertaining as Porthos', but it is a lot more true than his."

"Christos, Christophe," Porthos said, and for the first time all day Aramis spoke gently, rebuking Porthos for using the name of God, the savior, in vain. Porthos dismissed the words with a wave of his hand and continued right on with what he had been saying. "Now you're being a spoilsport. That's Athos' job. *Non*, wait, don't tell me. He put you up to it?"

"Not quite, *petit chou*," Laurel countered with less levity and more endearment than she had intended.

"I think the point has been made and made again or rather beaten into the ground." Athos stopped the exchange from going further. "I don't think now is a good time for an argument, no matter how amusing the rejoinders you throw at one another may be. I know I'm tired and in danger of contracting a headache. So if you feel you must continue your lively debate, please make it just a little quieter."

The large musketeer sat back on his heels. Everyone seemed—forget seemed—they were pretty grouchy tonight. Of course, Athos had not touched more than a glass of wine in days so he was entitled to a little grumpiness, especially considering the miraculous reappearance of his wife for another go-round.

Since everyone seemed to want to be such sticks in the mud, and D'Artagnan seemed to have lapsed into silence, Porthos excused himself from the group and went to entertain himself elsewhere. Oddly enough, Athos promptly fell asleep, and Aramis wandered off to keep the horses company.

"Laurel sorry, I forgot; Christophe," D'Artagnan apologized for forgetting to call her by the correct name. He lowered himself to sit beside her, and stretched out his legs to their full length. Thoughtfully, with as much tact as he had ever used, a surprising amount at that and sensitivity to boot, he asked, "Is there something going on between you and Aramis?"

"*Quoi*? *Comment*? Come again?" she said, as if startled or she hadn't heard right, and he repeated his query. "Why do you ask?"

"You just seem, well, you just seem different around him. Like today I could swear you were watching him every time he wasn't looking." He stopped as if something had hit him, something very foolish or very strange. "Are you falling in love with him?"

"What?" she said, more surprised than he'd ever seen her. They knew how she felt about love. "Well no. I was just worried about him, is all. He didn't have too good of a night last night so I wanted to keep an eye on him. Did you think I was falling in love with him?"

He shrugged his shoulders and said, "It was just a possible explanation. I know it's not a very good one. Oh never mind," he concluded, sheepish, and Laurel smiled as she assured him there were no hard feelings. She got to her feet and headed towards some trees. D'Artagnan didn't bother to ask her where she was going, not this time. He'd made a fool of himself enough in one night, but still her words left him uneasy. Was there something more than she suspected terribly amiss with Aramis?

Laurel altered her direction once she was hidden by the trees. Hopefully her sense of direction was true and she remembered where the horses were. Several twigs crunched beneath her feet, and she bypassed a fallen branch. Laurel had no desire to wander lost in the forest or accidentally stumble upon villagers. Phew! She had remembered. The leaves rustled, and she stepped from the trees to find a sword leveled at her throat. She froze, and Aramis sheathed the blade after a moment's hesitation.

"Christophe, you had best beware of sneaking up on people. I could have run you through," Aramis said in his usual tone, as he stepped back to allow her more room.

Ever so briefly he pursed his lips, and Laurel once again found herself thinking she was imagining things. Aramis at a loss—it did not seem possible. They both stood as if waiting for the other to speak, or to explain matters. Then the moment was past and Aramis addressed her with his customary aplomb. "To what do I owe the pleasure of your visit?"

"So we're back to that," she commented in a subdued voice.

"I am sorry, did you say something?" he inquired, and she quickly covered her tracks, shaking her head briskly, a mite too briskly, but fortunately Aramis did not comment upon it.

"How's your head?" she asked.

"There is no need to worry. I am quite all right."

"I don't know about you being quite all right," she informed him, "but there you go again not answering my questions. I know what happened last night, Aramis. I was there. You were not only abysmally drunk, but you were grief stricken. That kind of grief

131

doesn't go away in a day, and that kind of drinking does cause a hangover." She'd seen it before in many of the soldiers she'd known. Not to mention she'd had one go-round with the experience herself and had decided never to fall into that trap again.

"What is it you want of me?" he said almost as if he were resigned to her being contrary and not being happy no matter what he did.

"You know what I really wish? I really wish you could find it in your heart to trust me—to not always play the gentleman. However, it'd be more than enough if you just decided to be your real self."

There was no noise except the crickets for long seconds.

"You know what I wish, Laurel?" he said, forgetting to call her Christophe. "I wish you'd be happy letting me be the way I am, that you could possibly accept and like me for it."

"Wait, I never said I didn't like you." She defended her last words. "I do like you." Laurel responded before she could think to censor any comment. *Mince.* Well, finish the task at hand. "I just don't always like the way you act. You don't let anyone see inside your facade, and it's just . . . false. Just, oh, just forget it; you still don't understand." She raised her palms and spoke again with purpose. "Aramis, Athos saw me leave your room last night. I didn't know what to tell him. I think he just decided to forget it or to ignore it. But then D'Artagnan asked me tonight if there is something between us. I don't know what to say, Aramis. They're your best friends, not my best friends. I've no right to tell them. But maybe . . ."

"I'll think about it," he said gently and excused himself.

"Aramis," Porthos greeted the man who joined him beside a little creek. "Lad. Pull up a seat and join me. We can both pretend to sail these high seas." The man made an inclusive gesture that spanned the creek. "Ah, the life of a pirate."

The other musketeer shrugged his shoulders and sat next to the large man. "The life of a pirate would be unlikely to suit me," Aramis said, his voice expressionless.

Porthos hit his open palm against his forehead in his own exaggerated fashion. "That's right. How stupid of me to forget: the life of a pirate would conflict with the holy orders, not to mention it'd probably be a bit too exciting for your tastes."

"True enough," Aramis conceded.

"Aramis, you *crétin*, you're not supposed to give in like that. Come on; let's see some challenge, some fight, some spirit. Pizzazz."

"Sorry to disoblige you. However, there is nothing to fight. What you said is completely accurate," Aramis informed Porthos. For a moment he stared at the stars. Blinking so contently, at peace and beautiful. To be a star! To touch a star!

"Actually," Aramis spoke again, his voice deadly serious, "I'm seriously considering giving up the priesthood and fulfilling the responsibilities of my name and station."

"Say what?" Porthos was in shock. Flabbergasted. "Look, don't get me wrong. I'd be more than glad to have you fighting at my side for years to come and not shut away in some monastery or whatever, driving yourself insane with chastity and boredom. But, man, what brought this up? You've always wanted to be a priest." Porthos hardly expected an answer or an explanation, so he lapsed into silence.

Then Aramis dished him up a bigger leveler than before. "I just found out that my father died in the past fortnight." His words were very tightly controlled. Dead. It was still hard to fathom and so permanent, at least during this earthly existence.

"*Sacrebleu*," Porthos said, closing his eyes. Despite all their problems and not knowing much about Aramis' family, Porthos had always known his friend was very attached to his father. "I'm sorry, Aramis. God be with you," he said, without his usual joking manner. "Is there anything I can do? Or Athos or D'Artagnan or Christophe?"

"Christophe already knows," he replied, adding, "I do not think there is anything anyone can do. Quite simply, I will have to go home after this mission and see to it that the estate is in order and then decide whether to give up the orders, whether or not to claim the title and holdings. Unfortunately, no one can decide that for me."

"Just what kind of responsibilities are you considering taking on?" his friend asked though he already had an inkling.

"The responsibilities of a *duc* with prosperous holdings all over France."

"*Dites donc*, good grief," Porthos exclaimed and whistled, eyes wide. "You're a *duc*."

"Not yet," he qualified. "Only if I claim my title and am acknowledged as the rightful heir by the king within a year." He had already taken his first steps to the priesthood so his grasp on his inheritance was not a standard case.

"Aramis, all I can say on that one is, don't do it unless that's what you really want to do it. Otherwise you'll only be miserable. But no matter what you decide, *mon frère* . . . I'll always be your friend."

"On second thought, maybe you can do something for me."

"What's that?" Porthos inquired.

"Tell Athos and D'Artagnan what the situation is. They have already got a few misconceptions about what's going on, and those ought to be straightened out," Aramis told him solemnly. Laurel could ruin her reputation without his assistance, if she hadn't done so already.

"Absolutely." Porthos got to his feet and squeezed Aramis' shoulder very briefly before returning to join his other companions in the clearing and to dispel Athos' mistaken notion about what Laurel had been doing in Aramis' room, as well as to explain why Laurel had been keeping such close tabs on the man. Right now, however, Aramis needed some time alone to think.

* * * * * * * * * * *

Nervously, tensely, the auburn-haired man scoured the street. "Quickly, get him in here. To the back room," the man instructed brusquely to his compatriot who was lugging a man's limp body inside. "Hurry, before someone gets curious and comes out and sees us. You," he pointed to the last man in the room, "don't let this blood stain the floor. Try to get it out as best as possible."

"*Oui, monsieur*," he acknowledged, hurrying to carry out the order as his superior made his way to the back room.

Sure that the back room was secure, the auburn-haired man turned to his comrade. "What happened?"

"I found him sprawled in the street, shot twice. I also found another man whom I didn't recognize close by, shot through the heart, Mazin."

"He's still alive then?" Mazin asked .

"For now. He's not in very good shape," the other man concluded as he set to work pulling the bloodstained clothes away from Thomas d'Anlass' wounds. Briskly he checked the tourniquets he had tied before he had dared move the man. Shot twice in the same shoulder, once near the collarbone, once closer to the elbow. At least most of the bleeding had stopped. Mazin rushed over to lend the man a hand.

"What are his chances?" Mazin questioned the man whose father had been a doctor as he set about cleansing the wounds and preparing to perform surgery. The balls had to come out.

"Not good. I'll do the best I can, but he's lost a lot of blood, and this wound near his collarbone appears to be very serious." Even if he survived, there was no guarantee he'd keep the arm.

"I'll help," Mazin offered. "What do you need me to do?"

* * * * * * * * * * * *

"Who goes into Beauvais?" Porthos asked of Athos.

"Christophe must," Athos addressed his four companions. His eyes rested a moment longer on Aramis. The man seemed to be holding himself together, and Aramis had assured him that he would in no way endanger this mission, his word of honor. His word seemed to be holding up. It always had in the past, and there was no reason to doubt it now. "He's the only one who knows exactly who is delivering the letter and where. The messenger won't deliver it to anyone except Christophe Moulins."

"Then you'll send Christophe off alone," D'Artagnan said critically. It'd be insane to send the woman alone, anyone alone, especially after the entire fiasco that had occurred in Meung.

"No. I can't take that risk. Christophe's too important to lose. Without him we don't have the complete information we need." Athos paused. "I'm going into Beauvais with you, Christophe."

"What about being recognized?" Laurel asked Athos. Athos was not known for his facility at disguise and dissimulation.

"We'll both have to disguise ourselves. Aramis will have to assist us with that."

"And what about the *Comtesse de* Winter?" Laurel inquired, not liking to ask the question that had to be asked.

"We'd better be very careful and have very good disguises. Other than that we can only hope that she isn't there. If she is, we can only hope she doesn't see us, even in our disguises," Athos responded pragmatically.

"Fine," she said, though matters were far from fine. If Athos ran into Sabine . . . well, there could be problems, to put it mildly.

And if Sabine recognized her? Heaven forbid, Laurel didn't know what her stepsister would do nor how she would react to her sister.

"D'Artagnan," Athos spoke again, and the young man came to attention. "I want you to enter Beauvais from the southeast while Christophe and I enter from the southwest. As soon as you can, find us. You'll know our disguises. When you catch sight of us, tail us."

"You want me to help him with a disguise too?" Aramis asked, and Athos nodded quickly one time.

Before Athos could go on, D'Artagnan queried, "And if you run into trouble?"

"I want you to ride out of Beauvais as quickly as you can and find Aramis and Porthos. Then together you decide how to go about getting us out of trouble." That matter taken care of, the oldest musketeer turned to Porthos and Aramis. "You two go to the abandoned windmill, northwest of the town. The rest of us will meet you there after our business is done."

The five comrades went back to the horses they had tethered on a nearby tree and Aramis set about transforming Athos, Laurel, and D'Artagnan and their mounts with Porthos and Laurel's able assistance. Belatedly, Athos remembered to turn over all the papers they had gathered so far to Aramis for safekeeping.

The task completed, Porthos stood back and said, "You three are ready. I must say you do look marvelous. A wonderful piece of work." He whistled, complimenting his own work—oh, and Aramis' too. Laurel's, if she insisted. . . . They looked nothing like nobles except for their posture, and Aramis had coached them on toning that down. "No one's going to recognize you unless you let them get close and they look real hard."

"Good," Athos declared, and Porthos extended his closed hand outward. Athos, Aramis, and D'Artagnan all placed their hands on his, and Laurel stepped away, heading for her horse so that the men could have a moment undisturbed.

"Wait," Aramis stayed his friends. "I think someone is missing." They nodded solemnly one after the other. "Christophe, come over here, and join us."

Laurel's eyebrows rose but the men's eyes asked, almost beseeched her to join them. She did not keep them waiting. She put her own hand on top of theirs and joined them in saying, "All for one, and one for all."

The group broke apart, mounted their horses and prepared to set off. "Let's do it." Athos told them, and they were off.

"Where are you going to pick up this message?" Athos directed his question at the young woman who sat mounted on her horse, dressed little better than a pitifully poor lad.

Her eyes scoured the street, up and down. She'd prefer no surprises this time, and if Milady were here, Laurel wanted to know about it before Milady saw her and realized who she was. "If he's here, he'll be in the most popular bar. He should be here, seeing as he normally waits three days for me or my father to pick up a message before leaving. However, I have to talk to him alone. He's expecting to deliver information to Christophe Moulins."

Athos blew air from his nostrils, moderately put out. The situation was far from ideal, but he would have to cope, as he always had, as he always would. "I'll follow you and wait outside to be sure that you're all right."

"If you must," she acceded. "Be aware, though, we have to check on a second letter from *Monsieur de* Treville, and that would be at the posting station, if he sent it." The woman shrugged her shoulders and wrinkled her nose at the stench emanating from the streets. Nauseous. Overpowering. "It's up to you. I don't know how much time you think is reasonably safe to remain here."

"You really do make things complicated sometimes," the musketeer said with a touch of exasperation. "Do you have the money you need to pay off your messenger?" Laurel said she did, and with a slight shake of his head, Athos added, "I'll check the post to see if Treville wrote. I assume the letter's addressed to Christophe Moulins." Laurel did not contradict him. "I'll meet you back here. Scratch that. You get the delivery and find me at the posting station. And be careful."

"You too," she replied, dismounting and heading towards the local tavern. She was not looking forward to the bitter taste of that alcoholic brew so many men favored. Calling it a drink was favoring it too highly in Laurel's estimation. More like fecal matter or poison. Her palate was far more discriminating.

Athos followed her progress with his slate-blue eyes, and only after she entered the dwelling did he turn his horse and hurry it through the streets towards the post office. Time to see if Treville had sent them a missive.

He entered the dingy little room, lit by one open window. The heat, the stuffy muggy heat, nearly bowled him over. Beads of sweat ran between his shoulder blades and down his dirt-encrusted tunic, eating away the dirt as it made its path. He approached a clerk who sat ramrod straight, inscribing figures into a leatherbound book.

"Excuse me," he said, exaggerating his speech and adding a drawl that he used to use as a child until his father's repeated beatings had finally broken him of the habit. The clerk kept on working, ignoring his presence.

Parbleu! He had no time to waste on this fruitless impudence. Suddenly he slammed the book shut on the surprised man and repeated, "I said excuse me, and I expect to be acknowledged." His expression brooked no defiance, and the clerk set his quill aside and fixed his attention on the musketeer. "Has the post been delivered here recently?" The clerk nodded, annoyed by this stranger's impertinence. "Have you received any letters posted from Paris?"

"*Oui*," the clerk admitted. "Have you a name?"

"Christophe Moulins."

"I'll see what I can do for you." The clerk pushed his chair away and opened a door leading to another room without even so much as extending Athos the common courtesy of politeness. Impatiently Athos waited, and time slipped by, every minute more precious than the last. What was taking so long?

The clerk reappeared and all but tossed the letter at Athos who caught it before it fell to the floor. "There's your letter. It arrived yesterday." The man turned back to his work, and Athos was sorely tempted to teach the rude youngster a lesson in manners he'd not soon forget. Unfortunately, there was no time and it would be quite hypocritical to tell D'Artagnan not to be reckless and then be reckless himself. Therefore he demonstrated a remarkable forbearance and retreated from the office without beating the man to a pulp.

Laurel plunged her hand inside her tunic. The packet from her father was still there. Once she put this information together with the rest, she'd have as complete a picture as possible of the traitor to her homeland, hopefully. Absently, she wondered what D'Artagnan had done when she and Athos had split up or if he had even been able to find their trail.

As she neared the post she slowed Rebelle, carefully letting her gaze wander from person to person. This time she refused to be taken unaware. One day maybe her observation skills would equal or surpass those of her father's. Until then she would continue to practice and improve.

Dumbly, her mouth dropped open. Sabine. And she was headed straight for Athos. To compound the problem Athos had not seen the woman or the men who trailed along after her. "Don't panic," she warned herself. "Think. Plan. But quickly!" Don't call him by name. Still she had to get his attention, warn him.

"*Monsieur.*" She pointed at Athos, drawing closer to him and keeping a tight rein on her gelding. Her tone was accusatory, mirroring her hostile posture. "*Oui,* you, you dishonorable cur. I call you to account for your despicable actions against my sister." Laurel threw her glove at the musketeer's feet. "Name your weapon, and meet me within the hour if you have any semblance of honor."

"You're just a boy. Go home. I have no wish to kill or maim a young lad. Go home to your father," Athos responded, his mind racing to discover why Laurel was making such a scene that the eyes of all passersby were drawn to them.

At least the crowd stopped the *comtesse* for the moment, Laurel consoled herself, but she and Athos were left with the challenge of getting out of Beauvais. "Afraid to put your skills where your mouth is," she challenged, her posture becoming more erect and proud.

Her eyes, however, were not on Athos. Rather they were on her stepsister, and he cautiously glanced in the same direction and was unable to stop himself from starting. Sabine. "Name your place, boy," Athos recovered his voice.

"And have an audience," the disguised woman said derisively. "*Non.* Follow me, and I'll show you. I'll not give you time to turn tail and get away scot-free."

Athos mounted his horse without interference, and Laurel led their retreat as swiftly as was appropriate. As the riders rode away, Milady gestured to her men, instructing them to try to cut the riders off. They scrambled to perform the task, a task which was complicated by the crowd that had only begun to disperse. A duel was always an interesting spectacle, especially since Richelieu had banned them.

As they approached the outskirts of the town, Athos and Laurel picked up their pace only to see their escape cut off by several mounted men. The companions brought their horses to a sudden stop and turned to head back the way they came from, but their way was blocked by four soldiers and a woman mounted sidesaddle.

Deftly Milady de Winter urged her mare towards her prey, drawing her pistol and priming it as she did so. As she stopped beside Athos, she placed the pistol in a position where she could easily fire it against the man if she needed to. Carefully she surveyed his face, and her eyes narrowed. "Athos, how nice to see you again, and this must be young Christophe," Sabine remarked, barely glancing at the younger woman she'd considered her sister.

"Don't play games with me, Sabine. I know you too well. What do you want?"

"What do I want, Athos? What do you think I want?" He flinched at her words, knowing she wanted him to take back the wrongs he had perpetrated against her. Change the past—take away the hate, hurt, lies . . . "However, that will have to wait," never saying what would have to wait, but the musketeer knew it was retribution. In some way, perhaps, he deserved it, he was honest enough to admit now.

Sabine paused, and Laurel stared at Athos, praying he wouldn't fall apart. "You will deliver a message to D'Artagnan for me. He gives himself over to me or Constance Bonacieux dies." Just to assure him that Constance was in her custody she handed him the young woman's locket and a lock of her deep brown hair.

"What about Christophe?" he asked stiffly.

"I assure you'll he'll be safe. He's much too valuable alive. Oh, and you'd best not think about rescuing him. If any other than D'Artagnan enters Beauvais, the lady will be turned over to Richelieu immediately." Milady gestured for her men to take Laurel, and disarming her, they led her away. The *comtesse* lingered a moment. "We will meet again," she said and followed her departing henchmen.

As Athos drew away from the town, he spurred his horse, urging the beast as quickly as possible towards his destination. The old windmill. He could not afford to have D'Artagnan arrive ahead of him and bring Aramis and Porthos to Beauvais. That could effectively seal Constance's death warrant and would put

Laurel into Richelieu's hands immediately. And Laurel still had that packet she had received from Belgium. By now the packet was probably in Sabine's hands and on its way to Richelieu, and the spy was getting that much closer to Buckingham while they were stalled here.

Gritting his teeth and bending forward, he spurred the poor animal faster yet, regretting the necessity to drive it so hard. But the animal sensed his urgency (she'd known him long enough), and the mare spurted forward. The beaten hat was blown from his head, and he did not bother to go back for it. He had better hats elsewhere and a dangerous race to win.

"Hold," Athos yelled as he saw three men preparing to mount their horses. All three turned to look at the man who bore down on them and stopped next to them, kicking up a flurry of dust and pebbles as he did so.

"Athos." D'Artagnan was stunned. "How did you escape from Beauvais? I saw Milady overtake the two of you." He paused, noting the man was alone. "Where is Christophe?"

The oldest musketeer jumped from his horse. "I think you'd all better cancel your little excursion. We've got to talk." Now, or even sooner. The men crouched around Athos in rapt attention, knowing they would hear nothing good.

"What happened?" Aramis prompted, and the blond-haired man recounted the tale of the trip to Beauvais and his meeting with Milady. After a pause he added the fact he had picked a letter up from Treville. Reminded, he paused again in his tale and withdrew the letter from Paris and broke its seal. Scanned the contents and threw the letter on the ground with disgust, pacing in his vexation.

"More problems," Aramis stated, and Athos told him to see for himself. "Gentlemen," Aramis said after reading the message, "including today we've got about nine days to return to Paris before the king sends out a warrant for our arrest on the charge of desertion and conduct unbecoming a musketeer." He passed the letter on to both Porthos and D'Artagnan, who confirmed the unsettling details for themselves.

"We'll just have to go rescue Christophe tonight," D'Artagnan concluded, "and then go to Calais all out."

"I'm afraid it's not that easy," the older man contradicted. There was simply no way to soften the blow, but he tried to soften it anyway. "If any one of us is spotted near Beauvais, Laurel will be sent immediately to Richelieu. And if you, D'Artagnan, do not willingly give yourself up to Sabine by dawn tomorrow, she will kill Constance Bonacieux. She gave me this to prove the truth of her claims."

Athos placed the locket and the lock of hair in D'Artagnan's limp hand, and the young man opened it. A moment later, he jumped to his feet announcing, "I've got to go to Beauvais then. I've got no other choice."

Athos bodily restrained D'Artagnan pulling him back to the ground. "No one, that includes you, D'Artagnan, is going off anywhere right now." His voice and eyes brooked no defiance. "Sabine may have us trapped right now, but I do not intend to stay trapped. I say we create our own choice. This is going to take all of us. Suggestions, gentlemen?"

Laurel ached all over, in places she never knew existed, from her rough handlement. She rubbed her arms and legs, trying to soothe away the ache, hurt, and fatigue. Sabine had the packet from Thomas now. She had to get it back and get out of this place. This prison, however, had no window and no outside door. Only the door that led from the main room and that door had been barred behind her.

The dank smell of mildew offended her nostrils and her stomach rumbled. She could almost choke on the extreme heat of the stuffy air. Nor could she see much in the dark even now that her eyes had adjusted to the low light.

"Sabine," she said aloud, aware no one could hear her words, "what are you doing? Why are you doing this? You used to be so wonderful, giving, and kind." Had she really been tarred and feathered with the same unforgivable flaws as her father or done something more unforgivable to offend Sabine?

The bar slid from the door, and it opened allowing a woman bearing a torch to enter. The door closed behind her and the bar slid back into place. She slipped the torch in an outcropping that jutted out from the wall. Laurel whirled on the intruder, her braided hair falling down her back and tendrils of hair darting to escape the confines. Stubbornly she stared the shorter woman down, her eyes shouting accusations.

"Greetings, *ma belle sœur*," the *comtesse* said to her sister, and Laurel elected to remain mute. The claim to kinship stung, no matter how innocent.

"I thought you might like to know your fate." Laurel's posture stiffened, but she still refused to speak to the older woman. "You have become a very valuable commodity, Laurel. There are a great many people looking for you. Many rewards for your capture." Milady paused, allowing her words to sink in. Finally the *comtesse* announced, "Tomorrow you will be sent to Richelieu."

Laurel gasped. "Sabine, *non*. Why?" With a look from Milady, her question was answered. "He wants to use me to trap Papa. Don't let him do it, Sabine. Please think, Sabine. I'm your sister in all the ways that count. I love you and always have. Moreover, you love me. I know you do. Please, you can't turn me over to Richelieu, not after all we've been to each other for so many years."

Silence. Long. Hostile. Tense. Drew out even longer.

"My choices are limited, Laurel," she said her shoulders sagging and her eyes overwhelmed with sadness. She looked so old and tired, so resigned to a fate beyond her control. "It's you or my son, Laurel. My three-year-old son. He'll be four soon," she added absently to herself.

"Richelieu has your son?" Laurel was flabbergasted. She had not wanted to think that one man could be so devoid of common human decency, though she had seen much in her years to show her the evil side of man. Wait. Could this boy also be Athos' son? She counted back in her mind. Given what she knew, Sabine and Athos having a son was quite possible.

"*Oui*, Laurel, and I must keep him safe even if it means giving you to the cardinal," Milady told her. It was the conclusion she herself had finally reached after many an argument with herself and her pride.

"It doesn't have to be that way, Sabine. You don't have to let him win. Let me help you." Sabine shot her a contemptuous glance that said, "And what could you do?" "Sabine, remember how we used to plan and plot when we were young, how good we were at scheming? Together we can save your son, and you can regain your dignity and control over your own destiny." Her eyes pleaded with the older woman.

"I'm listening. This had better be good, Laurel."

Her mind raced, and the young woman desperately searched for a solution. She had to talk fast and think faster. "How long do you have before the cardinal would take his vengeance out on your son if you don't turn me over to him?"

"I have about a week to turn you over to him."

"In Paris?" Laurel pressed, and Milady looked at her as if she were stupid. "Sabine, of course I know I'd be sent to Paris. What I need to know is if your son is in Paris."

The *Comtesse de* Winter sat across from the other woman. "The last I heard or saw, he was being kept in Richelieu's residence in Paris." She grabbed Laurel's wrist tightly in her hand. "Don't even think it. You can't get in there. You're not a man." She would have tried herself had it been any other way.

"Is his eminence behind this entire plot against France and sending a spy to England?"

The question hung between them, and for several more moments there was silence.

Long moments.

Slowly Milady said, her voice just above a whisper, "It can't be proven. He's eradicated the entire trail that leads back to him, but he's behind it all. He wants to be king so he's striking a deal with Buckingham that will ultimately divide Europe between the two of them. That one has always been ambitious." And frighteningly competent.

Laurel took both her sister's hands in her own, refusing to release them. "Do you really want Richelieu to be king of France and rule half of Europe the way he rules France now?" she demanded, and Milady did not respond, so she repeated the question. Still the older woman did not reply, so Laurel shook her and said, "Answer me. Do you really want that man to be king? To rule other people and destroy their lives like he's been destroying yours? Is that the way you want your son growing up?"

"No." Sabine's voice was soft, but firm.

"Then hear me out completely before you dismiss my plan or blow up at me." Laurel waited, and her sister finally nodded tersely. "Is Athos the father of that boy?"

"*Oui*," Milady replied brusquely. The only thing that kept her from leaving was her word to her stepsister.

Laurel took a deep breath. "Let me tell Athos about his son."

"Why?" she snapped. "Athos threw me out without listening to me. He forfeited his *right* to have anything to do with my child."

The younger woman interrupted. "He is Athos' child too, and if Athos knows that Richelieu is holding his son hostage he will do anything to get that boy away from Richelieu. You know that he could get into Richelieu's residence, Sabine. Try to deny my words, but if you do you are lying to yourself. It is not too late. Not yet. Don't bring an even worse fate upon you and your son."

Milady de Winter did not deny the words, and Laurel decided to present the rest of her plan. "Set me free, and send me to Calais as quickly as possible with the information you took from me. Then when D'Artagnan comes, send him back to his friends with a message to head to Calais. There we will meet and catch the spy and foil Richelieu's plot. And don't try to convince me you wouldn't enjoy defeating Richelieu in his scheme."

The *comtesse* ignored Laurel's last words, a goad. "And where does my son come in?"

"I give you my word, and you know my word is good, I will personally go to Paris with Athos, and we will free your son after we catch the spy, who threatens us all."

Milady rose majestically to her feet and called to the guard. Just before the door opened, she turned quickly and said, "I will consider your plan."

* * * * * * * * * * *

The man forded the river and drew the stallion to a much-needed stop. He dismounted and allowed the fine animal to drink from the fast flowing water. Carefully he surveyed the landscape. He was getting closer. Probably a three-day or so ride to Calais and then the crossing of the channel to Dover.

Mentally he reviewed the unsigned missive from his eminence. The cardinal had seen fit to inform him that four musketeers had run into Laurel d'Anlass, daughter of the best spy France had ever known, and were now more than likely in pursuit of him. It was also highly likely they were well informed about his own dealings and identity, according to the cardinal. So, evidently, the same four musketeers who had put an end to Rochefort and an end to the plot to assassinate the king were now trailing him. Aramis, Athos, D'Artagnan, and Porthos. In addition, if Laurel was anything like her illustrious father, she had found a way to tag along with the musketeers regardless of their wishes. Another moment his mind dwelt on Aramis' name. It struck him as rather familiar. But from where? He was not sure. But he would find out.

As for Laurel . . .

Poor girl. Well, he supposed she was well into womanhood now and nearing spinsterhood. All her effort would be for naught. Louis would fall, and her dear enemy, Richelieu, would rise and bring him along on the ascension. The spy made his way back to his stallion and stroked its neck. "Ready to go, boy? We've got an important message to deliver to England," the man said, remounting his horse.

This time there would be no Marquis de Langeac on his tail. Pity, almost, that the Prussian had deprived him of the satisfaction of eliminating Thomas d'Anlass himself. Well, maybe he was partially responsible; his had been the second shot to find its mark. Nonetheless the marquis was dead now, according to his sources in Belgium.

Henceforth, there was only Thomas' daughter to challenge him or try to challenge him. It could almost be interesting to see what she was capable of, but then again she was totally without her father's help or experience now. "Ah, well," he murmured, forestalling further speculation as he took off northward.

* * * * * * * * * * * *

"Remember two hours, and then we come in after you. Best make this distraction quite good, youngster."

"Wouldn't want to disappoint you, Porthos," D'Artagnan assured him. The young man looked at Athos. Poor Athos. What he must be going through. "Where am I supposed to go, Athos?" He repeated his friend's name when at first he did not respond.

He clucked his tongue against the roof of his mouth. "Just into Beauvais. Milady's men will be looking for you, and seeing as you don't have a disguise, they should be able to spot you pretty easily." D'Artagnan nodded bravely. "Don't forget to draw as much attention to yourself as possible so that we can sneak in without being noticed."

Again the young musketeer nodded, and Athos and Porthos drew away from him. Only Aramis lingered. "D'Artagnan. Do not worry yourself over Christophe right now. Worry about keeping Constance safe and making sure Milady does not send the contents of Thomas' message to Richelieu. We have got to assume Christophe can take care of himself right now. As you reminded us, he is really very resourceful." One of these days he might get used to saying that, but he had been saying something like that entirely too often to suit himself. That headstrong, young lady needed protection and no small bit of taming.

D'Artagnan swallowed stiffly. It hardly seemed right to leave a woman in custody, but then again Laurel was not in danger of death, and Sabine de Winter was her stepsister. Hopefully, that counted for something. Nor would Laurel thank him for putting her personal safety above the safety of France and the French people. "I understand," the young musketeer finally replied, completely solemn for once.

Aramis released his light grasp on D'Artagnan's horse, and as D'Artagnan drew away, he called, "God be with you, *mon ami*."

"And you, also," he replied, though Aramis probably could not hear.

As Aramis joined them, Athos turned to Porthos, who was showing off the prize he had so recently secured. A small bundle of feathers almost obscured by his big hands. A carrier pigeon. "The bird is well enough to fly, and it will fly?"

"Why, Athos, I should be insulted. How could you possibly think that I would not know my animals?" Porthos sputtered, hamming up the role, milking it. Aramis' lips twitched. Porthos and his offended dignity. "I've only been raising all sorts of animals since I was a wee little lad, albeit courtesy of my father. The pigeon is perfectly well and will carry a message exactly where we want it to go."

"You are sure this pirate friend of yours can be trusted?" Aramis addressed the large man.

"Aramis, dear man, there *is* honor between fellow pirates. We owe each other more than our lives many times over. He will help us." Aramis gave him a look that said he just wanted to be sure, and the large musketeer directed himself to Athos. "So what do you say, oh great leader? Shall I release this little gem and enlist the aid of my once-upon-a-time swashbuckling companion?"

"You did tell him to keep certain soldiers occupied?" Athos asked.

"Of course."

"Release the bird," Athos commanded, and Porthos sent the pigeon on its way. Athos sent a silent prayer that the bird would do its job well. It was about time something actually went their way.

Milady de Winter stood regally before the sergeant of the cardinal's personal guard. Not so much as a tremor or a blink of her eyes betrayed what the woman was thinking. She merely offered him her hand; he kissed it and released it quickly. He knew better than to grasp her hand a moment longer than strictly proper. He valued his manhood, not to mention his life.

She allowed her hand to drop to her side while her other hand brushed through her hair and over the hair clip in what was easily mistaken for a nervous gesture. Had the sergeant tried anything suspicious he would have found that little clip was a vicious dagger. Milady smiled; only her lips showed the gesture. "Six of your men have taken Constance Bonacieux to my residence in Chartres to secure her there?"

"It is all done, as your ladyship requested. The woman has proved no problem. She trusts your word implicitly. She believes that you are helping her even as you are imprisoning her," the sergeant reported.

"Your other men are ready to escort our hot headed young D'Artagnan?" The sergeant nodded. "And the prisoner we took earlier today? Did you do as I instructed with the lad?"

"He has been escorted to the outskirts of the city on a fresh horse. I watched him head for Calais myself." He was very careful not to voice approval or disapproval of the woman's plan. The cardinal must know what he was doing by involving this woman, and she was no fool. Quite the contrary, she was an extremely dangerous and deadly woman.

"Good," she said. "Bring D'Artagnan to me as soon as he arrives."

D'Artagnan's hand kept wandering to the hilt of his sword. The sensation of the cool metal against his palm failed to comfort him. He was riding into a trap, and he knew it. The knowledge did not sit well with him. Yet he had volunteered, actually, suggested that he was the only logical bait. Perhaps he should have thought the thing through more before he just jumped in. One of these days he was going to learn better, and it better be soon. He could not fail Constance, and he could not fail his friends. Moreover, he could not fail his king, country, and honor. He was no coward. He could do this, and it was his duty.

How soon before they found him? Couldn't be long now, and he still had to be able to draw a great deal of attention to himself. Not that he wasn't getting a lot of attention simply by riding into a strange town decked out like an aristocrat who'd gone for a long ride in the country and had decided to drop by town for something rather then sending a servant. True, he had inherited his father's title and lands, but it didn't mean he always wanted people staring at him like he was some despicably unnatural freak.

Out of the corner of his eyes he saw the movements of several men. Those were probably the men who had been sent to find him and bring him to Milady. Well, it was time for him to implement a distraction. He did not have a chance to.

The musketeer started and barely was able to keep his horse from bolting as two dozen drunken men poured into the streets from the bar, yelling, screaming profanities, and brawling. Generally making a great public disturbance. The young man urged his horse farther away from the spectacle. To get caught up in it would be near suicidal, and contrary to what his friends might claim, he didn't wish for an early death. The men he had been watching made their own frantic effort to escape the fray and pursue the young musketeer.

Noisily, the hooves of his mare cracked against the stone, and he was forced to slow his pace to avoid running down several pedestrians. Well, Porthos did say his pirate friend could provide a distraction, though he hadn't quite expected that. Steadying himself, he drew Aramis' pistol and loaded it, quickly making sure the powder stayed dry. Then he fired the pistol into the air and howled like a banshee, drawing all eyes to him.

The onlookers burst into action and moved to surround the man to see what could possibly be wrong with him. Touched by the moon? Only after several minutes did the men who were pursuing him reach him and relieve him of the gun and his sword.

"You will come with us, and no more antics if you value your life and the life of your lovely lady," one of the men said as he urged the musketeer away from the noise of the street and to the deserted alley that led to Milady's hideout.

Roughly the three men removed him from his saddle, and he feebly protested until he thought better of it. He would rather be conscious this time. Could be a distinct advantage. The young man stumbled as he was pushed into a dusty ill-lit room. *Zut*. This wasn't turning out very well. He was going to end up falling over his own two feet and making a fool of himself in front of Constance.

Quickly he banished his romantic daydreams as he was brought before Milady de Winter. "D'Artagnan," she said sweetly, almost too sweetly. "Welcome, be seated. I do apologize for the rough treatment you may have received. It is simply so hard to find good help sometimes." She sighed. D'Artagnan had the niggling feeling that the sigh was well rehearsed, but it was still effective. It was still hard to believe that this beautiful woman could be so deadly and dangerous.

"Worry not, my handsome young man. Your lady love is unharmed. In fact, I can see to it that you join her." She smiled. It still didn't touch her eyes and certainly not her heart.

"What do you want, *Comtesse de* Winter?" he commanded brashly, ignoring the fact he was in no position to issue demands.

She ordered the soldiers from the room, assuring them she would summon them immediately if she needed help. "Believe it or not, young man, I'm going to help you and your friends. It is my understanding that you and your friends are in pursuit of a spy and traitor to France. Are you not?" His stubborn silence was answer enough. "Let's say I have an interest in apprehending this spy, a personal interest."

"Why should I believe you?"

"Because I set Laurel free. She is on her way to Calais even as we speak. I gave her my finest horse. In fact I expect that your friends will soon join her."

"You don't honestly expect me to believe you set Laurel free out of the goodness of your heart even if she is your sister. Nor can you expect me to believe that you'd send us after her, not after all you've done to hinder us. I'm not that gullible." Not this time.

She shrugged her shoulders. "Given. However, let's assume, for a moment, that I really do have a personal interest in the success of your mission. In fact, I have a proposal for you."

"What?" he asked cautiously.

"You have two choices. First, you can go to your friends and tell them what has happened and head after Laurel to Calais."

He broke in, "And what happens to Constance?"

"She'll remain safe, but you may never see her again. Your other option is to be taken away from Beauvais by my escort, and you will join Constance. In the meantime, I'll go to your friends and accompany them to Calais personally," Milady offered.

"Why would I tell you how to get to my friends?"

From inside her pouch she took a wad of papers and placed one of them in D'Artagnan's hands. He looked at it and looked back at the *comtesse*. "I have half the papers Laurel recently received from her father. Without them the chances of catching this spy are not very good. Wouldn't you agree?"

The musketeer closed his eyes in disgust. "All right, you win. I'll tell you where you can find Athos, Porthos, and Aramis," he replied. He hated having his hand forced. After a moment he informed her of the plan the four of them had constructed to sneak the other three into Beauvais in pursuit of D'Artagnan.

Satisfied, she plucked the paper from his nerveless hand and called to the guards who escorted the young man out and saw to it that he was well on his way to prison in Chartres before his friends got too far into Beauvais. With D'Artagnan in her hands, the musketeers dared not betray her.

Blast Sabine! This time she had gone too far with her twisted schemes. Her bitterness could end up destroying them all. That was another thing she had to hold against his eminence; he was greatly responsible for the monster her sister had transformed into.

Laurel winced as a pebble was driven upward by the horse's hooves and impacted with her shin. Half the papers did her little good, as Sabine knew, and still she had only returned half of them. Such a large hole in her knowledge could prove very deadly.

It hardly bore thinking what Milady might do with the rest of the information. Her sister could have given the papers to D'Artagnan, but then she'd have lost her leverage. No, more likely that her sister had used them to blackmail D'Artagnan and his friends into cooperating with her scheme. Whatever her scheme was. At least Constance was safe, even if she had been exiled to who knows where. The only good thing to come out of this catastrophe so far.

"Come on," she urged the horse, and sensing her urgency, it picked up its pace and headed northward faster, hooves flying over rough ground. She tried not to think about losing Rebelle . . . more important matters at the moment. She had to make it to a place to shelter for the night. It could not be safe to sleep in the woods alone at night. Not that it would really be much safer at an inn for a lone, young boy.

However, money could buy a certain amount of security. Plus, she could sleep in the stables and be near her horse at all times just in case anything went wrong. *Sapristi* and dang, she was getting so tired of "just in case." Couldn't God let her, this once, have everything work out all right?

Then again, she could hardly forget that God was often busy, and He helped those who helped themselves. She scowled. Aramis was beginning to rub off on her. They were all beginning to rub off on her for that matter. How would she ever go back to her dull, sedate life of the past two years after this was over? Drat it all! The good Lord must have a strange sense of humor. She'd miss those musketeers. Laurel scolded herself firmly. The mission wasn't over yet. In a lot of ways, it was just beginning.

Clouds obscured the rising moon, and Laurel grimaced. It was going to rain; she felt it in her bones. Not only would she be tired and sore when she finally arrived at the village that she knew was close by, but she would also be soaked to the skin. A drowned rat. That was definitely one way to get a bath, and not a very desirable one at that.

"You couldn't have held off even a little longer," Laurel ranted at the rain that was driving down from the sky, soaking her cloak and pasting it to her clothes.

All too soon, not even the smallest fraction of her would remember what it was to be dry. "*Non.*" She continued her tirade. She was allowed to make a fool of herself, especially when no one else was watching. "You had to pour down on me and make my job harder as if it wasn't hard enough already. You have a lot of nerve." She lapsed into silence as she almost choked on a stream of water that cascaded from her borrowed hat down her face and to her mouth.

Ducking her head, she drove onward. Couldn't be too much farther now.

At last! The mud-stained and thoroughly soaked young woman traipsed into the inn yard and led the pretty mare, well, formerly pretty, seeing as she was mud-caked, into the stable. As soon as the horse was out of the elements, she shook herself and sprayed dirty water all over Laurel, who frowned more deeply.

This really wasn't her day. Fortunately, there was a stable boy whom she paid well to take care of the horse and tipped a bit more thus ensuring that she could sleep in the stables and use his fire to dry herself. Thank goodness it was a warm night.

Section Five

"This way," Athos instructed, and Porthos and Aramis followed him, unnoticed due to all the chaos caused by a good two dozen-plus drunkards mobbing the street in frenzied excitement. Porthos' friend had come through. Only this time, Porthos was kind enough not to inform his two companions that they had been completely foolish to doubt that his friends would come through. Pirates assisted each other unless they were trying to plunder a ship that another pirate had appropriated first. Most of the time.

Porthos leaned fractionally towards Aramis as they speedily weaved through the crowd, having no trouble keeping his seat despite the ruckus. "So just where is it that you think we are being led to, or is this the blind leading the blind?"

"Porthos, I never knew you were so fascinated by the scriptures. Have you ever considered becoming a priest?" Aramis teased his friend, and Porthos actually knew the man was teasing him this time, so he passed the comment off. "It would be my supposition that Athos is leading us to the last place that he remembers being in contact with Milady."

"Ah." Porthos sat up straight in his saddle, still sore from the past days' hard riding. How did Athos and Aramis take it so calmly? Aramis especially. "And from there we seek out the nasty lady's hideout and rescue noble D'Artagnan, the beautiful Constance, and the reckless little lad, Christophe. Have I told you recently how much I love my job?" he demanded of Aramis.

"*Oui*, Porthos, you have told us both numerous times how much you love your job," Athos scolded lightly. "However, now is the time for action, not talk. Let's move, gentlemen."

The three companions drew to a halt, and three hands went to the hilts of their blades. Each man was prepared to draw as a strange man, cultivated, yet dressed almost as a poor apprentice, stepped in their path. In a lightly accented voice, the stranger asked, "Are either of you, by any chance, the noble and honorable Athos?"

"Who wants to know?" Athos replied rudely.

"Come now," Aramis chided. "Where are your manners?" The dark-haired man turned to the little man below him. "I apologize for my friend's lack of manners. We've been on the road all day, and he tends to get grumpy after a long ride." The stranger murmured that that was quite all right. "Now what can I do for you, my good man?"

"We," Porthos corrected.

"Quite right. What can we do for you?" Aramis rephrased the question.

"I have a message for Athos from a *Madame de* Winter. However, if none of you can help me, I suppose I must look elsewhere," the stranger said, eyes downcast.

"Wait," Athos instructed. "I'm Athos. What does Sabine, the *Comtesse de* Winter, want?" Surprisingly, the title did not get stuck in his throat. Nor did the idea that she married again, be it morally legitimate or not, cause more than a twinge.

"Follow me, all of you." The strange man gestured as he started off down a side street. "I will do better than that. I can take you to her."

"Something tells me we're not going to like this," Porthos commented aloud.

"Something tells me, you are right," Aramis agreed as they came to a halt outside an old door which the strange man knocked upon three times. Short and swift.

The door opened and a stout, not quite fat man opened the door. "I've brought the people your mistress requested," the strange man said as he was handed several coins.

The odd man disappeared around the corner in a matter of seconds. Immediately, the three musketeers were ushered inside, and the door closed and locked behind them. From the shadows, a woman of startlingly exquisite beauty stepped. Milady de Winter. There was no mistaking her.

"Welcome, gentlemen. I'm so glad you could join me," she said casually.

"Cut through the insincere crap, Sabine. What do you want?" Athos tore into her for her purported attempt at polite conversation.

Touché. "I'm coming with you to Calais," the *comtesse* announced, and Porthos told himself that he had been right. His guts always knew when a bad situation was on the horizon. Still, he'd much rather have been proved wrong this one time.

Porthos recovered his voice first and crossed his arms across his chest. "*Madame*, I think maybe you just might want to tell us why you think we're going to let you come to Calais with us."

She smiled, and Athos shivered internally. He knew that smile. It did not augur anything good. "Without me Laurel has only half the papers she needs to intercept the spy who is en route to Dover."

"Of course, it would be far too simple to give us the papers and let us go after him, wouldn't it, Sabine?" Athos said, his voice heavy with undisguised disgust.

"You always were very quick to jump to conclusions, now, weren't you, Athos?" She waited for her words to really hit him, then went on. "However, this time you are right. I've got a personal stake in seeing this mission succeed; therefore I have decided to see to it that it will. If I don't come with you to Calais, you could still go after my lovely younger sister, but she still would not get all the information she needs. Whereas if I come with you, she will get the remainder of the information she needs."

"When would you have us leave?" Aramis inquired without emotion, pragmatic as always despite his poetic and charming side.

"Tomorrow, about dawn," she informed them. "Oh and if I were you, I would not think about stealing the papers from me and then abandoning me. Then I would most unfortunately be forced to tell my men to eliminate D'Artagnan and his poor innocent lady. Naturally, if they don't hear from me in the next few days, your friend could well meet with a very unfortunate accident."

A vein throbbed in Athos' neck. He was so tempted to try to seize her by both arms and shake her furiously until Sabine came to her senses, but she was beyond redemption, and she held all the high cards. "And afterward, if all turns out to your satisfaction?" Athos asked, his voice harsh to even his ears.

"D'Artagnan and Constance shall be released and return safely to Paris, only after all is done to my satisfaction."

"How do we know that you'll fulfill your part of the bargain, Sabine?" Athos leveled her with a fury-filled gaze.

"For once in your life, Athos, you'll have to trust me," she informed him. Of course, that could prove very difficult for him. Athos got to his feet and stormed from the room. Porthos was the one who pursued him, leaving Aramis alone with the *comtesse*.

"Be ready to go no later than dawn, *madame*. You'd best not slow us down." Aramis prepared to leave and Milady also stood. "You still love him, *Comtesse de* Winter, don't you." It was not a question, and she did not see fit to respond. Aramis stepped towards her. "I charge you by the love you once felt and the love you still feel to fulfill your pledge."

All she did was laugh, a distorted, chilling laugh. "That's rich, Aramis. Charge me in the name of love. You who has never actually believed in love in his life and who goes through each new woman like some men go through a bottle of wine."

The musketeer shook his head ever so slowly. "May God have mercy on you, *Comtesse de* Winter. May He allow you to find it in your heart to forgive and to do the right thing." He exited the room, her words ringing in his ears, telling him to leave the Almighty out of this for He took little interest in the affairs of men.

"Athos." Porthos hurried after the blond-haired man who dashed an ugly vase to the floor, shattering it into hundreds of pieces. Athos quickly pivoted to glare at his friend. "Temper, temper. We must do this. Come now, my old friend." It wasn't often he saw the older man reduced to such a state.

"*Merci pour* that enlightenment, Porthos. As if that were ever under debate. Don't worry, I'll be coming with all three of you tomorrow. I have no intention of letting that, *that* woman destroy her sister's life the way she and I have destroyed our own."

"Athos, please. Do watch your temper," the younger musketeer cautioned him. "Don't let it cloud your good judgement. We need you and every scrap of your wisdom too much right now."

Athos leveled a finger at the large man. "You just see to it that she keeps her bargain, and that she stays out of my way, and we'll be fine."

"I hope I'm not interrupting anything important," Aramis remarked as he came upon Athos grilling Porthos, and the two men both forgot each other and looked at him. "We'll be leaving at dawn tomorrow from this location. I confirmed it with Milady. I think we all should get a good night's rest." Aramis' eyes rested on Athos for a moment, and Athos read their message loud and clear: no drinking tonight. The man needed to be clearheaded in the morning. In addition, if he even tried, Athos knew Aramis would forcibly remove the liquor from him, regardless of any bodily harm either of them might receive.

Porthos acknowledged the advice. "Can do, good man. Say a few prayers to God for me tonight. I think we may need them."

* * * * * * * * * * *

Sun dribbled through the cracks in the wooden slats. Its rays touched the ground and the figure that lay motionless by the embers of a fire. That same figure that lay curled in a cloak, a basket hilt longsword tucked underneath a leg. The person stirred and shook the dampness from her bones. She felt so sticky and dirty and lethargic. Maybe listless was a better word.

Suddenly, Laurel was fully awake and sitting in the damp straw. She clambered to her feet and outside into the bright light. She stopped short as a wave of heat washed over her. Not only hot, but unbearably muggy after yesterday's chilling storm. The young woman straightened the sword at her side and dashed back into the stables, searching each stall.

In relief, she flung the door open and urged the pretty mare out. At least her horse was still here and well rested. But she was late. Very late. It was already well past dawn, and she should have left hours ago.

Quickly, she lugged the saddle from its post to the horse and cinched it into place, adjusting the stirrups. Her stomach grumbled, and she ignored it, fastening her saddlepacks back on the mare. She jumped into the saddle and directed her horse from the stables, ducking the beam as she exited the dirty stables and went out to brave the sun's fury. Food would simply have to wait. She had to be in Calais and soon. Even if that meant riding hard all day, pausing only when absolutely unavoidable.

The mare snorted, and Laurel remembered to be sure she had brought the canteen of water with her. She and the horse would need it today. "Eya," she yelled and dug her heels into the horse's flanks. The mare's muscles rippled beneath the woman, and they were off in a race for the coast. If only she had Rebelle, then she knew she would still be able to make it to Calais. But that wasn't the case. Reality had to be dealt with. As always.

No, the man wouldn't be giving him away. The spy holstered his discharged pistol. Dead men couldn't talk. He walked away from the body, not looking back. No one took note of the man who emerged from behind the run-down hovel. He clucked, and a large stallion came towards him, pawing the ground anxiously.

"*Oui*, I know you're anxious to be on your way, as am I," he told the horse, patting it lovingly. The stallion was a good horse and quite particular. It had been the horse that had alerted him that he was being spied upon. Thus, a messy problem had been avoided—well for the most part. Nevertheless, he had been detained longer than he had planned because he'd had to track the man down after he had bolted. Such an inconvenience. However, he should still be able to make the ship in Calais. He was not in too much a hurry that he would skip eating either. Plus, he could use some information.

Thus, the spy led his horse to a nearby tavern and handed him to a stable boy. "Be nice to him," he warned the lad as he entered the tavern and sat down at a nearby table, ordering a mug of ale, a slab of pork, and several rolls.

Two strangers entered the room talking loudly, and several of the other customers shot a glance at them before they returned their attention to their own business. The spy did not look up from his drink. He did, however, listen very discreetly to the words that passed between the two men who had just entered the room and sat themselves at a nearby table.

"Never knew so many people was interested in Calais this time of year," one of the men commented.

"Think, you dolt. Course there's always people interested in Calais," his friend criticized, and the spy listened more carefully to their exchange. "Just ain't n'ver seen so many upperclass nobs so suddenly interested in a visit to the port city this time of year. They's usually as far away from cities as they can get this time of year. Ain't n'ver been hardy enough to take the summer heat."

The spy got up from his table and approached the two men. "Scuse me," he said and asked their permission to join them and offered to buy them a drink. "I couldn't help but hear's how you was mentionin' Calais," he said in a perfect imitation of the lower-class accent. The two men surveyed the dark-haired, green-eyed man and said nothing. "It so happens I've done run into a group of aristos headin' to Calais just this morning. Can't think why's they'd be interested in going there this time of year," the green-eyed man lied masterfully.

The man's reluctance fell away at this revelation. "Me, name's Jean, and Louis here was just talking bout the same thing."

"Really?' the spy said in feigned surprise. "Did several aristos try to order your services to take them there?"

"Nah," the man named Louis replied. "We just saw a party of three men and a lady widow who was riding all out for Calais. They'd done stopped a few leagues back to get one of their horses reshod. Think them dumb aristos would know better than to ride a horse that ain't properly shod. But you can't really xpect more from em." Louis leaned forward, taking a deep drink of ale, and wiped his mouth on the corner of his sleeve. "Anyway, they's said something about looking for the lady's sister. Me, I thinks something big is going on in Calais, and those nobs don't want none of us findin out bout it."

The green-eyed man deftly pretended to take a swig of his own drink. Time to find out just how much these men knew. "These men didn't happen to mention any names, now, did they?"

"Why do you ask?" the more suspicious companion, Jean, demanded.

"Because them men I ran into this morning was talking bout meeting another party in Calais," the spy replied glibly.

"You know, now that you mention it, I do recall them mentioning a name or so," Louis admitted. "Kept mentioning some man called D'Artagnan, and a lady—what's that name they kept saying, Jean?"

Jean scratched his head. "It was something d'Anlass. Couldn't hear them real well, cause they got all quiet when they mentioned them names, all secret like wasn't nobody supposed to know," Jean commented.

"Anyway," Louis continued, "think as they were saying something about finding this woman in Calais cause they had important information for her."

The spy turned the conversation to other more mundane matters as several meals arrived. So it seemed Laurel d'Anlass was already well on her way to Calais and reinforcements were coming right after her. Now whose help could she have enlisted?

D'Artagnan. His mind turned the other name over. D'Artagnan, he could recall Richelieu mentioning a boy by that name. Wasn't he the boy who'd recently become a musketeer and saved the king as well? So apparently, she truly had joined forces with several of the musketeers. Richelieu's letter had been correct in its surmise. Still, that didn't explain who the other woman was.

His meal finished, the green-eyed man excused himself from the two men, thanking them for their conversation and company. He threw a few coins down on the table and ducked outside.

Quickly, he mounted his horse and urged the stallion to Calais. He was still ahead of four of his pursuers. Futhermore, he intended to stay ahead of them. Perhaps he could plan a nice little distraction for them. *Oui*, he would do that. Still, he supposed he'd have to watch for Laurel d'Anlass; she could well arrive in Calais before him. It would not do to underestimate Thomas d'Anlass' daughter. In fact, in his experience, the women had often proven more dangerous than the men.

* * * * * * * * * * *

It really was challenging to ride a horse when your hands were tied and for all purposes you were being led to who knew where. Not to mention his rear end was really hurting, due to the awkward way he was forced to sit so that he could exert some measure of control over his horse. And his head still hurt from being trussed unceremoniously and knocked unconscious.

No wonder his head hurt like . . . like . . . *Zut et rezut*! He couldn't think straight. D'Artagnan shuddered to think what would have happened if his horse had not been well trained, since these soldiers had put him on the animal unconscious.

Thanks to that little maneuver, which had rendered him senseless, he had no clue how long he'd been on the road or even where he was going. At a guess, he'd put it somewhere southward, but more than that he couldn't be sure. Nor did he have any idea how long he'd been riding. Although, his stomach was rumbling, so he'd obviously missed an important meal. Judging by the sun, it was well past early morning, probably later.

"Stop here," the man in charge, a sergeant, instructed, and it took all D'Artagnan's skills to bring his horse to a stop and not tumble off. "Get him down," the sergeant instructed his men, and they unbound his wrists and tugged him roughly from his horse, setting him on his unsteady feet. He stumbled and then recovered his balance. For once, he managed to keep his own counsel as they prodded him to a nearby clearing.

Another brown-haired man materialized in front of the sergeant, and D'Artagnan was positive he was not one of the soldiers who had been escorting him. Quickly he counted. There were eight men now. Only six had been on the road with him. Odd. A rustling of leaves drew his attention to several more soldiers, who emerged escorting a shorter and daintier figure between them.

"D'Artagnan," the voice said in surprise as the small figure drew close to him.

"Constance," he replied, kneeling beside her and taking her hands, enclosing them in his. "Are you all right?" The guards didn't pay them much mind. They kept their distance, but were close-enough that they could prevent any attempt at escape.

"Quite all right for the most part," she said, a shy smile on her lips. They both spoke at once. "What happened?" Then they both tried to urge the other to explain first until Constance pointed out that a gentleman tried to always follow a lady's wishes where reasonable.

D'Artagnan explained that he was a hostage to ensure that his friends would fulfill a mission. Only when the mission was complete, would he then be released. "But how is it that we ran into you here? I was under the impression that you were a day ahead of us at least."

She shrugged her shoulders, a mirthful twinkle in her eyes. "Well you see, I had to stall them somehow. Only if I stalled them did I have a hope of being rescued, and now you're here." She lowered her voice to a whisper. "Together we can outwit these men and escape."

He nodded in agreement, assuring her they were definitely going to get out one way or another. "But, Constance, that still doesn't explain how you delayed these men. They obviously know their duty and are good at it."

She shrugged her shoulders and smiled broadly. "Women's problems," she revealed, her eyes twinkling with a healthy dose of glee. "I acted like I had women's problems, and I haven't met a man yet who knows how to handle that."

With these words, the two were broken apart and silenced. Shortly thereafter, they were given a bit of bread and water as a meal. Some meal, D'Artagnan grumbled to himself, but finished it nonetheless and willingly remounted his horse some time later. Two of the twelve men led their fellows and their two prisoners silently towards an unknown destination, and D'Artagnan plotted. He'd find a way out of this yet or he wasn't worthy of the mantle he'd recently won or his father's good name and Gascogne blood.

"Stay out of this, Sabine," Athos warned the woman, but she crouched next to the musketeers anyway and brushed her skirts downward. They were hopelessly wrinkled. So far she hadn't delayed them at all. Rather, it had been Porthos' horse throwing a shoe that had put them behind schedule. Athos never had been very good at tolerating delays. Another reason he was cross. Not that he blamed Porthos. They had been riding hard for weeks now, and that took a toll even on a well-cared-for and well-shod horse. "What do you want?"

"Don't you think it might be wise to allow me to help you plan a strategy? I do happen to know my little sister better than any of you. We grew up together. That would be a good number of years," Milady leveled her arguments.

He wanted to say, "What good would your brand of help do, Laurel? It could only get her killed." However, he did not. This was no time to lose his temper that had suddenly become volatile again, and Milady de Winter was obviously a talented schemer. Athos elected to say nothing.

"Perhaps you have a good suggestion that will be agreeable to dear Athos." Porthos looked at the woman.

Before she could respond, Aramis spoke to her. "How much do you value your stepsister's life, *Comtesse de* Winter?" Aramis referred to the true relation between the two women.

"Pardon?" she replied.

"Do you value your sister's life enough to set aside your grievances against us for the time being? And do you really want to prevent Richelieu's plan from succeeding?"

"Why?" Sabine's eyes narrowed as she asked the one-word question. Athos looked at his wife. He thought he knew what Aramis might be doing. He almost resented Aramis' efforts as peacekeeper, but he knew this group needed it too desperately to not come to peace with one another.

"Only if we can work together, in at least a semblance of trust, do we have a reasonably good chance to keep your sister from death and to capture a very cunning spy. If not, this spy will pick us off one by one." Aramis related cold, logical facts without emotion, sending home the truth of how dire their situation was.

"Divide and conquer. Of course. The oldest trick in pirating," Porthos told himself.

Sabine had to admit this would-be priest was a crafty devil with a gift for speaking the right words at the right time. Given time he might even become a very, very effective leader, if he wished to lead. Porthos finally took Aramis' cue and took Sabine's hand in his. The woman refrained from stabbing him, fortunately.

"*Madame, Comtesse de* Winter," he said with almost exaggerated ceremony. "I pledge to you on my honor I will protect you and be loyal to any plan we devise until such time as the entire plan is completed. I will do this even if I must die to do so."

"As do I also give you my word, Milady. Will you give us yours that you will not betray us?" Aramis inquired.

"Will Athos?" she asked simply.

All eyes turned to Athos as he wrestled with himself. Could he give his trust to a woman he had betrayed and who had turned around and betrayed him in return? *Non.* But perhaps he could set aside his unbending rules for the moment. They needed Sabine too much, and if working with her was what it took to save the king and his country, so be it. Apparently, the only way to do that was to give his word.

"Sabine, I pledge to you on my word of honor that until this mission is complete I will do all in my power to protect you, to death if needed. And you know the value of my word, Sabine," Athos reminded her needlessly.

Oui, she knew it all too well. She could never remember a time when Athos had broken his solemn word of honor. He had not even broken it when his father nearly disowned him for taking a permanent post with the musketeers without his permission or when helping with his older sister's secret marriage and then spiriting off his young nephew to relatives in England, effectively out of the reach of any further harm his father could wreak. "I give you my word. And if you ever have reason to doubt it, then do what you must," she told them and withdrew.

The lady arranged a cloak by the fire and lay upon it. It had been a long time since she had slept on the ground. Still, she would not complain. She had endured worse. She'd been humiliated and branded a murderer by her stepfather, and she'd been thrown in prison. Sleeping on the ground was nothing more than a mild inconvenience. Sleep claimed her quickly, but she had just long enough before she slumbered to grasp a dagger in her hand. No telling who could be roaming this countryside.

Following her lead, Aramis and Porthos drew themselves up a piece of ground and quickly fell to sleep. A light sleep, given, but a restful sleep nonetheless. Athos remained where he was, staring at the stars for a very long time. Somehow he didn't think he'd get much sleep this night. What he wouldn't give for that very stiff drink he'd been longing for, but he had promised Aramis he would drink in moderation if at all. Finally, Athos left his seated position and wandered aimlessly for several moments.

When he stopped and looked down, he was surprised to find that he was standing just above his wife's sleeping form. She looked so peaceful, so innocent, like the woman he had pledged his heart and hand to when he was still a young man who believed in love. She had changed so much, but she remained the most beautiful and desirable woman he'd ever seen. A breeze slapped at his face and blew hair across Sabine's eyes. Tenderly, he brushed the wisps of hair away, and his hand lingered for a moment.

On impulse he touched his lips to her cheek, and with the night air as his only witness whispered, "I'm sorry, Sabine. So sorry. Please forgive me, my. love." The words said, his momentary lapse was pushed aside, and he retreated. Athos needed some time alone to think. He'd been doing a lot of that lately. Maybe he was destined to brood until the end of his days.

As Athos' steps faded into the distance, Milady touched her hand to her cheek where Athos' lips had so recently touched her. "If only it were that easy," she said aloud, knowing he was too far away to hear her words. "If only love could be enough for us." A tear trailed down her cheek, and she brushed it away. Aramis was right: she did still love him. If only she had not turned into the monster that he had once mistaken her for, he might have taken her back after finding out he had been wrong in his original accusations.

Now, though, it was impossible. Their love did not stand a chance against the magnitude of her crimes and his honor, sense of justice, and sense of duty. Reality was harsh and unforgiving. Satan had well sealed their downfall, and she had little doubt she'd burn for her part some day.

Horse and rider, both equally exhausted and filthy, dragged into the port city of Calais.

Laurel shook herself firmly, taking her weary body to task. Had to stay awake. If she were to fall asleep and then fall out of her saddle . . . No, she refused to think about that right now. She was tired, hot, dirty, and depressed. Time to find a place where she could scrounge up some food and clear the cobwebs from her head before she tried to find a boat named Diana and another boat called Minerva. According to her father's message, one of the two boats was the one the spy was supposed to meet and cross the channel in.

The mare's hooves plodding along the ground and her own mind half gone, Laurel guided the animal down the streets aimlessly, searching for a relatively safe place to rest a bit. The stables didn't appeal tonight. She really just wanted a nice real bed and a bath. Okay, the first order of business was to become presentable. That meant find a relatively private place where she could make herself presentable and get rid of this travel dirt.

Her weary mind caught sight of the private residence that appeared to have been vacated for the summer. The rush of water falling drew her, and she peered between the hedges. Perfect! The only ones left would be the few servants needed to maintain the house in the master's absence.

If she was quick about it, she could be in and out before she was discovered. As Laurel watched, a servant entered the garden and then left, closing the door to the house behind him.

Laurel left her horse by the hedges with firm instruction to behave herself and patted the animal, promising her a good grooming and well-deserved rest, soon. The young woman grabbed her only other change of clothing, the one that had made her look like a presentable lad at Porthos' family home, and squeezed between the hedges and climbed over the stone rail.

Looking both ways to ascertain no one was coming, she dashed to the fountain. Hastily she stripped herself, every single article of clothing this time, except the bindings that secured her breasts. They were just too filthy to bear against her skin a moment longer and were in need of a thorough washing too.

As quickly as she had stripped she thrust herself under the cold spray of the fountain and dunked her entire abused body underneath the pool of water. With her hands she scrubbed every part of her body until the caked dirt was driven away. What she wouldn't give for real soap or even to linger here. Yet each second she lingered it was more likely that she'd be found.

Reluctantly, she hopped from the fountain, and without taking even the slightest instant to dry off, she dressed herself in the clean clothes, after checking to be sure that the wet bindings that held her breasts in place were still there.

Up she glanced. Someone was approaching. Time to leave. She wadded the old clothes under one arm, and in the other she grabbed her boots and hat. Then she dashed for dear life across the cobblestones and over the wall. Through the hedge and to her horse, arriving out of breath but basically clean and much refreshed.

Not a second too soon, for a servant was peering around the garden suspiciously, mumbling he could have sworn he'd heard someone out here. As for Laurel, she yanked on her boots and set her new cavalier hat atop her wet braided hair. She stuffed the clothes into her saddlebags, but not before she retrieved her sword from them and fastened it securely around her. Hopefully, no one would get too curious as to why a young lad was carrying such a fine weapon. If they did, she'd just have to say her father had lent it to her, sort of.

Her fatigued arms labored as she hefted herself onto the mare and leaned over to whisper in her ear. "How do you feel about a nice stable and good grooming and all the feed you can eat?"

The animal's ears perked up, and she seemed lighter on her feet as Laurel led them off in search of a place where she could do just that. "I thought you might like that." She smiled to herself, ignoring the looks she was getting from passersby for talking to herself. Let them think what they wanted; she knew she was sane for the moment.

Now was the real doozy, convincing the wife of the inn proprietor to let her stay, and she was running out of coins. Athos, Aramis, Porthos, and D'Artagnan had the rest of the money she had scavenged from Langeac. Once this was gone . . . *Non*, she wouldn't think negatively yet. Couldn't.

* * * * * * * * * * *

The cardinal swept down the hall, followed by several novitiates. He stopped and turned, dismissing them with a few imperious words. Richelieu continued on, down the corridor and through a door to the room the commander of his personal guard used as his office.

The *capitaine* came to his feet and bowed low before the cardinal as he entered. "Your eminence. What a pleasure. What can I do for you?"

Richelieu closed the door behind him, checking to be sure no one was eavesdropping. "Have you received any messages for me recently?"

"One moment, please, your eminence. Let me check." The *capitaine* ruffled through his papers and found a small letter which he placed in the cardinal's hand. His search finished, the *capitaine* leaned back in his chair.

His eminence broke the seal and read the unsigned, unaddressed letter from the spy he had sent to Buckingham.

> By the time you receive this letter I should be in Calais and readying to depart for Dover. I have all the necessary information and will present that to Buckingham upon my arrival in England. Success should be ours shortly. I will write you more after I reach the Duke of Buckingham. Also, for your information, my man in Belgium has informed me that the Prussian agent, Joseph, has shot and killed Thomas d'Anlass and was in turn killed himself, but not before Thomas sent information out of the country.

The letter ended as abruptly as it had been started, and Richelieu would soon see to it that it found its way into the fire. So Joseph had taken his own initiative and killed the marquis against his orders to capture the Frenchman. The man had betrayed him. Too bad he was dead already and beyond vengeance. Still there had to be a way to secure the British fleet even with Thomas dead. Perhaps he could give them Laurel d'Anlass and one of the king's other top agents. He would propose that to Buckingham's brother. And the Englishman had best accept or someone would pay.

"Is this all you have gotten?" Richelieu asked as he stashed the letter.

"There is nothing more, your eminence."

"Nothing from Milady?" The *capitaine* shook his head, and the cardinal left the office. Leaving the palace, he called for his carriage and ordered the driver to take him to his residence. A residence no woman was ever allowed to enter.

"Your eminence," voices called as he entered the residence, passing by numerous students, priests, and novices with a swift nod of his head.

He entered his chambers where a servant helped him undress and another prepared a hot bath for him. Might as well appear at his best for his meeting tonight, actually for both meetings. Until the water became tepid, he soaked in the tub and then called for his robe. It was slipped around his shoulders as he stepped from the bath.

Two servants held his robe as he slipped his arms into the red robes that signified his office. He allowed the servants to arrange the robes and then place his crucifix on over his head. To one of the servants he most trusted, he said, "I want the boy brought to me here, now."

"As your eminence requests." The servants bowed and both exited.

The minutes passed by, and the cardinal adjusted his signet ring upon his finger. The door opened and a young boy dressed somberly was shown in. Once again he dismissed the servants and turned his attention to the very young lad.

"Welcome, young master Guillaume," the cardinal said and the little boy made a bow that was quite well executed for his age.

"*Maman* is back? I get to see her?" he asked eagerly.

The cardinal sighed and took the boy upon his lap in a fatherly gesture that Guillaume did not quite seem comfortable with. "I'm afraid not, Guillaume. Your mother may not be coming back, ever."

* * * * * * * * * * *

"Constance," a voice whispered softly in her ear and a hand covered her mouth. Her first startled instinct was to scream, but upon seeing D'Artagnan crouched over her, a finger to his lips, she didn't. "Tonight we leave this little party," he told her.

"How?" she mouthed, sitting up, her muscles stiff from lying upon the ground. She would never complain about a lumpy bed again.

"In about an hour when the moon should be providing some light, I'll free my horse and subdue the guards. We'll both ride my horse out of here."

"But how will you subdue the guards?" she whispered frantically.

"I'm afraid I'm going to need your help," D'Artagnan admitted reluctantly. Seemed like no matter what he did anymore it was always risky, almost in the extreme.

"What do you need me to do?"

He pointed to the sleeping figure of the sergeant. "Since you are very quiet and light-fingered, I need you to get my sword from that man and bring it to me as soon as you can." Constance assured the musketeer she would do so as soon as she saw an opportunity. With a small salute he wished her good luck. God protect her.

"I'll be over there." The young musketeer pointed, not wanting to take any more chances that he'd be seen talking to Constance. She nodded as he left.

The young woman lay awake, listening to the crickets and the sound of men snoring. Waiting had always been hard, but she had to wait for the right moment when no one was paying attention or she would be caught.

The steps of the guard drifted farther away, and she crept to her feet and stole to the sergeant's side. Poised, she stood over him, glancing side to side to be sure no one was awake. She bent her ear right above his face and upper chest. Good. He truly was asleep. She had learned her lesson from the times she had thought her older brother was asleep only to have him catch her by surprise. Stealthily, she reached out her hand and touched the hilt of the sword.

The sergeant stirred in his sleep, and Constance froze. Her heart beat rapidly, and her pulse hammered so hard it drowned out her thoughts. Calm—she urged herself. It was just like sneaking into her brother's room and taking his favorite pillow while he slept. No difference. The man shifted again, giving her the perfect opening, and she snatched the sword, surprised that it was so heavy for such a fragile-looking thing. Good—he was still asleep, and no one was coming yet.

Quickly, she dashed to D'Artagnan and shook his shoulder, stirring him from a light and intermittent sleep. "Shh," she warned and slipped the hilt into his right hand.

"*Merci*," he mouthed and crawled to his feet.

"I'm coming with you," she told him, and he couldn't argue with her about the danger without bringing more danger down upon them. All he could do was warn her to stay well behind him and be quiet.

The two crept through the trees and underbrush, and the leaves rustled. Both froze, but the guard luckily did not see them. Instead he saw a rat rush from the underbrush, so he turned away. Silently, the young people released their breaths and hurried on as quickly as they could without making noise.

D'Artagnan motioned for Constance to keep herself hidden behind the tree, and she did so. He lifted the sword above his head and bounced on his feet in readiness. A guard passed by, and he slammed the hilt of the sword down on the back of the man's head. The guard fell at his feet with a moan, knocked unconscious. One down, one to go.

Once again the couple continued their slow progress towards the second set of footsteps. The steps stopped, and both young people ducked just in time to avoid being seen. That was simply too close for his comfort.

Maybe this plan hadn't been such a good idea. However, there was no backing out now. D'Artagnan jerked his head, and Constance crouched down. The man stood poised, his pulse throbbing wildly. One step. Crunch, another, and another. Closer. Not quite yet. Silently he urged the man to come just a step closer.

The guard stepped forward and stopped as D'Artagnan prepared to bludgeon him. Slowly the soldier started to look in the musketeer's direction, and desperately Constance chucked a stone as far as she could. It landed with a crunch a good few lengths beyond the guard, and he snapped his neck to look for the source of the sound. In that instant, D'Artagnan struck him senseless.

Grabbing Constance's hand, he raced towards where his horse was tethered with the other soldiers' horses. Constance soothed the other horses as D'Artagnan fumbled with the knot that restrained his mount. Finally, it slipped undone, and he led the horse to the dirt road, Constance behind him. He handed the lady up upon the horse and mounted behind her. Digging his heels into the sides of the horse, he urged it away and the animal, sensing the need for stealth, very quietly proceeded down the road.

When he thought himself far enough away he urged his mount faster, and the hooves pounded against the dirt. Time to prove that he could ride in the dark without getting killed. The musketeer stopped where two roads crossed and Constance asked, "Which way?"

"Your guess is as good as mine. Do you know which direction you came from?" The young woman shrugged her shoulders in a helpless gesture. D'Artagnan glanced to the stars, looking for the North Star Porthos had once pointed out to him.

That could be it. "Let's go right," the young man said. Before he was able to go anywhere, Constance turned and kissed him every so briefly on the lips. "*Merci*, D'Artagnan. Let's get out of here," Constance said as she righted herself in the saddle, and the horse surged forward. Everything was going to be fine now.

Drat it all! She would have to discover one of the few women who wanted to mother every lone girl or boy who crossed her path; Laurel sulked, trying to think of how she could get out of the room without the kindly woman noticing her as she tried to slip away. She simply had to get to the docks this morning without being waylaid.

Okay, so maybe she was desperate enough, Laurel concluded as she stared out the window at the bales of straw that were loaded in the wagon below. One more time, she made sure her sword was secure and scoured the room to be sure she had left nothing important behind.

The woman climbed into the sill of the window and closed her eyes. She couldn't believe she was actually going to do this. She must really have a death wish, she thought as she stepped from the window and plummeted into the straw below her. The wagon shook under her impact, but the straw still managed to cushion her fall. Though, whoever thought straw provided a good cushion was sadly mistaken. It stuck you through your clothes, and her body felt bruised and abused from her fall.

Laurel righted her hat and crawled from the wagon, barely clambering out of it before it pulled away. She stumbled and regained her balance. A moment later, she was off running through the almost empty early morning streets and towards the docks. She'd have to come back for her horse since for some reason she thought she'd be discovered if she went for the mare now, and that was the last thing she wanted.

As she got closer to the docks, she slowed and caught her breath. So many ships. How to find two out of all of them? Well, first things first, she had to go down to the docks. Laurel's attention was distracted by a marvelous black stallion and a rider perched upon it. What a fabulous horse. And the man was a superb rider. She hadn't realized she was staring until the man turned and captured her in his green-eyed gaze. Quickly, she lowered her eyes, and the rider passed by. Where was he going? It looked like the *tabac* shop.

Laurel shook her head to break her trance and walked towards the docks. Time to find someone to waylay and ask about the two ships. "Lad, move out of the way." Laurel jumped out of the burly sailor's way. Probably not a wise place to stop. She moved on. The sailors wouldn't talk to her unless she were a cabin boy or a wealthy benefactor trying to contract their services and she wasn't. That was it, maybe she could talk to a cabin boy.

"*Bonjour,*" she called to the boy who was checking a net for holes. He looked up from his work and caught sight of Laurel, sword buckled at her side. What an odd picture the lad made, with a sword tied to his side and his young, innocent face.

"Yeah," the boy responded to Laurel.

"Perhaps you could help me?"

"I can't book you passage, and I can't get you a job. Can't help you stow away neither," the cabin boy said.

"Oh, that's all right. I was wondering if you might be able to tell me if the Minerva and the Diana have arrived."

"Diana docked two days ago," the boy replied turning his attention to a knot in the net before going on. "Minerva arrived about three days ago."

"They're still here then?" she asked, and the boy nodded. "Do you know when they leave?"

"They's scheduled to leave by two days from now, maybe sooner," he responded.

She was about to thank him when an older sailor emerged from the hold and took the boy to task for talking with strangers rather than attending to his work. The cabin boy vanished below deck, and the sailor turned to her. "You get yourself out of here before I set the constable on you, boy."

Laurel was not about to argue. She beat a hasty retreat from the docks and sat huffing, her back against a stone wall. At least the ships were still there. That had to mean she had beaten the spy, but by how much? She didn't know. At the most, she had two days to work with. And how would she discover which ship he'd take or even who he was? She just didn't have all the information, and she couldn't quite remember everything she had read before. If that didn't beat all, she needed Athos and his friends. How could she have grown so dependent on those men after only a few weeks? She really hadn't a clue.

Laurel scrambled to her feet and slowly crept back through the streets that were steadily becoming more crowded. Sabine better have sent the musketeers after her, and they'd better get here soon. Of course God alone knew how she'd find them if—no—when they arrived.

* * * * * * * * * * *

"I tell you I've got a bad feeling about going into Calais," Milady informed the three musketeers, but they seemed unconvinced. "He knows we're coming for him."

"How could the spy know?" Porthos contradicted her.

"I don't know, *monseigneur*," she half snapped and then regained her composure. "All I know is that I've been in this business long enough to learn to listen to what my instincts tell me. And my instincts tell me he knows we're coming and is setting a trap for us."

"Enough," Athos forestalled further argument between Porthos, Aramis, and Sabine. "We will trust Sabine's instincts for now. We can't afford to take chances. That means we don't just ride into Calais. We need to sneak in. Suggestions?"

"We could all split up and go in from different directions, but that could be far too risky if the spy wants to divide us and conquer as Porthos so aptly told us was a common pirate's tool," Aramis was the first to speak.

"Or we could split into two groups and go in from different directions," Milady de Winter suggested after a moment. "Then we could meet at some easily recognizable place, like the docks."

"Possible," Porthos conceded, "But that won't help us find Christophe and get him the rest of the information."

"I think we just may have to go in together," Aramis said. "As discretely as possible, of course. After we get in, maybe then we should split up and look for Christophe."

"Sabine?" Athos asked for his wife's opinion.

"That will have to do. We'll all have to be alert, though, and if anyone falls into trouble we have to be able to signal the others that we've run into danger." Milady removed the last of her monogrammed handkerchiefs and handed one to each of the musketeers. "Drop this if you are in danger. If I run into anything I'll drop my smelling salts. The bag has my initials."

"Let's move," Athos said, directing Milady and Aramis to lead the way in since they were the best at sneaking into places unnoticed.

The four allies entered Calais. This time Porthos, Aramis, and Athos were playing the roles of servants and bodyguards to the wealthy *Comtesse de* Winter. The *comtesse* gestured imperiously, and the group proceeded into the market. Time to lose themselves in anonymity. Through sheer tenacity and no small dose of luck, Aramis was able to stick closest to Sabine, though the crowd threatened to pull them apart.

Athos and Porthos were not so fortunate.

The waves of bodies pushed them away from their two companions and nearly succeeded in parting Athos from Porthos.

Sabine leaned towards the one remaining musketeer. "A few more doors down," she said. "I have a contact that I can get in touch with about getting more information on the men that pass through Calais and on to England."

She dismounted; the crowd was comparatively sparse here. "Are you sure it's wise to go in alone?" Aramis asked.

"If you come with me, he'll tell me nothing. He doesn't like men that serve the king. He has a personal vendetta against the musketeers. Believe me, he'd recognize you." Milady ducked inside, leaving Aramis outside to wait for her.

"Fall back," Athos yelled over the noise to Porthos.

Porthos obeyed, and the musketeers maneuvered their way out of the crowd. They would happen to come to the market in Calais right in the middle of a festival. They really must have lousy timing.

"If we go around and double back," Porthos suggested, "we should be able to meet up with Aramis and the *Comtesse de* Winter. At least if they keep heading in the same direction as they were heading."

"We'll have to assume so. Let's go. Unless we get this mission done to Sabine's satisfaction, D'Artagnan dies," Athos reminded them unnecessarily, and they began a circuit to intercept their allies.

Two sets of ears were listening very closely to the conversation, especially when one of the men mentioned the name D'Artagnan.

Laurel raced across the close-crafted roofs and looked down to see a large man with a goatee and a blond-bearded man pass. She was right. That was Athos and Porthos. And they had been referring to Milady and Aramis. So those two had to be somewhere close by. Now how did she get down from these roofs? She had to draw their attention, and to call out to them would be very unwise.

Instead the young woman continued to follow their progress and witnessed as they were waylaid by several brigands in an empty alley. The odds were not good. Six to two. And each of the assailants was armed with primed pistols of pretty good quality. Athos and Porthos had only their swords.

Laurel watched helplessly as they were easily subdued and rendered unconscious. Suddenly, a seventh man appeared and instructed the brigands to take the two men away. Steadily, she stared at the man's back. He looked familiar. At that moment, he turned, and she caught sight of a pair of green eyes. She ducked down just in time to avoid his gaze, and then the alley was empty except for a single white handkerchief.

Laurel rolled to her feet and took off the way she had come. She had to find Aramis and Milady soon. Else she had a sinking suspicion they'd fall victim to the man with green eyes. Who was that man? A spy, hired hand, or some entirely unknown enemy?

Laurel jumped to another roof that overlooked the market. That was where Athos and Porthos had said they had gotten separated from their companions. She was nearly sure of it. Now, where could they be? They would have disguised themselves, and Sabine and Aramis were both so talented at disguising themselves that it could make her sick. Nor would she possibly recognize Sabine's horse, though she might recognize Aramis'.

She'd better recognize Aramis' horse, or things were going to get worse at an alarming rate. Her eyes caught the movements of several horses, grime-stained horses. A saddle shifted revealing a pure chestnut coat, and then the saddle shifted back. There! Aramis rode a chestnut mare.

Time to get off these roofs she had trapped herself on somehow. True, they were a good way to travel much of Calais without being seen, but you never were out of the sun nor were there any facilities. Why was it that it was always easier to get up than it was to get back down? There were no ladders, no ropes, nor anything she could make use of to climb down. Nor did she have time to trace her steps back to the blocks she had used to climb onto the rooftops originally.

She glanced down, and there was her good friend from earlier that morning—the very same straw cart. Laurel groaned. Maybe she really was insane or she had just lost all of her healthy respect for heights. On second thought, she was desperate, and that cart was about to leave. She flung herself from the roof, grabbing her hat to her head and gritting her teeth to keep from screaming.

"Umph." The air was forced from her, and she lay stunned for a moment, straw poking her, jabbing her all over. She spit several pieces out of her mouth and sat up, brushing the straw from her clothes. Only then did she notice the cart had stopped trying to move forward. Before she could bolt, a large peasant looked in the back of the cart and caught sight of her. She was in for it now.

This was not her day, she thought as he dragged her from the cart, yelling at her for ruining his product and demanding recompense. Of course, it was pretty ridiculous to say that she had ruined straw, but humans did the most ridiculous things; she was proof of that. The entire situation was proof of it! He shook her, and Laurel offered an apology, which he did not accept.

The burly man continued to rant about undisciplined heathens and called for the constable to come pick "this blasted lad" up and throw him in prison until he could repay the damage. As if throwing her in prision would get him his money . . . Laurel sincerely wished she had a gold piece on her, but she had spent the last of her money on the room and food.

Nevertheless, she had no intention of getting thrown in prison. With all her might, she kicked the man's shin and yelled at the top of her lungs, "Let me go or you'll be answering to my father." The man loosened his grasp long enough for her to wriggle free, and she bolted with the cart driver following right behind her.

Suddenly, a tall lean man stepped between Laurel and her pursuer. He snagged Laurel's arm firmly in his grasp, nearly yanking it out of its socket in his effort to bring Laurel to a halt.

He put his other hand up to stall the man. "I must apologize for the inconvenience and any damages that have been caused. I'm afraid my brother is still in an unfortunately rebellious stage."

"Your brother ruined my crop," the man protested.

"We are working at instilling some discipline in him. However," the tall man drew a pouch out and removed several pistoles and a gold piece, "I believe this should cover any damages and inconvenience my brother has put you through." The man goggled at the amount of money, but he took it and left without comment, despite his desire to throttle the young boy. No sense in pressing his luck.

The youth squirmed in his rescuer's grasp, and the man pulled Laurel just out of sight of the curious onlookers who had finally gone back to their business. "Enough, Christophe," he warned, and Laurel stared at the man's face and recognized the piercing dark eyes with gold flecks. Aramis.

Sudden relief left her limp. "Don't you dare faint on me now," he teased, and she glared at him and then settled for leading him further aside so that she could talk with him.

Once Laurel was satisfied with their relative privacy, she leaned against the wall and took several deep breaths. "If you were trying to draw attention to yourself by snagging a ride on that cart, you did succeed quite admirably."

"Aramis, you well know I didn't do that. I thought I saw your horse from the roofs and that was the only way I could think of to get down. So I jumped and you know what happened after that," she finished lamely.

"I will not even ask what you were doing on the rooftops," Aramis commented. He didn't really want to know. "Still I am glad I found you. Milady de Winter's got the papers you need. She should be out of the office momentarily, and then you can get them from her."

"One positive thing at least," she mumbled, and Aramis shot a glance at the woman. "Aramis, someone is after all of you. I don't know how he singled you out. I don't even know why. All I know is it has a great deal to do with a man with green eyes."

"What's this about a man with green eyes?" Milady interrupted as she saw Aramis talking to a young lad Sabine recognized as her sister. She seemed to recall something from Thomas' message that mentioned a man with green eyes.

Laurel shifted her attention to the other woman and then back to the musketeer. "He's captured Athos and Porthos just about, I'd say, a half hour or hour ago."

"And now he's after me and Aramis?" Sabine asked for confirmation, and Laurel supported her conclusion. "We'd better get out of here," the *comtesse* said, mounting her horse and seating herself as comfortably as possible on the sidesaddle. Aramis mounted his own horse and pulled Laurel up after him.

The trio set off, Milady in the lead. Aramis leaned forward, his chest brushing Laurel's back, and whispered in her ear. "Where did you leave your horse, or should I even bother asking?"

Laurel's immediate response was a groan. She cocked her neck back to look at him while she was speaking. "We kind of got separated after I jumped out a window this morning." Aramis didn't even bother to comment on her multiple jumping episodes of the day. His eyes said it all.

Laurel walked into the inn, and the first person she ran into was the innkeeper's wife. Swiftly, perhaps a bit too eagerly, she introduced Aramis as her brother and Sabine as her sister. The woman took Aramis to task for letting a young lad loose on the streets, and he silently took it. Gracefully, he apologized for his brother's behavior, and the trio made their way to the room Laurel had let. Aramis was beginning to suspect why Laurel might have jumped out of a window this morning, and he wouldn't be at all surprised to find a certain overprotective woman at the root of it.

Laurel sank into the bed and leaned her head against the bedpost. It was wonderful to be out of the beating sun. "Sabine, what do you know about a man with green eyes?"

Sabine did not answer. Instead she asked Aramis if he had the papers Athos had given into Aramis' care. He did. The *comtesse* took out her own papers and added them to the documents Aramis had placed on the bed beside Laurel.

"I do believe that between the three of us we have all the information that Thomas uncovered about this spy," Milady said, glancing at the collection of papers. "Plus, my source gave me the name of several ships that are bound for England with mysterious passengers that are not really passengers booked aboard. Oh, and as to a man with green eyes, Laurel. Your father mentioned that the closest he ever got to the spy he suspects is responsible for smuggling state secrets to England was close enough to see his green eyes, not a face, just the eyes."

"So we've found our spy then," Aramis remarked.

"Actually he found Porthos and Athos, and he's looking for all of us. I'm sure of it," Laurel contradicted.

"What did you find out about the ships?" Aramis asked Milady.

"The Treader, the Trade Wind, and the Minerva all leave with pseudo passengers within the next thirty hours. Maybe sooner," Milady replied.

Laurel's head shot away from the post, and the fatigue drained from her face. She was suddenly alert. "Did you say the Minerva?" Milady nodded. "Then we know which ship our nameless, faceless spy with green eyes will be taking to England. Which leaves us with several problems. How do we surprise him and keep him from England, for starters?"

"And what happened to Porthos and Athos, and how do we avoid his trap while setting our own?" Aramis added.

* * * * * * * * * * *

Constance stirred and opened her eyes to find her head lolling against D'Artagnan's chest. Stripes of sunlight caressed her cheeks. The horse was slowly plodding along, and she noticed D'Artagnan was fighting a losing battle to keep his eyes open. How long had they been riding? Apparently they'd made it through the night without being captured or killed or falling from the horse, but she'd no idea how far away they might have gotten.

The young dark-haired woman faced forward in the saddle and placed her own hands on the reins, bringing the mare to a stop. She soothed the horse and turned and gently shook the young musketeer. "D'Artagnan, D'Artagnan," she called softly.

"Hmm." The man started and came to wakefulness, looking down into Constance's brown eyes. "What?"

"Do you have any idea how long we've been going?"

The musketeer looked around him and up at the clouded sky. That was a distinct relief. For once he was glad to have an overcast day; it kept things cooler. "I'd guess it's approaching midday or maybe even past. We seem to have made pretty good time. I even recognize this territory. Athos, Porthos, Aramis, Christophe, and I came through here on our way up from Marseille."

"So we're quite a few leagues away from where we last were?" she wanted him to confirm. And who was Christophe? She knew Athos, Porthos, and Aramis, but no one named Christophe. Plus, it was rather annoying to have heard the name several times and still be absolutely clueless as to who the person was.

"I'd say we're actually about back where we started. Must be somewhere near Beauvais." Porthos' instructions about the North Star had actually worked, or so it seemed thus far. D'Artagnan closed his eyes briefly. He had to find his friends, but he couldn't abandon Constance either, but to take her with him?

"D'Artagnan, what's wrong?" There was concern in the woman's voice and in her light touch to his cheek. "Is it what you told me about Milady de Winter and your friends?" she asked, still finding it hard to believe the *comtesse* could have so easily deceived her and those aforementioned friends. Such gullibility was rather mortifying to her sensibility.

"I have to find my friends, but to bring you with me is dangerous to your reputation and your life," he told her honestly. "Do you have any safe place that you could stay anywhere near here?" D'Artagnan directed the question at her while squeezing his knees against the horse's flanks and urging it forward at a moderate pace that didn't deter him from being able to continue his conversation with Constance.

She shook her head. "My family lives mostly in the east near Alsace, and the only other place I could really go is Paris and back to the queen. Where are you headed?" she asked, hoping he might be able to prompt her with an idea to solve their problem if she knew their direction.

"Calais." By his tone she could tell that he felt he had to get there and very quickly, and she knew she truly would only be in the way. She simply wasn't a superb rider; nor did she have any fighting skills or any experience in danger outside of palace intrigue. As much as she wanted to go along with him, she knew that would be very foolhardy. Romantic fool, moonling, she may have been, but she was fairly realistic, most days.

The couple rode on, and the day dragged into later afternoon. As evening arrived the two young people had made it past Beauvais without a sign of pursuit, and their only stops had been a very brief water, food, and facilities stop. "D'Artagnan," Constance broke the silence. "Isn't there a convent near here?"

He shrugged his shoulders. "I think there is, about a league or so southwest of here."

The woman pointed in the direction and said, "Take me there."

The musketeer directed his horse as she spoke, and did just that, and shortly thereafter Constance was proven correct as a stone structure loomed before them. The couple continued to the door, and D'Artagnan helped Constance dismount after doing so himself. Constance turned to D'Artagnan and from a secret pouch took several gold coins and gave them to the young man. "Take them, D'Artagnan, and get to Calais as quickly as you can. I'll be waiting for you. Good luck, dearest," she said, kissing him on the cheek, and turned to rap the knocker against the door.

It opened and a sister looked at the young couple that stood on the doorstep. The young woman appealed to the sister for shelter, and the sister's disapproval vanished. It was not a couple set on eloping. The sister took Constance in and D'Artagnan remounted his horse, setting off as quickly as he could for Calais. *Grâce à Dieu*, his horse was well rested after the slow pace of the past day or two. Or at least he hoped it would prove the case.

* * * * * * * * * * *

Thunk. Drip. Clunk. The floor vibrated under the impact of several unidentified objects a distance away. Drip. Drip. Beads of water slithered down the wall and pooled together at the bottom.

"Aagh." Porthos flung the rat from his chest, waking all at once to a massive headache and a darkened, humid cell. Experimentally he tested his wrists and ankles. They were no longer bound, however, they protested the sudden return of circulation. Instinctively, he reached for his sword, discovering it was not there and neither were all his other assorted weapons nor his money. Even his hat and favorite sash, a gift from the queen of America, according to him, were nowhere to be found.

Tired of gazing at the ceiling of the dimly lit room, he pulled himself up to a crouch and surveyed his surroundings. He was upon a bale of straw that served as a bed. Nearby there was a single bucket that would have to serve the purpose of a bedpan. In another pail sat filthy, film-covered water.

Closer to the barred door lay an unmoving figure. Porthos made his way over to the motionless man. Athos in a state of undress and dishevelment he usually only achieved after a very hard bout of drinking. He grasped the man's wrist and felt the steady pulse beneath his fingertips.

The large man crouched back on his heels, and his stomach grumbled. He suppressed his thoughts of food and forced himself to assess how badly Athos was injured. The only sign of injury he found was a large egg-sized lump on the back of Athos' head. Obviously he'd been subdued a little more harshly than Porthos.

The large musketeer scooched the pail over to Athos' side and dipped his fingers in the water, sprinkling Athos' face with the liquid while saying, "Time to wake up, *mon cher* Athos, even though I know how much you *really* want your beauty sleep."

Porthos shook another handful of water on the older musketeer's face, and, sputtering, he came to consciousness. Athos' dull blue eyes fixed blurrily on the figure looming over him before finally coming to clarity. "By all that is sacred, Porthos, you would have to employ rather distasteful methods to wake a man up," he said, wiping the slimy water from his face. "Where are we?"

"Sadly, I do believe that we have been detained for an indeterminate amount of time." Porthos even had no idea whether it was night or day, as there were no windows in the stuffy cramped cell. "Unfortunately, I was not informed as to where I was being taken when we were so rudely abducted, or I'd love to share the information with you."

"Thanks a lot, Porthos," Athos said in a tone that was far from being one of thankfulness. He sat rubbing the back of his head where the nice lump was. "I don't suppose you've found a way out of here either?"

"I regret to inform you that I have entirely failed in that duty. We are nicely outwitted and trapped by an unknown assailant for an unknown reason," Porthos replied with a longer answer than necessary, as usual. Though he had a few general ideas about why they were rotting away in this cell.

"Lovely," Athos remarked, never a man of more words than strictly necessary.

A plate on the cell door slid open and both musketeers looked up at the sound and saw a pair of green eyes observing them. "Greetings, gentlemen," the green-eyed man said. "I hope you enjoy your accommodations. I do regret I shall have to be leaving you very soon, but you should have company quite shortly. Until then, I leave you." With that the green-eyed man slid two bowls of gruel through the grating, which Athos and Porthos grasped, and the grating was slid back into place.

"He's after Aramis and Milady," Athos commented, and Porthos did not gainsay him. Athos was right. This was beginning to make a frightening amount of sense. They hadn't found the spy. He had found them and was putting them out of commission. The only question that remained was how he would dispose of them.

"It is set." Aramis informed Milady and Laurel that he had indeed talked to the *capitaine* of the Minerva and paid him handsomely to put two more passengers on his ship without notifying the authorities or anyone else to the fact he was taking on passengers bound for Dover.

"How long until we are to board?" Milady inquired.

"I managed to convince him to allow us to board early. That means we board tonight, at dusk, and shortly thereafter he plans to sail for England," Aramis enlightened them using a polite euphemism rather than saying he had manipulated and bribed the *capitaine* into allowing them to board early and letting him know the precise time of departure.

"Laurel," Milady called, and her stepsister looked up from the paper she had been intently studying as if she were searching for any clue that might pinpoint the spy's weaknesses and allow her to understand how his mind operated.

"Sabine, please try to remember to call me Christophe. If someone discovers I am not exactly what I seem, you well know it could mean all our lives." Milady stood corrected; she did know better, it had just momentarily slipped her mind. If anyone ever overheard a slip like that, everything was over before it really even got started. "So you and Aramis are booked aboard the ship? Were either of you two able to find any clue as to where Athos and Porthos are or what happened to them?"

"My sources have nothing," Sabine said, contempt underlying the words. "All I was able to find was the handkerchief, one of them used to signal that there was danger." Wait. There was something, maybe. "Christophe, you were there when they were captured, right?"

"Right."

"You have gotten a chance to know the city quite well due to your trips here with Thomas?" Again Laurel confirmed this fact. It had been a while though. "How far do you think two men like Athos and Porthos could have been taken and not be seen? In other words, how could they have disappeared so quickly when you were watching everything, barring a very brief instant of time?" Milady asked.

"They couldn't have. In that area of Calais too many people are nearby, and the only way the buildings are connected is by roof. There are no tunnels or secret doors in that area of town." At least none that she knew of.

"Then they have to be nearby," Aramis observed. "Any idea where?"

"None," Laurel replied. "There are so many cellars and old below-ground prisons in that area, and to go snooping around in each of those would arouse a great deal of suspicion." There was a pause, and Laurel stashed the precious documents and said, "I'm not stowing away this evening."

"Then what about the plan?" Milady said, voicing Aramis' concern as well.

"You're not going to like the way I'm changing it."

"I did not think we would," Aramis commented dourly. "So what is it?"

The swishing waters of the tide rolling in and out against the shore could be heard for a good league as Calais settled down for the night, clearing the remnants of the festival away. Dusk was fast approaching, and the last of the peasants were packing up their carts and heading for home. Two passengers were hustled aboard a ship, very discreetly, so that no one would catch sight of them.

The sun sank further on the horizon in a brilliant blaze of gold, red, orange, and yellow. The air was still as Laurel slipped through the streets, shadowlike and unnoticed. She was taking a great gamble, but then again there were only two groups that might sell out the services of hidden prisons at short notice and do so very quietly—to her way of logic, that was. Only one of those locations was near the alley where her friends had been attacked. If she was right, the spy had hurriedly arranged this trap at the last minute and therefore had to turn to the high-priced groups that would provide such a service.

Her feet brought her back to the alley, and she tiptoed down the rough path, drawing closer to a nearby door. Now where had her father said he suspected a secret dungeon to have been built?

Laurel closed her eyes. Three steps to the right. A lunge. Turn ninety degrees. Two more steps right and several small steps forward. She opened her eyes, looking for the obvious. Her father had been convinced he had found the entrance, yet he had never had time to investigate, just those cryptic directions. Now what could he have meant?

The hiss of a cat made her catch her breath. Timing was crucial. Hopefully, the green-eyed man had just left for the docks, and she'd be able to get in, then out with her friends and back to the docks before the Minerva was ready to cast off.

Of course, the refuse pile. It would have to be the refuse pile. The woman rolled up her sleeves and braced herself for the distasteful task of moving it aside. She worked quickly, ignoring the gritty feeling and the stench. The pile was shifted in a matter of a few minutes, and below was a trap door.

Pay dirt! Laurel knelt down and released the catch. If she'd known exactly where to look, she'd only have had to move two items and the door would have been accessible. She examined the mechanism. It was simple, but ingenious, set to trigger a slight disturbance that would cause the refuse to fall back on top of it when you closed it—that is if you had left most of the refuse undisturbed—She hadn't.

Wasting no further time, she climbed down the ladder, closing the door after her. She emerged into a dank, ill-lit stone corridor that merged with a main corridor after only a few steps. The woman glanced around the corner. To her left were four cells. To her right a guard sat slumped over a mug of ale, and several empty, uncorked bottles littered the floor. Lady luck was really favoring her tonight. But no need to press her luck too far. In and out, quickly.

Stealthily, she crawled upon the floor until she was just below the snoring guard. The ring of keys dangled out of his pocket, nearly falling out. Now, to make him shift so the keys would fall. With one hand she tickled the back of his neck very lightly, and the other she placed directly under the key ring. The man shifted in an effort to fend off the tickling fingers, and the key ring fell into her waiting hand. For several moments she waited, but he stirred no more. Firmly she grasped the keys so they wouldn't jingle, and she scurried in the opposite direction, towards the cells.

First she glanced in one cell, then the next, and the next. She stopped at the last door. If this wasn't it, she just might want to shoot herself. She peered through a crack in the grating and saw two men. *Oui!* It was them. Quickly she experimented with the keys and found one that fit. She then opened the grate a fraction and whispered, "Athos." The man looked up. "It's me," she informed the man as she turned the key. The lock slid open, and she opened the door.

With uncustomary quietness, Porthos told her, "You are darn lucky you warned us you were coming in or we could have strangled you, and you are darn lucky we recognized your voice."

Athos made no recriminations. There wasn't time. "Which way is out?"

Laurel gestured with her head and led them back to the trap door, which she pushed open, letting in the outside air. The three companions climbed the ladder, one after the other, and emerged into the alley, closing the door behind them. Laurel took off at a run, and her two companions followed her, surprisingly quietly. They rounded several corners and stopped. "I'm sorry I couldn't get your horses. I couldn't risk it. Nor could I get you your swords. However," she lifted the lid off the barrel and drew two new swords of reasonable quality, handing one to each man, "Aramis was able to purchase these."

Athos inspected the blade. "They'll do. Where is Aramis?"

"Where we're headed right now . . . the docks," she said. There was no need for her to tell them to be careful. They well knew the man they were stalking was canny and had probably taken precautions against anyone who might follow him to his ship. Which probably indicated that he did not travel alone.

A cloaked man trailed by several other men approached the docked ship. The cloaked man stopped and called out asking for permission to come aboard. It was granted, and he surveyed the ship that was hidden in the early night shadows; the sun had just finished setting. Motioning for the men to follow him, he stepped aboard and was greeted by the *capitaine*. No other sailors were in sight. The green-eyed man noted their absence. Something was decidedly off. A trap!

He drew his sword and put it to the *capitaine's* throat. The seven hired men also drew their swords and waited. "Who's paying you to trap me?" The *capitaine* did not respond so the sword was pushed further into the rough skin of the *capitaine's* throat, and he repeated his question.

"No one," the *capitaine* broke down and stuttered. "Honest. A man bribed his way to get on board early as a passenger, but when he came aboard he and his lady friend eliminated my men one by one. Said if I didn't do exactly as they said, my men would die and me after them," the *capitaine* blubbered, recalling the coldness of the lady when she had delivered her ultimatum. He'd not doubted for an instant she had meant what she said, that she would follow through on her threat.

The green-eyed man smiled, closer to a smirk, and saying, "*Merci,*" plunged the sword into the man's throat, killing him almost instantly, before the *capitaine* had a chance to scream. The corpse fell to the deck, and the spy turned to his men. "Tear this ship apart. I want that man and his *chère-amie* found."

The spy swept the rigging aside, his bloody blade still in hand. Behind him he heard a soft thud, and he whirled to see a tall black haired-man wielding a sword. "I don't think it will be necessary to tear this ship apart," Aramis said, his voice very cold. Murder was something he found impossible to condone.

"You're a dead man," the green-eyed man told him. There was no trace of boasting in his tone.

"We will see about that," Aramis replied, parrying the blade, knowing that all too soon the other swordfighters would be drawn to the commotion. Laurel had better arrive and with his friends, and that meant now. "You've got a lot to answer to God for, and I intend to let Him wreak His justice."

Milady cursed fluently to herself as she slipped among the ship's riggings right above several fighters. She was no fighter, and Aramis simply could not fight eight men alone no matter how good he was. Already, the other men were starting to offer assistance to the spy. Well, there was no avoiding it; she'd have to reveal her location, she thought grimly.

She loosed the comb that served as a miniature dagger from her hair and sawed a rope with it. Strand by strand it broke apart and finally the rope was severed, sending a sandbag plummeting down on one unsuspecting man, putting him out of commission.

Another man pointed in her direction and three men set off in pursuit of her. At least she had distracted three of the men from Aramis, but he would soon be surrounded.

"Ladies and gentlemen, here comes the cavalry," Porthos announced, stepping on board and leveling his sword against one of Aramis' would-be opponents. *"En garde,"* he said as Athos and Laurel slipped on board behind him and engaged several of the men, leaving Aramis alone to deal with the spy.

The three soldiers who had been in pursuit of Milady stopped and turned back, approaching the new threat. The air was filled with the clashing of swords, labored breathing, grunts of exertion, punctuated by screams of pain.

In his usual blustery, showy, fashion Porthos went after two of the soldiers while Athos contented himself by dealing with one. Amazing what a brief period of incarceration and little food could do to one's endurance.

Laurel had little choice in her opponents; two went after her, thinking her the easiest of their prey. Yet despite fatigue and lack of adequate nourishment in the past days she held her own against them, but the depravation had taken a toll on her quickness. All that seemed to keep her from falling to the pair of mercenaries was her greater skill at fencing.

Another man crept towards Athos, and Porthos yelled a warning to his friend just in time for Athos to avoid a downward sword thrust. The final soldier made his way towards Aramis.

Athos lunged away from another thrust and caught sight of another fighter pushing a sandbag away and getting to his feet, preparing to join the fray. The odds just kept getting worse.

At the same moment, Aramis was forced to retreat, and his foot got tangled in a length of rope. He stumbled and quickly regained his balance. He was not quick enough to avoid the entirety of the spy's attack, and he felt the blade cut a line upward from his right breast to right shoulder. "Ayee," he screamed, but was able to continue. This man was good, very good, Aramis remarked. Apparently, his luck had run out.

With a quick thrust, Porthos gutted one of his assailants and turned his complete attention to battling another. However, he forbore taunting the soldier. He didn't have the breath to do so. His companions failed to notice that the man who had been unconscious had recovered his sword and was heading for Porthos.

The fighter was about to plunge the blade into Porthos' back when a man yelled, and the attacker was distracted just long enough for the man to dance from the railing to the deck. Quickly, he engaged and parried expertly, driving the unsteady soldier backward and back again. The young man made a rapid, penetrating slash against the mercenary, wounding him from thigh to gut. The wounded man wobbled unsteadily, and Porthos' rescuer took advantage of the situation, pushing him over the edge of the boat and into the channel.

Meanwhile Laurel danced away from one opponent and confronted another. *Saperlipopette*, she wanted a breather. Lunge and glide. Another swift stroke, parry from behind, then from in front. Fighting two good opponents was about as much fun as a one-way ticket to hell. There it was. An opening! She took it and with one deft thrust cut the man open from groin to chest.

Porthos tidily dispatched his other opponent and turned, his bloody sword in hand, to face his rescuer. "*Nom de nom,* D'Artagnan! So you finally got here. What took you so long?"

"I hardly had any control over that. I had to rescue Constance and then escape. Then I almost ran my horse to death and had to get another to ride to the ground in order to get to Calais now." D'Artagnan paused for breath and took several steps towards Athos. "Porthos, what do you say we help Athos out?"

"Ooh, I like your thinking. Shall we?" he inquired, and they both charged into the fray, drawing away one soldier and allowing Athos to eliminate his other opponent.

Athos stood, gasping for breath as he watched D'Artagnan and Porthos dispose of the soldier. Momentarily unoccupied, they turned their attention to their other two companions. The spy had just been relieved by one of the two remaining mercenaries, and with a desperate lunge Laurel finished off her second opponent. The exhausted woman laid her longsword at her feet and clutched her knees, chest heaving and gasping for breath.

"I do believe they have it under control," Porthos told his companions, but they stood ready to offer any assistance should it become needed.

Milady made her way down from above as Aramis threw his sword from his right hand to his left and neatly sliced the man's neck from ear to ear. "Aramis," Milady yelled at the musketeer closest to her sister and pointed. "The spy's after Christophe, and Christophe doesn't see the man."

Having no time to pamper his shoulder, Aramis dashed after the green-eyed man who made a slash downward just as Laurel frantically grabbed her blade and deflected it somewhat. However, her sword flew from her hand, and the spy's sword cut her from shoulder to elbow. The man prepared to deal her a deathblow when Aramis parried the stroke, and the spy turned with surprise on the musketeer. "I suggest you drop your sword. You are sadly outnumbered."

Thinking his right shoulder out of action, the spy lunged in that direction at Aramis, but Aramis swiftly switched hands again, tearing the wound farther open, but enabling himself to hit the spy's sword with such impact that the sword shot from the spy's hand. Aramis leveled his sword at the man's neck and was sorely tempted to saw his head from his neck, but he didn't. Instead he said to his friends, "Take this man into custody in the name of the King of France. The charge is treason and murder."

As Porthos and D'Artagnan rushed to do so, Milady came to Athos' side. At the same instant the spy said, "Aramis, you just don't have the courage to finish me off, do you?"

Aramis recognized that voice. He hadn't really paid much attention to it earlier, but now that he thought about it, he knew that voice. Aramis stared closely at the green-eyed man Porthos and D'Artagnan had now grasped firmly. *Le Duc* d'Amiens. It wasn't possible! Truly not possible. Treason in the highest ranks of the French government. "I think not, Georges. I'll leave the king to decide what to do with you. It is the least I can do for my country and king," he said his voice liberally tinged with disgust.

Aramis turned from the *duc* and knelt beside the wounded woman who was clutching her shoulder, her left shoulder. He set his sword aside and touched her right arm. "Christophe, are you all right?" he asked with real concern.

"Aramis, look who's talking. Your wound's as bad as mine. No, worse. I'll be all right," she assured him, clambering to her feet with Aramis' assistance. Of course, she was not at all happy that her sword arm was put out of commission. Sure, she could fight right-handed, but her left was better.

Athos, as was often the case, took charge, instructing Porthos and D'Artagnan to escort their prisoner to a nice holding cell while Sabine escorted the injured members off the ship and into better light where she could get a closer look at their wounds. All in all, a good night's work. Still Athos had a bargain to fulfill, and Sabine would see to it that he and Laurel did so. That, and Laurel had a feeling this entire thing had been far too easy.

Section Six

"Sit down," Athos ordered Aramis. The unbending voice allowed for no defiance, and Aramis sank back down heavily. "Christophe," he said to the woman as she got up to try to sneak out of the room, "that goes doubly for you." This always happened whenever Aramis was injured—which wasn't very often. He was a lousy patient, and Laurel was trying, and succeeding remarkably well, to outdo him in that department.

"Okay, both of you, let's get something straight. Until you allow us to change your bandages and stitch the wounds we can't and won't go anywhere." Plus, Athos still had to wait for Porthos to come back with his sash, their horses, and their swords.

"What about getting back to Paris before the king sends out warrants for our arrest?" Aramis contended. "We have no time to spare."

"My point exactly," the irritated Athos informed the walking wounded. "Put it this way, until this task is taken care of we are going nowhere. I want both of you healthy enough to ride pretty hard for Paris, and with those wounds unstitched it's too likely you'll injure yourself worse, and then we truly will never get back in time." Nor did he want to see Aramis and the woman injure themselves worse due to an irritating level of stubbornness. He turned to Laurel. "Well, do you have anything to add?"

Her first instinct was to say *oui*, insist she was in a lot better shape than Aramis, and that her shoulder was not that bad, but she reconsidered. Porthos had already threatened to strangle her if she protested one more time and that had been while Milady had been bandaging her shoulder earlier this evening; and her sister had seconded the man. Now Athos looked ready to do the same thing.

The prospect of braving Athos' ire was not one even she wished to take on at this juncture in time. She was not up to it. Deciding on this wiser course of action, she reluctantly shook her head, and the oldest musketeer had Sabine see to her sister while he saw to Aramis. D'Artagnan wasn't missing anything by being outside by the cellar guarding the spy. Athos almost wished he were with either Porthos or D'Artagnan. Anywhere except attending these two aggravating patients who were rubbing his fraying temper even more raw.

Athos finished sewing Aramis up and rebandaged the wound before allowing his friend to don his clean tunic, very carefully so as to avoid stretching the gash and tearing the stitches from his breast. Laurel came up behind the man, gently cradling the arm that Sabine had just finished tending to. "Actually, Athos, I do have something to add," she began and quickly rushed on. "It's nothing having to do with the wound. I need to talk with you in private, at the earliest possible moment."

The blond-haired man glanced from his wife to Aramis and asked if they would mind leaving him and Christophe alone for a few minutes. They excused themselves with admirable aplomb and left Laurel and Athos alone in the room. "Why do I have a feeling I'm not going to like what you have to say?"

"Probably because you're right," she said in a tone that said she hated being the bearer of bad tidings. Messengers bearing bad tidings often had bad things happen to them. Finally, she gathered her courage and met Athos' eyes with her own, never dropping her gaze. "I made Sabine a promise, on my word, and I cannot go back on it. Nor do I think you would want to ask me to."

"Let me be the judge of that," he replied gesturing, for the woman to go on. He was beginning to hate it when Laurel employed that particular tone.

Her chest heaved once, but her gaze didn't waver. Blunt it would have to be. "You have a son, Athos, you and Sabine." Leveled, the man stared into her eyes for a few long seconds, then dropped heavily into a nearby chair and propped his chin on his hand as he forced his attention to focus back on the woman.

"*Comment*?" How . . .

"He's almost four years old, and when Richelieu spared Sabine, he spared her son as well," Laurel continued, despite the expression of surprise and disbelief that had escaped Athos. "So now he's using her son as insurance to make sure that she does not dare cross him. I promised her that you and I would free the boy from the cardinal's residence in Paris after we captured the spy."

A long moment, the older musketeer seemed too stunned to speak. "I should have known," Athos finally chastised himself bitterly. He should have suspected Sabine had been pregnant, but he'd still thrown her out without letting her try to explain to him.

Laurel gripped his broad muscular shoulder tightly with her right hand. She shook him and shook him fairly hard, trying to break through his melancholy. "Stop this, Athos. Stop this, you hear? Hating yourself and feeling guilty does not help the situation. Your son needs to be rescued before the cardinal discovers Sabine has betrayed him, and he decides to take his revenge on the child."

Athos regained his control and asked rhetorically, "So Sabine gets away again without atoning for her crimes, and she'll take my son with her?"

"I don't know," Laurel said helplessly, replying to the rhetorical question, forbearing to point out that it was their son. "All I can advise you to do is to talk to her. She's not as corrupted and warped as she appears. She still cares and has a healthy sense of right and wrong." Though she often didn't pay it any heed.

"I'll be letting you know when I need your help in this," the man informed her, surprising himself by the words that came out next, the level of confidence that he was showing already in this young woman. "But right now I just need to be alone to think, okay, Laurel? I've got to come to grips with this myself before I can turn to any of my friends. Just go . . . I beg you."

Pursing her lips, she nodded and withdrew from the room.

The next day, an hour before midday, the musketeers set off at a brisk pace for Paris. Athos and D'Artagnan rode in front, and Porthos and Milady picked up the rear while Aramis and Laurel were placed in the middle so they could be most protected. Not to mention, it allowed them to keep the pace more moderate so that their injured companions didn't injure themselves more by trying to push the pace. Between and slightly in front of Aramis and Laurel, right where four people could watch him, the spy rode bound to his horse. Their formation was tight enough that the *Duc* d'Amiens could not force his horse out between the other riders' mounts. Theoretically.

"Athos," D'Artagnan looked askance to Athos, "what about getting Constance from the convent?"

"Unfortunately, unless we get back in roughly three days, getting Constance won't do any good. You'll have to go back for her after we report to *Capitaine de* Treville."

The young musketeer lapsed into silence, resigned to the inevitable. Athos was right. He just didn't like it. Too much to go wrong, especially with Milady still free. That was another thing he didn't understand. Why had Athos prevented them from putting her under arrest too? It didn't make sense. So very little did anymore—if it ever had in the first place.

A sudden violent wind kicked up, and Laurel was unable to prevent her hat from flying from her head and smack into the middle of Georges' back as he rode stiffly in front of her. The green-eyed man looked back in time to see Laurel's long hair torn down from its bun by the wind as her hat landed in his lap.

He should have guessed earlier, Georges criticized himself. Of course, the lad was Thomas' d'Anlass' daughter disguised. Thomas always had been a queer one—one of the few men who would have condoned such behavior in a daughter. Georges slowed his horse so that he came even with the woman, offering her the hat awkwardy with bound hands. After the briefest of hesitations, she snatched it from his grasp and placed it swiftly on her head.

Quietly enough so that only she could hear, he spoke. "So nice to finally meet Thomas d'Anlass' daughter. He was a worthy opponent; he almost caught me." Laurel maintained a stony silence. Do not respond, she coached herself. "You know he'd really be quite proud of you, if he were still alive," Georges commented and she shot a glare at him. As he had planned, her glance was drawn to a small item he attemped to roll between his fingers. "Don't tell me you didn't know your father was killed in Belgium? Shot twice as I recall." Again her eyes went to the item. *Non*! Her father's signet ring. But . . .

Laurel wanted to deny his words and the truth of the token in the man's hands, wanted to accuse him of lying. Yet even without that subtle prod she knew with an unearthly certainty she'd never be able to explain that Thomas' death had to have been part of the reason she had felt so uneasy, edgy, for some time now. *Satané homme*. "Go to the devil," she commanded him and took off from the group, allowing her horse to go as quickly as it pleased, outdistancing her party. Too bad she didn't have Rebelle. He would have understood and really given her a good gallop.

Georges simply smirked, calmly self-satisfied by destroying another person's life and what little peace they had been able to find. Porthos rode up quickly to flank Georges and draw him to a stop demanding to know what he'd said to Laurel. The spy stared in silence and remarkably deftly slipped the signet ring up his sleeve as Sabine rode up to inform Athos and D'Artagnan what had happened. As for Aramis, he quickly took off in pursuit of the young woman, wondering what had set her off, his brow furrowed with concern. Once again that out-of-control temper of hers was putting her in danger.

Milady succinctly apprised Athos and D'Artagnan of the situation as they rode back to circle the spy and his stationary horse. At that precise moment, D'Artagnan caught sight of Aramis riding all out after Laurel and turned to pursue him when Athos and Porthos both stayed him.

This time Porthos took Athos' words right out of his mouth. "Let Aramis take care of this. We can't afford to have any less then four of us watching our delightful guest here. I'm sure he'll be more than willing to cooperate with us." And as Porthos spoke, Athos drew the pistol he'd purchased in Calais, primed it, and leveled it at the spy, a preventative measure to ensure their guest decided to stay in their company while Aramis was tangling with the Laurel situation.

Aramis spurred his mare on faster, recklessly fast, gaining on Laurel's smaller horse. The muscles of the horse rolled and bulged beneath him, and he winced as he jarred his injured shoulder. That woman was really moving, moving so hard and fast that the hat had been blown free again and that her braid had been blown from her hair, leaving it to trail along behind her like a banner. Yet it looked like her horse was slowing and possibly fatigued, so he urged his laboring mare faster, gaining on her and finally drawing up beside her.

In an instant he appraised the situation. Dangerous. Explosive. But there seemed to be no other viable choice left to him. His good hand snagged outward, and he grabbed for the reins of the other horse and urged the animal to a stop even as he pulled his own mount to a halt. Still holding the reins, he jumped from his horse to the ground. Laurel altered her grip on the reins and sent a command to the animal to urge the mare on again. Halfway through the motions, Aramis interrupted, placing a restraining hand on the halter and halting the mare before she could obey.

Startled by the sudden loss of balance and control, the woman floundered and impacted against the musketeer's chest. Barely, the man remained standing as her body jarred his wounded shoulder more than the hard ride had. Almost, Aramis didn't remain upright as he felt her fists pounding his pain-filled body. He was going to be a lucky man if the stitches didn't tear, if they hadn't torn already. On second thought, he was really not a very lucky man. Not if one threw the unpredictable Laurel into the mix, at any rate. Dangerous woman.

"*Ca suffit*, that's enough, Laurel," he told her firmly to stop. "Stop struggling. I'll let you go if you promise not to run off again. Promise me, Laurel," he said, shaking her much more roughly than he had intended. "*Votre parole*," he repeated implacably, insisting that she give her word.

"I promise," she said softly in a tone that belied her frantic state. He set her to her feet, and she looked up at him. "What do you want?" Why had he come? Her tone was accusatory and venomous. Never had she been very tolerant of being at the disadvantage. And this man had a way of rubbing her the wrong way—a gift to be sure.

"You can't just go galloping off like that. That spy could have escaped. He still could."

"You should have killed him when you had the chance," she flung the words at him like the barbs they were. That man, Georges, had no touch with normal human feelings. Cold blooded. · She fought back the shiver, knowing the *Duc* d'Amiens would be capable of doing something even more unspeakable to her and would if he were given the chance. Evil man, perhaps even beyond redemption. Sabine had nothing on the man. Maybe her stepsister even realized that.

"It wasn't my right to administer justice," he protested, his usual controlled demeanor obliterated. "Laurel, that's not what this is about. What happened to make you tear off like that? It's not like you to be that careless. Reckless, yes, but definitely not that careless."

"You wouldn't under . . ." She cut herself off.

"What *wouldn't* I understand?" he asked, his tone low and soothing.

"Just leave me alone, Aramis. Leave me alone, you b—" The rest of the invective was lost in an almost growl. "I don't want your comfort. I don't want your regrets or your pity. Go away! Well, didn't you hear me? I said, go away!" Devil was going to use her words against her. That much she saw coming and desperately wanted to head it off.

"No," he said firmly. "That's it, you're afraid I'd understand, and you don't want me to." She switched her gaze to the ground, unable to meet his eyes. For if he saw her eyes he'd know he was exactly right, as he was so annoyingly often. "Remember when you asked me to trust you? How can I ever possibly learn to trust you if you won't even try to trust me? *Chérie*, it goes both ways."

She turned her back on him, resting her forearms on the mare Sabine had lent to her. "He . . ." she stopped as if changing her mind about speaking, and Aramis took a step closer to her, close enough to hear her next very solemn words. "He has my father's signet ring, and Papa never let that out of his possession. . . . They murdered my father in Belgium. Shot him twice. He's dead. Funny, you know, I should have been ready for this. I always knew my father had a very lethal job. Really, it's surprising he lived as long as he did when you consider his line of work," she reasoned, trying to convince herself more than trying to convince Aramis. However, her voice broke, indicating that her reasoning did no good, and Aramis turned her around to face him, both hands on her shoulders.

"My condolences, Laurel. I wish I could take the hurt away. But I cannot. The hurt, the emptiness is real. I cannot even tell you it gets better. I just know you learn to cope and someday move beyond it, for you do heal. And I know if I am strong enough to go on, you are too. Let go and let God." He dropped to silence. "*Mon Dieu*, give me the right words," he pleaded with God.

He didn't realize he'd spoken the last plea aloud until she turned her face up towards him. "There are no right words, Aramis," she spoke with a bitterness that might well have chilled even Athos. "If there were I would have said them to you when you told me about your father." She choked and closed her eyes firmly against threatening tears. She would not cry, not now. She never cried. Too easy. Too weak. Certainly not in front of anyone.

Helplessly, Aramis floundered, trying to figure out anything to do. Then he put one hand on her check and the other on her uninjured shoulder. "Don't," he warned. "Don't you dare. It is going to hurt, and it is going to hurt like the devil. Don't lock it inside. It only gets worse if you do. Believe me. I know. It has happened to me."

Suddenly she buried her head against his left breast, and her thin body shook as it was racked by tears. Aramis wrapped an arm around her, pulling her close, and with his other hand stroked her long hair. Tears stained his own eyes and fell down his face, silently drop by drop. Finally, her sobs subsided, and she took a small step back, but not far enough to break Aramis' hold. She surveyed his face and saw the red lines where tears had stained the man's face. With a finger she touched his cheek, almost as if trying to push away his sorrow or as if she were sorry that she had brought his pain to the surface. She had not meant to remind him of the recent terrible loss he had suffered. For once in her life she was terribly ashamed of her own selfishness.

Gently he grasped the hand in his own and felt his hand shake in concert with her own shaking hand. "I will be all right. And you?" he said, his voice raw.

Without realizing what she was doing, her other hand went to his face and rested on his cheek. She raised herself upward on tiptoes and kissed him on the cheek. Maybe he wasn't such a bad man to have around. "*Merci*, Aramis."

He kissed the palm that was still in his hand and said emphatically, "No, Laurel. *Merci*." He released her hand, and she threw her arms around his neck, holding him close, clinging to him for dear life. For a long time they stood, hugging one another, trying to take solace in the touch of another human being.

It was a very subdued group that made its way to the inn and took shelter there for the night. Roughly, Porthos and D'Artagnan guided their prisoner to the cellar that would serve as his cell. As they passed by Aramis, Laurel, Sabine, and Athos, Aramis fixed cold, unforgiving eyes on *Duc* d'Amiens.

"You just keep him away from me," Aramis told the large man with a deadly calm intensity, and Porthos knew Aramis was capable of killing the spy right then and there without compunction. He nodded, and he and the young musketeer finished their trek to the cellar after D'Artagnan paused long enough to slip the cold metal band that Aramis had instructed them to look for into Aramis' hand.

As he shut and locked the cellar door, Porthos wondered what Georges had done to first send Laurel off on a tirade that ultimately ended in injuring both herself and Aramis more and then succeeded in making unperturbable Aramis so bloodthirsty.

Pauvre Porthos, Aramis refrained from saying the words. He was not in the mood to explain his actions. His equilibrium had been too severely disturbed by the recent circumstances. It wasn't every day you ran into the man whom you held responsible for the corruption and eventual death of your older brother, seducing him into gambling, whoring, and drinking for starters. Then there was whatever he had done to Laurel (not just the murder or the treason, but turning things deeply personal), a woman who had touched him more quickly than any person other than his closest friends had—had won his respect despite it all.

Athos led all but Porthos and D'Artagnan inside, being sure that they got settled. Between himself and Sabine they had agreed that Laurel must remain in her guise of a boy. It was only logical seeing as she had no dresses with her, and there was still the price on her head to be avoided. However, he only procured two rooms—one for Aramis and himself and another for Laurel and the *Comtesse de* Winter to share. Given, they'd have to be very careful that no one saw Laurel and Milady spend the entire night together; people might get too curious despite the fact he was passing the two women off as brother and sister. He just couldn't leave Laurel alone tonight. Too dangerous. Especially after her stunt this afternoon, regardless of whether she had good reason or not, though that remained to be seen, as neither she nor Aramis had been very specific.

For once the younger woman meekly submitted to the plan. Not a single word of protest fell from her lips. In fact, she didn't speak at all. Mutely, she entered a room with Milady and shut the door behind her. That in itself worried Athos, and he paused in the corridor, and his friend paused with him. "Do you think she'll be all right, Aramis?"

The man took a moment to mull over the question. "*Oui.* She'll be all right eventually. She's still in shock."

"Eventually." Athos sighed. Eventually had better arrive fairly soon.

"Time is the only thing that is truly going to help, Athos," the other man stated in a lowly confident voice. "*Non*, I cannot say much more without her permission. You'll have to ask her directly if you feel it is important to know those sort of details. One thing, however, I can assure you of is that she won't slow us down or let us down. Her honor would never let her do something like that." Aramis leaned against the wall and flinched as the irritated wound was jarred anew. If things kept going the way they had today, he'd be lucky if his injury didn't leave him crippled for life.

"You look like you could use some rest yourself, *mon ami*," Athos said, and Aramis nodded and headed for his room before Athos even requested he do so. Now that was a little creepy as well. Aramis retiring without a fight when there was a prisoner to guard. Even when he was injured he usually insisted on sharing guard duty.

For a moment Athos stared at the space where his friend had been, trying to figure out why and how the "rules" he had come to know pertaining to his comrades had suddenly changed. Finally, he turned and went back down the stairs, making his way back to the two musketeers he had left outside. D'Artagnan looked worn to the bone after his drive to get to Calais and after the frantic pace and tension of trying to make it to Paris without being killed and before a warrant for his arrest went out.

"D'Artagnan." The man looked at Athos. "I've sadly neglected my duty here. I'll take guard duty tonight. You take my room. No arguments," the older man insisted. "Get several hours sleep and then come relieve Porthos so he can get some sleep too."

"And what about you, Athos?" both D'Artagnan and Porthos asked in concert.

"I'll be fine. I wouldn't be able to sleep tonight anyway," he told them, and they had no doubt it was the truth.

D'Artagnan dawdled just long enough to get directions to the room and then departed. Later he'd talk to Athos and maybe they could figure out what was tearing or seemed to be tearing their normally tight relationships apart.

A man fingered the paper in his hands, and glanced over the sketches again. It was them. All of them he decided. All except the woman, Laurel d'Anlass, that is. The blond-haired widow and the boy simply didn't fit into the scheme. But the four men definitely did. Smiling, he tucked the paper away and gathered his friend, sharing with the other man what he had seen. For several moments the two compatriots talked and, to seal their bargain, drank down a mug of ale each. Two thousand gold pieces each would make them rich men. This was going to be a good night.

Oddly enough, Laurel fell straight into an exhausted sleep, but Sabine, unable to sleep, left the room and wandered outside. Fresh air had helped often enough before so perhaps it would help again. Worth a try. The night was still and cool, and a gentle breeze nipped across her skin, lifting tendrils of her hair, which she didn't bother to push back into place.

She still didn't know what to make of Athos' conversation with her. She had expected him to lose his temper with her after finding out she hadn't told him about his son, but he hadn't. Instead he had appealed—yes, that was the word—appealed to her, asking her at the very least to let him get to know his own son even if she insisted on living a life on the run from justice. It would be a hard life, to let her son live with Athos sometimes and then pick Guillaume up herself and disappear and then deliver the boy to Athos again some time later. Hard on her and their son. If it were even possible.

Her musings were interrupted by a movement in the distance. Milady froze and looked long and hard towards the movement. Two shadowy figures came closer, heading towards the cellar. Coming in behind the two musketeers, quietly with what might have been pistols in their grasp.

In a split second, the woman bolted for the stairs. There was a little time, hopefully enough; she couldn't take those men on herself nor could she warn Athos and Porthos without showing herself and probably getting herself shot as well. The woman took the stairs as fast as her long skirts would allow. Banged upon D'Artagnan's door and dragged the newly woken man down the stairs after her, barely giving him time to put on his boots and grab his sword. As they hurried down the stairs, she told D'Artagnan what she had witnessed.

As the young musketeer dashed to intercept the assailants, Milady ran towards the two musketeers who were guarding the cellar. She saw Athos grappling with one of the men, wrestling back and forth, trying to knock the gun from his hand. However, the second assailant leveled his gun at Athos' back and Sabine yelled out of breath, "Athos, behind you."

Just in time, he whirled and knocked the man's gun hand aside. The ball discharged into the air with a loud report.

Arms and hands intertangled, Athos grappled with the bigger man who had almost killed him. He couldn't draw his sword.

Tired of the deadlock, Athos kicked the man's feet out from under him, sending the assailant sprawling to the ground. Athos didn't even bother to draw his blade. Instead when his opponent tried to regain his feet, he delivered a vicious right hook upside the man's face and then followed that up with a left hook. The fallen man wavered and fell back to the ground unconscious. Gasping and rubbing his knuckles, Athos decided that maybe he enjoyed his work almost as much as Porthos at times. Been a long time since he had resorted to using brawling techniques, but some things stayed with a man.

His sword drawn, Porthos looked about him and saw Athos had things well in control. D'Artagnan, however, was fast losing ground against a stronger opponent. Yelling, he ran towards the two men who were wrestling, brandishing his sword wildly.

The assailant jumped, startled, and fell back several steps, pushed by D'Artagnan. It gave Porthos just the opening he wanted. As he raised his sword he spoke, "Unwelcome guest meet sword. Do enjoy." Porthos brought the hilt down with incredible force as the assailant turned to look at the man who had spoken such odd words. The hilt hit him upside the head, splitting his face from ear to mouth, and he stumbled but didn't fall. D'Artagnan grabbed his own sword firmly in his hands and brought the hilt down on the back of his attacker's head, sending the man wobbling and reeling into unconsciousness.

Both musketeers dropped back as the man fell between them. Porthos offered a hand to his companion and said, "Good work, youngster."

"We do work well together, don't we?" D'Artagnan gasped as his hand was shaken furiously.

"Of course." As if anything else could be the case. The large man crouched, slipping his free arm underneath the bleeding man's shoulder. D'Artagnan followed his lead and together they dragged the man they had wounded towards the cellar. Porthos and D'Artagnan dropped their load beside the other senseless man and looked to Athos.

"Well, gentlemen, it looks like we're going to have to be more careful to avoid bounty hunters. They almost took us all by surprise," Athos addressed his companions and glanced at Milady, and she dropped a coil of rope at their feet.

"I thought you three might find this useful," she spoke and began to leave them when Athos stayed her.

His blue eyes met hers, and without bitterness he said, "*Merci*, Sabine. You saved our lives. *Merci.*"

She nodded and left the scene as the musketeers handily trussed the two unconscious men. As she departed she could have sworn she heard a loud voice bluster, "I love my work." She smiled and mounted the stairs, her decision finally made. This time it was one she could live with. One that was honorable. Or at least she sincerely hoped so.

* * * * * * * * * * *

Louis tapped his riding crop on the table atop of which his feet were crossed. He barely heard what his minister was telling him. It was about some state function, another ball or party for some notable or another. Suddenly, he noticed the minister wasn't talking, and he lowered his feet, sitting upright in his chair. "Is that all?" the king asked and his minister told him it was, knowing the king thought the entire matter trifling. "Good then, check with Covert, and get back to me."

"*Oui, votre majesté*," the man replied, bowing and departing.

"We thought we asked not to be interrupted," the king replied, annoyed when shortly after the minister left he heard someone else enter the chamber.

"Please forgive me, *votre majesté*, but I thought this matter most urgent, so urgent you would want me to interrupt you," *Monsieur de* Treville addressed Louis XIII.

"*Monsieur de* Treville," the king acknowledged and looked at the man's unfamiliar companion. "And this is?"

"Milord Compton from Marseille." Compton bowed as the *capitaine* of the musketeers introduced him.

Yes, now Louis knew who the man was, the coordinator of his secret police and the best spies in France. The man had never before personally visited him, always had relayed messages in the past. What had caused him to suddenly make a personal visit?

"Urgent business brings you two here then?" Louis sat and gestured for the other two men to follow suit. He had only a moment to wait for Treville's reply.

"Unfortunately, *votre majesté*, Compton and I have reason to believe that you are in imminent danger," Treville began.

The king allowed him to proceed no further. "Explain."

"I leave that to Milord Compton." Treville turned the conversation over to the nobleman recently arrived from Marseille.

"In the past few months secret government documents and plans from Austria, Prussia, and Spain have been smuggled into France and given to an agent who is working for England. Not only did this man receive these secrets, he was also able to appropriate highly sensitive information on France. We further believe that this information will set up a coup d'état if it gets to Buckingham."

Louis scowled and jumped to his feet, pacing the length of the room. "So you're saying a highly trusted man in our government is betraying me and all of France to our worst enemy? Who is it?"

Compton sighed, shrugging his shoulders helplessly. "That's what we don't know. We know he's a man we've been after before. That's why we sent our best agent, the Marquis de Langeac, after him. Thomas d'Anlass has been gathering information for the past few years that could lead us to the spy."

Still agitated, the king sat while Compton explained how Laurel d'Anlass had come to him in Marseille after seeing her father and how he sent her to Calais so that between her and the marquis they could capture and finally eliminate this spy and prevent him from delivering the sensitive information.

"However, I was just recently alerted that Thomas d'Anlass was murdered in Belgium and his daughter has disappeared. I have no sure way of knowing whether Thomas was successful in his last attempt and was able to get Laurel the information she needed. Nor do I have any idea if she received anything he sent. Within the next few days, I'm recommending calling a state of emergency under strict military rule unless we get this spy in our custody."

Louis sat in stunned silence, and tension electrified the air. "Where does that bring you in, *Monsieur de* Treville, other than enforcing military order?"

The *capitaine* folded his hands and leaned forward, resting his elbows on his knees. "Milord Compton came to me since we are good friends and associates, and he explained the situation in detail." Treville shifted his position. "It so happens that one of my musketeers ran into Laurel d'Anlass and wrote telling me that she would be sent to my protection while he went to Calais. However, the woman did not arrive and a fortnight or so later I received another letter from Meung that said Laurel would not be sent to me. So Compton and I are hoping that she joined forces with my musketeers and that they were able to get to Calais and apprehend this traitor. That's why we ask you to wait two or three days before having me impose military order. We would not want to unduly alarm your subjects."

"Gentlemen, you have my permission to wait two days. If this spy has not been turned over to me or if proof of his death is not presented, I will declare France a military state. Is that clear?" his *majesté* asked.

"*Oui votre majesté,*" both men responded as Louis stormed out of the room, calling for his horse. His *majesté* always went hunting when he was perturbed or worried. Just think what he would have done if Louis had known the plan was to divide Europe in half between Buckingham and the new leader of France.

* * * * * * * * * * * *

Other than refusing to ride near Georges, Laurel remained adamantly quiet as she rode alongside Porthos, the ring Aramis had slipped to her that morning clutched in a hand. The man was completely unable to goad so much as a smile or retort out of her. So as it happened, it was Aramis and D'Artagnan who rode in the middle, just behind the spy while Milady and Athos led the group at an ever more rapid pace towards Paris.

Porthos glanced at Laurel. This brisk pace had to be straining her healing shoulder, but she made no complaint and gritted her teeth. She and Aramis would not slow them down, and they were determined to prove it. How had he gotten stuck with such bullheaded companions? Of course, he wasn't in the least bit stubborn himself. Couldn't possibly be.

A sudden crack of thunder shattered the sky, and the horses pawed against the ground in an unanticipated fit of skittishness. Yet each rider was able to maintain control as dark billowy clouds rolled across the late afternoon sky. The temperature plummeted, and the sun blinked out of existence temporarily. A gust of wind tore through the branches of a somewhat distant grove of trees, and they shook back and forth.

Thunder rumbled forth again. Then a streak of lightning crisscrossed the sky. A bolt exploded against a nearby tree, setting it afire.

All the companions' attention was focused on controlling the spooked animals as the fire jumped from tree to tree, and the smell of acrid smoke permeated the air. Porthos and D'Artagnan regained control of their horses swiftly, but not as swiftly as Georges, who had urged his horse into a gallop.

Making for the opening in his escort's formation, the *Duc* d'Amiens spurred his horse. Swiftly, the beast responded, darting through the small space and making for a different path where the horse could have his head.

"D'Artagnan," Porthos yelled, seeing the young man was in control of his animal. "This way. We've got to cut him off before he gets to the river."

This said, the men took off in pursuit of the spy, urging their mounts against the terror and in pursuit.

The high-strung mare that had become Laurel's responsibility started anew as the confusion swirled about her. Laurel put every ounce of her effort into calming the mare and directing her slowly from the blazing trees.

As for Athos, he helped Sabine keep her seat and led their horses from the fire. When he was clear he galloped after his companions who were almost out of sight.

Another bolt of lightning sizzled through the air severing, a huge limb from a tree and sending it plummeting straight for Aramis. Just in time the musketeer jerked the reins backward, causing the horse to swerve, and narrowly avoided being hit by the branch. By the time he and Laurel joined Milady—Athos, Porthos, D'Artagnan, and the spy were all nowhere to be seen.

Frantically the *Duc* d'Amiens worked at the bonds on his wrists, and the ropes cut deeply into his skin, coating his flesh with sticky scarlet fluid. He had to get better control of the horse soon, and that meant freeing his hands. Desperately, he put his mouth against the knot, gripping it between his teeth, and pulled. Strands of rope frayed in his teeth, and he spit them out, freeing his mangled wrists as he did so. The broken rope fell to the ground, almost tangling in the horse's feet.

Placing the reins in one hand, he turned his attention to untying the bonds on his legs so he could have more control over the horse's speed. The knot undone, he slipped the ropes from his legs and spurred his fine stallion to a quicker pace. However, the lost time had cost him.

The stallion whinnied in protest as Georges yanked on the reins to avoid D'Artagnan who had somehow gotten in front of him and was blocking his path to the river. Once again he allowed the stallion to have its head, knowing that the animal could outdistance the musketeer's smaller mare.

A branch snapped in his face, and he ducked to avoid it, permitting D'Artagnan a chance to pull even with him and draw his sword, slashing at the spy. The young man missed his target but scored the horse along its flank. The stallion screamed but pushed on, blood trickling down its leg.

D'Artagnan saw the briefest flicker of metal as a streak of sunlight burst from behind the clouds. Porthos. If he could just drive the stallion in that direction. Dropping the reins, he grabbed the hand crossbow Porthos had given him and loaded it. Praying that he could do this right, he fired, missing horse and rider, but not by much. It was enough to drive the stallion towards Porthos.

Remarkably, Georges maintained control of the fabulously trained animal and swerved away from Porthos, heading straight for the river. The musketeers raced to beat him, but they knew their horses weren't quick enough to outdistance the stallion.

A ball burst through the air, and the horse trembled and collapsed, throwing its rider. D'Artagnan and Porthos jumped from their horses and pounced on the stunned man before he could get to his feet. Porthos slammed his fist down on the man, sending him into the realm of dreams.

Athos rode up beside the three men, a smoking gun in his hand. Shame he'd had to harm such a quality mount. "Nice shot," Porthos told him. "Almost as good as my own, I might say." Not that he even owned a gun at this particular moment. Athos, in fact, was the only one in the entire group who possessed a pistol right now, Aramis and Laurel having both lost their guns en route to Calais.

"I wish I hadn't had to kill the stallion to stop him though. It was a good horse, and now someone will have to ride double," Athos responded as he dismounted to help them secure the prisoner again. He silently cursed himself for not putting the spy on a lesser horse earlier that day.

When the spy was tied again, Athos spoke, "We'll put him on my horse with me. My horse is the strongest of all of ours, and I'm strong enough to watch him and not so big that the horse will be run into the ground."

* * * * * * * * * * *

Capitaine de Treville made a circuit around the courtyard flanked by his friend. Every so often the two men stopped, and

Treville would issue some pointers to a musketeer or have him try a new defensive technique or present a different way of looking at an attack.

"You have good men here," Compton observed. "They respect you greatly."

"I know. I'm very lucky. Few men are ever so blessed as to get such loyalty. I'm still not sure what I did to earn it."

"You didn't do anything to earn that kind of loyalty and respect. It's who you are, Treville." Compton shook his head and laughed as Treville issued another pointer to a young man who was holding one shoulder too high. Treville turned back to the other man, and they continued their circuit around the busy courtyard. "Does his *majesté* ever come here?"

"Every once in a while," the *capitaine* replied, "he comes every so often to inspect the fighters and to assure himself that I'm doing an adequate job. Most of the time he leaves it up to me to pick the best men for whatever job that needs done."

Compton carefully took note of the fact that it was most of the time and not always. "Where are your best men?"

"That seems to be the question around here. I haven't heard from any of them in more than a week, and if they aren't back within two days Louis is going to discover they are missing and issue warrants for their arrest despite our little talk with him. Richelieu still has that much influence over him. Nonetheless, they will be arrested."

"For desertion?"

"For desertion and conduct unbefitting a king's musketeer," Treville confirmed.

"*Capitaine,*" a voice warned, and Compton and Treville whirled to see a horse charging right for them. They stood, frozen, and at the last second the rider pulled the horse to a stop. The rider half fell from his saddle, and Compton raced to support the young man, as did Treville.

"D'Artagnan?" Treville surveyed the exhausted man.

"*Capitaine.*" The young man gasped. "I'm sorry I came in that way, but I had to see you as quickly as possible."

"Slow down and tell me what's going on," the man instructed D'Artagnan calmly. "Is it Athos, Porthos, and Aramis?"

The musketeer licked his lips. "*Oui* and three others. You see, we caught a spy and have the papers to prove it. It's just that Aramis and Christophe are injured, and because we lost a horse,

Athos and the others had to stop so they could keep an eye on the spy. Actually, the spy kept trying to escape, so they stopped and sent me ahead to get help," he finished with a sharp intake of breath.

"Where are they, lad?" D'Artagnan informed his superior that they were a few leagues north of the city. "Good job," Treville told him. "Let's get you cleaned up. I'll see to it that this gets taken care of." D'Artagnan nodded and allowed Compton to help him to his room while Treville rushed off to gather a dozen musketeers to dispatch to Athos' aid.

"Good news, *votre majesté*," Treville said almost forgetting to bow after the king granted him an audience.

Louis shuffled through several letters and asked, "Have your musketeers returned, and are they now able to go on another mission?"

"Not exactly," Treville responded, and Louis asked what exactly the news was then. "My men have just retrieved Athos, Porthos, Aramis, and three of their traveling companions. One of them is the spy who was to deliver the papers to England."

"He is in your custody then?" Louis queried. "Who is he?"

"Georges, *le Duc* d'Amiens, sire. We just put him in the dungeon under heavy guard."

Louis' eyes flashed angrily at the deep betrayal. *Le Duc* d'Amiens. It was unthinkable. "And the four musketeers in question?" he finally asked.

"Unfortunately D'Artagnan rode himself into the ground and is still in need of rest. And Aramis is recuperating from a nasty sword gash across his right breast. So I regret to inform you half of those men are out of commission."

"But you say they apprehended the spy?"

"*Oui*, with the help of a lad they call Christophe and the *Comtesse de* Winter."

"They'll be present for the trial, of course?"

"Of course," Treville replied. Nothing would stop his best musketeers from going to this trial.

"Good. Afterward I'd like to thank them all personally. It seems I owe them a great debt," Louis said, more thoughtfully than was his wont.

"*Oui, votre majesté*," the *capitaine* said with pride and excused himself gracefully.

D'Artagnan wiped the sleep out of his eyes and emerged into the courtyard and the late afternoon sunshine. He still had to go get Constance, but that would have to wait a while until after the trial with the spy was resolved. His blurry eyes came to focus, revealing three men, side by side, sporting long-unworn musketeer mantles. Smiling, he walked towards them, trying not to hurry. "It is good to see you," D'Artagnan told his friends.

"It's very good to be back." Porthos slung an arm around the young man's shoulder. "You did good, kid. You're learning. Someday you might even be a match for me."

"Only a match for you, eh, Porthos. A little cocky, are we?" Aramis took up in his usual fashion of confusing Porthos as to whether or not he was being insulted. "Why the lad is already a match for you in more areas than one," he finished innocently with a completely straight face, and Athos couldn't control a bark of laughter. Leave it to Aramis, the oldest man remarked.

"Hey, where's Christophe and Milady?" the young man inquired, noting their absence for the first time.

"Some of our comrades in arms have escorted young Christophe to the barracks to have his wound tended to. Unfortunately, our young friend is quite near passing out on his feet, and Aramis here is hardly better off. In fact, we'll be sending him to the barracks very soon to have his own wound tended to. But since he was still on his feet, we decided to allow him to see for himself that you were all right," Athos said, surprising himself a bit with the length of his speech. He hadn't thought he had that much to say.

Aramis made no comment, and Porthos proceeded to enlighten D'Artagnan about what had become of the *comtesse.* "Milady is staying with a relative of her family in the city. Of course, that is what she said. What she'll do could be another matter, but she'll stick around Paris long enough for Athos to fulfill a promise he made to her."

The four men were interrupted by Compton requesting to "borrow" D'Artagnan, Porthos, and Athos for a bit.

"You know?" Aramis started with nonchalance. "I'm really beginning to get the idea that I am not wanted."

"Oh no, you're wanted," Compton contradicted him. "I just don't think you're up to what I need done until your wound heals more completely. And you won't be alone long, anyhow. Treville said he wanted to talk with you. He should be along shortly." With these words Compton departed, taking Aramis' friends with him.

The musketeer put the boy, who had just passed out, on a cot. Lad was close to being skin and bones, and there was a splotch of blood seeping through the fabric of the boy's fraying tunic. Another musketeer, who served as a doctor, came up behind his comrade. "What do we have here?" the new arrival asked.

"This boy was wounded while helping Athos and the others. I'd also say he needs to put on a few pounds though," the man who had delivered the boy responded.

The doctor quickly glanced over the unconscious boy noting a little blood seeping through the cloth covering the left shoulder. He couldn't see anything else wrong, but he would have to be completely sure how bad the lad's wounds were. The doctor looked at his companion. "You by any chance know the extent of his wounds or how he got them?"

"Don't know about the extent of the wounds, but I believe they're sword wounds. Boy was exhausted and close-mouthed." Preferred to treat himself. The musketeer left the last part out though. Very few people actually liked doctors.

"We'll just have to do an examination then," muttered the doctor. "Give me a hand with this," the doctor informed the other musketeer to help lift the boy up while he proceeded to try to take the tunic and doublet off.

Laurel's head swam as she came back to reality. Her first realization was that several strange men were trying to undress her. Undress her . . . Her muzzy mind slowly kicked into action. No one was taking her clothes off, not at this moment in time.

Her hands reached for the sword no one, oddly enough, had removed from her person. One by one, her fingers wrapped around the hilt of the weapon. In a fluid motion, she slid the blade from its sheath, pushing herself up into a seated position, and leveled the sword at the doctor. The shock rendered him speechless and halted the sawbones in mid-action. "I will thank you both for removing your hands from my personage. Now," she ordered. The doctor took a step back and called for assistance while the other man tried to grab her sword.

"I wouldn't recommend it," Laurel said, making a swipe at him that narrowly missed his nose. A surge of adrenaline took her and the young woman made it to her feet. Twirling, she dropped gracefully to the floor, holding her sword in the ready position. The woman looked at the men who closed in around her, the men who were coming closer to her with each step. "I'm capable of seeing to my own wounds. Now, if you gentlemen will be so kind as to direct me to the way out, I'll leave you."

"Quick, disarm the boy," someone yelled. And several swords were drawn against Laurel. The men lunged at her, and she twirled out of their way, deflecting blade after blade. A parry here, a riposte there.

She danced back and forth on the balls of her feet. Waiting for one attack and fending it off, then fending off the next attack. Neatly, she held the four opponents at bay, playing them off one another and foiling them with her quickness. Consequently, she gave them the hairy task of trying to subdue a good and desperate fighter without hurting her.

"What's going on here?" a commanding voice demanded to know, and several unarmed musketeers split apart to allow *Monsieur de* Treville and Aramis passage. Treville was taken aback to see a young boy fending off four trained musketeers, and his arm was even wounded. His left arm, given, but the boy was wounded. "That will be enough," the *capitaine* ordered, but Laurel refused to disengage. Revealing, or having it revealed that she was a woman at this crucial juncture could cost her far more than her reputation. Only now did she truly begin to understand the threat to her life this masquerade posed—now that her father was no longer there to protect her from certain consequences. Repercussions. Actions had them.

Aramis tapped his commander on the shoulder, cringing inwardly at the scene as he did so. He should have known Laurel would do something like this, should have expected it. "Let me see what I can do," he half asked his commander, and the *capitaine* gestured for him to go right ahead and make it quick.

Aramis stepped forward as close as he dared get to the foray. "Christophe," he called loudly, and the young woman paused long enough to recognize him. "Put the sword away."

"I'm not having any doctor trying to butcher me up," she repeated stubbornly. She wasn't about to reveal she was a woman, Aramis read between the lines. Not that he particularly blamed her for wishing to hold onto that secret.

"Okay," he replied, well aware she was not much mollified. "Just put the sword away before I come after you myself." He would, too, any way that worked.

Laurel sheathed the sword, and Aramis rushed forward, escorting her away from the musketeers to an alcove where *Capitaine de* Treville joined them. "Well, lad, I must admit you're a talented young fighter, but I won't have you fighting my men in my barracks. Do I make myself clear?" the *capitaine* quizzed her.

"*Oui, monsieur*," Laurel replied contritely. Consequences had been avoided for the moment.

Treville let her stew for a while, allowing her to feel guilty for her behavior. "With a little work, and a few pounds, you could almost be a musketeer."

"*Monsieur*, I'm better than that," she contradicted him with the most respect she could muster. She hated being misjudged by the right-handed world for starters. "My right hand is not my sword hand, though it was the hand I was first trained on. I am a superb left-handed swordfighter."

Treville turned to Aramis, asking him if it was true and Aramis reluctantly confirmed Laurel's words. Worse and worse. Would Laurel never learn that sometimes it was better to hold one's tongue? "In that case I invite you to apprentice yourself to the musketeers once your arm is healed and provided you can learn a little discipline."

Aramis groaned. Laurel was stunned into speechlessness. *Incroyable*, she'd really done it now.

"Go ahead and take some time to think about it. Get yourself well. That goes for you too, Aramis," the *capitaine* concluded, leaving Aramis and Laurel alone so he could attend to other pressing business.

"Move," Aramis told her, not giving the woman any choice as he grasped her good arm and half pushed, half urged her out of the barracks and into his own room. A little privacy was required for taking her to task. God willing, she'd listen to a little good sense for once.

He closed the door behind him. "What was the meaning of that?"

"I couldn't lie."

"But you did not have to go and tell him he was wrong. You could have said nothing," Aramis criticized, condemning her prickly pride and her too-frequent impulsiveness.

"I couldn't keep him in the dark. It just didn't seem right, so I told him the truth. I'm good at fighting. I didn't expect him to ask me to join the musketeers. That was the furthest thing from my mind," she defended.

He fixed his deep brown eyes on her as if trying to stare her down, but she didn't flinch. "Since it was the last thing from your mind, you'll tell him no, of course."

She clenched her jaw. How dare he presume to dictate her life! "I will do no such thing."

"What?"

"You heard me. I said I'll do no such thing. It'd be kind of nice to be a musketeer for a year or two," Laurel said.

He threw his hands in the air after remembering at the last instant that her left shoulder was injured and it would not quite be the thing to shake her senseless. "You stubborn little wench. Where in the name of all that is holy is your sense?"

"*Merci.*"

"*Merci?*" Aramis was confused.

"You finally said it, Aramis. You've finally honestly told me what you think. *Merci.*"

Aramis was exasperated. "That's hardly a description to be thankful for, Laurel." She shrugged her shoulders, saying "so what" without words. He dropped to his bed, shaking his head. "Damn it. You know you are a very frustrating woman." Now she had him cursing in front of a lady, and he rarely ever cursed.

"I never said I wasn't. I've always been eccentric, and eccentrics are frustrating." As she began to speak again Aramis muttered that some eccentrics were more frustrating than others. "Heck, I even tried to help every peasant I saw until my father put a stop to it, saying we didn't possibly have enough money to help them all and informed me they'd just resent it."

"That is not what we were talking about," Aramis informed her, not permitting her to lead the conversation further astray. "What are you going to do about being a musketeer? It would be incredibly dangerous for you to try to keep the masquerade, and it might only work a year or two before people start wondering why you are not getting taller, broader and everything else." Aramis was not about to give her a lesson on male anatomy and development, provided her eccentric father hadn't already enlightened her.

"I know, Aramis," she admitted and sat down next to him. "Believe me, I know. It's just so hard for me to think what I'm going to do when my arm's healed and this is all over. I could go back to Langeac and be a marquise if Louis XIII permits it— honors my father's last wishes, and grants this last favor." She stumbled a moment then went on, "But home won't ever really be home again. Don't you ever get that way, wondering if you even want to go home and try to pick up where your father left off?" She cocked her face up at him.

"*Oui*," he admitted quietly. "I can't stop thinking about it. I would be a *duc* if I claimed my inheritance, Laurel. A *duc* with responsibilities and unable to enter the priesthood."

"At least you'd always have the musketeers," she mumbled, but he caught the words. "Do you really want to enter the priesthood, honestly?"

He offered her a feeble half smile. "I used to. Now . . ." Now indeed. . . . Her eyes were intense as they rested on him, almost looking right through him. "I don't think it is for me anymore. Too much has changed. I have changed. I don't know; I'm just . . ."

"Confused," she finished for him, empathizing with him. She checked her impulsive reaction to reach out and touch his shoulder, sensing he'd not appreciate the action. Instead she said, "I'll go to *Monsieur de* Treville and tell him I can't join the musketeers, politely. If he insists, I'll tell him who I truly am."

"And after that?" he prompted.

"I think I'll go to Compton and have him take me on. He can't rightly refuse me," she told Aramis, and he knew if Compton tried, she'd pull no punches. She was her father's daughter, and once she set her mind and talents to something, she was . . . difficult to dissuade would be the mildest way to put the situation.

He gently grasped her by the shoulders, favoring his right side. "Laurel, you are going to get yourself killed or worse that way. Do you really want to die so young?" His eyes locked on to hers. Who turned away first from that battle of wills, neither knew.

"Aramis, you'd be killed just as easily in your line of work," she finally retorted as both broke that eye contact. "Ooh, you egotistical swine," she shot back at him and yanked herself out of his light grasp. "Don't you dare go back to treating me like some china doll."

"Laurel," he cried silencing her tirade. "I am not treating you like a china doll. I am worried about you. I do not like the idea of seeing you die, or finding out you've died. It would hurt a great deal more than I care to think about.

"Try to deny you see me as a woman to be coddled, protected, and restricted," she raged, without concern as to her reasonableness or lack thereof. Excesses rarely followed rhyme or reason.

"I cannot, Laurel," Aramis said and took the hat from her head. "You are a woman, and that is not a bad thing. Why does it bother you so much that I see you as a beautiful woman?"

"Stop trying to placate me with your flattery."

"I'm not placating you, *chérie*. You do not even want to know what I'm thinking." He rose to his feet and left his own room and an abruptly very confused young woman.

* * * * * * * * * * *

Athos left Compton and discovered his feet automatically taking him towards his wife and certain confrontation. The issue could not be avoided indefinitely, and she had asked him to come see her when he got a chance. Slightly bewildered, he stood in front of the door, contemplating it with a blank look on his face, for a moment. A moment long enough to draw the attention of those who passed by.

Finally, he raised his hand and hit the knocker against the door. A kindly, flirtatious maid showed him to the sitting room. Sabine entered before he really had a chance to prepare himself.

"Athos," she acknowledged him civilly.

"You asked to see me," he said, folding his hands, unable to take his eyes from her. After all this time she still had the power to take the breath from his body. He still wanted her.

"The trial for Georges is tomorrow, is it not?" The musketeer nodded. "I would come with you then."

"You don't need to be there. All four of us will testify and Laurel will too. By her own insistence." Athos informed her of this development and also remembered that Compton had been assured that Laurel would testify because she was crucial to making the case against the *duc*.

"I may not need to be there, but I want to be there. I want to do something that I can be proud of, Athos—the right thing for the first time in a very long time. I want to help see to it that the man is punished for the crimes he's committed, and I can condemn him. You see, at one point, I'm the one who went to Austria and Spain and stole documents which I gave to him; I will say that at the trial too."

Athos knelt down in front of her, beseeching her. "Why didn't you tell us before? Our lives could have depended on it."

"I didn't realize that particular information was going to England, and I never once thought it could be his grace that would smuggle the information to England, although I should have." She touched her hand to his cheek. "You will take me with you?"

"*Oui*," he finally said. "I give you my word." Sadly, she smiled. It was unspoken but it was there, as always, along with the guilt. His sense of honor, duty, justice, and fairness could not let her go unpunished for her murders and her numerous other lesser crimes. Yet he knew that her testimony would not condemn her; it would condemn the spy. Plus, in doing so she could be royally pardoned for her part in this affair, maybe even have her death sentence stayed, for a price.

Rapt, the exclusive audience including the King of France and several highly placed noblemen hung on his words. Not a one seemed to be aware that the orator had a gift for manipulating words, shifting blame.

As he continued the story became a conspiracy to discredit his family and him in particular, and a personal vendetta perpetrated by a man who blamed him erroneously for the death of a brother, and another person who blamed him for the discrediting and death of a father. Contritely, he hung his head, finishing his performance. "Haven't enough innocent men and women suffered? It is time and past that innocents stop suffering, that we lay the issue to rest as it would be were it not for the false accusations of grief-stricken and misled compatriots. I thank you for your time and consideration."

Back to his seat the man went, knowing that he had indeed wrung sympathy from the tribunal.

Just as he regained his seat and felt his confidence growing, two women entered the closed chamber. Both were thin and endowed with unusually long blond hair and blue eyes. One was as tall as the average man the other was a bit shorter. Yet both held all eyes with not just their bearing but also their beauty. They could both have been easily mistaken for sisters by blood.

Laurel d'Anlass proceeded to the center of the room after bowing to his *majesté,* remarkably poised. Formally, she introduced herself to those assembled. With a quiet intensity, she presented her case against the *Duc* d'Amiens. Gave them the information her father had amassed on this man and how long he had worked to get it, contradicting the self-same man who had twisted her accusations back at her.

Tension hung thick. It dawned on her that Georges had very effectively spiked the game and had cast doubt on her credibility and that of her father. For that matter he had probably tried to throw doubt on all those who would be speaking against him. In midword she halted. Desperate measures then.

She'd not intended to present sensitive and rather personal documents and letters of her father's—not in their entirety. "*Messieurs, votre majesté.* I have in my possession certain papers which can confirm the truth of my claims. If you will permit?"

"We permit. Present us your documents," Louis granted the request.

Carefully, with the schooled poise instilled by her father, she withdrew the packet of information from her pocket and approached the monarch. Kneeling before him, she waited until the king signaled for the papers to be turned over.

She remained on her knees as the king fingered through the papers and passed them to a servant with instructions that the others on the tribunal look at the evidence presented him. "Have you anything else to present us?"

Other than the fact that Richelieu, the untouchable, was equally responsible as the *Duc* of Amiens? A fact she could not even begin to substantiate with any form of proof other than her word. "That is all *votre majesté, messieurs.* But there is one who knows even more than I of this situation. I would beg your indulgence and ask that you hear the witness of my stepsister."

"So be it." The king had already intended to hear from the lady's stepsister, the *Comtesse de* Winter.

Thus, the shorter woman took her place in the center of the room. Coolly, she spoke of her own rather dubious role against France and her associations with Georges. Equally unperturbed, she fielded the inquisition of questions thrown her way and in her turn handed over a cache of documents.

The session drew to a close, and Louis XIII rose to his feet and addressed all present. "We will consider your evidence and return to render our decision shortly." The king departed the audience chamber alone. In this he left little doubt he was going to exercise his absolute authority as judge, jury, and possibly executioner.

Scarcely an hour later the monarch returned, accompanied by a personal assistant. The members of the room—noblemen all except Milady and Laurel—came to their feet. Louis XIII handed a scroll to the man beside him and he unfurled it and read:

"*En l'an de grâce*, sixteen hundred and thirty–eight and our most noble monarch Louis XIII, we do decree that Georges, *Duc* d'Amiens, by virtue of the evidence presented against him, is guilty of betraying his monarch and his country. Thus, with all due haste *le Duc* d'Amiens is sentenced to a traitor's death in the public square tomorrow at dawn—to die by the blow of an ax. Henceforth, his title and holdings revert to the crown. Thus, his *majesté,* Louis XIII, decrees in the name of God and of France. May His will be done," the man finished and handed the scroll back to his king.

"Remove him from my sight," Louis said with disgust, commanding Treville and his soldiers (not any of the four musketeers in question) to take Georges to his prison to await his death and a priest.

The guards left, escorting the declared traitor. Moments later, Laurel and Milady departed, leaving the men to their final discussion. Laurel, however, could not resist snatching her sword from where it rested in the hall and taking it with her as she and her sister left the palace grounds.

Georges and his armed escort of six left the empty corridors of the palace and exited to the equally empty street. The rhythmic thump of their feet echoed off the stones. No one disturbed them. It was midday and most people had left the streets to take their meal. Yet Treville was still uneasy. It was too easy, far too easy. Georges was a cannier man than the facts seemed to indicate. His brilliant testimony, which had nearly swung the king in his favor, was proof of that.

That was when the street erupted with mercenaries, and his men were quickly overwhelmed. Treville himself frantically fought against the attackers—in vain.

Suddenly his world went black, and his limp body fell to the ground. A man saluted the former *Duc* d'Amiens and freed him from his bonds. This done, he presented Georges with a rapier. The man addressed the spy. "Compliments of his eminence. The rest is up to you."

The commander gestured for his men to follow him and the street was soon empty except for Georges and dead and senseless soldiers that had once been his escort. Georges took the rapier in hand and departed the streets with all possible haste, heading for a horse and transport to the border between Belgium and France.

Sabine and Laurel walked without hurrying through the streets. Wordlessly, they looked at one another, confirming their instincts. Something was wrong. Only they didn't know what. As they rounded the corner, their sense of unease grew, and the women picked up their pace, their skirts swirling around their feet.

The two women froze as a man with green eyes holding a sword materialized in front of them. He appeared as surprised to see them as they were to see him. Laurel unsheathed the sword she had been carrying and set the scabbard aside, grasping the blade in her right hand. Taking her cue, Milady departed at a run. Her sister would need help, and quickly, or Georges could well escape.

The spy looked Laurel up and down. Dressed in a court gown and her hair done up, she was far from presenting a threatening picture, and the sword in her hand looked distinctly out of place. Not to mention that her shoulder was wounded. "You don't really think you can stop me, *mademoiselle*," he informed her in his most condescending tones and moved to pass her.

She raised her weapon, barring his way. "You don't seriously think that I'm going to let you walk away after the crimes you've committed against me and mine." They stood staring at each other.

Neither gave and Laurel moved to disarm the man. Automatically, Georges parried. Swiftly, trying not to stumble, she retreated at his attack, cursing the skirts that hampered her movements, hampering her quickness and giving the half-starved and tired man a significant advantage.

She whirled backward, narrowly avoiding his stroke. Disengage, and she backed up several steps, allowing herself just enough time to slit her skirts to reveal the pantalets underneath. The skirts fell at her feet and she jumped away from another lunge. Better, though by no means as good as breeches, a good tunic, and sturdy pair of boots. Men didn't realize how lucky they had it. Of course they got the better end of the deal in everything.

Her arm wavered as his sword thrust upward, and she linked her blade with his to block the blow. The blow sent little shock waves tingling up her arm. Her right arm simply wasn't as strong as her left, and she was out of practice in fighting right-handed.

If she ever got out of this and was able to heal, she swore to herself that she'd not neglect her fencing skills for either hand. The balls of her feet ached as she felt every stone and pebble through the thin slippers. Blast fashion for its absurdities! Blast men for dictating not only their own fashion but the fashions of women as well. She lunged, swiping upward, and her stroke was easily knocked aside, almost dislodging her sword in the process.

Her grip failing, she still managed to block the next blow and dance around behind him. Okay, enough was enough. She threw her sword in the air and caught it in her left hand, and Georges looked at her like she was a complete fool. His sword at ready, he circled her. "You really think you still have a chance. *Mademoiselle*, it seems you are doubly foolish now."

"Then a fool I will be," she huffed, attacking him and driving him back, to his surprise.

Nom de nom! The woman was better at fighting with her left hand than with her right; Georges chastised himself for being completely unprepared for a left handed fighter, for forgetting that that boy on the ship was one and the same as his current enemy.

She pushed him back another step, negating his longer reach and almost slicing his arm from elbow to wrist. Capitalizing on his superior strength, he pushed her away. With a cry she fell back, blood seeping from the reopened wound to her sword arm. He followed up immediately, hoping to catch her off guard due to her pain, but she neatly parried and danced out of reach.

No more did Laurel attack. She simply couldn't complete a full range of motion with her left arm, left shoulder throbbing and throbbing with pain that threatened to blur all her senses.

Clumsily, she slipped and fell to her knees, barely blocking the next stroke. She thought she heard footsteps and a scream but it was all so distant. Apparently Georges heard it, and for a moment was distracted, but it was long enough, and she sent his blade flying from his hand. She went limp as she saw *Monsieur de* Treville knock the man senseless.

The *capitaine* regarded the woman, recalling how she had come to him the night before and told him she could not enter the musketeers and revealed to him her true identity. He knelt by the woman and helped her support herself against the wall as he tore a strip of cloth and tied it tightly around her bleeding shoulder. "You really are one of the finest young fighters I have seen in a long time. If only . . ."

Laurel shook her head, not really wanting to hear the words, "But I'm not a man." Her roles would always be limited due to that simple fact of chance, of nature.

Four musketeers followed by the king himself rushed around the corner, forestalling, by their appearance, anything further she might have said.

None of the men including the king said a word about Laurel's part in combatting the traitor. The king looked at Athos and his companions. "Take this man and lock him in my palace prison. We'll execute him when he awakes. No more chances," the king told them. The three healthy musketeers hefted the deadweight of the spy between them while Louis addressed Treville concerning the daughter of his one-time best spy and a man who had saved his life several times over. "How is she?"

"She'll recover fully with adequate rest and care. And her shoulder will heal without complication if no one lets her touch a sword for at least the next fortnight."

"You have my thanks, *madame*," and that was all Louis had to say on the matter other than instructing Aramis and the *capitaine* to help her get adequate care. Later he supposed he'd have to deal with Thomas d'Anlass' last requests and the special favor he had requested.

Treville lifted the woman to her feet, and Aramis supported her with his left arm as they fell in behind the king who was following the other three musketeers and trailed by his personal assistant.

Treville leveled both Aramis and Laurel with a gaze that made them flinch. "If either of you even so much as looks at a sword the wrong way until I say you can, I will set you under lock and key, and you will rot there for the next six months." Neither argued with him, and when they had returned to the palace it was two rather quiet young people who allowed themselves to be tended by the king's personal physician.

The mantel clock tolled two when the priest entered the cell, asking the man if he had any last words. The green-eyed man turned him away, and several guards then entered and guided him outside to the plaza to a raised platform upon which sat a cutting block stained by blood. A large but unusually subdued crowd surrounded the platform. Executions were usually primarily a social event, but to find that a well-respected *duc* was guilty of treason made them uneasy.

From the safety of his entourage his *majesté* looked on. Porthos, Athos, and D'Artagnan stood by his side ready to defend him to their deaths. Laurel stood next to Anne d'Autriche, her *majesté,* decked out in a somber dress and her left arm hanging in a sling. Aramis flanked Louis, dressed in his musketeer mantle, but lacking a sword; like Laurel, his arm was in a sling. There was one difference: it was his right arm.

The guards escorted the prisoner up the stairs, his hands bound behind his back. Murmurs passed through the crowd as a woman marked off a ruler at his neck and took the ruler to measure it against coffin sizes. The guards forced Georges to his knees in front of the block and stepped back. A large man with a black mask inspected his ax, and his assistant forced the traitor's head onto the block.

For a moment D'Artagnan watched, transfixed. He remembered when he had been on that block and had thought he was going to die. Of course, Athos, Porthos, and Aramis had rescued him. There would, however, be no rescue this time. The young musketeer saw the ax arc down, cleaving head from shoulders, and blood exploded across the block and platform. The man closed his eyes against the sight of the empty eyes looking up in shock. Laurel too turned her eyes from the sight. Justice was done. Death, though, always more death. There had to be a better way. Something that might actually bring solace.

* * * * * * * * * * * *

Richelieu signed the letter and handed it to his *capitaine.* "Send it immediately. Remember, no names," the cardinal warned. The *capitaine* took the letter and made himself scarce. His eminence was in a foul mood.

The man in question stood and slashed his hand across the desk, knocking papers, paperweight, and the inkwell to the floor with a crash. Those infuriating musketeers again and the daughter of the former Marquis d'Anlass. They had ruined it. Georges was dead a week, and Buckingham had withdrawn any pledge of support. And then there was the *Comtesse de* Winter. She had turned against him despite the fact he still held her son. Well, she would, quite simply, never see her son again. After the middle of the next week the boy would live the rest of his formative years in a remote monastery until Richelieu or his successor had need of a loyal man to call upon. How sweet it would be to have a man raised to be unquestionably loyal to the cardinal above all.

The cardinal marched to the window and threw the doors to the balcony open. The sky was overcast, and only a few brave rays of sun peeked from behind their covering. The streets of Paris stretched before him, streets that should have been his. Now he'd have to wait again until Louis was not wary to launch a bid for the crown. His fist slapped against his open palm. The musketeers would pay, starting with the youngest one who had foiled his first plan, and then Porthos and then Aramis, and then only after he'd watched all his friends die, then Athos would finally die.

Now where was that assassin who was supposed to arrive? A man with a heavy burr and a scar from ear to scalp addressed the man at the window. "Your eminence has a job that needs to be conducted with expediency and confidentiality?"

"*Oui*, two to start with." Richelieu slipped a catch under his desk and caught a sack of gold coins, which he set on the desk. "This is for the first two. You will receive five thousand more gold coins upon successful completion of your task and the elimination of two more men. Do we have an agreement?"

The scarred man counted each coin, letting them run through his hands. The man paid well. There would be no questions asked. As far as he was concerned the man who hired him ceased to exist after he took the job. "I'm at your disposal. The marks?"

"First D'Artagnan and about two days later Porthos," the cardinal responded and gave the assassin the complete instructions on which men he wanted eliminated, when, and where he would get his next payment.

* * * * * * * * * * *

"Where's Athos going?" D'Artagnan asked Porthos and Aramis as he watched the oldest musketeer draw further away from them.

"I do believe the man is seriously contemplating taking on Richelieu." Porthos adjusted his new sash about his waist as a breeze blew through the courtyard.

"On his own?" D'Artagnan said, taken aback by the idea that Athos could fall to the level of using tactics that he himself would use and then regret later if he survived.

"He has not done anything yet," Aramis interjected a voice of reason. "I dare say he has gone to see his wife. I believe he has a promise to her to honor."

"That's not very reassuring, Aramis," Porthos criticized in a somewhat odd role reversal.

"Then take assurance from the fact that Athos will not leave without at least telling one of us beforehand. We do know him well enough to know he would at least do that even if he will not say where he is going or what he is up to," Aramis said, resisting the urge to scratch at the bandages covering his right breast. They'd been on for ten days, and he was chaffing at the restriction.

"Hate to tell you this, Aramis, my good friend." Porthos nudged the man and D'Artagnan's lips quirked. "But glaring at that sling isn't going to help your wound heal any faster." He abruptly changed his tone. "*Pauvre* Aramis. But look at it this way, man. If you're a good boy, you can stop wearing the sling tomorrow, and if you're even better Treville might let you have your sword back by the end of the month."

"I am so glad you are here to tell me these things, Porthos. What would I do without you?" Aramis said.

"Good gracious, don't even think of it." Porthos slapped his hand to his heart dramatically. "You poor lads might die of seriousness if I weren't here to make you laugh. Then where would you be?"

"I cry mercy, Porthos," Aramis said, raising his good hand. "The point is yours this time."

Porthos bent down and thrust his face right in D'Artagnan's face. "Good morning, D'Artagnan," he said loudly, and the musketeer started and fell back several steps. "You were supposed to laugh."

"Sorry," he replied apologetically. "I was just thinking." He closed his mouth, and a slight blush tinged his cheeks.

"Of course." Porthos clapped his young companion on the back. "Your beautiful, young lady. What is her name? Constance, that's it. She arrives back at court today. Actually I believe she arrived earlier this evening. Well, you'd best not keep the lady waiting, youngster. A gentleman never makes a lady wait, especially not a queen and her lady in waiting."

D'Artagnan excused himself hastily to find out if Porthos was right.

Aramis expelled a breath between his perfect teeth. "Ah, Porthos, you could teach us all something about tact," he commented sarcastically.

Anne d'Autriche smiled, a regretful little smile, as she saw Laurel d'Anlass, her arm freshly out of the sling, yet still bandaged, staring longingly down at the two men who were fencing in the gardens in the crisp late morning sun. What must it be like for her to have to live her life the way she had to now after the way she'd been raised? Not that Laurel said much about her past, but Anne could imagine just from the rumors she had heard from her own private sources. If Laurel were a man, Anne would be willing to wager she could become one of the best musketeers around within a few years.

Poor woman. Oft she had stood there in exactly that same manner for the past week—actually, closer to about eleven days.

"You are not happy here," her *majesté* noticed.

She turned and sat next to the woman who was not all that much older than she. "No, I'm not. My life has not been very happy recently. Nor am I used to playing this game of practiced perfection. The complacent life is not for me. Yet where can a woman like me turn for fulfillment then?"

Another pretty brown-haired woman, Constance, looked up from the cloth she was stitching. "Is there nothing you really desire that you would be able to do?"

"I could follow in my father's footsteps. Compton, however, does not take single ladies, only widows and married women and that he does rarely." Laurel flicked an invisible piece of lint from the long skirt, still debating how she was going to overcome that obstacle.

Anne grasped the Marquise de Langeac's right hand in her own. Steadily she asked, "Is that what you want, to become a member of the secret spy service?"

"*Oui*," she said, no doubt in her voice, body, or eyes.

"Then I will see to it that Compton takes you on as soon as you are well," the queen concluded, and Laurel knew it'd be done.

"*Merci*, Anne," she said gratefully, and Anne smiled at the marquise. The queen had so few friends, and she was glad to welcome Laurel as one of them, even if she had only known the woman a short time.

A rap came upon the door, and the three women looked up as the queen called for the messenger to enter.

The messenger announced, "D'Artagnan, *Comte de* Garonne, requests the presence of *Mademoiselle* Constance Bonacieux in the formal parlor." His announcement complete, he left and Constance's eyes glowed as she set her sewing away, enraptured.

"Go to him," Anne insisted and wouldn't hear of it when Constance said she could not abandon her. "I have Laurel to watch over me. Now, go to him. You hardly want him to think you forgot him." Happily, Constance rushed off to meet the musketeer.

A young man stood in the large room, hat in hand, alone, and feeling insignificant when a woman rushed through a set of pillars and down the stairs. She ran towards him with dainty steps, and D'Artagnan's face lit up as she threw her arms around his neck, and he swirled her in a circle and off her feet and then set her back down reluctantly.

Wordlessly, they stood in each other's arms and then remembered where they were and separated to a more appropriate distance. D'Artagnan extended his hand, and Constance slipped hers in it, and the two began to walk towards a painting. Once there he released her hand, and she turned to face him, placing her back against the wall.

Suddenly the woman's brow furrowed. "D'Artagnan, what is that?" She pointed, and D'Artagnan slowly turned to see what she was pointing towards. "*Sacré bon . . .*," he cursed and threw Constance to the floor, ducking to the left as he did so. Constance peeped in surprise.

An instant latter D'Artagnan gasped, his face turning unnaturally white, and he fell forward into Constance's arms, blood pouring from a bullet wound near his upper left breast, narrowly missing his shoulder blade. It was a bullet that had ripped clear through his body to lodge in the painting.

"D'Artagnan!" she screamed as she frantically tried to stop the bleeding. At least he was still alive. Thinking and acting quickly enough that she could block the attacker's escape, she yelled at the top of her voice, "Guards." They rushed into the room en masse.

Firmly, she ordered some of them to catch the assassin; he would not escape. The others she instructed to get D'Artagnan to a doctor. He had to live. She wouldn't let him die. The guards extracted the young woman from him, assuring Constance he would get the best care possible. One of the guards escorted the distraught woman back to the queen.

Anne rose to her feet at the sight of the beautiful young woman with a scarlet stain streaked down the front of her dress and an unnaturally pale face. The guard left at Anne's signal, and Constance told the two women in a voice racked with pain that D'Artagnan had been shot and badly wounded.

Anne glanced from Constance to Laurel, and Laurel implored quietly, the strain evident in the inflection of her voice, "Let me go to the musketeers. Athos, Aramis, and Porthos should know what happened, and I would be the best choice to tell them." The queen nodded, and Constance finally broke into tears, which Anne did her best to comfort. If she were a man. If only she were a man, this country would be run differently, starting by getting rid of that cardinal, one way or another.

Section Seven

"What are you doing sneaking up on people like that?" Porthos said as his impertinent and unrepentant gaze raked the slight figure dressed in what appeared to be a stable hand's cast-offs. Too much to expect, to hope, Laurel had given up her escapades as a member of the opposite sex. Crying shame to hide that exquisite body of hers underneath such rags, anyhow. One might even presume that the queen was not up to contending with the over feisty noblewoman.

"Besides," the large man contested, "I thought you'd given up the masquerade, charming though it may be. You haven't gone and snuck out and in the middle of the night? You've really gone and done it this time, lad, have you not? Offended your hostesses." Closer to just after dusk, in reality, though Laurel did not attempt to correct the large man.

"*Non*, nothing like that," she assured the large man soberly, dampening his ardor before the musketeer got on a roll that could not be stopped. "My hostess knows exactly where I've gone and why. I simply thought it inappropriate to come over here with an entourage when I've come to see you for—personal reasons." Not to mention the fact that it was easier than coming in more conventional ways, but Laurel elected not to tell him that. He'd never believe that it drew less attention or that she might actually have a reason to try to draw the least amount of attention to her this time. "Is there someplace private that I could speak with you, Athos, and Aramis?"

"Don't ask much, now, do you?" Porthos, seeing the dark look cloud her features, changed tracks. "Right now?" She nodded, and Porthos told her he'd see what he could find. Several musketeers cast them suspicious glances, sent them speculating as to whether this was the same the young lad who'd set the barracks upside down by drawing a sword against the doctor and then, to make matters worse, had tried to fight his way out of the barracks.

Inside a building where several men were lounging nonchalantly, Porthos peeked his head. "Athos. Aramis," he diverted their attention from fellow musketeers. Excusing themselves from their colleagues, they approached their friend.

"*Oui*?" Athos directed himself towards Porthos while Aramis hung a step back. Something was decidedly off, though Aramis could not identify exactly what it was.

"We've got ourselves a little visitor from the palace, it seems. Can we use one of your rooms to talk privately?" Porthos directed the query to both men.

"My room. It is the closest," Aramis said, and the musketeers and Laurel made their way to Aramis' room.

Upon the floor away from the closed door, Laurel made herself a seat, completely unconcerned with her appearance or what things might well be on the floor. "I think we'd best all sit. I'm afraid I bear no good news."

"How bad?" Athos asked, complying with the younger woman's suggestion, and Aramis and Porthos followed suit.

"Very bad," the woman began, lifting her gaze from her hands and forcing herself to stop wringing those very same limbs. Nervousness was not usually in her habits, nor was this gnawing feeling at her innards.

For the briefest of moments, she almost asked for a drink to steady those nerves that had been stressed by more these past few months than during most of her life. Instead she cleared her throat and spoke, "An assassin snuck into the palace today. He was captured only after he shot D'Artagnan. From what I've been told, the situation is rather dire, and D'Artagnan will be lucky if he survives. The prognosis is not good. But he's got a chance," she stressed to them, that is, if all went very well. Ominous, the words hung, like a death knell, even to her own ears.

Shock left them speechless. It didn't seem possible that a companion and friend they had come to know and love in the past year might likely die due to an assassin's bullet. He was so young. "The assassin was captured, you said?" Porthos finally asked.

"*Oui*, but not alive," was Laurel's reply.

"Who was the bullet meant for?" Porthos addressed Laurel again, trying to make some sense out of something that seemed not to have any really sense to it.

"The official version or my version?" asked the woman.

"Why don't you give us the official version and then your own." Athos did not request it. He expected it.

She didn't argue. The official version was that an assassin had sneaked into the palace looking for the queen; however, he mistook Constance for the queen and would have shot her if D'Artagnan hadn't pushed her out of the way. At least that was the official version she'd heard. Rumors were not often trustable.

"And so D'Artagnan took the bullet for her," Aramis said; his deceptively mild inflection demonstrated he plainly did not believe the story, not any more than the woman who had recounted it.

Grimly, Porthos said, "Let's hear the not-so-official version." There was something bloodthirsty in his words and intonation that caused Laurel to pause a moment. Odd that she had forgotten just how big, powerful, and intimidating the heir to the *Comte de* Vendôme was capable of being.

"I took a look at the scene where the shooting took place, and after Constance calmed down, I talked to her as well." Laurel paused again, regathering her thoughts and a semblance of calm control. "From what she told me and what I saw, it's pure luck D'Artagnan isn't dead right now. If Constance hadn't made him turn around, that bullet would have went straight through the back of his heart. Believe me, for I stood exactly where Constance said he was standing, and right where his heart would have been, lodged in the painting, was the bullet."

"So D'Artagnan was the mark," Athos concluded. "Sounds like Richelieu wants us dead," he said, the leap of intuition not at all implausible to him nor his friends.

"For some reason I was afraid you'd reach that conclusion too." Laurel wrapped her arms around her knees. What she still couldn't quite figure out was the cardinal's complete motivations in this or what purpose it furthered. Richelieu was far from being a stupid or reckless man. Vengeance seemed too simple and too risky when a man of his position could easily arrange convenient accidents.

"Tomorrow, I'm going," Athos spoke, and Laurel was the only one who understood he was going to go after his son, prompted from his inaction by the latest development.

"You shouldn't go in alone, Athos. Your chances of success are better with a small group or at least one other person," Laurel reminded him. Nor did she care to see Athos suffer a fate such as D'Artagnan's by rushing in. She was unreasonably fond of him. Had she ever really had a brother, she would have chosen the blond-haired man.

"Would you two kindly let the rest of us in on this or should we just leave?" Porthos said. Patience was not his strong suit. Big surprise. The woman glanced at Athos, her eyes beseeching him to tell his friends what was going on.

"Richelieu has my son by Sabine hostage in his Paris residence," Athos told them bluntly. "I'm getting him out tomorrow. I'll welcome help, healthy help. But I won't be talked out of it. Richelieu will not keep my son a moment longer, and I gave my word."

"I'm coming with you," Porthos said, a smile crossing his face. Checking Richelieu might possibly give him a measure of satisfaction. That and he wasn't about to abandon Athos. Distracted by this new task, between the four of them they laid out a plan of tackling the problem.

Some time later, Porthos and Athos made their way out of the room to make preparations for the excursion they'd be taking on the morrow. Laurel was on the verge of heading back for the palace when a loud, persistent rap came upon the door. Aramis jerked his head, signaling her to duck out of sight, and she rolled under the bed, wincing as she jolted her tender arm, but surprised nonetheless that her shoulder seemed to be behaving quite nicely all in all.

Aramis slipped out of his doublet and threw it over the chair. Quickly, his fingers undid the strings at the top of his tunic. Mussing his hair and kicking his boots from his feet, he completed the picture of a gentleman getting ready for a nap or having just awoken from one. Finally, he opened the door, blinking his eyes, and recognized Milord Compton.

"Okay, where is she?" Compton demanded.

"Excuse me?" Aramis responded.

Compton shot the tall man a suspicious, mistrustful look. "Where is she?" he demanded again and pushed past Aramis into the room and saw nothing on first inspection.

"Milord, really," Aramis reminded him, "this is my room. You could at least have asked me before barging in."

"Sorry," his lordship said quickly and looked at the man who leaned against the doorjamb, the picture of nonchalance. He was too polished sometimes. "I was looking for Laurel d'Anlass. I had thought she had left in the guise of Christophe and came here."

"Why would you think that Milord?"

"Obviously I was mistaken. She isn't here." The man shook his head and said apologetically, "I apologize for my rude behavior. That woman is quite simply infuriating. Breaks all the rules."

"Quite all right," Aramis responded. "I understand perfectly. I did travel with her for quite a few weeks." The musketeer extended his hand, and they shook firmly.

"*Merci* for your time and indulgence," Compton thanked the musketeer and left the premises. Softly, Aramis closed the door behind him.

Laurel rolled out from under the bed and was in the process of retrieving her hat from under the bed when Aramis turned around.

The woman scrambled to her knees, clutching her hat. She stopped short of putting the hat back on and noted Aramis, his hands perched on the table, ankles crossed, looking straight at her with a look she didn't trust. Made her feel like he was looking right through her. Suddenly, she was reminded of the last time she had been in the room and how he had gotten the last words and left her in a state of bafflement. What did he want? Did she really want to know? Maybe not.

"Perhaps you could be so kind as to tell me what that little visit was all about." Aramis pushed away from the table and stood looking down on her.

Quickly, she clambered to her feet. It was bad enough that he was taller than her. But to have him towering directly over her while she was kneeling . . . "I don't know. I haven't seen Compton since the trial."

"You do not know," he said in a tone that clearly implied otherwise. "You can do better than that, Laurel. Use your imagination a little. Perhaps you absconded with his best sword or sent a letter demanding half his holdings for the ransom of his son and heir."

"I did nothing of the sort," she retorted. "And you well know that."

"*Oui*," he prompted, aware that at a certain level he was baiting her and not at all adverse to provoking her.

"Oh, you arrogant pig," she said with disgust and dropped to the bed. Sometimes arguing with Aramis was like arguing with a brick wall. "Have to know everything. Well, if you must know, I went over his head and pulled a few strings. I asked her *majesté*,

Anne d'Autriche, to see to it that Compton instate me in the secret spy service. Although, I must confess I didn't think she would talk to him so soon. Well, no matter, the thing is done."

"Honestly, Laurel, you do beat all. Don't you know better than to go over the head of a man like Compton? There are other ways."

"Excuse me if I can't always think of the perfect thing to say, so I did what was effective," Laurel stated and shrugged her shoulders and decided what the heck, she'd play along. Besides, she had a strange feeling he was goading her. "Okay, so maybe there was a better way. But seeing as you're so well versed in that area, why don't you enlighten me?" She leaned back a bit, waiting for her poor, feeble mind to be illuminated by certain greatness.

"Smart aleck," he muttered, and fortunately she didn't hear the remark, or he'd never have lived it down. At least not in this particular lifetime. He perched one foot on the bed next to her and looked down at her. "Well, you could try a little tact."

She harrumphed, folding her arms across her chest and sitting up straight. "Like the tact you so admirably demonstrated the other day when you turned tail and fled."

His eyes narrowed, and he cast her a threatening look that boded no good for Laurel. He was very tempted to . . . But he was a gentleman, whether the woman approved or not. "As a matter of fact, *oui*, Laurel. That was a very good demonstration of tact in avoiding what could have escalated into a very complicated and messy situation."

"Call it what you wish," Laurel said studying her fingernails. Served him right if she turned the tables on him. "I call it cowardice."

He suddenly sat down next to her and grabbed both her hands. "Look at me." She complied reluctantly. "I highly recommend you do not bait me, Laurel."

"I'm not baiting you," she protested. "I have a difference of opinion. And I don't appreciate it when people walk out on me in the middle of a conversation. It's rude, for starters."

"Is that what you really want?" he asked the woman, and she replied with a "What?" "Is that what you really want—to pick up our last conversation where we left off? Because it can be arranged, but I warn you that my thoughts and the direction of the conversation may not be very respectable."

"Aramis," she said, her eyes wide with confusion, and then she understood. She laughed nervously. "I don't think so."

"Now she gets it," he spoke as if there were an audience. Porthos' ways had apparently rubbed off on him more than he had suspected.

Laurel suddenly made a move to get to her feet and announced, "I'd better go."

"Now look who is running away," he observed casually.

"I'm not running away," she insisted firmly reseating herself on the bed.

"Then what are you afraid of?"

"I can take whatever you dish out, Aramis. I am not a coward."

"Okay, you are not a coward. But you are quite naive, my lovely innocent." He lifted one of her hands to his lips and kissed it, expertly. His eyes fixed on her. "You should know better than to stick around with a man who desperately wants to kiss you speechless, *chérie*."

Her mouth fell open in surprise. "Kiss me?" she repeated, too shocked to say anything else. How had she forgotten that amongst the inseparable foursome, the would-be priest was a consummate seductor?

"*Oui*," he said, his eyes never wavering from hers as he leaned closer, sinking down on the bed beside her. His face a hair's breadth from hers. Frozen, mesmerized, Laurel forgot to even so much as breathe. With a feather-light touch, he brushed his lips against hers. He released her hand, and it fell to her lap. This time he placed his own hand on her chin and lifted her lips to meet his again.

He broke the kiss off, still staring at her with that eerie intensity, and for a moment she sat there still transfixed, and then she bolted out the door and down the stairs two at a time, almost forgetting to put on her hat until the last second.

"Heaven have mercy," Porthos cried as a swiftly moving body impacted with him, and he grabbed the person stopping him, no, her, he discovered, when he saw Laurel's deep blue eyes.

"Pardon," she apologized, not even trying to hide her distraction.

"Where are you off to in such a hurry? Being chased by the devil?" he tweaked.

"Understand—I'd love to talk, but some other time," she said, distracted, glancing one way then another as if she truly did fear pursuit. "I've got to get back to Anne and Constance before they wonder where I am."

The large man dropped his hands, and Laurel took off at a more conservative pace at first, which became an all-out run by the time she had reached the gates.

"What was that all about?" Athos said coming up to Porthos' shoulder.

"I haven't a clue." Porthos was baffled. "Aramis?" He was the last person they knew she was with. It was always possible he knew something.

"No, it's okay." Athos rested his hand on his friend's shoulder. "Let me talk to him. You finish our preparations."

"Aramis," Athos called, pushing open the door to see his dark-haired friend seated on his bed in a state of disrepair. He was unmoving except for looking up to acknowledge the older man.

"Athos." Aramis was a little surprised to see the man before the mission to rescue his son had even been attempted. "Is there something we forgot to go over?"

"No," he replied, asking if he could sit down, and Aramis gestured for him to make himself comfortable by all means. "Did something happen in here after Porthos and I left?"

Aramis ran his fingers through his hair and linked his hands behind his head. "Compton showed up demanding to see Laurel, and I covered for her."

"Hmm." Athos blinked several times. "That still doesn't explain why she ran out of here like the devil incarnate was after her, Aramis." He fixed his gaze on the man, seeing his state, really seeing his state for the first time. "You didn't . . ." Athos wanted Aramis to tell him he was completely wrong in his suppositions. Aramis didn't speak. " . . . You did. *Diantre!*" He got to his feet and at the doorjamb turned around. "You be careful, Aramis. Be very careful." Being stuck in the middle was not a role he fancied.

Constance brushed sweat-stained hair away from the man's face. His forehead was hot, too hot, to her touch and the color was all but completely blanched from his cheeks. The young man moaned, tossing, and Constance stilled him. *Non, non, non.* This was not the way things were supposed to happen. But the fever played no favorites, and it ignored her wishes entirely.

The blanket fell back, revealing D'Artagnan's chest, swathed in bandages from shoulder to almost the bottom of his rib cage. Gently she pulled the blanket back up and dipped a rag in the basin of tepid water. Twisting it, she wrung the excess water from the cloth and placed the damp cloth on his forehead, wiping the beads of perspiration from his face before placing the wadded cloth back in the basin. The physician had almost barred her from the room. As it was, it had taken all of Constance's persuasive powers to convince the old man to permit her to see D'Artagnan.

But she hadn't thought, hadn't realized, that seeing him like this would be so difficult. Racked with pain that she couldn't take away and murmuring words that were disjointed, desperate, and nonsensical. Nor did he recognize her. Not that she shouldn't have expected such a thing. He slept, if you could call it sleep. And the few moments when he had woken, he saw nothing—delirious.

Scuffling of footsteps out in the hallway caught her attention, and she looked up from her ministrations—from her attempts to calm the man and prevent him from throwing off the blanket and catching the chills. For a moment, he lapsed into undisturbed sleep, and the door opened and an old man with a permanent squint and receding dark hair entered the room, frowning at the young woman. "Move out of the way," he commanded in a tone that plainly told her she was a nuisance, and if she didn't move immediately he'd have her thrown from the room.

Constance scooched away from the bed, never taking her eyes from the young musketeer she had grown to love. How her hands itched to box that man's ears and tell him what she really felt. He was mean and arrogant and crude and foul-tempered to begin with. She brought her thoughts to a halt and watched as the doctor unwrapped several layers of the swathed cloth until he could see the angry red swelling that surrounded a blood caked hole.

Now, why hadn't he sewn the wound shut? Seemed like that would be the logical thing to do. Something about letting it breathe and being able to bleed the foul spirits out of it. His chubby dirt-stained hands probed the inflammation, and Constance scrambled to her feet and from the room, unable to watch any longer. The doctor ignored her, except to be glad that the woman was gone.

"I don't like that man. I don't like him at all," the woman announced, upset, as she joined the queen in her chambers. Constance unclenched her fists and sat next to Anne.

"Which man is that?" Anne asked, concern in her voice.

"That so-called doctor that's tending to D'Artagnan. He's foul-tempered and crude and nasty. And a boor. A lot like a maggot in many ways, and I don't trust him. I don't think he really even cares if D'Artagnan lives or not." Constance wrang her hands together and trembled with emotion. "Ooh, if I were a man I'd show him a thing or two."

Actually, if that were the case she'd probably have throttled him by now, Anne concluded as Laurel d'Anlass shot them a look that said she would have already tried to throttle this "doctor" regardless of the fact she wasn't a man—that is, if he was that bad. "He is truly that bad?" Anne asked.

"He's worse," Constance said emphatically. "Why I'd trust you or Laurel or even me more than that, that, that . . . Ooh, words fail to describe that thing." At this point she almost wished she knew some of the profanity that seemed to pepper Laurel's vocabulary every so often.

Anne fixed her gaze on the blond-haired woman. The marquis' daughter had traveled to many countries and was obviously a person of uncommon experiences, along with being decisive and strong-willed. "Laurel." The woman approached the queen, withdrawing from her observation of the fighters in the garden. "Have you ever attended victims of gunshot wounds before?"

"More times than I'd care to recall sometimes. My father and I both," she admitted. There was a war going on in Europe now—had been for all her formative years. "And more recently than I'd like to remember. I had to tend Athos' shoulder when he took a ball on the way to Calais."

Constance looked hopefully from Laurel to the queen. "Then you'll tend D'Artagnan," Constance said eagerly.

Anne hushed her lady in waiting gently. "Only if she wants to and thinks she's up to it."

There was a pause, and Constance's eyes beseeched Laurel. "I'll do it, but you get rid of that doctor, and don't let anyone gainsay me no matter what peculiar things I may do," Laurel finally spoke, and the queen rose, declaring it was settled. Anne hurried off to tend to the matter immediately, leaving Constance and Laurel to arrange any other minor details. Maybe the queen still had some influence in this palace—more than could be rightly expected, considering her childless state and where she was from.

* * * * * * * * * * * *

Porthos hated cowls. They itched, and they were hot too, especially when the morning sun was focused on them. So what if they were loose-fitting and provided good cover for a sword and other such items; they were annoying, to say the least. Of course, Athos seemed right at home in his assumed role and not at all uncomfortable, Porthos mused morosely to himself.

Why couldn't some of Aramis' implacability, impassiveness, whatever, rub off on him as well? Only seemed fair. After all, he'd been friends with the man as long as Athos had. Actually this would have been the perfect role for Aramis, had he been well enough to play it, considering he had once been a student of the cardinal's and actually had a desire to enter the style of life required by the orders. Plus, he knew the grounds.

"Porthos, your Bible," Athos reminded, him noticing that Porthos was about to lose his grasp on the book for the third time that morning. The large man grasped the book to him again as reverently as he could manage, and the companions continued to trace their way through the streets of Paris, mostly unremarked. Athos stopped and bowed his head reverently as the matins tolled, and Porthos belatedly followed suit. The bells ground to a halt, and the men started on their way again.

They drew to a halt at a set of double doors, and Athos withdrew the letter that Aramis had forged, signing in the name of an abbot from Gascogne that would be familiar to the cardinal but not very. Athos rapped on the door, and a novice opened it, asking them what their business was here. The musketeers told him of their journey to see the great spiritual leader of France and how their abbot had recommended they strengthen their faith by a pilgrimage to Paris to see his eminence, Cardinal Richelieu.

The novice asked for a letter confirming this story, and Athos mutely handed over the forged letter. The man opened it and read through the contents, diligently. The novice folded the letter and gave it back to them, granting them entrance.

Porthos sighed inwardly. Aramis' forgery had been perfect; if it hadn't been, they'd be in prison again by now. The novice led the two visitors down the hall, explaining, "His eminence is occupied today, and his schedule is quite busy. However, there are many spiritual activities to enlighten you in the city until such time as he can see you himself."

The trio entered through a pair of pillars into a room containing various large baths much like the Muslim baths in Africa. Public, open, extensive. Men in various states of undress lounged around the baths either fully emersed, wading, toweling off or even getting a massage. "So this is what worthy cause? His eminence uses church tithes for a pleasure pool," Porthos whispered bitingly in Athos' ear, and Athos gave him a quick jab in the ribs, warning him to hold his tongue.

Gesturing, the novice told his brethren, "You must be weary after your long journey. Please feel free to make use of these facilities to clean up and relax. All the brethren do," he concluded in a tone that clearly implied any who did not make full use of the facilities were thrown out for insulting their host, Richelieu.

Now Athos and Porthos understood why no woman would ever be able to sneak in here. They'd never pass for a man in a state of undress. "*Merci*, my brother, I think we shall enjoy a chance to rest our tired muscles," Athos replied, and the brother waited for them to follow up their words with action. Athos and Porthos stripped carefully so as to avoid revealing their swords.

Moments later they joined the throng of men bathing in the hot soothing waters, and the novice departed. As he entered the waters, Porthos grumbled that Laurel would have enjoyed this (after she had grumbled at the expense and the misuse of funds), and that she should have been the one to come here if this place had permitted women.

His Eminence arrived back from mass and set aside his heavy stole that marked the season in the Church. His duties were never done; always more sheep to lead back to the fold of the Good Lord and the Holy Church. But someone had to be responsible for the salvation of their souls. That was the price of being chosen as God's representative. Of course, it had been so tragic to hear that D'Artagnan was badly wounded and could very well die; actually, according to the doctor, there was little hope. So sad. He smiled and closed the Bible that sat upon the podium.

From his adjoining chambers Richelieu heard the sound of a man entering. "Set it on the far table," he called, instructing the servant where to place the basin of hot water he had sent for. Richelieu loosened the tie that bound his cassock and strode to the next room, startled to see that the lay brother had not yet left the room after completing his task. "Did you have a concern to share with me, my son," Richelieu addressed the man with exaggerated sincerity.

The lay brother turned around to face him, not in the least meek or mild. He lowered the hood of his cowl. "As a matter of fact, I have a great concern to 'discuss' with you," Athos informed his eminence, stepping closer to the hawk-nosed man.

"Ah, my dear Athos, had you wanted to see me, you hardly needed to have gone to all the trouble as to have snuck in here. You could have come to me after mass or during confession."

"*Merci*, but I decided to invite myself here. I didn't think you'd be quite receptive to the subject in public," he said, putting his hand to the hilt of his sword in case he might have to use the weapon.

The cardinal reached out his hands, palms upward, in a mocking gesture of welcome. "Well, now that you're here, what seems to be the problem?"

"Where have you put my son?" He wasted no time in getting to the heart of the problem.

"Your son, *cher* Athos? I was not aware that you had any children."

"Let's dispense with the games, shall we, Richelieu," he ordered. "We both know that I was and still am a *comte,* for all practical purposes. I don't think you remained in the dark for long about the woman you saved from execution somewhere around four years ago, maybe five. Remember her, Richelieu?"

"Oh, do go on. This is really all quite fascinating." The cardinal waved his hand.

"I'm sure it didn't take you long to realize that I was the *comte* that Sabine de Winter had been married to, once you met me." The one he was still legally married to, in all likelihood.

"Ah, *oui*, the beautiful *Comtesse de* Winter. She has had a habit of going through husbands and lovers very quickly and then dispensing of them." He paused and twisted the ring on his finger. "How odd that you're still alive then."

Athos came closer to the cardinal, menace in his posture. "Enough chitchat, as enlightening as it may be. I have come for Guillaume. Either you tell me where he is now or we can do this the hard way." Athos drew his sword, emphasizing the serious nature of the threat.

The cardinal left the bedchamber without hurry and proceeded back into the adjoining study. If he had hoped to lose the musketeer, he had hoped in vain, for the man followed him. His eminence placed the desk between himself and Athos and shuffled several papers containing the remains of sermons. "You have no claim to the boy. His mother left him in my care."

"His mother is still my wife. We never divorced like some Englishmen, nor was our marriage annulled. The boy is mine, and I will have him back," Athos said, prompting Richelieu out from behind the desk with the tip of his sharp saber. "I'm glad to see we understand one another. Now where were we? *Oui*. That's right, you were about to tell me where you are holding my son." Athos smiled and Richelieu glanced at the door. "I wouldn't recommend calling out."

However, the cardinal did not take the musketeer's recommendation, and he called for the guard outside to enter. Another man wrapped in a black cowl came in, taking stock of the situation as he entered.

As he pushed his hood down, Porthos said, "Drat. And I was so hoping that his eminence would decide to be cooperative. So disappointing to be proved wrong. People these days just never live up to your expectations."

Athos shrugged his shoulders at the cardinal's look of mounting fury at his temporary helplessness. "I did warn you, your eminence." Athos instructed his large friend, "Porthos, why don't you check through all those papers and that desk and wherever else you feel the desire to look? I'll keep our friend here entertained."

Porthos set to work, jovially searching through the papers with gusto and discarding those inscribed with Latin sermons unceremoniously. From there, he started yanking out drawers and dumping their contents out for inspection. His thigh bumped against the desk and a compartment slid open. The musketeer reached inside and took out a letter and a ring. He read through the letter and palmed the ring.

"Why, your eminence," Porthos called to the cardinal, admiring the ring in the rays of sunlight that came in the room, "how nice of you to keep Aramis' ring and letter safe for him until he could claim them. I'll remind him to thank you. However, I can take the duty off your hands now," he remarked, securing the letter and ring inside a pocket in his tunic.

The cardinal clenched his jaw and a vein throbbed in his temple. "You don't approve?" Athos inquired as Porthos continued his search. "What a shame. Now why don't we talk about the assassin you hired. Okay, how bout we make sure no more assassins get in my way." Richelieu met the musketeer's gaze, not daring to provoke him. "It would be so unfortunate for me to have to return here to pay you another visit if that were to happen again. You just might not survive the encounter," Athos said, and Richelieu clearly understood the message. No more assassins would be sent after the musketeers, or he'd pay for it with his life. For Athos quite simply wouldn't care if he lived or died, if he had to come after the cardinal again.

Porthos crowed in triumph. "I've found it, Athos." He left his search to approach his friend.

"Wonderful," Athos told Porthos. "Thank you so much for your hospitality, your eminence. But we must be going now," Athos concluded as Porthos swung the hilt of his sword downward on the cardinal's head, asking the Lord's forgiveness for striking "a man of God." Someone had to take up Aramis' role. Richelieu crumpled to the ground, completely unconscious. "Ah, Porthos, I wanted to do that," Athos told his friend.

"Sorry," the man said, only mildly contrite. There was nothing he could do now. "Shall we go?" Both men resheathed their swords and pulled their hoods over their heads before sneaking back out to the corridors and quickly down the halls.

"Aramis." Laurel stopped on the threshold of the room as she saw Anne and Constance talking with the tall, handsome musketeer.

Before she could ask why he was there, he said, "Why so surprised to see me, Laurel? D'Artagnan is my friend. I wanted to see how he was. I understand you are in charge of his care now."

"*Oui*," she replied, glancing at the blood that she hadn't quite been able to scrub off her hands or from under her nails. She rubbed her eyes. Tired. That's what she was, but at least she was doing something. She shouldn't be surprised to see Aramis here; after all, he'd hardly be able to sit around and wait calmly for Athos and Porthos to return.

Anne gestured to some chairs, urging her newfound friend and Aramis to be seated. "Please have a seat, Laurel. You look like you could use some rest," Anne said, wondering at the newly appointed marquise's reaction to the musketeer. "How is the young man?" the queen asked as diplomatically as she could, considering the fact that Constance and Aramis were both in the room, and both deeply cared for the injured man. In fact, she suspected Laurel also cherished D'Artagnan like she would a well-loved younger brother.

"His fever still hasn't broken." Her voice sounded very tired as she imparted the information. If anything, his fever had worsened. Though Laurel was unwilling to admit that yet. "I think I've gotten the inflammation down and have been able to drain the wound. I just finished stitching it up, but I don't know if he's going to be strong enough to fight off the fever and the effects of blood loss and mild festering. I just don't know," she repeated. Helplessness did not suit her personality.

Constance's face went several shades whiter and she stuttered, "Does that mean he's going to die?"

Anne, seeing the signs of imminent hysterics, went to Constance and slipped her arms around the other woman, leading her back to her chambers so that she could calm the woman.

Anne and Constance vanished from sight. "Why am I always getting left alone with you?" Laurel said in a combination of exasperation and a half dozen other emotions she couldn't name.

"Fate," he suggested in a teasing tone and then became serious. "Is he really that bad? Will he probably die?"

"Unfortunately, he's very bad, Aramis, and that first incompetent fool did no good for him. But as to if he'll die, I honestly don't know. He's got a very strong will to live. He may pull through." She chose not to respond to his teasing, but did tell him more of her opinion on D'Artagnan's chances, and she hoped she was wrong about him being in terrible condition. "You really do care about him, don't you? You really care so deeply, and you almost never show it," Laurel said in wonder.

"*Oui*, I care deeply, Laurel, but as you well know: 'Show how much you care and then you get hurt.' People use it against you," Aramis revealed to her with complete frankness. "Now can you understand that I might possibly be worried about you?"

Oui, she could. She truly could. For she didn't know how she would have dealt with her father's death if Aramis hadn't been there. Nor did she know what she'd do if Aramis should die. Nor did she know if she could stand to have Aramis and the other musketeers just walk out of her life when this crisis ended. "Don't look at me that way."

"Pardon." Aramis shook his head a fraction.

"I wish you wouldn't look through me like I'm not even here. It's eerie, like you can see every little thing," Laurel told him, accidentally saying more than she had intended.

"You care too," Aramis' lips curled into a half smile set off by the twinkle in his gold-flecked eyes. He was thankful that he was still capable of having a sense of humor at this rather dire moment. "You do not like showing it any better than I do, *chérie*."

"Well, of course I care. I have a heart." Laurel got up from her chair and strode towards the balcony, completely aware that Aramis was following her. The cool air brushed against her skin. Summer would end soon and fall was on its way. Not many perfect days like this would occur in the near future. She turned and leaned against the rail, fixing her gaze on Aramis. Something in her stomach did a flip-flop, and she forced herself to be as impassive and formal as possible. "But D'Artagnan, he's your friend. I don't know that I can possibly imagine how much you four care about each other."

He leaned his elbow on the rail so that he was at equal height with her. "I do not know about that, Laurel. Is what you claim really true?"

A pause hovered between them—one which was so very long. "I don't know what I'll do when you guys go," she admitted, finally allowing herself to consciously acknowledge the words. "*Zut et zut alors*. It shouldn't be this way."

"Shouldn't be what way?"

"Shouldn't . . . well it shouldn't be possible to be so bloody scared about losing four men who've only been a part of my life for less than three months, barely two. It can't be possible to feel this numbness in the pit of my stomach, this certainty that so much meaning would leave when I think that D'Artagnan may not live, but I do. Sometimes I think that if I were to lose all of you, it'd take more meaning out of my life than my father's death, and that doesn't make sense." She wrenched her hands from the rail and hit her fist against her open palm, brutally. Stupid! Never should she have said what she had. Had she learned nothing about wariness from her father?

"*Oui*, it does," he contradicted and stopped her from hitting herself again. "It is not being disloyal to your father or saying that you did not love him. You see, Laurel, though we may never say it, Athos, Porthos, D'Artagnan and myself are very close, and if I were to lose them all or even one of them, it would be much worse than losing my father."

Laurel was at a loss for words. She'd thought she'd be prepared for the real Aramis, but she wasn't. His intensity and conviction, and his capacity to care were far more than she had imagined. The woman caught sight of the queen, and Aramis caught sight of Anne a moment later. Laurel rushed—well, not quite rushed, more like hurried with control into the chamber with Aramis once again following her. "Is Constance going to be all right, Anne?"

The dark-haired dainty woman nodded her head. "I think so. She was overwrought. She's sleeping now and should be out for a while."

"Is there something going on between the two of you that I should be aware of?" Anne addressed the young marquise.

"Something going on? Between the two of who?" Laurel was genuinely confused. It had been a long day, and there was still a lot of the day left and a critically wounded man to tend to. So many hopes and expectations leveled on her shoulders, above and beyond her own exacting ones. "I think I'm missing something."

"I was just wondering if you and the musketeer who left earlier, Aramis, were having any problems or something of that nature," Anne clarified, or at least tried to. Laurel could be surprisingly obtuse when she wanted to be.

"I was surprised to see him. It didn't even occur to me that he'd come to see D'Artagnan, but it should have. And, well, Aramis has this talent for rubbing me the wrong way."

"How so?"

Laurel stopped gathering cloth to roll into bandages and faced the brown-haired woman. "Well, for one thing he always is so infuriatingly smooth and suave. Always does the proper thing, a perfect gentleman. All cultivated grace and charm. Makes me sick. Don't you ever get that way around people like that?"

Anne smiled her alluring smile, touched by a trace of ever-present sadness. "*Oui*, as a matter of fact I do know what you mean. Unfortunately, in my position I don't have the luxury of ever being able to confront the person or slap him across the face. I have to smile and do the pretty thing or risk offending some powerful diplomats and alienating some powerful countries." A gilded cage was a cage nonetheless. Anne paused, cocking her head slyly. "You do have to admit he's a very handsome man and honorable, too."

Laurel narrowed her eyes, reluctant to talk about attractive men and flirting and the such. She had never much talked of those things before, not even with Sabine, but Anne was waiting. "Okay, so he is handsome and honorable and loyal and all that. But too much of a good thing is still too much. He gets so honorable that he can't even tell where his image, his facade, stops and the real person starts. Is it really such a bad thing to want to see people be themselves?" Not to mention his charm and seduction ability were another reason to be very wary.

"Not at all," Anne said with force. "Unfortunately, in our world very few people ever are genuine. Everyone presents a facade. It's imperative to play the game to even survive. Image and reputation make or break lives here." She waved her hands, dismissing the topic. "Enough on society. Tell me more of this perfection Aramis has crafted."

"Okay, aside from being arrogantly sure of himself," she really was getting emotion behind it, hand gestures and all "he thinks he knows it all. Not that he says it that way, but he gives you that impression. And he's too observant for one's peace of mind, cause you never know what he's thinking. And those blasted eyes of his that look right through you."

By this point Anne was laughing so hard she was clutching her sides, and Laurel broke into laughter with her. Neither quite knew what was so funny, they simply laughed. She did know, however, that it felt good to laugh without reserve. It'd been too long. They brought themselves under some semblance of control. Anne's lips twitched as she asked, "And what does this gentleman think of you?" She held back her observation that the man seemed quite taken with Laurel.

"To use his own words, 'Laurel, you do beat all,' 'you stubborn little wench,' and 'you are a frustrating woman' or 'where is your sense?' Actually, I am frustrating, I suppose. I guess I like confusing him to no end. He needs a little something in his life to knock him out of his well-planned existence and force him to be the real Aramis," Laurel confessed, and then went on to swap stories with Anne about the things that really annoyed them about men, what they had done to those men, or what they had wanted to do to those men. By the time they were done, both felt much better. They had really needed the laughter to lighten the atmosphere of the place and alleviate the tension. Maybe it wasn't such a terrible thing to talk about men after all.

"Here." Athos looked to Porthos for confirmation that the door was the one he was looking for. Porthos nodded and Athos opened the door, trying not to cough at the dust that kicked up as a result of the action. "You have a torch?" Athos called back as he squinted into the darkness.

"Now I do." Porthos grabbed an unlit one from the main corridor and diligently struck a flint and lit it, carrying it into the dark recess that had once been a well-traveled passage. On second thought, he grabbed another and lit it from the first, then handed it to Athos.

Porthos swiped a cobweb out of the way. "Looks like our illustrious cardinal hasn't had much use for these old corridors in years."

"Probably didn't want anyone knowing about this wing, even the servants," Athos said as they walked farther down the aged corridor that sported several paintings dating back before Joan d'Arc. "It's a better place to hide people and things when no one knows the place you're hiding them exists."

"Ain't that the truth," Porthos said as he stopped to admire a picture of Joan d'Arc. He whistled. "There's a fortune's worth of valuable paintings and such here. Enough plunder to fulfill a pirate's dream and keep him living high for years."

"Come on. No time to admire the scenery. Nor are we here to pillage."

The two men continued on and came to a point where the corridor branched in two directions, and each hallway was peppered with doors here and there. They stopped, and Porthos raised his eyebrow, silently asking what next. "Looks like we split up. Meet back here as soon as you've searched the extent of that corridor." Porthos crossed his sword with Athos' and both men set off, torch in one hand and sword in the other.

Drat and double drat, this cowl was really getting in the way. Porthos stopped long enough to rid himself of the scratchy garment before he opened one door after the other, quickly. He knew he was pressed for time. As soon as the cardinal awoke, someone would be after them, and the cardinal knew exactly where they'd be.

He reached out to open another door and found it was locked. He broke the lock with a mighty kick and looked inside. Nothing. He went on and tried the next door. Another empty room. Near the end of the corridor he spotted another door and tried the handle. It too was locked. Once again he kicked it brutally several times until the handle split from the wood and permitted him access to the lock. He reached in the broken frame and slipped the lock from its place.

A startled little face looked up at him from behind a stool. Suddenly, the boy got up and ran behind the bed. Hiding from the strange but menacing man. Porthos sheathed his sword and approached the young lad. "Ah, Guillaume; that is your name? *Bon.* How'd you like to play a game with your Uncle Porthos?"

"Uncle Porthos?" he said in a small and suspicious voice.

"*Oui*, your papa and *maman* sent me to find you. They want to see you out of this dismal place."

"Don't have no papa," the boy insisted.

"Well, see, that's what I'm here to tell you. You're *maman* wants to have you meet your father. She asked him to find you so that she could see you again. And seeing as I'm a friend of your *maman* and papa, I am your uncle." Porthos crouched down so that he didn't tower over the blond-haired hazel-eyed boy.

"Why didn't *maman* come then?" Guillaume pouted.

"Ah, you see, that's part of the game. I'd hardly want to spoil her surprise. But if you don't want to play, I suppose I'd better go." Porthos turned and pretended to prepare to leave.

"Wait." The little boy came out from behind the bed and asked. "What game?"

"How'd you like to play 'Hide from Cardinal Richelieu?' And if you win you get to leave this room and go to a new house and be with a real family."

"Want to win. How?" the boy asked.

Porthos extended his free hand. "Hitch a ride with me, and I can do better than tell you how to win. I can help you win." Guillaume took it, and Porthos hefted the boy from the ground and left the room, heading back for the intersection. He stopped when he got there.

"Why're we waiting?" his new friend asked the large man, and Porthos said it was part of the game. And he hoped to God Athos hurried it up. It couldn't be long before they were found.

"Who's that?" The boy pointed at the new arrival.

"This," Porthos said, "is your papa."

"Are you sure?"

"Trust me." He smiled at the boy, actually grinned outrageously and tussled the boy's hair. Athos raised an eyebrow, but made no comment. Porthos would never own up to being a softy for children.

"If you say so," the boy agreed as they set off back down the dark hall.

Boot steps that weren't their own echoed through the hall, coming towards them from a distance, and Athos cursed so fluently that his friend almost thought the man drunk for a moment. "Where to now?" Athos asked for advice.

"What do you need?" Guillaume asked the stranger who was supposedly his father.

"A good way out," he replied.

"To hide from Richelieu?" the boy inquired, wondering if this was part of the game, and Athos nodded. "Pointed lady."

"What?" Both musketeers exclaimed at the same time.

"Pointed lady," the boy insisted.

"What pointed lady?" Porthos asked the hazel-eyed boy, and he pointed at the painting of Joan d'Arc that they stood in front of.

"What about the pointed lady?" Athos urged as he felt time steadily running out.

"Knows the way out."

"Of course," Athos and Porthos said one after the other, and Athos reached behind the painting, tripping a lever, and a door slid open.

The companions rushed through the opening, and Athos tripped the lever behind him; the door rumbled shut. Up the slope at the end of the passage the afternoon light poured in. The men dropped their torches and put them out, making a run for the light.

All three, including Guillaume, emerged into the light, blinking as their eyes adjusted. Athos assessed their location, and quickly they set off towards the place where they had agreed to meet Aramis—the residence where Sabine was staying. As they rushed on their way, Guillaume tapped Porthos' shoulder, and the large man shot a friendly glance at the boy. "We won the game?"

"I do believe so," he responded. "But your *maman* can be the one to give you your prize."

A smile transfigured the boy. He'd missed his mother. That was obvious. Guillaume tapped Porthos' shoulder again. "Where're we going?"

"To see your *maman*." Guillaume's face lit up again and he lapsed into a content silence.

* * * * * * * * * * * *

"No news yet?"

"None," Milady de Winter informed Aramis as she ran her hand over the back of the sofa lounger. "There is still time, however. And your plot is not a quick one. Laurel will not be joining you?"

"*Non*." He shook his head while he spoke, his hands neatly clasped in his lap. "She's working herself to the bone trying to save D'Artagnan's life. Apparently, the queen pulled a few strings and got rid of the doctor, putting Laurel in his place," Aramis answered the question before it was asked.

Sabine sat, bowing her head. "Perhaps it is better that way," she said softly. She was aware of Thomas' penchant for teaching his only daughter an interesting mix of "unladylike" skills.

"Better what way, Milady?"

"That she won't be here to witness a terrible scene." She put her finger to her lips, silently telling him she would say no more on that subject at the moment, so he'd best not ask. "You, Porthos, Athos, and D'Artagnan are good friends?"

"The best," he said without inflection, but with complete sincerity. Somehow he knew the woman would not ever use the information against him. "We'll die for each other, but we'll also live for each other. All for one and one for all. That is more than our motto and how we've chosen to live our lives, Milady; it is who we are."

The comtesse sighed. If only . . . But "if onlies" were not for her. Her son was what mattered now. Her son, her sister, and Athos. Athos would be all right, eventually, especially with his friends standing by him. But Laurel . . .? "May I ask where Laurel fits into your group?"

"She didn't." Milady looked almost crestfallen, and Aramis decided for once not to withhold information. "At first she didn't.

She was a stubborn, unconventional inconvenience. But we couldn't lose her, and then she saved Athos' life. After that she proved her abilities to fight and track and observe, time and again. She was loyal, honest, honorable, blunt, and trustworthy. And somewhere along the way the little hothead won our respect."

"And now, what do you think your friends think of her?" Sabine asked, and Aramis somehow got the impression the answer to her question was of great importance, beyond anything that the woman would admit.

"They would lay down their lives for her and trust her at their back any day, though they might never admit it to anyone who didn't personally know them and Laurel as well. Athos, I think, sees her as his younger sister and would always be there for her. You'd better believe he'd protect her. As for Porthos, he seems to view her as a very good fellow companion. In fact, it would be quite likely that he sees in her the same kinship he sees in each of us. D'Artagnan likes, respects, and looks up to her, at first as an older sister, but now more as a well-loved, slightly older brother."

"Then be sure you do not just walk out on her. For she needs your friendship. She has no real family left now that Thomas is dead."

"But you are her family."

"I haven't been her family for years, and she'd never be happy with my lifestyle." Sabine changed the tenor abruptly. "Would you all really go back to your old routines and let her try to forge out a new life alone?" Milady asked.

"I do not think so. We will at least always be in touch and let her know she is free to see us or call on us, with proper escort, that is. And I'm sure if she doesn't call on us, at the very least Porthos will most certainly call on her."

She fixed her gaze on Aramis and took his hand between her hands, enclosing it. "How do you feel about my sister, Aramis?"

"I respect her like I've respected no other woman," he told her, revealing nothing Sabine didn't already know.

"So you feel nothing like your companions then?" Her eyes never blinked while they searched his face. He was good. So very good at hiding what he felt and thought.

"Your sister is a very frustrating, nonsensical, hot-tempered, smart, yet naive woman. I have already risked my life for her. I have already trusted her with my life and many of my hardships. I am no less attached to her than my friends. I could never turn my back on her."

Milady released his hand and remained silent for several long moments. Moments that dragged on until they took on their own life. "I ask you to watch over her. To help her. I think you understand her better and more fully than the others, and she's going to need someone to lean on. Promise me you will help her whether she asks for your help or not. *Non*. Don't ask me why. I can't tell you, not yet. I need to talk to Athos first."

"And I will understand after that?" Sabine nodded. "Then I promise, Milady."

"*Maman*." A little form bolted right for Sabine and threw his arms around her, clinging to her, his face illuminated by a smile. "I just played the greatest game with Uncle Porthos."

"Oh?" Uncle Porthos now, was it? Milady played along. "And what was that?"

"We played 'Hide from Richelieu,' " he said as if it were a secret, a conspiracy of some sort. "And Uncle Porthos even took me on his horse. . . ." Suddenly, the boy stopped as if realizing he had a crowd, and then he glanced at Athos. "Uncle Porthos said you sent Papa after me. Is that true?" Guillaume suddenly demanded.

Sabine sat her son down beside her on the couch and warned him to be still. From there she proceeded to formally introduce Porthos and then Aramis. She called Athos over, and he crouched by her side, not even daring to hope. "Guillaume," she said, serious, "your Uncle Porthos was right. I did send your father after you. This is your father, Athos."

Guillaume stared at the blond-haired man who had helped in the game "Hide from Richelieu." He'd never had a papa before and now . . . "If you're my papa, why didn't you come to find me sooner?"

"Guillaume," his mother warned, and Athos stopped her, stating it was all right.

"I wish I had come for you sooner, Guillaume, but I didn't even know I had a son until very recently. You see, your *maman* and I haven't been able to see each other for a very long time, so she wasn't able to even tell me about you until a little while ago."

Guillaume was confused, and with as much dignity as a four-year-old could manage, asked, "Why was I with Richelieu then? I want to know." At this point Milady interfered and explained that the cardinal was a bad man who took her in when she got lost one day and then took Guilluame prisoner so that he could control her. In other words, the boy learned that he was a hostage to a man called Cardinal Richelieu, and that this man had tried to hurt *maman* and Papa was his conclusion.

"Won't go back," the boy said stubbornly. "Bad man. He hurt you. He hurt Papa."

"You don't ever have to go back," his mother and father assured him.

"Guillaume." Sabine made sure the boy was paying very close attention to her. "I need to talk to your papa alone for a little while. You stay here and play with Uncle Porthos and Uncle Aramis. Will you do that for us?" Finally he nodded, and she said he was a good boy as he hopped down to go to his new playmates while his mother led his father from the room.

"He's a wonderful boy, Sabine." Athos was the first to speak.

"I know," she said softly. Which was why she could not bring herself to stigmatize her son forever. "*Merci* for getting him from Richelieu." The couple fell into an awkward silence. Both started to talk at once, and then Sabine told her husband to go ahead.

"Will you be going now?" the man asked stiffly, and the *comtesse* read the very real pain and longing in her husband's eyes.

She had really hurt him, hurt him badly by her actions, and now he was going to lose the son he had just found to her. Milady didn't answer the question. Instead she gently touched Athos' cheek her eyes meeting his. "Can you never forgive me for lying to you Athos? All I ever wanted was your love. I didn't want to end up hurting you." It might well have been wrong to accept his marriage proposal all those years ago or at the very least not to have listened to Garrett.

Athos placed his own calloused hand over the small hand that still rested on his cheek. "I forgave you a long time ago Sabine," he said as if every word were painful for him. "But by then it was too late, and I thought you were dead, thought it was my fault. And when I saw you again and found out what you had become because of my rejection . . ." He choked.

Milady put her fingers to his mouth, stopping him from saying more. Her eyes were almost luminescent as she spoke again. "*Non*, Athos. You need not say it. I understand. I always knew you had a big heart, but that you stood by justice, truth, and honor first and foremost, especially in those you loved. I know you could act no other way than you did when you found me last. If you had done any differently, you wouldn't have been my Athos."

"Can you forgive me?"

"Athos, as soon as I realized you were doing only as your nature dictated, I had to forgive you. Must I say again that if you had done differently you wouldn't be the man I fell in love with? I would have ended up hating you for compromising ideals and betraying the man I still love." He wiped the single tear from her face and held her face between his hands. "I have forgiven you. I was just lying to myself so I wouldn't have to see what I'd become, the terrible murderess and vengeful woman." Milady stopped and sat herself on a nearby chair, and Athos sat on a chair across from her. "I am not permitted to leave Paris."

There was confusion in Athos' eyes, and he folded his hands in his lap, stilling their shaking. "Cannot leave Paris? You were only staying until Guillaume was safe."

"*Seigneur de* Winter's brother discovered I was still alive and presented his case against me to the king. I am under arrest until such time as the king decides my fate." She spoke almost as if she were speaking to the air, and was somewhere very far away.

"So you will take Guillaume and leave then?" Athos voice was strained, and he struggled to maintain his composure. He didn't succeed and his shoulders sagged.

His body shook with the suppressed emotion and Sabine knelt in front of him, grasping his arms, one in each hand. "I cannot run any longer, Athos. That is not the life I want for my son. And he deserves to know his father, to love the man that I love."

For the first time the meaning of her words hit him. She still loved him, loved him enough that she wanted him to be a real father to their son. Loved him even though he had rejected her and condemned her to death. At that moment, had Sabine asked him to go to the king and get him to spare her life, he would have done so. Sabine raised her face and kissed his lips. "*Non*, Athos, please do not say it. I know that you still love me, but I cannot have you betray yourself by saving me." She took a deep breath. "I have decided I will abide by his *majesté's* decision."

"You will die for the crimes," Athos said, his throat sore from clenching so hard.

"I know that, Athos, and I am guilty. But I can no longer live with the woman I have become. I hate her. You and Laurel made me really see her for the first time, and I do hate her. If I run again, I would only hate myself more. I need to face my fate now, with honor, and then maybe I can respect myself again, respect myself and be at peace with myself as well."

Athos hugged his wife to him tightly, both their faces streaming with tears that neither tried to wipe away. "What of Guillaume?" Athos whispered in her ear.

"Raise him with love, and tell him about how it was between you and me when things were good." Sabine stopped, overwhelmed for a long time. How was she going to explain this to her son, explain that he would never see his mother again?

"The king could always decide to exile you. In fact, it's the more likely choice. . . ."

"*Non*, Athos," Sabine's face was set stubbornly. "If I am exiled I will never see my son again, and he will have to live with the stigma of having a mother who was a traitor to France. No one would ever let him forget that. I cannot do that to Guillaume."

Athos touched her cheek. "There has to be another option, Sabine, *ma chère*."

"Not for me, Athos. I am resigned to my fate, Athos. This is not a decision made in haste. Can you understand that? *Non*, listen and consider. Can you understand?"

"*Oui*, but—" She silenced him with a kiss.

"Please . . . no more. I am not afraid of death. Not anymore." Her eyes remained locked on her husband's. "Tell him his mother died serving France, Athos," she finally said, and reluctantly he nodded holding her even tighter for a long time before she extracted herself, and she and Athos gathered their tattered emotions and went to face their fate. If only . . . But that was not how it would be. Time did not go backward, and it was too late now. Sabine continued to hold him close and made one last request that he see to it that Laurel's mount, Rebelle, who was in her stables, be returned to Laurel.

The Monday morning was overcast as Athos left his friends and walked the round-about way to the palace. His feet led him there while his mind remained subdued. He did not complain about the day. It fit his mood. Absently he presented himself at the palace doors with a letter in his hand that showed Louis had asked to see him today.

He didn't even notice as the servant led him down the corridors and around up the weaving staircase to his *majesté's* room. Rather his body went through the motions, and he stopped when the servant stopped. The servant rapped on the door and announced the musketeer to Louis and then came back out. "He will see you now," the servant said, bowing as Athos thanked him. The servant disappeared, and Athos finally entered the chamber.

Louis dispensed with the formalities and invited his guest to sit. The king pushed his papers away. They could be taken care of later. With unusual aplomb, the king asked, "You know why I have asked you to come to me today, Athos, *Comte* d'Avignon?"

"I believe so," the *comte* told his pledged sovereign in a voice that was strong yet weary just the same.

"Sabine de Winter is still your wife legally," Louis said as gently as he could, deciding to gloss over the bigamy she was obviously guilty of. "Is she guilty of the charges brought against her?"

Athos met Louis' eyes, knowing that for once the king did not want to ask this of him and was trying to spare him. Finally, Athos said, "*Oui*, she has told me so herself."

Louis nodded and sighed, setting down the document that laid out the charges against Sabine. "I owe you much, *Monseigneur* Athos. I would have your input on what you would have me do about the charges leveled against your wife."

"You are asking me if I would have her life spared?" Athos responded with a question.

"I would be willing to do so, *monseigneur*. She could be exiled instead and justice would be served, if that is what you wish," his *majesté* added.

Athos was silent. He had been offered a way to spare her life and still satisfy a small part of justice. He could spare her life, but would she want him to do so? Torn, he thought for a long time before speaking. "She would not have me spare her life, my liege. She would accept the punishment for her crimes, but without an audience and without formal accusation."

Louis would rather exile her. Still, one look at Athos told him that the man did not want his wife to die, but she would not have it any other way. Finally, the king nodded and broke from his role as sovereign, going to sit beside the man who had served him well as one of his best musketeers for bordering on eight years. Louis placed a hand of comfort and understanding on the man's shoulder. "Is there nothing I can do for you, then, nothing at all, *mon ami*?"

"I cannot ask you to treat me differently than the rest of your subjects," Athos said. He was well aware the king would never be so sympathetic to him again, never demonstrate again his friendship for the younger man.

"But you are different, Athos. Be assured that I will not condemn you for your wife's actions. I restore your lands back to you and to your son. And we would let you keep your title with honor. Justice will still be served, Athos." Louis paused. "She will still die for her crimes."

Athos met Louis' eyes. "Then I ask again that she be allowed to die in private with dignity, rather than in the public plaza."

"It will be done," Louis said. "This matter will be kept between you and me and the present *Comte de* Winter. None need ever know that Sabine was anything other than a loving devoted wife and a woman who saved France in the year of our Lord, sixteen hundred and thirty–eight. It is the least I can offer your wife after the help she offered in capturing Georges and bringing him to justice," the king said, thereby stopping Athos from trying to be honorable and prevent the king from showing him too much favor. "God be with you, Athos," the king said as the musketeer left. From this moment on they would be nothing more than king and subject.

The small group gathered in a secluded glen outside of Paris far removed from any prying eyes. Porthos, Aramis, and the *Comte de* Winter led the procession. Athos trailed several steps behind, his eyes not seeing the few rays of light that shined through the clouds blanketing the sky. Behind, Laurel talked with her sister, coming to terms with Sabine's decision and sharing a last few precious moments.

The party stopped, and the executioner retrieved Sabine from Laurel's side. With dignity and grace, Sabine walked to the circle of stones and knelt, watching the faces around her. God grant that Athos and Laurel could be strong and that their friends would support them. A melancholy breeze ruffled the woman's hair, and finally it was Aramis who spoke. He asked God to forgive her soul and take her unto His divine presence in the name of His son. Silently, he added a prayer that God help Athos and Laurel and Guillaume through the hardship and to heal. This time there would be no escaping. Not like the last.

Each man bowed his head as did Laurel, and the executioner made sure that the blade was very sharp. He would not have the woman suffer. It was a sad duty, was this. But justice would be done. The woman had insisted upon it despite a personal offer from the king, offering to spare her life and exile her. Lord have mercy on them all, the hooded man said and fulfilled his sworn duty to the crown, sending Sabine de Winter to a peaceful rest without any tarrying.

Both Athos and Laurel turned away, hiding their faces as the blade fell, ending any hopes they might have had. Laurel walked mechanically from the stones and leaned against a tree while Aramis and Porthos led Athos away from the scene so that the *Comte de* Winter and the executioner could bury Milady de Winter with a semblance of honor and spare Athos and Laurel the grim task.

The task complete, the *Comte de* Winter offered sincere condolences to the woman Louis had recently appointed Marquise de Langeac, and to Athos. The men shook hands, no blame placed, and then the *Comte de* Winter departed with the executioner, leaving the four friends to find what comfort they could.

Aramis slipped from Porthos and Athos' side, going to Laurel who stood still, leaning against the tree several strides away. She stared at the sky, but Aramis had the suspicion the woman didn't see it at all.

It was all too clear why Sabine had extracted the promise from him. She had known she was choosing to die for her crimes and had known that her sister would be overwhelmed by the loss. For now Laurel truly was alone, the last living member of her family, barring a profligate cousin Thomas had asked that Louis disinherit in his will. His boots crunched in the leaves, and he stopped right behind her, not daring to touch her. "I am sorry, Laurel," were the only words he could offer her, and she turned to face the man.

Her eyes were dry. The pain was too unreal for tears, the loss too bizarre and fresh on top of all the others. The woman looked older, more wary of the world. What an initiation to the real world, to the world Laurel must learn to live in. "I know what Sabine made you promise," Laurel said quietly. "She told me, and I release you from that bond."

After a moment's indecision, he reached a hand out towards her, taking her hand in his. "Let me help, Laurel. Do not turn the world away," Aramis entreated, and she could almost hear, if she let herself, the words: do not turn me away.

Laurel slipped her hand from his grasp. "I'll stay long enough to see D'Artagnan through to health or death, if God wills. After that I must go, Aramis. I have a new life to live. But I will never forget any of you. I promise. You will always be dear to me. I will always cherish what we had." Her voice was firm, confident as if she had finally won a long struggle.

Aramis knew there would be no reasoning with her now, no way to convince her not to leave everything in this life behind. No way to break through the icy detachment she had encased herself in. "As you wish, Laurel. Remember, though, I will always be here. And I will wait," Aramis assured. And he would wait. Wait for her to come to terms with her grief, wait for her to grow up and come to grips with a world that was foreign to her at this moment. Silently, he offered her his hand and led her from the woods.

* * * * * * * * * * *

Monsieur de Treville watched as Aramis fenced superbly with Porthos. The last soreness of his wound had healed well, and the man was back up to his old form. He hadn't, however, quite been prepared when Aramis had asked him to stand as a witness before the king as he claimed his inheritance. Still hard to believe that Aramis had taken on his father's *duché* and forever closed the door on any aspiration to the holy orders.

The two fighters saluted, ending their bout, and a third man joined them—Athos. Athos, Porthos, and Aramis. They had been virtually inseparable since the day they had met. Three men with pasts they didn't much discuss. One a *duc,* one a *comte*, and only their closest friends knew the real extent of the details. Someday he'd turn the command of the musketeers over to one of those men, if he could ever choose one of them to single out.

The *capitaine* continued on his walk, glancing back at the three men every so often. Yet the three were no longer complete. Somewhere along the way the three inseparables had become the four inseparables, and that fourth part had been missing for two months now. And it might always remain missing. Slowly Treville headed inside, and the three musketeers watched him disappear.

"Well, Treville knows we are all well enough to fight now," Athos commented to his friends. "It will only be matter of time before he sends us out again."

"True," Porthos and Aramis said together, but without heart.

They all looked up as the *capitaine* headed directly for them, a grimly determined look on his face. Well, apparently, it was time. They came smartly to attention. "Gentlemen," Treville said, "if you'll come with me, I have a task for your special talents."

They nodded their heads and followed the man into his office. One after the other, they froze on the threshold of the door. First Aramis, then Porthos, and finally Athos.

"Well, don't just stand there, come in," Treville told them, knocking them out of their state of limbo. The musketeers came in, and Treville went back to the door. "I'll leave you all some time alone. I'll be back later," the *capitaine* said and marched back out the door, closing it behind him.

"Glad to see that you all are so happy to see me," D'Artagnan commented smiling at his friends. "Maybe I should just go back to the palace and be waited upon hand and foot again."

"Oh, no you don't, young pup," Porthos said. "Just give us a moment to get used to seeing you back from the dead. It's been quite some weeks, young man." Truth was that they had all basically given him up for dead. Sometimes, though, it was very nice to be proven wrong.

Porthos slung an arm around first Athos and then Aramis and drew them to a corner in a huddle. D'Artagnan watched the curious scene, unable to hear a word the men were saying. The three men hit their hands together and turned to face the seated and confused D'Artagnan. They pulled him to his feet and at the exact same moment enclosed him in a massive three-person bear hug. "Welcome back, D'Artagnan. And if you ever scare us like that again . . ." Porthos spoke for all of them.

"Oh, never mind the lectures, Porthos," Aramis said. "We all know it's one for all and all for one. Let's just get our friend back into shape as fast as his health permits."

The men nodded and escorted D'Artagnan outside, knowing even as they did so that Laurel had departed them without even saying goodbye, not even to D'Artagnan.

Epilogue
1639 A.D.

The man stood leaning against the wall away from the bright, and hot, light of the August sun. His eyes silently watched the courtyard and those that bustled by. It had happened again. He was tired. So very tired. And he felt so incredibly old despite his youth. Maybe he was just bored and in need of an adventure to spice up his life, he told himself. But then he took himself to task, reminding himself that the toll of his last adventure had been high enough.

Far too high, in many respects. This time Porthos hadn't even attempted to employ his usual methods to knock Aramis out of his sulks. Could he really be becoming as big a brooder as Athos?

No, wait. Now, scratch that thought. Athos didn't brood so much anymore. He still thought of Sabine, but little Guillaume had done wonders for the man. Athos smiled more often now, seemed younger and happier than he'd been for years. He was glad for his friend. Athos deserved the happiness, and, apparently, Anne and Constance loved having little Guillaume in their care while Athos was occupied with his obligations as a musketeer.

Who would have thought Athos would be such a good father, but he was. Despite all his duties, he always made time for his son; Guillaume was a lucky boy, all things considered. Got to play and have fun. Appeared his father was letting him be a kid and letting the boy grow up in his own good time, knowing soon enough Guillaume would have to deal with the duties of being heir to the *Comte* d'Avignon. Adulthood came far too quickly anyhow.

"Come out of it, Aramis," he criticized aloud, trying to knock himself out of his melancholy mood. He had no reason to be brooding. Life was going well. Porthos was happy. Athos was happy. D'Artagnan would soon be married to Constance—four weeks to be exact. For that was when she would be released from her service to the queen. All his friends were happy. He should be ecstatic for them and he was, really. He was just tired, he assured himself as he pushed away from the wall and kicked a pebble out of his way. He took several steps on his hike back to the barracks. He ought to visit his lands soon. Duties were still there.

"Stop right there," he heard someone say.

"*Oui*, you in the black hat, with the swaggering walk. How dare you, arrogant swine, turn your back on me and walk away without even acknowledging me."

Aramis whirled, taken completely off guard. A tall youngster dressed in dirty breeches and a tunic and doublet that had seen better days and a sword that looked out of place stood staring him down. "What's the problem? Didn't you hear me?" the youngster insisted, taking a step towards the musketeer. "Always knew I shouldn't have left you on your own. Went right back to being that stuffy, old, perfect gentleman who was bored out of his skull. Now we're right back where we started." Aramis' interrogator advanced towards him, bravado in each step.

He suddenly grasped the youngster's arms and shook the person in question. "Laurel, you little wench. What are you doing here?" His voice was soft, belying the emotional chaos her sudden appearance set off. The woman hadn't even talked with him or communicated with him in about a year, including those last two months she had tended D'Artagnan. . . . Yet, he had waited, as he had promised, holding out hope against hope that she would see her way out of the emotional turmoil of the last year.

"Well, maybe we aren't right back where we started," Laurel reconsidered her hasty assessment. She dearly hoped she hadn't made a grievous, unforgivable error almost ten months ago by leaving the way she had—without even saying *merci* or goodbye. She had no excuses. She just hadn't been up to it, and she'd made a big mistake, perhaps the biggest of her life.

"Why are you here?" the man repeated, always in control of his emotions, giving no hint of his thoughts.

"You did tell me you would be here for me and that you'd wait. I hope I wasn't wrong to assume that I could take you up on that offer," she said, not even wanting to dare to hope, and he dropped his hands from her shoulders.

His eyes were hard and distant, but he nodded. "I meant what I said. I do not go back on my word." A man's word was his bond of honor.

Immediately he noticed a deep lassitude sweep over the woman, and an aura of despondent despair. "Wait." He reached out his hand to prevent her from walking away. "I did not mean that the way it sounded. It just hurt, hurt us all when you left so suddenly without a word." He stopped. "Is that the only reason you came back?"

His brown eyes looked at her with an intensity that she would have drawn away from a year ago, but this time her gaze didn't falter. He couldn't really see right through her.

Courage, she reminded herself; the worst he would do was turn her away, politely. She shook her head. "I missed you," she replied simply and touched his face with her palm. "My life seemed empty without your arrogant little presence." This time Aramis was at a loss for words.

Laurel, too, said nothing more. . . . A long time they both paused, as if they were carefully assessing the other.

Finally, she simply gathered herself up and took his face in her hands. Raising herself on tiptoes, she touched her lips to his and felt herself fall forward. Then she wasn't falling anymore, and her arms were around his neck, and he was holding her tightly, kissing her back with a ferocity that startled him.

"My, my, Aramis. Your taste has really changed." Porthos' loud voice startled them apart.

Laurel blushed bright red, but quickly recovered her composure. "Oh, do shut up, Porthos. You are always jumping to conclusions."

"Did you hear what that little *chipie* just said to me?" Porthos asked Athos and D'Artagnan, his voice filled with mock hurt. But he was grinning from ear to ear at the sight of Laurel. No grudges held by him. In a way, he understood her better than any of his other companions, even the man she had been kissing.

"Yeah." Both men nodded and each man took one of Porthos' arms, saying, "I think we'll let them work this one out on their own, Porthos." The two men spoke in unison in a somewhat feeble effort to try to explain the matter to their pirate friend. Not at all unexpectedly, the effort was a complete waste of time. Thus, they began leading Porthos away. And as the trio left, Aramis caught Athos' wink and smiled.

Aramis turned back toward Laurel. "You know that you have just completely ruined your reputation by doing that. My friends are not the only ones who saw."

"I know, but only if they have figured out the details of my true identity." She shrugged her shoulders. She doubted they suspected she was anything other than Aramis' mistress. Last thing to cross their mind would be the fact the noble, respected, and much sought after Marquise de Langeac—titled noblewoman without a husband—would dare such a thing. She'd been very careful with her image in society's eyes.

"You are still the most infuriating, nonsensical woman I've ever met. . . . And if you think for one instant that I'm letting you run off again, you have got a lot to learn. Actually you have a lot to learn, regardless." He knew she was right in the last. A disguise spared the damage to her reputation so long as he and his friends were careful and did a little bit of rumor spreading.

"*Oui, monseigneur,*" she responded in a voice that left no doubt she had a lot to teach him as well. She'd never be a complacent little thing. He'd better accept that. And maybe she knew what she was getting into. Could it really hurt to have a serious suitor she showed favor to?

He shook his head and led her away from the stares of the onlookers. Aramis knew he might well live to regret taking her on, accepting the dare, but his life would never be boring at least. And he'd always have someone to fence with, in more ways than one.

This could well get complicated; as if it weren't already. Plus, things probably wouldn't work out as planned, but then again he had a suspicion neither of them really had a plan or knew what to expect. But what the heck? God sometimes only gives you one chance, and he wasn't going to let this one pass him by. At least he could try and see what happened. The Marquise de Langeac was, after all, a beauty, rich, titled, and a prize much sought after, and the *duc* needed, had, a duty to his lineage. They needed each other. *Duc* and marquise, who happened to be a spy. . . . Stranger things had happened.

Historical Afterword
A note from the author

Much time and research has gone into the crafting of this novel and assuring the accuracy of historical events and customs of the time. However, for the sake of the story, some changes have been made.

Furthermore, fans of Dumas' *Three Musketeers* will have noted some deviations from Dumas' stories. As fans may have noticed, this story takes place roughly after the action of *The Three Musketeers*. Nevertheless, some events are treated as if they had never happened and others were altered. Also, it is assumed that none of the events written of in *The Man in the Iron Mask* ever occurred.

I hope you have enjoyed this fictionalized version of 17th century France. *Vive la France. Vive les mousquetaires.* Or, if you prefer: Long live France. Long live the musketeers.

Watch for these new novels by the author, coming by December, 2004.

You met some unforgettable friends in *For Honor*. Bring them back into your life again in these exciting new stories.

See **www.forhonor.com** for availability information.
Order books from www.buybooksontheweb.com
Or call 877-BUY BOOK   (877-289-2665)

Gambit for Love of a Queen by Kat Jaske

. . . Aramis frowned. . . . Laurel. He should have known that Laurel would never send a messenger if she really wanted to get in touch with him. He nodded and escorted her to a room where they would be out of sight of the servants so he could speak with her. "I understand there is a matter of some urgency that you needed to talk to me about," he said without inflection.

"Don't be so pompous and condescending, Aramis," she retorted and stalled his rebuttal. There was no time for another argument between them. "The matter is of international importance. If it is not resolved, France could become embroiled in another nasty drawn out war and it could prompt an internal revolt . . . The Prussians have kidnapped Anne d'Autriche." . . .

Does trouble just follow Laurel? See 17th-century France and the musketeers through the eyes of a spirited young woman. Her dear friend, the Queen of France, has been abducted. How long can they keep it quiet while they search for her, and what happens to France, Laurel, and the musketeers if they fail? The author brings the heroes to life again in this swashbuckling, spellbinding adventure. Ms. Jaske expertly weaves several plots within plots into the totally unexpected conclusion. The love/hate relationship between two of the main characters threatens the success of the entire mission, and, yes, sometimes heroes do die, and sometimes people really do get what they wished for, ready or not. You will shed a few tears for and with the heroes, your friends.

267

<u>Righting Time</u> by Kat Jaske

. . . Panic did no good: that point had been vividly driven home to her by harsh experience over the course of her ten years with the Guild of History and Time Observation. Before long, the time fluctuations would manifest and the true time—her time or her present—would be inextricably altered. Right now there was still some chance to try for correction and containment. "Find me the date of the first time fluctuation in the timeline and pinpoint the locale on the main screen." Daryl nodded and did so swiftly. The trio turned to the screen as the map blipped into place. It was a very old map. At a guess, Keith would place it at least eight hundred years old.

"Old-world France?" Jala questioned, and Daryl nodded as the woman came close to the screen.

"France in 1641, eight hundred and seventy-three years ago, to be exact," Daryl enlightened his companions. Jala punched a button and another section of the screen leapt to life. United States of America, 2060. Those dates were linked. Linked very closely. Jala's eyebrows came together in deep thought. Without needing to be told, Daryl set about determining exactly how they were related.

At the same moment, Keith and Jala lifted their heads and looked at one another. "Something or someone from 1640 or 1641 was thrust forward into the year 2060," they said together. "Make that a person from 1640 was thrust forward, but a secondary big-time disturbance occurred in 1641, then manifest further in 2060," Jala said as she scanned over the data Daryl had discovered.

"But who was pulled from the seventeenth?" Daryl asked. . . .

Science fiction and adventure with a creative twist mark this unforgettable story. The author weaves a tale that becomes so intriguing and thought provoking, your whole concept of time may be altered. How does one go about finding someone in time when you don't even know who you are looking for? What you do know is that whatever this person did in their future of 2060 is slowly winding its way to the future, your present, and you could very well cease to exist. Jala must enlist some help from the past, from people you are quite familiar with from previous books, or people you will soon come to know and love if this is your first book. The heroine discovers powers she never knew she had, but if she fails to learn how to control and use these powers, the past, present, and future could be altered with tragic consequences. The ending will bring tears to your eyes, tears that are somehow sad and happy at the same time. There will be more stories to bring back your favorite characters (friends) again and again.

<u>Out of Phase</u> by Kat Jaske

. . . Jean-Pierre met his father's eyes for the first time, looking down on the man just an inch or two, perhaps three. Porthos read the unspoken message there—the one about whether he really wanted that information said here. Porthos nodded his head in response to the unasked question, and the young man took a deep breath. "I'm your son."

"*Parbleu*," Aramis whispered and the whole room dropped into silence, eyes fixed on the two largest men they'd ever met.

Porthos finally found his voice. "How old are you?"

"Two and twenty," was the automatic response. Nearly three and twenty, but Jean-Pierre wasn't going to quibble.

"Who's your mother?" The whole room seemed to wait tensely for the man's response to that question. Laurel met Jean-Pierre's gaze, and in that instant the young man knew that she already knew who he was and *when* he was from. Even with her powers somewhat latent, the beautiful duchesse knew.

"Cynthia," he said softly.

"Cynthia," Porthos echoed and his son nodded. At the same time, Aramis, Athos, and D'Artagnan all seemed to grasp the significance of the boy's parentage. Porthos' son. Porthos' son from over eight hundred and eighty-five years in the future. "By all that is . . ."

This story has everything for the science-fiction fan. Aliens, time travel, wars for survival of the universe, and powers of the mind not yet even dreamed of. The love story of two people from the past woven throughout has implications for survival of the human race itself. The author has plots and subplots going on in the far future, near future, and the distant past. The outcome of each affects all the others. True science-fiction fans will find the story challenging, thought-provoking, and just plain fun to read.

Kat Jaske won the national prize for a poem she wrote while at Wake Forest University, and she won the Upper Arlington High School top-five senior thesis award for her book. Kat is fluent in French, and earned certificates from Jean Paul Valéry University in Montpellier, France. She is currently finishing her M Ed degree in education and will be teaching English and French. Kat is an avid runner, and ran on the Ohio state-champion cross-country team in high school. She also enjoys writing, fencing, singing, and playing piano. Kat lives in Las Vegas with her black cat, Minnesota.